NOWHERE TO HIDE

Alex Walters was educated in Nottingham and at Cambridge University. After leaving university, he worked in management roles in the oil industry, broadcasting and banking, before moving into management consultancy. Having worked for various global practices, he now runs his own specialist consultancy company, working in the UK and abroad. His consultancy work in recent years has specialised in various aspects of the criminal justice sector, including police, prisons and probation, as well as various public bodies including the UK parliament. He lives in Manchester with his three sons.

By the same author:

Trust No One

ALEX WALTERS

Nowhere To Hide

A V O N

AVON

A division of HarperCollins*Publishers*
77–85 Fulham Palace Road,
London W6 8JB

www.harpercollins.co.uk

A Paperback Original 2012

1

First published in Great Britain by
HarperCollins*Publishers* 2012

Copyright © Michael Walters 2012

Michael Walters asserts the moral right to
be identified as the author of this work

A catalogue record for this book is
available from the British Library

ISBN-13: 978-1-84756-287-6

Set in Minion by Palimpsest Book Production Limited,
Falkirk, Stirlingshire

Printed and bound in Great Britain by
Clays Ltd, St Ives plc

As always, I must thank the various anonymous sources who fed me with the information and titbits that I've carefully fictionalised. You know who you are. And of course thanks to Sammia Rafique, my terrific editor at Avon, and to my agent, Peter Buckman, who between them manage to keep me roughly on the straight and narrow.

As always, to James, Adam and Jonny for their support. And, of course, to Christine who made it all possible.

Prologue

They were some miles from the port terminal, out on the open road, before Hanlon felt able to relax slightly. 'Shit,' he said. 'I really thought they were on to us back there.' He was a short wiry man, muscular, with the air of having drunk one too many strong coffees during the journey over.

At first he thought that Mo was asleep. But the older man opened one eye, peering at him from under his trademark trilby hat. 'You worry too much, man.'

'Jesus, Mo. We've got plenty to worry about.'

Mo opened both eyes and shrugged. 'I'd say not, wouldn't you? All gone smooth as clockwork.' He eased himself back in the passenger seat and jerked his thumb over his shoulder. 'Not even any noise from back there.'

Hanlon glanced back over his shoulder. The two women were asleep. Partly exhaustion. Mainly the sedatives Mo had fed them as they were leaving the port. Christ, how had he allowed himself to get mixed up in this? Apart from anything else, it seemed so half-fucking-baked. 'This worth the hassle, then, you reckon?'

Mo's eyes were half-closed again, the hat slid low across his forehead. 'What's that, man?'

'You think it's worth it? All this?'

'Not ours to judge, man. Being paid for it, aren't you?'

'Not enough,' Hanlon said. 'Like I say, I thought they were on to us back there.'

'That was nothing. I been through far worse with those bastards. They didn't suspect a fucking thing. Even with you shaking like a bare-assed Eskimo.' Mo tried to sound like he was on the sidewalks of Harlem, but his North Wales intonation kept breaking through.

He was right, though, Hanlon thought. The passports had been convincing enough. The Immigration Officers had waved them through with no more than a couple of questions and a glance into the back of the car. He'd been worried that the two women might make a fuss, either on the ferry or when they reached the border. After all, it was their one chance to get free. But they'd played the game, just as Mo had said they would. Maybe because they were scared of Mo. They had plenty of reason to be scared. But Hanlon thought they'd just lost the will to resist. They'd been through too much. There was no future for them other than this.

'Feels like there should be a better way of doing it,' Hanlon went on. He just wanted to keep the conversation going to calm his nerve, keep focused for the long drive. Mo looked like he wanted to sleep. 'Something less risky.'

'What you suggest, man? Parcel post? Rolling 'em up in a fucking carpet?' Mo slid the hat fully across his face, a gesture indicating that the conversation was at an end.

He was right about that as well. As long as the women played ball, this was low risk and cheap. Two couples returning from a long weekend in Dublin. Apparently legitimate British passports. Even the ferry tickets had been bought at a discount.

Hanlon was new to this. He didn't even know how often they carried out these kinds of transactions. Not very, he guessed. They'd have other means of getting the women into the country in the first place. Most probably they arrived legitimately, lured by the prospect of jobs and money. Then, before they knew it, they'd vanished off the grid, exploited by thugs like Mo and the people he worked for.

Christ, he thought again, how the *hell* had he allowed himself to get mixed up in this?

Money. That was the short answer. A way to make the quick buck he needed. Low risk, they'd said, though he hadn't really believed that. Just help them move the merchandise about. That had been the word. Merchandise. One of the less unpleasant words.

Hanlon didn't know the background and he didn't want to. Some deal had been done across the Irish Sea, and now they were bringing these two women – hardly more than girls – to work in some brass-house in Manchester. For them, probably no different from doing the same thing in Dublin. Crap either way.

They'd had cheap tickets on the last ferry of the day, so it would be into the small hours before they reached Manchester. God, he felt tired. Mo was snoring gently now, hat flat across his face. The privilege of being the senior partner, Hanlon assumed. You got to snooze your way across North Wales, while the junior oppo kept his eyes on the road. As far as he knew, the car belonged to Mo, though Hanlon assumed the car was stolen or the plates pirated in some way. Presumably, like the faked passports, nothing would be traceable. He didn't even know for certain who Mo worked for. He had his ideas, but better not to ask too many questions, as long as they paid what was owed.

It was the first and last time, though. They'd suckered him just like they'd suckered those poor cows in the back seat. The difference was that he had an exit route. If they paid him what they'd promised, he'd have enough to settle his debts and get things back on track. Maybe even make an attempt to patch things up with Cath, if it wasn't too late for that. At least stop her playing silly buggers about giving access to Josh. Not that he had any rights in that department, after everything he'd done.

'Shit.' He'd been driving on autopilot, his mind full of his unmissed past and half-imagined future. For a minute or two, he hadn't registered the flashing blue light in the rear view mirror. He glanced down at the speedometer. It would be fucking typical to be pulled over for speeding. But, no, that was okay.

He leaned over and nudged Mo. 'Fucking pigs,' he hissed. 'Behind us.'

Mo sat up with an alacrity that suggested he perhaps hadn't been sleeping after all. He looked over his shoulder and peered through the rear window. 'Christ's sake, man. Relax. They're not after us. Probably just the end of their fucking shift. Keen to get back to their loved ones. Or even their wives.' He snorted at his own wit and prepared to stretch himself back across the seat.

But the police car was already overtaking and slowing in front of them, in an unmistakable signal for them to pull over.

'Jesus, Mo,' Hanlon said. 'What the fuck do we do now?'

Mo was sitting bolt upright, looking less relaxed. 'Let me do the talking. Keep calm and keep it zipped.' He looked across at Hanlon, his gaze unwavering. 'Nothing to worry about, man. Long as you leave it to me.'

'But the car—'

Mo shook his head. 'We're not fucking amateurs, man. Vehicle's stolen, but it's a ringer. Licence plates match the type and colour. Name of registered owner's the same as the passport. It's all sorted. There's nothing to worry about.'

'So why the fuck are they stopping us?' Hanlon was already pulling into the hard shoulder, carefully following the police vehicle.

'Probably just routine. Not much opportunity to hassle a black guy out here in the sticks.' He frowned suddenly, leaning forward in his seat. 'That not right, man. Who is that guy?' He watched for a moment as a figure climbed slowly out of the car in front, then turned to Hanlon. 'Shit, man. Get started. Just fucking drive!'

Hanlon stared back at him, bewildered. He'd already cut the engine. Now, in the face of Mo's unexpected panic, he frantically twisted the ignition. He slammed his foot on to the accelerator, misjudging the movement, and the engine stalled.

'Fuck, man. Just get it started.'

Hanlon turned the ignition again, but he'd flooded the engine and the starter turned ineffectually. In the dark outside, the figure had reached the car. Hanlon made another attempt to start the car, trying to remember what to do about a flooded ignition. Then, suddenly, the engine burst into life. As he struggled to put the car into first gear, his mind and actions refusing to coordinate, the car door beside him was pulled open. He jammed the gear stick into what he thought was first, banged his foot hard down on the accelerator and let out the clutch.

The engine coughed and died.

The figure outside said: 'Need a few more lessons, mate. Don't take off in third.'

Hanlon looked across at Mo, baffled now. Mo had his head in his hands, his body hunched as if anticipating a blow.

'Fucking cowboys,' the figure said. 'Shouldn't be let out on your own. Give us all a bad name.'

Hanlon raised his head and stared through the windscreen at the car parked ahead of their own. Not a police car. Not a police car after all. Just a plain dark saloon with one of those magnetic blue beacons that doctors and plainclothes cops use to get through the traffic.

He looked up at the figure standing next to him. Black suit. A baseball cap. Dark glasses. No one he'd be able to recognise in daylight. Beside him, Hanlon could hear Mo breathing rapidly, murmuring something, a voice on the edge of losing it.

'Nice of you two to do the heavy lifting, though,' the figure said. He leaned forward and peered into the back seat. There was a gun in his hand, Hanlon noticed, feeling oddly calm now. 'Bringing these two charming ladies over. I'm sure we'll use them wisely.'

He straightened up, juggling the gun gently in his hand. Then he looked back down at Hanlon. 'Sorry about this, son,' he said, gently. 'Nothing personal.'

Hanlon stared back, surprised by the softness of the man's tone. He suddenly had the sense that it was all going to be all right. The man would simply take the women and leave. Okay, he and Mo would lose the payment because they'd fucked up. But he could live with that. He could fucking live.

But the man had already taken a step back and Hanlon knew that, really, nothing would be all right again. He watched as the man crouched slightly, then raised the gun and pointed it past Hanlon into the car.

Hanlon was screaming before the gun was fired. Before he felt the rush of air and heard the explosion. Before he sensed the impact and the sudden jerk from Mo's body beside him. Before the windows and seats and his own face were showered in Mo's blood and bone and grey matter.

He was still screaming as he tried ineffectually to free himself from his seat belt, throwing himself sideways in a vain attempt to drag himself from the nightmarish, blood-drenched interior of the car.

And he stopped screaming only when the man outside raised the gun and fired for a second time.

Ken had left his car in one of these back streets, but for the moment he couldn't quite remember where. Earlier, it had seemed the obvious place, just around the corner from the club, handy for when he came out. But now he'd walked round the block twice and he still couldn't work it out.

Maybe someone had stolen it. Always possible in an area like this. Not likely, though. Not the kind of car to attract thieves. Too new to be easy pickings, but not so modern or sexy that anyone would be particularly drawn to it. Not one for the boy-racers, or for the professionals who blagged prestige cars to order. A nondescript runabout for the middle-aged. Just the way Kev liked it.

Story of his life, in fact. Keep your head down. Don't draw attention to yourself. Get to know the right people. Word of mouth. Enough people knew who he was, but not too many. If he wanted some gear, he knew who to go to. If he had some gear to shift, people came to him. Otherwise, he drifted out of sight, unnoticed. An inconspicuous link in the chain.

He didn't feel particularly inconspicuous tonight, though. He'd made a mistake, lost a bit of control. He wasn't a good drinker. A cheap drunk, Kev, they always said. A few pints and he's anybody's. That wasn't quite true. Kev was always his own man, no matter what he'd drunk. But on a night like this that just meant there was no one to look out for him.

Shit. He stumbled on a loose paving slab and clutched at a shop front to steady himself. He didn't really believe the car had been stolen. In any case he was in no state to drive. But he'd wanted to reassure himself that it was still safely there. Now all he could do was hope that his memory would improve once he'd sobered up.

He turned round, trying to get his bearings. Where was he, exactly? He didn't know Stockport well. He wasn't even sure why he'd come along this evening. A gentleman's club, Harvey had said. The audience hadn't seemed to contain many gentlemen, and the women on stage hadn't been Kev's idea of ladies. Expensive bloody drinks, as well, especially when the big man, whoever he was, had moved them on to rounds of shorts. Harvey had told him he'd meet some useful people there. Maybe he had, but in the morning he'd have no bloody idea who they were.

He tottered his way towards the next street corner, looking for some recognisable landmark. There was a knot of street lights at the far end of the street. Probably the A6, the characterless trunk-road that sliced through the town on its way to Manchester. Once he reached that, he'd find a minicab office. This was going to cost him a bloody fortune. A taxi back home, and then another cab back in the morning. Why had he let Harvey talk him into this?

It never paid to stray outside your own territory. He should know that by now. Up in the city, he knew what was what. Who to talk to, who to avoid. Tonight, he'd talked to a few people, suggested a few deals, but he hadn't known what they thought. He hadn't even been able to work out who were the real players. Not the mouthy ones, for sure. There'd been a few of those, making the right noises, but that counted for nothing. It was the ones in the background who mattered, the ones who watched you, made their judgements, and said nothing. It was only later that you'd find out whether they were happy or not.

What the fuck had happened to Harvey anyway? He'd been there earlier, had done the introductions, settled Kev in with a crowd who looked mostly like chancers. Then at some point he'd buggered off. Probably found himself some woman. Someone not too choosy.

Shit. This was the last time. Harvey always made out he was doing you a bloody favour, and nine times out of ten you ended up out of pocket.

He stopped again. The lights he'd thought marked the A6 had turned out to be at the corner of some other junction entirely. It was vaguely familiar, but only vaguely. Somewhere he'd driven through maybe. Certainly nowhere he'd ever been on foot. There was a closed down pub opposite, the back end of some industrial buildings. Not the kind of place you'd find a minicab.

He turned, peering through the pale darkness down each of the streets in turn. There wasn't even anyone around to ask, this time of night. The only sign of life was a car pulling slowly out of a side street further down the road. Judging from the speed, the driver was nearly as pissed as he was. Kev had been half-thinking about trying to flag the car down, ask for directions, even try to cadge a life to the nearest minicab office. But who would pull up for a drunk at this time of the night?

Well, maybe someone who was in the same condition. To Kev's mild surprise, the car drew up next to him, the electric window slowly descending. If you're after directions, pal, Kev thought, you've come to the wrong fucking bloke.

Kev was on the passenger side of the car and could see only the shape of the driver through the open window. Baseball cap, he noticed irrelevantly. Dark glasses. Who the fuck wears dark glasses to drive at night?

From inside, a flat voice, devoid of intonation, said: 'Kevin Sheerin.' It was a statement rather than a question.

Kev suddenly felt uneasy. He glanced both ways along the street, but there was no sign of anyone. Just the stationary car in front of him. A dark saloon. Cavalier or Mondeo or somesuch.

'Who's asking?' he said finally. The wrong response, he realised straight away. No one was asking, but he'd already given all the answer that was needed. The car window was already closing. 'What the fuck—?'

But that question needed no answer either. Kev, sensing what was coming, had already started to run, but his drunken feet betrayed him and he stumbled on the edge of the pavement, tumbling awkwardly into the road. He rolled over, head scraping against the rough tarmac, trying to drag himself out of the way. He could already taste blood in his mouth.

It was too late. The headlights, full beam, were blinding his eyes. The engine, unexpectedly loud, the only thing he could hear. The moment seemed to last forever, and he told himself that he'd been wrong, that it wasn't going to happen after all. Then he was at the kerbside, trying to drag himself upright, and the car slammed hard into his crouching body.

For an instant, he felt nothing and he thought that, somehow, miraculously, he'd escaped unscathed. Then he tried to pull himself upright and immediately the pain hit him, agonising, unbearable, a shockwave through his legs and back. He fell forwards again, hitting his head on the curb, scarcely conscious now, thinking; *shit*, my back—

He had no time to think anything more. The car had reversed a few yards, and now jerked forwards again, the front wing smashing into his legs. He lay motionless as the car rode bumpily over his prone body and disappeared into the night, leaving his mangled, bloody corpse crumpled in the gutter.

Steve woke too early, like every night since they brought him here. It was the silence, he thought. The silence and the darkness. He'd never be comfortable in this place. He

11

was a city boy, used to the traffic-drone that never died away, the wasteful small hours glare of the street lights and office blocks.

He rolled over, pulling the cheap duvet around his body, burrowing in search of further sleep. But the moment had passed. He was awake, mind already racing through the same thoughts, the same anxieties. Feeling a sudden claustrophobia, he threw back the covers and sat up in the pitch black. The room faced east, across the open valley, and the curtains were as cheap and flimsy as the duvet. But there was no sign of dawn, no promise of the rising sun.

He fumbled around the unfamiliar bedside table until he found a switch for the lamp. The sudden glare was blinding but, after a moment, reassuring. The bedroom was as bland and anonymous as ever. Off-white walls, forgettable chain store pictures, inoffensive flat-pack furniture. There'd been a half-hearted attempt to make it homely, but that only highlighted its bleakness, confirmed beyond doubt that no one would ever stay in this place by choice.

It was cold too, he thought, as he reached for his dressing gown. The central heating hadn't yet come on, and he could taste the damp in the air. He crossed to the window and peered out. A clear night, the sky moonless but full of stars, less dark than he had imagined. In the faint light, he could make out the valley, the faint gleam of the Goyt in the distance. Miles from anywhere. The end of the line, past all civilisation.

He pulled the dressing gown more tightly around him, and stepped out on to the landing. This was his routine. Waking in the middle of the bloody night, making himself a black coffee, sitting and waiting for the sun to rise on another empty day.

The unease struck him halfway down the stairs. Nothing he could put his finger on, just a sudden sense of something wrong. He hesitated momentarily, then forced himself to continue down. Of course something was wrong. Everything was fucking wrong. He didn't even know why he'd done it. It wasn't the money – he knew there would be little enough of that, now they didn't need him any more. It wasn't the supposed guarantees. He'd few illusions about what those would be worth when the excrement hit the extractor. It wasn't even that he was doing the right thing. He'd just managed to get himself wedged firmly up shit creek and then discovered that there never had been any paddle.

He pushed his way into the tiny kitchen and went wearily through the familiar ritual – filling the kettle, spooning coffee into the cup, adding two sugars. While the kettle boiled, he stared out of the kitchen window, across the postage stamp of an unkempt garden, towards the Peaks. The eastern sky was lighter now, a pale glow over the bleak moorland.

He stirred the coffee and paused for a moment longer, sipping the hot sweet liquid, gazing vacantly at the darkness. The sense of unease had remained, a thought lurking at the edge of his mind. Something more focused than the usual ever-present anxiety. Some idea that had struck him and receded before he could catch it.

He picked up the coffee and forced himself back into his routine. He would go into the living room, sit on the chilly plastic sofa, switch on the television and watch the silent moving figures, with no interest in turning up the volume. Waiting for yet another bloody morning.

He pushed open the sitting room door, and his mind finally grasped the thought that had been troubling him. The door. He'd closed the sitting room door before going to bed. Another part of his routine, some unquestioned wisdom retained from childhood. Close the downstairs doors in case of fire. Waste of bloody time in a place like this, he'd reasoned. Whole place would be up like a tinderbox before you could draw a breath. But he still closed the doors.

Halfway down the stairs he'd registered, without even knowing what he'd seen, that the living room door was ajar.

He thought of stepping back, but knew it was already too late. In that moment another, more tangible sensation struck him. The acrid scent of cigarette smoke, instantly recognisable in this ascetic, smoke-free official house.

He thrust the door wide and stepped inside. The small table lamp was burning in the corner of the room, The man was sprawled across the tacky sofa, toying lazily with a revolver.

'Up early, Steve,' he commented. He was a large man in a black tracksuit, wearing dark glasses, with a baseball cap pulled low over his eyes. His face was neatly shaven and boyish, but there was nothing soft about him. 'Guilty conscience?'

'Not so's you'd notice,' Steve said. 'You?'

'Sleep of the just, mate,' the man said. 'Sleep of the fucking just.'

A moment before, Steve had been contemplating how to

get out of this. Whether to try to get back into the kitchen or upstairs. Out of the front door, or through the patio windows.

But there was no point. The man knew his name. Knew who he was. Why he was here. Someone had grassed. Why else had he come? Someone would always grass. He ought to know that better than anyone.

There was no way out. No future. There never had been any future, not to speak of, once he'd taken that step. He'd known it then and there was no escaping it now.

Steve felt oddly calm, detached, observing all this from a distance. He saw the man playing aimlessly with his gun. He saw it all, and he felt untroubled. He had no illusions about what the man would do. Perhaps no more than he deserved.

So he stood there, motionless, waiting for it to start. And in that moment – before the flare and the noise, before the impact, before his blood began to seep into the worn fibres of the cheap grey carpet – Steve felt almost relieved.

He'd almost missed it.

Something caught the corner of his eye, some movement. A twitch. He moved himself to the right to try to gain a better vantage through the spyhole.

It was well after midnight. The dead hours of routine patrols when nothing much ever happens. Maybe just some scrote with insomnia – and, Christ knew, all of this bunch ought to have trouble sleeping – shouting the odds, wanting to share his misery with the rest of the fucking world.

But usually nothing much. A fifteen minute stroll along

15

the dimly lit landing, glance into the cells, check that no one was up to no good. There was never any real trouble.

Sometimes Pete tried to kid people that this was a responsible job, stuck up here all night by himself on the landing. If anything happens, it's up to me to sort it out. Yeah, he thought, up to me to press the bell and summon backup. He was an OSG. Operational Support Grade. Bottom of the pile, with – at least in theory – minimal prisoner contact. Didn't always work out that way, of course. But nobody expected much of him. Especially not the Prison Officers.

Like that one earlier, who'd been coming up here just as he was ending his previous patrol. Pete had been running a bit late, had lingered a bit too long over his coffee and copy of *The Sun*. Nobody really cared at this time of the night, but he didn't like to let things slide, so he'd been a bit out of breath, dragging his overweight body hurriedly round the landings then down the stairs.

He hadn't recognised the officer who'd met him on the stairs. He thought he knew most of them, but they kept buggering the shifts about and this one was new to him. Christ knew what he was doing going up to the landings at this hour.

Pete had tried to offer a cheery greeting – they were both stuck on this arse end of a roster, after all – but the guy had just blanked him, hardly seeming to register that Pete was there. Well, fuck you as well, Pete had thought, puffing down the last few stairs. He'd heard the officer unlocking the landing doors above him.

Afterwards, he'd been worried that the officer might report him for being late. It was a stupid concern. The guy probably wouldn't even have known what time Pete was supposed to carry out the patrol. But there was something about him, something about the way he'd ignored Pete on the stairs, that had seemed unnerving. Just the kind of officious bastard who'd grass you up for the sheer hell of it.

So, just in case the guy was still up there, Pete had kicked off his next patrol a little early so he could get it finished on time without busting a gut. But of course the landing had been deserted. Whatever the officer had been doing, he'd finished it and buggered off.

There was nothing else to do. Pete shuffled with effort round the landing, stopping to check on each cell in turn. Everyone sleeping like a baby.

He'd reached the last cell and was preparing to move on to the next landing, when he stopped and looked again.

Yeah, he'd almost missed it. The cell was in darkness and he'd assumed the occupant was securely in bed. Then he'd caught some movement in the periphery of his vision. He hadn't even been sure he'd seen it at first. He'd shifted his body to get a better view.

Jesus.

There was something – someone – there, jerking and struggling. Someone pressed against the wall behind the door, almost invisible. And now Pete could hear the sound of choking, the awful sound of a wordless, gasping scream . . .

He reacted better than he'd have expected, racing across the landing to sound the alarm. Then back to the cell, fumbling with his own set of keys. He was supposed to enter the cells only in the direst of emergencies, but surely this counted as one of those. As he pushed open the door, it occurred to him that he might have been suckered. But the landing was sealed and backup would be there in minutes.

He knew straight away he'd done the right thing. The prisoner was hanging halfway up the wall – Christ knew how he'd managed it – some kind of cord tight around his neck. The man's head lolled to one side, his waxy face already blue in the dim light from the landing.

Pete threw his arms round the prisoner's body and tried to drag it down from whatever was holding the rope. He struggled at first, afraid that he was doing more harm than good, but knowing the prisoner would have no chance as long as his own weight continued to tighten the cord. Suddenly, as Pete strained to lift the prisoner's body, the rope gave way and the body toppled sideways, out of Pete's grip, on to the hard floor.

A nail. A fucking six inch nail hammered into the wall. Where the fuck had he got that from? And the rope, for that matter? Someone was for the high jump.

Pete crouched down by the body, fumbling to loosen the ligature from the prisoner's neck. The face was purple now, and the old guy looked like he might be a goner already. Pete fumbled around the plastic cord and finally found the knot. He could feel it beginning to give under his trembling fingers. At the same moment, he heard the sound of the landing gates behind unlocked.

By the time the two officers and the principal had reached the cell door, Pete had managed to loosen the rope. He looked up as the three men crowded the doorway: 'Trying to top himself.'

Pete moved back as the principal officer crouched over

the body and began to administer CPR, thrusting hard and rhythmically on the prisoner's chest. One of the officers was on his radio calling for an ambulance.

Pete dragged himself to his feet, only now beginning to take in what had happened. What he'd just dealt with. 'Jesus.' He glanced down at the supine figure, still bouncing under the pounding arms of the principal officer.

The officer with the radio nodded laconically towards Pete. 'Good work, son. Let's hope we're in time. We all get a bollocking if one of them tops himself.' He took a step back and glanced at the number of the cell. 'Mind you,' he added, 'won't be too many saying any prayers for this one.'

Pete looked up. 'That right?'

'Don't reckon so.' The officer moved to lean against the doorframe. 'This is Keith Welsby. Just another bent copper. There's one or two would be glad to help him on his fucking way.'

PART ONE

1

'So you were lying to me.'

Salter gazed back at her, his mouth working hard at a piece of gum. His expression was that of a bored spectator staring into an aquarium at an unfamiliar species of fish. 'If it wasn't the kind of thing that gets me branded as sexist,' he said, finally, 'I'd say that sounded a tad hysterical, sis.'

She eased herself back in Salter's uncomfortable visitor's chair, wondering how to extricate herself from this conversation. There was no way of combatting Salter in this kind of exchange. The most you could hope for was to slow him momentarily on his path to victory.

'It was a condition of my joining your team,' she said. 'I made that clear.' Which was true, but there was no way of proving it now.

He shrugged, chewing at the gum. 'Nobody makes conditions in this business. You know that. We do what we're told.'

'I'm not trying to be difficult, Hugh—'

'Never thought you were, sis. All seems easy enough from where I'm sitting.'

She didn't doubt that. Life tended to look pretty easy

from where Hugh Salter was sitting, if only because he was busy making life hard for everyone else. Like his insistence on calling her 'sis'. A hangover from that last undercover assignment. Salter had invented a family connection supposedly as cover in their telephone conversations. It was a joke now long past its sell-by date, but he knew she was irritated by the implied intimacy.

'You know my circumstances. There must be someone else.'

He waved his hand around as if the other potential candidates were gathered in the office with them. 'Believe me, sis, I've looked. There's no one else with your talents.' He made the last word sound like a double entendre. 'No one with half your experience.'

That wasn't entirely bullshit, she knew. Apart from herself, Salter's team was pretty wet behind the ears. That was how Salter picked them. Bright young things smart enough to do a decent job, but without the confidence to answer back. She tried another tack. 'Anyway, it's too risky. It's against procedures.'

Salter's smile was unwavering. '"Procedures"? Who gives a fuck about procedures? The other side don't follow procedures.'

And that's why they're on the other side, she thought. Out loud, she said, 'It's not about bureaucracy, Hugh. It's about not jeopardising the work. Or me, for that matter.'

'Look, sis, if there was an alternative, I'd jump at it. I don't want to do this any more than you do.'

Like hell, she thought. That's what this came down to. Another of Hugh Salter's games. She sometimes thought it was what really motivated him. Not career. Not money. Just the opportunity to screw other people around. None of this was a surprise. It was what she'd expected, one way or another, from the moment she'd finally agreed to join Salter's team.

It had taken him longer than she'd expected, though that was probably just another part of the game. It was six months since the business with Keith Welsby, their former boss and mentor. She'd been here in HQ all that time, working largely on backroom intelligence. Page after page of data on mobile phone numbers, banking transactions, email correspondence. It was important work and she was good at it, but that didn't make it any less boring. She'd learned to treat the boredom as part of the challenge. You ploughed your way through endless documentation, jotting a note here, a comment there, knowing that most of it was telling you nothing. But you had to keep your head engaged, waiting for the rare moment when something jumped out at you. Some trend, some pattern, some significant link with another piece of data, pages before.

It wasn't quite that basic, of course. The databases did a lot of the work, highlighting links and trends. Even so, when it came to the detail of a specific case, there was still a heavy dependency on the individual analyst. The most important links were often the least obvious. An odd piece of data – a name, a number – that had snagged in the back of your mind from another file. Sometimes it was little more than intuition, a feeling that there was a link you'd missed or a pattern you'd overlooked. She knew she was good at it. She could cope with the tedium, and she had a gift for finding information that others had missed.

In any case, after everything that had happened, she'd

needed a break. She'd nearly been killed, for Christ's sake. But then so had Salter, and he showed no obvious signs of mental trauma. And it was Salter, in the end, who'd killed Jeff Kerridge and exposed Welsby as corrupt. He'd been acclaimed as a hero and become the new rising star. Marie had watched uneasily from the sidelines, suspicious of Salter and his motives, convinced that, beneath that clean-cut ambition, he was as corrupt as their former boss. But Salter had sailed serenely on, enjoying the fruits of promotion, apparently untroubled by anything that had happened.

So she'd been happy to step back from the front line and lose herself in the rhythm of facts and figures. For the last six months, every day had been the same. The semi-comatose journey up the Northern Line, the short walk along the Embankment, takeaway latte from the staff restaurant. Settle at her desk and boot up the computer. Check emails, then access the database or pull out the files. The same every day. A sandwich at her desk, or lunch with a couple of the other analysts. More data-crunching till it was time to get the Tube home. Despite herself, she'd begun to enjoy the routine, the predictability.

Maybe Salter had hoped she'd be climbing the walls by now. She might have predicted it herself. She'd done this kind of work before and been happy with it, but that was a long time ago. She had been a different person then, she thought, with different expectations. But perhaps she'd changed less than she imagined.

In fairness, she'd always intended to return to the front line eventually. After they'd brought her in from the field, they'd had her formally assessed by Winsor, their pet psych.

In his inimitable style, Winsor had stated the blindingly obvious in language that no one fully understood. The upshot was that she'd suffered a major psychological trauma. Well, thanks for that, she'd thought. If you hadn't brought it up, I might not have noticed.

Winsor's conclusion was that she was a resilient character, and that there would be no long-term effects as long as they didn't push her too hard. She had no idea what evidence he had to support this assertion, but she felt no need to challenge it. If they wanted to stick her in a quiet office for a few months, that was fine by her. She had plenty of other problems on her plate, after all.

She looked up at Salter's blankly smiling face, wondering how to play this. There was no point in trying to match Salter at the gamesmanship. All she could do was play it straight down the line. 'I take it you've cleared this idea, Hugh?'

For a moment he shifted in his seat, his body-language suggesting that he couldn't fully answer her question. But she knew Salter well enough to recognise that he wouldn't go into something like this half-cocked. He'd always make sure his backside was covered. 'I've been through the procedures, if that's what you mean. What do you think this is?'

Well, that was the question. But, as Salter well knew, it was a question she couldn't begin to answer. 'It all just seems a bit irregular, Hugh. I mean, the protocols—'

'The protocols are there as guidance. We're professionals, Marie. We have to exercise judgement.' It was the first time he'd used her name. A sign that he was shifting things up a gear.

'And your judgement is that this is safe?' she asked.

'As safe as these things ever are. Christ, Marie, it's my neck on the block if things go wrong.'

She doubted that. If things went wrong, she would be the one at immediate risk. And she was willing to bet that Salter had made sure he wasn't in line for any professional blame. One way or another, he'd have everything covered. 'But it's the same area. And it's only been six months. That must be a risk.'

'There's always a risk,' he said. 'But it's not the same area. Not the same network at all. We've looked at it very carefully.'

'It's the north west. There are bound to be overlaps. It just takes one person—'

'We'll take care of it. You'll look different. You'll be a different person. Even if you should happen to stumble across somebody from before, there'll be no link. Nobody will have any reason to make the connection.'

It didn't sound convincing, she thought. They reason they had protocols was because, whatever the odds, shit still tended to happen. She'd experienced it herself. Some past contact eyeballing her suspiciously because she'd turned up somewhere she wasn't supposed to be. She could change her hair, her clothes, her lifestyle; but it wouldn't cut any ice if the wrong people became suspicious. 'But what if they do, Hugh? What if someone looks at me and thinks, wait a minute, that looks like old Marie who used to run the print shop in Trafford Park?'

'Christ, Marie. It's not going to happen, right. You're the best person for the job, that's what it comes down to. You can do it.'

Jesus, he was trying to flatter her now. Flattery wasn't

one of Salter's strong points. His compliments always sounded insincere, she assumed because he didn't really believe that any other person could match the towering talent that was Hugh Salter. 'Don't bullshit me, Hugh,' she said. 'You've just come to me because I'm convenient. If you tried to give this to one of your youngsters, you might actually have to put some effort into training them.' She paused, conscious that she was coming close to saying something that she really might regret. 'Do I actually have any choice in this?'

'There's always a choice, sis. But I really want you to give it a go.'

'I'll think about it.' She knew that she might as well have saved both their time and just said yes there and then, but at least she could string out his discomfort for a day or so. 'Chester?'

'Chester,' he agreed. 'It's a different world. Jesus, it's nearly Wales. Safe as houses. No contact with the Manchester bunch at all, so far as we know.'

So far as we know. Hardly the ring of bloody confidence. How much did they know? Three-fifths of fuck all, if past experience was anything to go by. 'Drug trafficking?'

'Mainly.' There was a look of relief on Salter's face, even though he was trying hard to hard to keep it hidden. He knew he had her hooked now. Once you started talking about the detail, there was no going back. 'One of those who'll bring in anything if the price is right. Some cigarettes and booze, but mainly the hard stuff. Comes across from the east coast ports, and then they distribute it around Chester and North Wales.'

'But not Manchester or Liverpool?'

'There are bigger fish operating up there. No point in this one trying to compete. He's got a nice little niche of his own, without antagonising the competition.'

It made sense. The north west was carved up pretty thoroughly by the big boys. That elite bunch had included the infamous Jeff Kerridge, until Salter had blown off the side of Kerridge's head, supposedly in self defence. They'd had intelligence that Kerridge's widow, the very redoubtable Helen, was continuing her late husband's good work. And now Pete Boyle, Kerridge's former protégé turned competitor, was out of prison and, by all accounts, also rebuilding his influence around Manchester.

That was the real source of her unease, even now. There'd been a point, six months before, when she was convinced that Salter was on Boyle's payroll. Salter had claimed that, with no one to trust, he'd been forced to go freelance to gather definitive evidence against Kerridge and their corrupt former boss, Keith Welsby. Welsby had ended up behind bars, and was still awaiting trial after a botched suicide attempt. Salter had emerged smelling of roses. But Marie had suspected that the scent concealed a more noxious stink. If Boyle had been looking to depose Kerridge, maybe Salter's intervention hadn't been so public-spirited after all. And that in turn raised questions about the manner of Kerridge's death.

She'd agreed to join Salter's team because she wanted some closure on all that. She wanted to find out the truth. But the last six months had proved nothing. As far as she could tell, Salter had played everything by the book. He was still tasked with rebuilding the case against Pete Boyle that had collapsed with Welsby's exposure and Kerridge's death. They'd arrested Boyle with the expectation of a successful prosecution, but the evidence had been irredeemably tainted by Welsby's corruption. In Marie's eyes, the whole affair had ended just too well for Boyle and she suspected that Salter had been part of that.

But she could prove nothing. He'd asked to take on the Boyle case, supposedly as unfinished business, but perhaps simply to ensure that it remained under his control. Whatever his motives, he'd appeared to make some progress. They'd gathered more intercept evidence against Boyle, they'd pinned down one or two more witnesses. A few more tiny pieces of the jigsaw had fallen into place. They were still a long way from having anything they could be confident would stand up in court. But, given that the Prosecution Service had already ended up with egg on its collective face once before, building a new case was always going to be a slow process.

It might be that Salter was simply going through the motions, recognising that he had to be seen to be doing something about Boyle. But Marie had seen and heard nothing that might confirm her suspicions.

And now this. Sending her back to the edge of Boyle's stamping ground. Pushing protocol to its limit by assigning her to an area where she might be recognised. It wasn't against the rules exactly, but it wasn't standard practice.

The generous explanation was that Salter was, in his inimitable style, just jerking her around. He knew the situation with Liam. He knew how difficult things were getting. His initial promise had been that, even when it was time for her to go back into the front line, he'd find some operational role that kept her reasonably close to home. She'd accepted that, at least for the time being, it wouldn't be possible for her to continue in an undercover position. She assumed they'd find her some investigation or enforcement job in London. It wasn't exactly the career move she was looking for, but it would do till, one way or another, things became easier on the domestic front.

So maybe this was just Salter pulling the rug from under her, handing her a whole new set of problems to contend with. The less benign interpretation was that he was using her. If her suspicions were correct, and Salter really was on Boyle's payroll, then maybe she'd been selected to do some of Boyle's dirty work. As Salter had implied, any drug dealers in Chester were operating on the edge of Boyle's territory. Perhaps Boyle was looking to expand his empire and her role was to help take out the competition.

Salter was leaning back in his chair, his relaxed manner suggesting that he was confident he'd achieved his objective, even though his words remained tentative. 'Just give it some thought, sis. That's all I want. Sleep on it overnight. We can chat about it again tomorrow.'

You smooth bastard, she thought. Whatever other qualities you might or might not have, you're good at this. You know how to play people. You know I want to be back in the field really; you know the kind of work I want to be doing. You may even know that I'm just looking for a way to trip you up, to prove some link between you and Boyle. You've pitched this just right, going out on a limb yourself so you can lure me out after you.

And maybe, her mind continued before she could control her thoughts, he knows what you want at home, too. Maybe he realises that all your talk of wanting to stay near home, of needing to be there for Liam, is so much bullshit. Maybe he knows that you're looking for a reason to get away.

Maybe. If so, Salter knew her better than she knew herself. She thought she'd reconciled herself to doing whatever it took to stay near Liam. To give him the support he needed. She'd come to terms with that – right up to the point where Salter had dangled this assignment in front of her.

She pushed herself up from her chair, determinedly looking Salter in the eye. 'Okay,' she said. 'I'll think about it. And I'll tell you tomorrow.'

Salter smiled back at her, his expression unrevealing. 'That's all I can ask of you, sis. All I can ask.'

2

'Just about there,' the DI said, pointing to an apparently unremarkable point on the hard shoulder. He gestured off towards the steady stream of traffic heading along the dual carriageway. 'Cool bastard. It was well out in full view. Wouldn't have been much traffic at that time of night, but even so . . .' His tone sounded almost admiring.

'You reckon a professional job?' Brennan asked. It was a miserable day for early autumn. Not raining yet, but leaden skies low over the horizon. Pity any poor bugger who'd just arrived here on holiday. They were standing in a gateway to a field beyond the road. A bleak landscape. Flat grassland, windblown hedges. The tang of the grey sea in the air.

Sheep were munching unheedingly behind them, and Brennan was growing conscious of the layer of mud caking his expensive shoes. Should have changed into an old pair before setting off, but he hadn't reckoned on getting brought on a field trip quite so quickly. Clearly, they were keen for him to see what he wanted and get out of their hair as speedily as possible.

'Not much doubt,' the DI said. 'All very efficient. Clean

34

as a whistle. Nothing much for forensics.' Not a Welshman, Brennan thought. Maybe a hint of Scouser there. Come over the border to do missionary work.

'What about the victims?' Brennan had read the files and, in his usual way, had memorised most of the salient points. But it was always useful to hear it from the horse's mouth. Sometimes you heard stuff that they didn't want to write down. 'Known?'

'One of them. Mo Tallent. Small time freelance: runs errands for anyone with a bob or two. The pride of Rhyl. No Talent, we called him.'

'Very droll.' Brennan moved to stand next to the DI, who was staring at the grass before him as if the two bodies were still lying there. 'What about the other?'

'No record. But one of the immigration officers at the port remembered him driving a car with Tallent in the passenger seat. False passports, so the names don't tally. False plates on the car, but a match with Tallent's passport and with the car type and colour if anyone did a cursory check.'

Brennan nodded. 'So they were on business.'

'Seems like it. Someone else's business. Tallent wasn't connected enough to set up those kind of arrangements on his own.'

'But we've an idea what the business was?' Brannan straightened up and looked at the DI. Like getting blood from a sodding pebble, he thought, even though we both know I've read the bloody file.

The DI nodded. 'Four of them in the car, according to the border records. Tallent. Mr X. And two women. Working girls, we're assuming. Probably illegals, being taken to a nice new home in the big city – Liverpool or Manchester. That's where Tallent did most of his bigger business.'

Brennan turned and surveyed the flat, unenticing landscape. There was some fine country in North Wales. This wasn't it. 'What about Tallent's associates?'

The DI shrugged. 'We're pursuing that, of course. But everyone's clammed up, as you'd expect.'

'And the women?' Brennan had already begun to walk back towards the road and their parked car. He couldn't imagine that he was likely to learn much more from being out here. Other than never to wear his best shoes to work.

'Nothing. We presume they were taken.'

'Jesus.' Brennan paused, his eyes fixed on the passing traffic. 'Pieces of meat.'

'Pretty much.' The DI caught up with him, sounding slightly out of breath. 'I imagine they've probably ended up in your neck of the woods.' He made the words sound slightly accusatory, as if Brennan had been casting aspersions on local morality.

'I dare say,' Brennan agreed. 'So what do we think this was, then? Turf war?'

'Something like that. But if so, it's a bloody serious one. This isn't just some local hoodlums giving the opposition a warning. This is two very bloody corpses. Expertly dispatched.' The DI paused, fumbling in his pocket for the car keys. 'But then I imagine that's why you're here.'

Brennan nodded, strolling back along the hard shoulder to where the DI's car was parked. Just a few yards from the spot where the victims' car had been parked. 'Well, I assume that's why I'm here,' he said, smiling now. 'But frankly, at the moment, your guess is almost as good as mine.'

'Shit. *Shit!*'

She could hear the voice from the rear of the house, and for a moment she was tempted to turn around, step silently back outside, and head for the pub. There was nothing wrong here that a good evening's drinking couldn't cure. Except, of course, that there was. She'd tried drinking it away once or twice. It brought a temporary respite, but everything was still there the next morning. And you had to face it with a hangover.

She closed the front door noisily, making sure she'd unmistakably announced her entrance. 'Liam?'

'In the back.' The fury of his previous utterance had drained away. There was another tone in his voice now. Something not too far removed from despair. Christ, she thought. Another fun-filled night in the Donovan household. Almost immediately she regretted the thought. This wasn't about her. Whatever this was like for her, it was a thousand times worse for Liam. Of course, she knew that. And of course it didn't help in the slightest.

She trudged her way slowly through the house and stood in the doorway of the former dining room that Liam had adopted as a studio. He was sitting slumped in his wheelchair in front of his easel. There was paint smeared across the canvas in a way that looked anything but artistic, unless Liam was attempting a radical shift in his painting style.

'I can't do it,' he said.

She didn't know how to respond. She could offer platitudes, try to tell him it wasn't true. But they both knew that it *was* true, at least up to a point. She was no judge of art, though she liked Liam's paintings. But even she could see that he'd lost something – a sureness of touch that characterised his best work. It wasn't that his recent work was bad. At least, Marie didn't think so. She could tell that the same vision was there, the same sense of imagery and perspective. But she recognised that he could no longer render his ideas with his old precision.

She'd tried to reassure him that it didn't matter. It would just mark a change in style. After all, weren't there theories that some of the old masters had developed their unique techniques as a result of various medical conditions – poor eyesight, colour-blindness, that sort of thing? Perhaps Liam could work within the confines of his condition to create something new.

It was bullshit, of course, and Liam's response had been so scathing that she'd never tried the same argument again. But that left her with not much else to say. Even so, Liam stared back over his shoulder at her, challenging her to disagree.

'What happened?' she said, finally.

'Christ knows. I thought I'd have a go at something new. At least try to make a start. I've been feeling knackered all week. But I just wanted—' He stopped, his mouth moving slightly, as if he didn't have the words to express what was in his mind. 'I can't just stop. I've got to keep trying.'

She moved forward and put a hand on his shoulder. 'Tell me what happened.'

'I've not done anything for weeks. Not really. I've played around putting a dab or here or there, pretending I was improving things—' He stopped again. It was as if his mouth ran ahead of his brain, so that he had to stop every minute or two for his thoughts to catch up. 'But I was just fooling myself. Most of it's not worth trying to improve, anyway.' He paused again, watching as she dragged a chair from the corner of the room and sat down beside him. 'So this afternoon I just thought – well, let's have a go.' He waved his hand towards the canvas. 'I'd been doing some sketches. They weren't very good, but I thought they'd at least be the basis of something. Shit—'

She looked up at the smears of red and brown paint across the blank sheet. 'I take it that wasn't what you intended?'

He stopped and smiled for the first time, recognising that she was trying to engage with him. 'No, not exactly. Christ, I wasn't even trying to do anything very complicated. Just a few initial brushstrokes. And I couldn't even do that properly. The lines were all over the place. In the end, I just scrubbed it out.' He looked back at her, the smile faded, the eyes despairing. 'Shit, Marie. It's the only thing I could do, and now I can't do it any more.'

There was nothing she could say. There was no point in denying it or in trying to offer any attempt at consolation. She knew from experience that he wouldn't be in any mood to listen to that. She grasped his hand in hers, squeezing slightly, trying to express physically the emotions she couldn't articulate in words. It wasn't worth, now, even trying to pretend that his condition might improve. The consultant had made that clear. Liam had gone well beyond the point where they might expect any remission. The best they could hope for – and even this seemed increasingly forlorn as week followed week – was that his condition might stabilise, that he might remain as he now was. Looking at him this evening, that hardly seemed a consoling thought.

'Come on,' she said. 'I'll get some supper on. Open a bottle of wine. You're exhausted now. You can try again tomorrow—' Even as she said the last words, she regretted them, knowing how Liam was likely to react.

'Jesus, Marie, haven't you worked it out yet? I'm always bloody exhausted. I sit around on my arse all day in this bloody contraption, watching fucking makeover shows on TV. And I'm still bloody knackered. It's not something a good night's sleep's going to sort out. Assuming I could even get a good night's sleep.'

Not even trying to respond to any of this, she climbed to her feet and pushed the wheelchair back through into the sitting room. Depression, she thought. On top of everything else, like some bad joke. Apparently, it wasn't uncommon for sufferers from multiple sclerosis also to suffer from clinical depression. Liam had had bouts of that before, long before he'd been diagnosed with MS. Just my artistic temperament, he'd half-joked, when they'd first talked about it. But now it looked as though it might have been just one more indicator of this bloody illness. Christ knew, he had enough to be depressed about.

She positioned him in front of the television, searching through the channels to find something that wasn't entirely mind numbing. That was another thing, she thought. Perhaps the most worrying of all.

She'd expected the physical disability. Maybe not the extent of it or the speed of its progression – but she'd known it was going to happen. She'd steeled herself for it, as best she could.

What she hadn't expected was the condition would affect him in other ways. His cognitive abilities, to use the jargon that had become so painfully familiar. It wasn't unusual for MS to have some impact of that kind, but usually the effects were relatively minor – the odd difficulty in remembering a word or in formulating a sentence, some increased forgetfulness. Not that different from the fate that awaits most of us as we grow older, she thought.

But in Liam's case it already seemed worse than that. He forgot things that had happened only minutes before. He struggled with words. There were activities, familiar day-to-day tasks that he seemed to have abandoned entirely – using their PC, operating the microwave, even using his mobile phone. Some of that resulted from the physical effects, of course. It was increasingly hard for him to get about the house, get into the kitchen, so he was less inclined to do things that previously would have seemed routine. And, as he'd snappily pointed out, if he hardly ever left the house, why would be need to use his mobile phone?

But it was more than that. She'd watched him, on a few occasions when he hadn't realised she'd been observing, and seen how he'd struggled with what should have been straightforward tasks. Sometimes trying over and over again to complete an action like making a phone call. She'd heard him getting into tangles trying to explain something to a caller – making arrangements for a delivery, say, or change a medical appointment. Once or twice, she'd had to intervene to sort something out, and she'd seen the mix of despair and irritation in his eyes.

He would barely admit that there was a problem. He couldn't deny the deterioration in his physical condition, but he refused to acknowledge any other problems. If she tried to raise the issue, he cut her off or insisted that it was tiredness. But she'd called the consultant back after their last joint visit – feeling as disloyal as an errant lover in doing so – and asked his view.

'There's definitely something there,' the consultant had confirmed. 'Some cognitive problems. A degree of disinhibition.'

'More than you'd usually expect?' she'd asked.

'Nothing's usual with MS. But, yes, definitely something more significant than the norm.'

It was the luck of the draw, the consultant had explained. It very much depended on which areas of the brain were being affected. Generally, the effects were primarily physical. But sometimes, if you were unlucky, there could be a significant cognitive effect as well.

'We could get the clinical psychologists to have a look at him,' the consultant had offered. 'Do some tests. Get a measure of how far things have progressed.'

She'd turned down the offer, at least for the present. She knew there was a problem. She could see no real benefit in finding out quite how much of one. It would be like rubbing Liam's nose in something he was trying hard to avoid. She'd go down that route only when it was really needed – which would no doubt be when she had to persuade social services to give Liam more support.

Now, though, watching him sit in front of some cosy police series on the TV, she was haunted by the consultant's concluding comments. She'd asked the doctor what the prognosis might be, what further deterioration might be expected.

As always, the consultant had been unforthcoming. 'There's no way of knowing. It might just stabilise—'

'Yes, I know that,' she'd interrupted. 'You've explained that. But what do you *think*?'

There'd been a pause, as if the consultant was considering the idiocy of her question. 'Well, the only guidance we've got is how quickly it's progressed over the last year or so. And that's been very rapid. So, well, if you *forced* me to give you a view, I'd say it's probable that it'll continue to progress at a similar rate.'

'And in terms of his – cognitive abilities? What can we expect there? If I *forced* you to give an opinion.'

Another pause. 'Well, the same, I suppose.'

'And what does that mean? What will it look like?'

'You need to understand. It's not like, say, Alzheimer's. You won't get the same types of confusion about, you know, who people are or where he is that you'd find in those kinds of dementia. This is more like – oh, I don't know – more like an old computer, gradually getting slower and slower. It's the white matter, the connections in the brain, that are being affected. So it's likely that he'll get increasingly passive, increasingly unresponsive. If things get more severe, that is.'

And that was what she'd seen, as the weeks had passed. Today's outburst had been unusual, a rare demonstration of energy and emotion, however negative. That happened from time to time, as Liam's frustration at his condition built inside his head to the point where he could no longer contain it. But those sudden explosions were

43

increasingly rare islands in an otherwise endless sea of calm.

It wasn't the Liam she'd known. The old Liam had been sparky, enthusiastic, full of ideas. He could be a pain to live with at times, their different personalities rubbing up against each other in a constant friction. But that had been the Liam she'd loved. The Liam who was always looking for a new challenge, a new opportunity. The Liam who continued to pursue his dream of being a successful artist even when, some might think, it had ceased to be realistic. The Liam who would do anything rather than sit slumped in front of some anodyne television programme.

She returned from the kitchen bearing an opened bottle of red wine and two glasses, a takeaway menu tucked under her arm. Liam already had a local authority carer who came in a couple of times a day to help him get something to eat, check he was okay. Increasingly, though, Marie had the sense that he shouldn't be left alone for too long. He needed more care, someone to be with him through the day.

Would that be her? She couldn't see it. She tried to imagine herself giving up her job, spending the day as Liam's full-time carer. The image simply wouldn't form in her head. Apart from the practical questions – what would they actually live on, for example? – that just wasn't the person she was. Maybe that was selfish – well, of course it was selfish – but she knew that if she tried to devote her life entirely to caring for Liam, she'd probably end up killing both of them.

It needed thinking about, though. She had to start planning for this. She'd intended to discuss Salter's proposed assignment with Liam before she gave Salter her answer.

But she knew there was no way she could raise it tonight, and, even if she did, no likelihood that Liam would be able to give her a sensible response.

Another decision postponed, then. But she was beginning to recognise, watching Liam gazing vacantly at the flickering TV screen, that nothing could be delayed forever.

3

'Get much from the sheep-shaggers?'

Brennan paused in the doorway, his blank expression suggesting that Salter was speaking some entirely unfamiliar language. Brennan closed the door behind him, paused to hang his jacket carefully on the coat stand, and walked across the room to the conference table where Salter was sitting. He paused for a moment, as if deciding whether or not to sit, and then lowered himself on to the chair opposite Salter. 'Not really. Nothing new, anyway. Mind you, it might have helped if I'd had the foggiest idea what I was supposed to be looking for.'

'Local colour,' Salter said. 'Mainly green out there, I imagine.'

Brennan bent down to unfasten his expensive-looking leather attaché case. Salter was dressed in the plainclothes cop's standard uniform. Jeans, open-necked shirt, leather jacket tossed casually around the back of chair. Brennan wondered whether he always dressed like that. He suspected not. Salter struck him as a Marks & Spencer man. Brennan's own suit was Paul Smith, and not off-the-shelf. 'I still don't really know why I'm here,' he said, placing a thin manila file on the table in front of him. 'Not just today, but the whole thing. Why have I been seconded over here? Don't tell me it's just because you're short-staffed.'

'We are, actually. Bloody short-staffed, now you come to mention it. And particularly short of bright young things like yourself.'

'I'm not sure I'm all that young any more, let alone bright. Anyway, I thought this place was wall-to-wall bright young things.'

'It's a mess over here, to be honest, Jack.' Salter's voice had taken on an ingratiating tone now. 'It's been a mess from the start. It was a political decision to set up the Agency, so everything was done at a rush. Bits and pieces from all over the place, cobbled together. Of course, there were some excellent people – there still *are* some excellent people – but we're holding it together with not much more than good intentions.'

Brennan noted that Salter had casually included himself in the category of 'excellent people'. Probably not without reason, from what he'd heard, but it was clear that Salter wasn't short of ego. Well, okay, Brennan thought. That makes two of us. 'And now it's going through another set of changes?'

'It's never stopped bloody changing,' Salter said. 'That's the trouble. As soon as the dust begins to settle, they start moving the deckchairs round again. If it's not the politicians, it's senior management trying to second guess what the politicians might want. People get pissed off.'

'Well, I'm sold,' Brennan said. 'I can't think of anywhere I'd rather be seconded to.'

'Yes, well, at least you're only being seconded,' Salter said. 'Means you've still got a way back.'

'And you haven't?'

Salter shrugged. 'There's nothing to stop me applying for jobs back in the police service. At the moment, I'd even be in with a shout. Despite everything, you get some good experience over here. But the longer I'm out of the main-stream, the harder it'll be to get back. That's why a lot of our best people have already voted with their feet.'

'And that's why you need some new blood, is it?' There was a cynical edge to Brennan's voice. Experience had taught him that management decision-making rarely stemmed from much more than short-term expediency. We've got a gap to fill. You got anyone suitable? Well, Jack Brennan's royally screwed his career. We could send him over to cool his heels for a few months. Keep everyone happy. He could imagine the conversation.

'It's why we need talented officers,' Salter said. 'And, yes, I've been fully informed about your background. It doesn't stop you being a very capable, committed and experienced officer.'

'It bloody well proves that's what I am,' Brennan said. 'That's the point, from where I'm sitting.'

Salter looked doubtful. 'Yes, well. Not everyone will see it that way. Even here.'

'I imagine not. I'm well past caring.'

'And it means we have something in common.'

Brennan gazed thoughtfully at Salter. 'So I understand. Funny how things work out, isn't it? From what I hear, you're quite the hero round here.'

'In some people's eyes. Not in everyone's, I imagine.'

'Your case was a little more spectacular than mine.'

'Not through choice,' Salter said. 'I just didn't know what I was taking on. Nearly went completely tits up. The outcome was the same for both of us.'

'A corrupt copper exposed. I guess so. My case wasn't so clear-cut. Apparently.'

'No. Well, things rarely are, are they?' Salter paused, a smile playing softly across his lips. 'Unless you're actually caught with your hands in the till.'

Brennan nodded, accepting that Salter was just playing games. He'd come across plenty like Salter over the years. Smart-arse graduate types who maybe weren't quite as smart as they thought, but who enjoyed yanking people around until they were found out. Christ, he'd probably been one of them himself, though it hadn't felt like it.

'Is that why I'm here, then?' Brennan said. 'Birds of a feather, and all that. Or did you just feel sorry for me?'

'Not my call. Though of course you're just what we needed. Like I say, the really experienced investigators are getting thin on the ground here. We're up to our ears in ex-Revenue types. They've been only too keen to stay with us. Well, it's more fun than chasing up some dodgy builder for accepting too much cash in hand. No, it's the honest-to-goodness coppers we're short of.'

'So now you've found an honest-to-goodness copper, what exactly do you want to do with me?'

Salter pushed himself slowly to his feet and walked over to the window. The meeting room was in the Manchester regional office, an anonymous industrial building in the furthest corner of an equally nondescript industrial estate, somewhere in the far reaches of Trafford Park. The window looked out over the rear of a small-scale distribution company – a couple of lorries lined up for loading, a forklift truck, a couple of piles of poorly stacked pallets. 'Kevin Sheerin,' Salter said.

'Go on.'

'You knew him?'

'We all knew him. Not that any of us particularly wanted to. Small time dealer. Occasional grass. No one's friend; probably a few people's enemy.'

'And now no longer with us.'

'Hit and run. Back streets of Stockport. Sheerin, pissed out of his head, fell into the road and was hit by a car. Driver didn't stop. Not entirely sure I blame him.'

'Accident, then?'

'Christ knows. Like I say, Sheerin had made a few enemies. Grassed up a few of the wrong people. Got away with it as long as he did only because he was so small-time. But he might well have pissed off one person too many. Not worth wasting a lot of resources on, either way.'

'So you weren't treating it as murder?'

'We were treating it as a hit and run. Inquest gave an open verdict. We made the usual efforts to find the driver – CCTV, any witnesses. But no dice yet, as far as I know.'

'Is Stockport Sheerin's usual stamping ground?'

'No. He's more of an inner-city Manc type. Cheetham Hill. That's another reason he survived as long as he did – kept on the right side of the people who matter up there.'

'So he was off piste when he was killed?'

'Off piste and well pissed. Definitely. We checked out the local pubs. Found a couple of witnesses who remembered him knocking back the pints earlier in the evening. Was

50

with a few others, but nobody knew who they were. Or so they said.' Brennan leaned back in the hard chair and stretched out his legs. 'Who knows? Might have been there on business, might have just gone out for a quiet pint or two with his mates.'

'In Stockport?'

'It's been known. Apparently. Though I'd stick to the real ale in the Crown. Is all this going somewhere?'

'Last case you were working on, before we called on your services.' Salter turned from the window. 'Stephen Kenning.'

'This your specialist subject? Recent cases of the Greater Manchester Police, Metropolitan Division?'

'Maybe. How am I doing?'

'Seems to me you're asking all the questions.'

Salter lowered himself back into the seat opposite Brennan. 'Okay, here's another one. Your starter for ten. Tell me about Stephen Kenning.'

'Another grass. Big time, though. Blew the whistle on a major drugs ring in Longsight, four or five years back. Was in witness protection, living all by himself in a little cottage out in the Peaks.'

'Picturesque.'

'Not this bit. But there was a decent view. So you could see anyone coming from a mile away. Except that he didn't.'

'No. Shot three times, I understand.'

Brennan nodded. 'Pro job. It was a couple of weeks before anyone found him. Postman noticed the smell eventually.'

'Anyone in the frame for it?'

'You must know the answer to that,' Brennan said. 'You seem to know quite a lot about all this.'

51

'Don't pretend you share everything with the likes of us. Any more than we share everything with the likes of you.'

'In this case, there was nothing to share. I mean, it's obvious who's behind it. But we can't prove any link, and we were never going to get near whoever actually pulled the trigger.'

'And it took a burden off your hands,' Salter pointed out. 'Pain in the arse, witness protection.'

'If you say so.' Brennan's face was expressionless. 'Anyway, we'd reached a dead end.'

'This drugs ring,' Salter said. 'You know who the key players were?'

'We know who went inside. That doesn't mean they were the key players. We took it as far as we could with our resources. I imagine you lot would have the bigger picture. What was it you said about not sharing stuff with the likes of us?'

'We just try to make connections. Name Jeff Kerridge mean anything to you?'

Brennan looked up. 'Not as much as he means to you. He was the guy you shot?'

'Yeah. He was the guy who'd got our corrupt cop on the payroll. They tried to kill me. Then, like you say, I killed him.'

'You're saying that it was Kerridge behind the drugs ring?'

'Kerridge didn't leave any more fingerprints than he could help. Looks that way, though.'

'But if Kerridge is dead, who killed Stephen Kenning?'

'Interesting question, isn't it?'

'Another interesting question.' Brennan fingered the file he'd placed on the table at the start of the meeting. 'What does all this have to do with our two fall guys in North Wales? I'm assuming you didn't send me out there just to enjoy the scenery?'

'Christ, no. Just wanted an objective view on what they were up to. Don't trust those Welsh bastards to share any more than they need to.'

'Well, they were very polite, just not very forthcoming. They gave me the basics, but not much more.' Brennan flipped over the file. 'Two bodies. One was a small-time crook, known to them. Name of Mo Tallent. The other's still unidentified. Not on their records. Not yet reported missing.'

'Nice to be loved,' Salter commented. 'What do you reckon, then?'

'Looked like a warning to me. Somebody frightening off the competition.'

'But the local plods claim they don't know who Tallent was likely to be working for?'

'When did you leave the diplomatic corps? Or have you forgotten that I'm still officially a local plod?'

'Ah, but not a Welsh one. Sad thing is, they're probably telling the truth. I bet they really don't know.'

Brennan shrugged. 'Don't really believe that, though, do you? They must have an idea who Tallent worked for. The DI over there told me that everyone had clammed up. Probably so. But the local plods will have a decent idea which clams are worth prising open. A better idea than you, at any rate.' Brennan flicked through the handful of papers in the file – witness statements, scene of crime reports, all the routine bumf, but nothing that was likely to be helpful. 'So, yes, if you want my honest opinion, I reckon he was holding something back. Probably no great significance in that, though. He most likely just couldn't see why he should share his speculations with a bunch who think the Welsh are largely bumbling sheep-shaggers. Not that he was Welsh, as it happens.' Brennan paused, as if a new thought had suddenly struck him. 'In much the same way, I imagine, as you're not bothering to share your specu-lations with a local plod like me. Or, at least, you're taking your time getting round to it.'

Salter smiled again, and this time there was a little more evidence of humour in his eyes. 'Yeah, I've got a few ideas. You know much about the prostitution scene in south Manchester? Professionally, I mean.'

Brennan ignored the jibe. 'Not really my field,' he said. 'No shortage of it, though, from what I understand.'

'That's one way of putting it. It's the usual mix – from desperate junkies on street corners to the more upmarket escort stuff. Amounts to the same thing in the end, though. It's the middle ground I'm interested in.'

'Professionally, you mean?' Brennan said. 'You mean the massage parlour type places?'

'Massage parlours. Brass-houses. The places one step up from the poor buggers on the streets. Again, it's what you might call a mixed economy. Some sole proprietors plying their sleazy trade in one or two establishments. Some who've done a bit better for themselves. High street chains, if you like. Of course, it's a very competitive environment.'

'Important to build your market share,' Brennan agreed. 'You've seen some turf wars, then. Recently, I mean.'

'There's been a bit of expansion over the last year or two. Mostly immigrant groups – the Chinese have always been big in Manchester and there've been some Romanians making a splash recently.'

'Not exactly your territory, all this. I don't see your lot busting massage parlours.'

'We leave that to you local plods. We're more interested in what the parlours are being used for. Apart from the obvious, I mean. Drugs. Money laundering. People trafficking. A lot of our targets see brothels as their retail outlets.'

'So you reckon that what happened in Wales was one of your targets putting the squeeze on the competition?' Brennan said. 'Would this be about your famous Jeff Kerridge again?'

'Yeah, another little thread in Kerridge's big commercial web. Again, we don't know for sure. Kerridge was much too smart to get himself directly mixed up in that kind of world. Everything was a step or two removed. But, one way or another, Kerridge had established his own little network of high street boutiques.'

'Except that Kerridge remains dead,' Brennan pointed out. 'So if someone's putting the squeeze on, it's not him.'

'That's the thing about Kerridge's sad departure,' Salter said. 'It really tossed the cat among the pigeons. Lots of jockeying for position. All the more so as Kerridge's supposed number two, Pete Boyle, was temporarily out of commission at the time.'

'Way I heard it,' Brennan said. 'Kerridge and Boyle weren't all that chummy towards the end anyhow?'

'You heard right. It was a question of who'd screw the other one first. But Boyle saw himself as the heir apparent. Trouble was, he wasn't the only one.' Salter laughed. 'Once

Kerridge popped his clogs, various parties stepped into the breach pretty quickly, even before Boyle was back walking the streets. Chief among them, Mrs K.'

Brennan raised an eyebrow. 'Kerridge's wife?'

'The fragrant Helen. Not a lady to be underestimated.'

'So you think all this is linked? Kenning and Sheerin and these two poor bastards in Wales. Collateral damage in the war of the Manc succession?'

'Something like that.'

'Bit thin, isn't it? I mean, you could well be right. But these were the kinds of buggers who made enemies every way they turned. Might have been a dozen people wanted to take them out.'

'Might have been. But Pete Boyle definitely did.'

'You reckon?'

'Done a bit of digging,' Salter said. 'Called in a few favours from a few scrotes. Informants.'

'Imagine our lot would have done the same. Not aware they found much.'

'Maybe not. But they didn't know the question to ask. They didn't think to ask about Pete Boyle.'

'Boyle's a big player in these parts,' Brennan pointed out. 'Especially now that Kerridge has gone. His name would have come up.'

'No doubt. But there'd be no direct connection between any of these cases and Boyle. Or Kerridge, for that matter. Not even Kenning the grass. I only made the link between Kerridge and that drug ring after the event. We hadn't got it pegged as one of Kerridge's outfits – still haven't, officially. It was only after I'd made the link between Kenning and Boyle that I went back and checked the detail of the case Kenning had been involved in. One or two of the players who went down were second-level associates of Kerridge's. It doesn't prove for certain that Kerridge had a finger in that particular pie, but I'd wager money on it.'

Brennan frowned. 'I'm not following this. You're saying that these cases are all linked to Boyle. But that it's not a direct business link.'

Salter was smiling broadly now. He had the air of a magician who was in the process of pulling off a particularly neat piece of misdirection. 'Not quite. Boyle's got a real business interest in all three cases. But that's not why they were picked.' He leaned forward and pulled Brennan's file towards him, then flicked through the pages until he found the short report on Mo Tallent. 'Tallent,' he said. 'Petty thief and grifter. Spent most of his adult life living in sunny Rhyl, for reasons best known to himself. But born and brought up in less sunny Hulme. Left in his early twenties. Partly because, for one reason or another, he'd seriously fucked off Peter Boyle. And, trust me, Peter Boyle is not someone you want to antagonise.'

Brennan shook his head. 'Some kind of personnel vendetta? Boyle waited twenty years to get even?'

'Not quite. Let's move on to Stephen Kenning. Bit more straightforward, that one. No one likes a grass. He'd sold Kerridge and Boyle down the river on that drugs deal. Even if there was no risk of them being implicated, they must have taken a financial hit. A decent enough motive for icing Kenning. But it turns out there's a bit more. Kenning is also a Hulme alumnus. The original school of hard fucking knocks. Turns out that Kenning and Boyle were bosom buddies as teenagers. They'd drifted apart over the years. But I'm told that Boyle still thought of Kenning as a mate, pretty much up the point where he shafted the drugs deal.'

'Did Kenning know he was shafting Boyle?'

'Who knows? But the effect's the same, either way. From what I know of Pete Boyle, there's no way he wouldn't have taken in personally.'

'Okay, so Boyle had a personal link with Tallent and Kenning. What about the third guy, Sheerin?'

'Surprise, surprise. Same again. Another graduate of the University of Hulme. Rough contemporary of Boyle's. Interesting one, this, though. Couldn't find much connection at first. No evidence they'd known each other. So I did more digging. Eventually found an older guy who'd been mates with Boyle's mother. Single parent. Tough as nails, by all accounts. Father had fucked off before Boyle was born, assuming that she ever knew who he was. Anyway, rumour was that Sheerin's old man had had some sort of fling with Boyle's mum. Treated her badly. Thought of himself as a hard man, but got short shift when he tried any rough stuff. So ran off with the housekeeping money or some such. Old codger I spoke to wasn't too clear on the details, but reckoned that Boyle would have reason not to be too enamoured of the old bastard. Or of his son.'

'So you're saying that all these three, one way or another, had bad blood with Boyle? Sounds a bit tenuous as a motive for murder.'

'Of course. But that wasn't the motive for the murders. That was just the reason why these three particular poor buggers got chosen.'

'So what is this? Boyle gets out of prison. Sees his hoped-for empire beginning to disintegrate. Barbarians at the gate, all that. So sends out some warning messages. That the idea?' Brennan looked sceptical.

'Pretty much. These three were well chosen. Whoever employed Tallent would be one of the interlopers into Kerridge's lucrative sex-trade operations. Sheerin was doing business for one of the gangs who've been drifting into Kerridge's traditional territories in Cheetham Hill. As for Kenning – well, like I say, no one loves a grass. There've been a few other incidents as well, less serious than these three. Premises getting torched. The odd beating up. One or two serious Saturday night injuries.'

Brennan's expression hadn't changed. 'You realise that serious Saturday night injuries aren't that uncommon in central Manchester? It's a trend even our lot have managed to spot.'

'Yeah, unlike any of this.' Salter bent down from the table and lifted a laptop bag on to the table. He unzipped it, fumbled inside for a moment, and then pulled out a plastic wallet stuffed with papers. 'I've been through a stack of those cases. Some I've dismissed. A couple of the fires look like genuine accidents or insurance jobs. Some of the beatings are just muggings or domestics of one sort or another. But I'm left with maybe eight or nine incidents, apart from our three biggies, which I could link back to Pete Boyle.' He pushed the wallet across the table towards Brennan. 'Have a look.'

Brennan pulled out the papers and flicked quickly through them, stopping every now and then to read one of the reports more carefully. Eventually, he looked up. 'Okay.

I don't deny it's interesting. But Boyle's a big fish in this pond. You could probably link anything back to him if you tried hard enough.'

'Three murder victims who grew up within half a mile of him? One went to school with him? Another's dad screwed Boyle's mum, in more ways than one? Hell of a coincidence.'

Brennan nodded. 'Let's say you've convinced me. Or half-convinced me. Where are we going with this?'

'This is why you're here. The secondment. It's why I wanted an experienced investigator. Someone local, with decent inside knowledge. Someone who could pull the right levers, if need be, with the local police.'

'I'm flattered,' Brennan said. 'Though I'm not sure you've got the right man. If I pull any levers at the moment, it's likely just to bring a bucket of crap down on my head. I'm not exactly flavour of the month.'

'They'll forgive you soon enough once you're not under their feet as a permanent fucking reminder.' Salter leaned back in his chair and watched Brennan carefully. 'I think we've got full-scale fucking gang warfare going on here. Boyle's taking out or warning off all his competition, one by one, step by step. It's diverse enough that it slips under the radar of you local plods – here, North Wales, Derbyshire, wherever the hell it is. But it's targeted so that no one on the receiving end of it will have much doubt what it means. And as an added bonus he's settling a few old scores on the way.'

'What about Kenning? The grass. He wasn't competition.'

'You reckon? Word was that Kenning didn't turn Queen's evidence out of the goodness of his heart, but because he'd been promised a nice little nest-egg by someone who wanted to corner the market.'

'I saw the place he was living,' Brennan countered. 'Must have been a fucking small nest-egg.'

'It's a sad world. People don't always deliver on their promises. One of our dirty little secrets. That the life of a superannuated supergrass isn't all it's cracked up to be.' Salter pushed back his chair and stood up, in the manner of one indicating that the meeting was coming to an end. 'So. You game for it?'

'I'm still not entirely clear what *it* is,' Brennan said.

'We're trying to build a case against Boyle. It's been a slow process. Not least because we fucked up so spectacularly last time. So this time we want to do it absolutely by the book. I want you to act as evidence officer. Work through what we've got. See if it stacks up. Tell us where the gaps are and what we need to do to fill them. I can give you some intelligence resource from my team, though not much. We'll give you authorisation to work with the local plods, so you can finagle any information you can from them. Though good luck with that.'

'I'm an experienced investigator. But I've not worked in your environment before. You must have people around who've got more of a track record in that kind of work.'

Salter nodded, smiling, as if this was a question that he'd been waiting for. 'Maybe. But we're stretched to the fucking limit. I've a national team, trying to juggle major operations from here to sodding Portsmouth. Half my lot are so wet behind the ears they've barely been weaned, and most of the other half are the kinds of alcoholics and deadbeats who couldn't swing a return back to proper policing. I've got a clutch of officers working undercover that I'm not even supposed to talk about. And I'm not even based up here. I spend half my life stuck in the fucking ivory tower in Westminster filling in forms and writing reports so my superiors can prove to the politicians that we're not squandering their tax money on liaison trips to the fucking Bahamas, or whatever it is that they think we do when they're not looking.' He paused and took a breath. It sounded like a prepared speech, or at least a speech that Salter had delivered before. 'That's why I need someone like you, up here, who can get some real nitty-gritty work done.'

Brennan pulled the wallet of papers back towards him. 'Okay. I'll give it a shot.' He looked up at Salter, with what looked like genuine amusement on his face. 'After all, given what I've come from, it's not like I'm got much fucking option, is it?'

4

The whole thing felt wrong. Too soon. Too risky. Too ill-prepared. Shit, the last time she'd done this they'd spent months preparing her for it. They'd had the legend worked out to the last detail. Every minute of her fictional past. Every last nuance of her character and personality. She'd had an answer worked out to every possible question that might be thrown at her.

They'd put her through exercise after exercise. Memory tests. Role playing. Even that bloody farce where they'd snatched her from the airport car park and terrorised the life out of her. By the time she'd hit the street, she'd been note-perfect.

And now, what? Just over three weeks of scrambled briefings, cobbled-together documentation, hurried liaisons with informants who clearly thought they had better things to do that make her life any easier. And here she was, sitting outside the head honcho's office about to stick her head firmly on the block. The whole thing felt so bloody *amateurish*.

The smart-suited young secretary emerged again from the main man's office and regarded Marie with a look of disdain. 'I'm terribly sorry,' she said, with no obvious sign of sincerity. 'He really won't be much longer.'

The secretary didn't bother to offer any explanation for the delay, but Marie hadn't really expected any. She'd already assumed, perhaps unfairly, that this man, McGrath, was most likely just sitting in there with his feet up reading the *Daily Star*. For all that she felt unprepared, Marie had seen through this place immediately.

She smiled at the secretary. McGrath doubtless called her his PA. 'Not a problem,' Marie said. 'I appreciate how busy Mr McGrath must be.' She smiled warmly at the young woman, who now smiled uneasily back, perhaps growing conscious that her assumptions about Marie might not be entirely justified.

That was the only consolation, Marie thought. She might feel as if she'd been tossed carelessly into the deep end, but she'd already seen enough to know that, for the moment at least, she wasn't out of her depth. Bunch of cowboys, she thought, glancing around at the large secretary's office. All show, and no substance.

It had taken her a few minutes to register the fact when she'd first arrived. On the surface, it had all looked impressive enough. A neat little unit in a serviced office block just off the main drag near the centre of Chester. Half a mile and a world away from the city of Roman remains and bijou fashion shops, but it probably still had what the property agents would describe as a prestigious address. The Victrix Business Park, for Christ's sake.

Inside, though, it wasn't quite right. The place was an old factory that had clearly been converted hurriedly. Okay, perhaps not quite as hurriedly as she'd been converted into

Maggie Yates – and, come to that, couldn't they have found a more prestigious name for her as well? – but more hurriedly than the building's pretensions required. She was no expert, but even sitting here Marie could see that the wallpaper was badly applied, the paintwork sloppy, the carpet cheap and already beginning to wear. Even the office furniture looked outdated. Not, she suspected, the kind of image that McGrath was hoping to project.

There were other signs, too. As the secretary had led her in from the chilly unattended lobby, Marie had glimpsed the rear courtyard through one of the windows. A miniature junkyard – an old fridge, a discarded sink unit, a broken table lined with paint pots, all overgrown with weeds. If the offices had been recently converted, she might have thought it was just waiting to be tidied, but this place was no longer new.

Even the staff weren't up to scratch. There had been no one at the reception desk in the lobby, and no response when Marie had pressed the electric bell on the desk. After a while, she'd used her mobile to phone the number she'd been given. The secretary had answered the call and, after a few minutes, had bustled officiously through into the lobby. Marie suspected that the secretary and McGrath himself were the only occupants of this part of the building.

She knew that these thoughts were partly just a displacement activity, a way of not thinking too hard about the fragility of the ice beneath her. Salter had been full of reassurance and had even wheeled out Winsor, the psychologist, to confirm just how emotionally resilient she would be in the face of diversity. Or something like that. Winsor had spouted his familiar professional gobbledygook and she'd nodded politely, knowing by then that it was all going to happen anyway.

Jesus, then there was Liam. When she'd finally broken the news that she was going back out into the field, he'd responded better than she'd feared. He'd taken the news calmly, shrugged, told her that, yes, of course she had to keep things going at work. He absolutely understood that. He wouldn't want it any other way.

She'd enjoyed a few seconds of relief at his reaction before she became concerned. At first, she thought that Liam was reverting to the passive-aggressive style he'd perfected in the early days of his illness. But this felt different. This felt sincere. And that raised questions about what was going on in Liam's head. There were times, already, when he seemed like a different person.

She'd tried to put all that from her mind as she'd made her way up here. She and Liam had danced round the issue of her departure, talking about the practicalities rather than the emotional impact of their separation. The practicalities had been challenging enough. She'd had to ensure that a suitable care regime was in place for Liam. He was already barely capable making his way around the house, even in the wheelchair, and was no longer able to look after himself reliably. He had two carers, funded by social services and supplied through some agency, who had been coming in twice a day to prepare him a meal and, essentially, check that he was okay. After a little negotiation, they'd managed to add another visit in the evening while Marie was away. Marie had had the impression that the main carer, Sue, hadn't been all that impressed by the idea of Liam being left alone overnight. But what other option did Marie have?

'Mrs Yates?'

Shit. She almost missed her cue. That was why, in some cases, undercover officers stuck with their real names, or at least their real forenames, to minimise the risk of that moment's hesitation. Or, worse still, of reacting to a name that wasn't supposed to be yours.

She recovered herself in time. 'Miss, actually,' she said. 'Divorced. I decided to go back to my maiden name. Don't ask.' She laughed, rising to her feet and holding out her hand for McGrath to shake. 'But please call me Maggie. Pleased to meet you.'

'Likewise.' McGrath was observing her with an expression that managed to remain just the right side of lecherous. 'Please come through – Maggie.' He gestured for her to precede him into his poky office. She could feel his eyes making a full appraisal of what was likely to lie underneath her clothes. If she'd harboured any doubts about actually getting the job, she began to feel more confident now that it was in the bag.

'Please. Take a seat,' he said from behind her. There was a faint trace of an Irish lilt in his voice, she thought, though you had to listen for it. Or know something of his history. She lowered herself into the chair facing McGrath's desk, and waited while he seated himself opposite. The desk was a mess – unsorted piles of paperwork, messy looking files, a discarded coffee cup.

'Good to meet you, Maggie,' McGrath said. He'd wasted no time in taking up her invitation to use her first name. 'You come highly recommended.'

She smiled. McGrath's non-professional interest in her was so transparent that it was difficult not to play up to it.

'Not too highly, I hope. I don't know if I can live up to it.'
She knew exactly how highly she'd been recommended,
and by whom. More of the string-pulling that they were
so adept at in the Agency. It was clever stuff. It was usually
a tame informant who'd set the wheels in motion, getting
the word about her out on the grapevine. In this case,
according to Salter, they'd got wind of the fact that McGrath
was looking for a discreet administrator to help him keep
the various strands of his business in order. Looking at this
place, she wasn't surprised. McGrath had positioned
himself, as so many of them did, as a legitimate businessman, running a more or less straight operation in
parallel with his seamier activities. But, looking at the desk,
she could imagine that administration wasn't McGrath's
strongest point.

The key word, of course, was discreet. In her short telephone conversation with McGrath, they'd maintained the
fiction that she would be looking after the above-board
element of McGrath's business – an import/export business
which, according to the records she'd checked at Companies'
House, had a turnover barely large enough to cover her
requested salary. But the grapevine had been very clear that
McGrath was looking for someone to help run all parts of
his business, including those elements that were kept hidden
from the light of day.

Maggie Yates came highly recommended to fulfil that
particular brief. The story was that she'd been the brains
behind her ex-husband's business, an East End mix of
legitimate market-trading and more clandestine dealing.
She'd given her husband loyal support, up to the point
where she'd caught him dipping his hands into the till to

subsidise his affair with some Dalston pole-dancer. She'd withdrawn a sizable sum from the business account, packed her suitcases, and headed north, leaving her ex with a pregnant pole-dancer and a pile of debts. It was a decent story, filtered skilfully through a succession of friends of friends. Creating an undercover legend was a little like money-laundering, she'd sometimes thought. The original source gets lost along the way, and the story becomes a little more legitimate each time it's passed on. The figure who'd recommended her to McGrath had sincerely believed everything he'd said, having received the story himself from someone he considered reliable.

Marie had been nervous about it, because again they'd had so little time to prepare the ground. It had been well-handled, but there was always the risk that someone would pick up the phone and speak to the wrong person, and the whole house of fictional cards would come tumbling down.

It might still happen, but she felt more confident now that everything had been running for a few weeks. The rules were different in this world. If you wanted the right person, you couldn't call the JobCentre or some local temp agency. All you could do was rely on word of mouth. And McGrath wasn't entirely stupid. He'd take his time, trust her only as far as he needed to until he was confident of her loyalty and discretion. The recommendation might get her through the door, but it was her own abilities that would keep her there. That, and the fact that already McGrath was virtually panting like a lascivious dog.

'We're a small but ambitious business,' McGrath was saying, in the tone he probably reserved for the local Chamber of Commerce. 'On the way up, you might say.'

'You said it was primarily import/export?' she asked, feeding back the line that McGrath had given her over the phone. 'What sort of things?'

'Pretty much anything that I can sell at a profit, if I'm honest,' McGrath said. 'We're probably more of a distribution business than a straight importer. Take stuff off people's hands, then sell it on for a bit more.'

Marie didn't doubt it. From what she understood, most of McGrath's legitimate business comprised the kind of tat that was sold on market stalls or by street vendors. Tawdry plastic items from China. 'A middle man?' she offered.

'That's about it. Cream off a little slice for myself, that's the idea. So, Maggie, tell me about yourself. I understand you've experience in this kind of line.'

She nodded, and began to trot out the well-rehearsed lines about her ex-husband. She didn't go into the detail of how and why she'd supposedly split up with the fictitious ex, but she knew that all that background would have been carefully fed to McGrath. He was clearly as interested in her marital status, or lack of it, as he was in whatever relevant work experience she might have.

That side of the job made her feel uneasy; but she knew that as a female undercover it was almost inevitable that you'd sometimes make use of your femininity to gain some advantage, particularly over men like McGrath. You couldn't be too precious in this line of work. If the likes of McGrath were so easily distracted by the simple fact that she was a half-presentable woman, it would be stupid not to benefit.

In any case, she told herself, this time it was just part of her new character. The glamorous divorcee. She knew she was pretty decent-looking – enough to attract a few overlong glances in a male-dominated office, at least. But her usual instinct was to play down her appearance – minimal make-up, neat but low-key business suits, nothing that might attract unwanted attention.

As Maggie Yates, though, she'd raised everything just a notch or two above how she would normally choose to appear. She was wearing a business outfit that was slightly more brash, that showed an inch or two more leg and cleavage, than she would normally consider. She was wearing a little more make-up, her hair dyed a shade or two lighter than usual. She'd even managed, to her great amusement, to persuade Salter to cough up for a couple of pairs of earrings on expenses.

She'd been surprised, when she'd first effected the changes, by how much her new outward appearance influenced the way she felt and behaved. She felt a different kind of confidence, aware of the impact her appearance had on a certain type of male. Even Salter had seemed more flustered in her presence. McGrath, on the same basis, looked as if he might dissolve into a small puddle on the office floor if she were to gaze at him too intently.

McGrath nodded as she finished her brief account. 'So, do you think you'd be up to handling things round here?' The innuendo was inescapable, even if unintentional.

She looked coolly around her – at the shabby office, at the piled mess on McGrath's desk. 'I wouldn't imagine there's anything here I couldn't handle,' she said. Jesus, she thought to herself, don't push it too far. McGrath might not be responsible for his actions. She smiled innocently. 'I can give you a little run through my past experience, if you like, Mr McGrath.'

'Andrew,' he coughed. 'Andy, that is. Please call me Andy. Everybody does.' He picked up a pile of papers from the desk and shuffled them as if trying to imbue the documents with some significance. 'I don't think that'll be necessary. I've already heard very good reports about you.'

'So what is it I'd be doing?' she said. 'If you were to offer me the job, I mean.'

'Well,' he coughed again, 'eventually, I'd be looking to you to keep the place ticking over. I'm out of the office quite a lot of the time, what with one thing and another. I have to be out there getting the deals. So I need someone who can keep the show on the road in my absence.'

Marie glanced towards the door. 'What about your secretary?'

McGrath shrugged. 'Lizzie's just a kid, really. She can answer the phone, type a few letters. Bright enough, you know, but not really able to keep on top of a place like this.'

'Well, that would suit me down to the ground,' she said. 'I'm used to running my own show, more or less, so I'm happy to do as much or as little as you need.'

McGrath frowned slightly and she wondered whether she might have overplayed her hand. 'Well, obviously there's a lot I'll need to hand over to you. It may take a while.'

She nodded, trying to look contrite. 'Yes, sorry. It's just that I'm keen to get this. It's been a difficult time . . . well, you can imagine. Need to build my confidence up a bit, probably. Prove that I'm still up to it—'

It was McGrath's turn to look embarrassed. 'No, I didn't mean – look, I'm sure you'll be perfect in the job. When can you start?'

She blinked, as if the offer had taken her by surprise.

'You mean I've got the job? Well, thank you. Really. I won't let you down. I can start more or less immediately if you'd like.'

McGrath rose from his chair, holding out his hand. 'Well, pleased to have you on board,' he said. 'I'm sure you'll be able to . . . lick us into shape.' The innuendo had returned, she noticed, now she'd accepted the job. She was beginning to suspect that this was going to be a long few months.

She took McGrath's hand. He shook her hand firmly, in the manner of one who'd seen fictional businessmen doing this kind of thing in films, then, almost inevitably, held on for just a few seconds too long. 'Yes, good to have you on board,' he repeated. 'One of the family and all that.' He paused, his smile broadening. 'Don't suppose you've made too many friends up here yet,' he added. 'Perhaps we should celebrate your arrival? Over dinner, maybe?'

Oh yes, she thought. It was going to be a bloody long few months.

5

He'd almost lost her. He'd had to look twice, maybe even three times, to be sure it was her. That surprised him. Usually one photograph was enough, if the likeness was a decent one. He had a superstition about that, always approaching it in the same way. He'd stare at the photograph for minutes on end, and then he'd hold the picture to his forehead, as if somehow absorbing its essence.

He knew that the last gesture was little more than superstition. But somehow it had developed as a habit, and now he felt it helped him memorise the face. He knew, though, that it was important to analyse what he was looking at. Not just the superficial trappings – the style or the colour of the hair, whether or not the person was wearing glasses, facial hair or the use of make-up. Those things could be changed.

Instead, he concentrated on the detail of the face itself – the shape of the chin, the nose, the ears, the mouth. Above all, the eyes – not so much the colour or the shape, but their look, their expression. It was harder with a poor photograph, but if the image was a good one, the eyes were the most revealing part of all. If he could look into their eyes, he would recognise them every time.

And he was good at this. They came to him because they knew he'd get it right. He'd identify the targets, no matter what they did. And many of them – most of them, maybe – were keen not to be spotted. They did their best to change themselves, and he had to laugh sometimes at the feebleness of their attempts. The ones who took to wearing sunglasses, or who dyed their hair or grew a beard. Even if he hadn't studied their features so closely, most wouldn't have fooled him. They were still essentially the same people – walking and speaking and behaving the same as before.

And once he'd identified them, he would be there, watching and waiting, for as long as it took. He knew what made him good at this, and it was a rare combination of qualities. First, it was all the slow things – patience, attention to detail, willingness to give as much time as it all needed. He would stick with them, wait for the ideal moment. That was when the other qualities kicked in. The fast things. Quick decisions, sudden action. Do what needed doing and get away. Slow and then fast. It was why they came to him. Why he was the best.

But, just for a moment, he'd felt wrong-footed. This should have been one of the easier jobs; maybe that was the problem. It had been a difficult few months. One tricky job after another. Nothing he couldn't handle, but all with additional complications. And now people were getting jittery. Looking out for him, or for someone like him. He couldn't depend on the usual element of surprise.

But this one should have been easy. He knew exactly what she looked like, who she was. He'd allowed himself to become complacent. He hadn't given it enough time. He thought he'd known what he was looking for.

Except that, as it turned out, he'd hadn't quite. He'd seen her come out of that surprisingly anonymous house and climb into that unfamiliar family car. And he'd thought: shit, I've got the wrong place. It was as if the ground had shifted under him. He'd memorised the house number and the road. Of course he had. But perhaps he'd got it wrong – round here, it was all Such-and-such Close and This-and-that Avenue, all variations on the same dull themes. Perhaps this was an Avenue when it should have been a Close, or maybe he'd transposed the numbers.

It had taken him a moment or two, concealed in his discreetly parked car, to realise that he'd been correct all along. It was her. Everything about her looked different – the hair, the clothes, the whole style – but she hadn't been able to hide who she really was. The way she walked, the way she moved her body. Even the way she'd climbed into the bloody car. He'd known all along. But, somehow, in those first few seconds she'd thrown him.

He swore loudly and started the car engine. The last thing he wanted was to have to chase after her down these lifeless streets. This kind of estate was a tough environment for surveillance. Too quiet, too anonymous. Too rigidly fucking conformist. People didn't park down here without a good reason, not in the street, anyway. Every driveway was spacious enough to accommodate at least two family cars. People like him stood out like dogshit in a goldfish bowl.

He'd found a way, though. He always did. Having observed the roads on foot for a day or so, he'd found a suitably ambig-uous place to leave his unremarkable car. A wider stretch of street where most of the houses seemed to have three or even more cars – teenage children and their friends coming and going. He reasoned that, for a day or two, no one would twig that his small saloon didn't belong to one of the neighbours' houses. It worked well enough, but he didn't want to draw attention to himself.

He caught up with her car as it reached the junction with the main road. He drew into the roadside for a moment, leaving sufficient distance between them. He had a good idea of where she was going. That information had been included in the brief file they'd sent.

As it was, he caught up with her easily enough. The mid-morning traffic had helped, preventing her from getting too far ahead, though he had to take care not to lose her in the endless sequence of traffic lights heading towards the city centre. It didn't help that her car – a black saloon nearly as anonymous as his own – blended inconspicuously with the countless others streaming through the suburbs. But he kept her in sight until she turned off the main road into the maze of streets that comprised the industrial estate. He felt more comfortable then, confident of where she was heading. He continued along the main road then, a few hundred yards further along, turned into the rear of the estate. He could park up, check where she'd left her car, and keep a discreet watch until she emerged.

He had no need to reproach himself. Even now, he couldn't quite believe how different she'd looked. Superficial stuff really, of course. Different clothes, different hair. A whole different style. A new image. She was good, that was the truth. She wasn't an amateur, like most of them were.

He reached across to the glove box and pulled out a Mars bar and the flask of coffee he'd prepared before setting out that morning. Creature comforts – part of the secret. Make life easy for yourself. Save the hard stuff for when it matters.

He took a first bite of the chocolate and sat back to wait.

As Marie climbed back into her car, she involuntarily glanced behind her. Instinct, or maybe just experience. Sure enough, McGrath was standing at the window of his office, gazing admiringly out at her. She'd managed to fob off his offer of dinner with some excuse about being in the middle of sorting out her new house. But that was only a temporary respite. McGrath didn't strike her as the type to give up at the first sign of discouragement.

Maybe this was all just Salter's idea of a joke. She couldn't believe that McGrath was a serious enough contender to justify their attention. She had him pegged as a small-time dealer with delusions of grandeur. But it was true that the likes of McGrath were often the weak links that allowed them to break apart much bigger chains. He'd have his own network of suppliers, customers and associates, and some of those might provide an entry route to more serious targets. Perhaps that was Salter's thinking. Perhaps.

In any case, she was stuck with this now. Building up her new life as Maggie Yates, establishing trust and credibility with McGrath, gathering whatever evidence she could along the way. It ought to be a piece of cake. Unless she messed up spectacularly, she couldn't imagine that McGrath would be bright enough to see through her cover. As long as she kept wearing these slightly too revealing outfits, his mind would be elsewhere. The only challenge would be keeping McGrath sweet while not letting him get too close.

As she drove out of the car park and turned back towards

the main road, she glanced in her rear view mirror. Something had made her feel uneasy, though she couldn't work out what. Perhaps the same instinct that had told her that McGrath would be watching her from the window.

She could see no immediate grounds for unease. The road behind her, which led deeper into the industrial estate, was deserted of traffic. There were a few cars parked here and there, but no other signs of life.

One of those cars, she thought. She had a half-sense she'd seen it before, at some point earlier in the day. Nothing she could pinpoint clearly. She didn't know where she'd seen it, or why it should have snagged even tentatively in her memory. It was nothing more than an aging silver-grey Mondeo. There were thousands like it.

She reached the junction with the main road, and looked in the mirror again. The car was still parked in the same spot, three or four hundred yards behind. She couldn't see whether there was anyone inside it.

She pulled out into the traffic. A little way ahead, there was a petrol station with a convenience store attached. She pulled off the road and parked in one of the spaces reserved for customers, reversing in to watch the passing cars.

At first, she thought she'd been wrong. A stream of cars went by, but there was no sign of the grey Mondeo. Then she saw it, or a car very like it, pass by. She had the impression that the driver glanced momentarily in her direction as the car passed, but she could make out nothing but the pale mask of a face. Not even whether the driver was male or female.

She waited a few moments and pulled back out on to the road. But she'd delayed too long and the car had vanished.

Although the traffic was moving freely, she didn't think the car could simply have disappeared from sight along the main road. More likely, the driver had turned off into one of side roads that led into the rows of Edwardian houses that dominated this part of town. She glanced to her left and right as she drove, searching for any sign of the car, but couldn't spot it.

She was letting her imagination run away with her, but the experience had left her feeling shaken. She was left with a sense that her instinct was right, that the car was significant. But if she really had been followed, then why? Who would have an interest in keeping track of her up here? There were various possible answers, none of them comforting.

The other possibility was that Winsor, the Agency's pet psychologist, had been wrong. Maybe she hadn't properly recovered from everything that had happened to her months before. Perhaps this creeping paranoia was some delayed form of traumatic shock. Perhaps she wasn't ready to go back to this work.

She knew there was no room for complacency. Christ, she'd learnt that the hard way. McGrath might be an idiot, but that didn't mean she should underestimate what she was involved in. This was dangerous territory – sometimes the idiots were the most dangerous of all – and she couldn't afford to forget that.

She reached the ring road and turned left, heading back to her new home, conscious suddenly of quite how lonely she was feeling.

6

'You can see why he picked it,' Brennan said. Somewhere behind him, he could hear Hodder struggling for breath. Brennan glanced over his shoulder. 'You okay?'

Hodder stumbled to a halt, wheezing slightly. 'Not as fit as I thought, obviously.' He straightened up and looked around. 'Jesus, where the hell are we?'

'Long way from anywhere. Just where I'd have wanted to be if I was Stephen Kenning.'

'I suppose,' Hodder said, doubtfully. He looked around at the sweep of the hillside, the drop to the road behind them. 'Impressive views, if you like that kind of thing.' His tone implied that he didn't include himself in that category.

'You can see a long way. That's what would have appealed to Kenning. He could see the bastards coming.'

'He didn't, though, did he?' Hodder had regained his breath and drawn level with Brennan.

'We all have to sleep sometime.'

'That the place?' Hodder gestured towards the white-rendered cottage another half mile or so ahead of them.

'Don't see any other candidates, do you?' As far as

Brennan could see, there was nothing else for miles. Just bare open moorland stretching off to the horizon. Apart from the single-track road where they'd left the car, there was no other sign of human habitation. The perfect hide-away – or not, as it turned out, but as good as Kenning was likely to find.

'Come on. Let's get this over with.' Brennan began to trudge slowly up the footpath towards the cottage, Hodder following a few feet behind. As they drew closer, he caught sight of a black-clad figure, pacing alongside the cottage. Brennan glanced at his watch. They were fifteen minutes late. Wakefield was, as always, on time.

They walked the last few hundred yards to the gate. The path continued on over the next hilltop. Probably a few walkers made their way up here, but not many.

By the time they reached the cottage, Wakefield had come forward to greet them. He was finishing off a cigarette, tossing the butt with practised nonchalance into the over-grown garden.

'You want to be careful,' Brennan said. 'You'll have the whole place up in smoke.'

Wakefield smiled, as at a well-rehearsed witticism. 'Rain we've had up here, you couldn't cause a fire with a fucking flamethrower.' He regarded Brennan for a moment. 'How you doing, Jack?'

Brennan shrugged. 'Not so bad. Considering.'

'*Considering*. Not dead yet, then?'

'That's probably disappointed a few people.'

'I imagine.' Wakefield pulled out his packet of cigarettes, waving it towards Brennan and Hodder, who both shook their heads. He was a tall thin man, with swept-back grey hair and sallow skin. He was probably forty or so, but looked older. 'There's still a few of us on your side.'

'Didn't see many putting their heads above the battlements. Present company excepted.'

'Not everyone's as dumb as I am. But there are a few who think you've been treated shittily.'

'That's a great consolation,' Brennan said.

Wakefield waved his lit cigarette towards Hodder. 'Didn't know it was "bring your kid to work" day.'

Brennan glanced round at Hodder. 'Pure jealousy. When you're a decrepit old has-been like Rog, the only pleasure you've got left is taking the piss out of the younger generation.' He ushered Hodder forward. 'Andy Hodder, a very capable officer despite his tender years. Roger Wakefield, a crap old copper, for all his decades of experience.'

Wakefield laughed and shook Hodder's hands. 'If you're coping with Jack Brennan, you must have something about you. He's got many good qualities, but not being a pain in the backside isn't one of them.' Wakefield turned back towards Brennan. 'Okay, Jack, you've dragged me up here to the arse-end of nowhere to open up for you. What's this about exactly?'

'Wild goose chase, probably. But since I'm kicking my heels over in the ivory towers, I thought I should come and see where Kenning met his unfortunate end.'

'Why the sudden interest in Kenning? It's not like there's any great mystery about his killing.'

'Except that you don't actually know who killed him.'

'No, and I don't suppose we ever will. I think I'll learn to live with that.' Wakefield was fumbling in his pocket for the keys to the cottage. 'He was a grass. He was living on borrowed time. He got taken out. Simple as that.'

'So who took him out?'

'Buggers he put behind bars,' Wakefield said. 'But we'll never prove it. It was a pro job, and a good one.' He led them to the door of the cottage and, after trying a couple of the keys on the chain, found the one that fitted the front door. He unlocked the door and led them inside.

'Who's the cottage belong to?' Hodder said from behind. 'The Force?'

'Funded from the witness protection programme', Wakefield said. 'We'd think about selling it but no one would want to buy up here. Keep it for the next daft bugger who blows the whistle.'

'Take it you've had the place cleaned up?' Brennan asked. The front door led straight into the living room of the cottage, a dark shabby-looking room with a worn sofa, two armchairs and, at the far end, a folding wooden table and a couple of chairs. Brennan walked over and peered at a dark stain on the dull mauve carpet. 'This where it happened?'

Wakefield nodded. There was still a faint scent of blood in the air, just detectable through the pervading stench of bleach and disinfectant. 'Yeah, you can see the bullet mark in the plaster behind. Best we can judge from the ballistics, the gunman was actually seated on the sofa.'

'Doesn't pay to exert yourself,' Brennan commented. 'What's that mean, then? Someone he knew?'

'You fishing, Jack? See what you can pump out of an old mate?'

'You know me better, Rog. If I want to know something, I just blurt it out.'

'True enough. Go on, then. Blurt.'

Brennan ignored him and moved to stand by the sofa, looking across to the stained carpet. He squatted for a moment, envisaging the passage of the bullet through the air. 'What weapon?'

'Nine mil. We think a Glock 17.'

Brennan raised an eyebrow. 'Police weapon?'

Wakefield laughed. 'Yeah, we use them. Not one of ours, though. Plenty out there.'

'You've not found the gun?'

'Like I said, Jack, this was a pro job. He'd have taken the bullet with him if he could. He barely left a trace. Some scraps of DNA, but nothing that matches.' He paused, then smiled across at Hodder who was standing awkwardly by the open front door. 'Why do I get the feeling that I'm doing all the talking, son?'

Brennan rose and moved to stand beside Hodder at the front door, peering at the lock. 'Decent seven-lever dead-lock,' he commented. 'Lockable bolts. Kenning cared about his security. Well, you would, wouldn't you? So how'd the killer get in?'

'Back door, we think,' Wakefield said. 'Security not quite as tight there. Pretty expert entry, though. Like I say, a pro.'

'No alarm system?'

'No. You know, I sometimes think that, if we want people to grass, we should look after them a bit better after they've done it. Just my opinion, you understand. Views expressed don't necessarily represent those of the management.' He pulled open the door that led out into the narrow hallway. 'Grand tour?'

'Might as well now we've paid.' Brennan and Hodder

followed Wakefield into the tiny kitchen at the rear of the house. It had been thoroughly cleaned, along with the rest of the house, but still carried a dingy air, the afternoon sunlight barely penetrating the grimy windows.

'Dream kitchen.' Wakefield pointed towards the back door. The lock had been replaced, but the splintered wood alongside it indicated that the door had been jemmied open. 'How he got in. Not subtle, but skilfully done. Minimum damage, minimum noise.'

'Not all that secure, though.'

'Once they found out where he was, it would take more than a few locks to keep them out. And if they couldn't get in, they'd just torch the place. Maybe Kenning wanted an exit route.'

Brennan surveyed the small kitchen. 'Christ, what a fucking life. Stuck in this dump. Not even a sheep for company. Knowing they're out there somewhere, waiting to track you down. Jesus.'

'His lucky day when the mystery assassin turned up. Least he had a bit of company.' Wakefield watched as Brennan prodded the doorframe. 'Okay, Jack, I've been very patient. Now cough up. Why the interest in Kenning? He's not the right league for your lot.'

'Not my lot,' Brennan pointed out. 'I'm only on secondment. I'm one of you.'

'Not most people's opinion,' Wakefield said. 'And I'm starting to have my doubts.'

Brennan glanced across at Hodder, as if he were about to make the young man complicit in some illicit action. 'I can trust you, Rog,' he said. 'Not to shoot your mouth off, I mean. Not just yet.'

'Depends what you're going to say.'

'Nothing very significant. But I get the impression that communications between my bosses and yours aren't as transparent as they might be. Don't want to step on any more toes than I can help, just at the moment.'

'Bit late for that, mate. But okay, if you're in the shit, at least try to tread water.'

'I've been asked to look at a series of killings. Kenning's one of them.'

'But your lot haven't told our lot.'

'Above my pay grade. But my boss has asked me to collate the evidence. Guy called Hugh Salter. You know him?'

'By reputation. DS in the Met, before he went over to your lot. He was involved in that corruption case last year, wasn't he? Jeff Kerridge and all that. On the rise, from what I hear.'

'Yeah. We already had a chat about the ironies of the situation.' Brennan looked across at Hodder again. 'Sorry if I'm talking out of school, Andy. Just trying to be straight with Rog here.'

Hodder looked slightly surprised at being consulted. 'Don't mind me,' he said, after a pause. 'Wouldn't trust Salter any further than I could throw him.'

'No way to talk about your elders and betters,' Brennan said. 'Interesting you think that, though.'

'He got me tangled up in that Kerridge business,' Hodder said. 'Had me tailing one of our undercover officers, Marie Donovan. I went along with it because – well, because he was senior to me, I suppose. I thought he'd got it officially

87

sanctioned, but he was off on his own. He covered for me, but mainly because he had to make his own story hang together. Didn't feel right, though. Still doesn't.'

'How'd you mean?'

'I don't know. The whole thing with Kerridge. Salter came out of it looking good. But there was something not right about it.' He shook his head, as if dealing with a subject beyond his comprehension.

Wakefield had been watching this dialogue with some interest. 'So what's Salter's interest in Kenning? The guy grassed on a small-time drug ring.'

'Salter reckons it wasn't all that small-time. That it was part of Kerridge's empire. And that Kenning was taken out by Pete Boyle, the guy who's trying to become the new Kerridge.'

'Anything's possible,' Wakefield said. 'Boyle marking his territory? Tomcat pissing up the wall sort of stuff?'

'Warning off the competition. Yeah.'

'So what's your role in all this?'

'Evidence officer. They're still trying to build a case against Boyle. Some days I just think he's come up with half-arsed task to keep me out of trouble. Then I think maybe he's using me. If anything comes of it, he can claim the glory. If it goes tits up or if you lot get arsey, he can always just blame me.'

'The perfect scapegoat,' Wakefield agreed. 'So what do you reckon? Does Salter's theory have legs?'

'It's not completely off the wall. Three incidents of small-timers killed by oddly professional murderers. Look at this one. You might expect Kenning to be taken out eventually, but a pro hit seems more than he merited.'

'Maybe,' Wakefield agreed. 'Though God knows you can't always fathom the logic of these people. These other cases, they look like pros too?'

'That's the thing with pros. If it's done well, you don't know it's been done at all. One was a hit and run. But the driver had picked the perfect spot, in the middle of bloody Stockport. No witnesses, no CCTV. Drove out by a route that gave us no shot of the car or its plates. Either a fluke or careful planning.'

'And nobody's linked these killings except Salter?'

'Three different areas. One possible accident. Two – or maybe three – killings that look like local vendettas. Victims all small-time scrotes better out of circulation anyway. No one's going to waste too much time worrying about the whys and wherefores.'

'Boyle was the guy who slipped out of the Agency's clutches last year, wasn't he? Bit of an embarrassment, from what I heard. Maybe not surprising that Salter's got a bee in his bonnet about it.'

'He's got that all right,' Hodder said. 'He made a big issue of it when the CPS dropped the Boyle case. That was why they gave it back to him. Money and mouth time.'

'So there you go,' Wakefield said. 'That's your job. To remove the bee from Salter's bonnet.'

'Sounds like it,' Brennan agreed glumly. 'Like I said, a wild fucking goose chase. I'm out of favour and out on a fucking limb. No resource, other than occasional dibs on Andy here. Oh, and I can call on the intel guys in London. Thanks a bunch. How am I supposed to go about collating evidence against Pete Boyle?'

Wakefield laughed. 'Jesus, Jack. You built a case against

your own Chief Super. This should be child's play by comparison.'

'Thanks for reminding me. That's how I got where I am today.' Brennan stopped and gazed gloomily around the grubby kitchen. 'Stuck in a shit hole on top of the High bloody Peak.'

7

She tried calling Liam to check how things were, but the phone rang out. After a moment, she heard her own voice: 'Please leave a message after the tone—' She ended the call, knowing that these days Liam never checked the messages. Maybe he was asleep or out of reach of the phone. She'd try again later.

It was all procrastination, anyway. Her real task today was to sort out this bloody house, make it at least look the kind of place she might want to live in. At the moment, it was about as inviting as a prison cell.

The Agency looked after her well enough, at least on the material front. If this house was less to her taste than the apartment they'd provided previously, it was still a decent enough place. And the kind of place the fictitious Maggie Yates might choose to live.

For the real Marie Donovan, it was all too clinical and anonymous. A two bedroom new build on an estate that could be anywhere in the country. Nicely fitted kitchen, modern bathrooms, inoffensive decor. A tiny garden at the rear designed for minimum maintenance. Enough driveway at the front to accommodate more cars than would ever be parked here. One among a row of not-quite-identical houses stretching as far as the eye could see. Further into the estate the houses became three-bedroomed, then four, then more, a physical metaphor for social aspiration. Most of her neighbours were young couples – cohabiting or recently married professionals getting their first rung on the housing ladder. As children arrived, they would look to move deeper into the estate, exchanging for the size of house that would meet their changing needs. Marie could see that it was practical, but it sent a chill down her spine.

She'd been here only a couple of weeks, and had met few of the neighbours. There was a retired couple living opposite, who had traded down from one of the larger houses as the children left home and the money grew thinner. They'd made a point of coming out to say hello as she'd arrived with the removal van, the wife bringing her a cup of tea. She'd also met the male half of her immediate neighbours while putting out the refuse bins a day or two earlier. They'd engaged in some brief, early morning conversation about which of the several coloured bins was scheduled to be collected that morning.

But it wasn't a place that encouraged sociability. The estate seemed designed to promote isolation – rows of small detached houses, high fences around the gardens to prevent them being overlooked, no one walking anywhere. If you wanted to do anything – shopping, leisure, recreation – you had to climb into your car. It was the outskirts of Chester but the beauties of the city – the Roman walls, the quaint shops, the rolling River Dee – might have been a million miles away from this drab modernity.

If she was honest, it wasn't all that different from her

house in London. Most of her neighbours there commuted into central London every day, and she usually saw them only if they happened to leave the house at the same time. But it didn't feel quite the same. At least there people walked to the Tube, and there were half a dozen pubs and restaurants within a short walk. You didn't meet the neighbours often, but you did see people around.

She had months of this to look forward to. She sat on the neat sofa in the unadorned living room and wondered quite how to make this place inhabitable. She'd buy some pictures – cheap prints, but at least something that she'd chosen. She'd brought up a box of books and CDs to help to make the place hers. And within a few days her natural untidiness would reduce the sterility of the place. But it still didn't feel enough. It didn't feel *real*.

Last time, up in Manchester, she'd had time to adjust to the part she was playing. And it hadn't felt that much of a stretch. Her fictional persona hadn't been all that different from the reality – a person she might have been if her life had taken one or two different turnings.

But Maggie Yates – well, she didn't really know who the hell Maggie Yates really was. She'd always laughed at actors pompously asking about their characters' motivation, but now she needed something like that. Maggie Yates felt like a hastily thrown-together concoction, an idea that seemed okay in the brainstorming sessions with Salter but which was now as insubstantial as a doodle. She couldn't believe she could sustain the role even for a few days, let alone for weeks on end. She'd got through that first interview with McGrath because his attention had been easily deflected by her more superficial characteristics. But even McGrath might eventually display some curiosity about who Maggie Yates really was.

She set about unpacking the small collection of items she'd brought with her. As she did so, she tried to imagine the sort of person Maggie Yates might be. She'd exercised some care in selecting the objects to bring with her. She couldn't have anything that was too revealing – no personal photographs, no items that might be inconsistent with her new life. But she wanted items that conveyed a sense of individuality – some books, some CDs, a few ornaments. But, in so far as those items reflected a personality at all, it was that of the all-too-real Marie Donovan. Maggie Yates remained nothing more than a shadow.

She finished unpacking and stood back to review the effect of her work. It looked like an unambitious stage-set adorned with bric-a-brac from the nearest charity shop. But perhaps that was right. The fictitious Maggie Yates was up here to start a new life. She was divorced and had chosen to leave most of the trappings of her former existence behind. This bland anonymity might be exactly how Maggie Yates would choose to live just at this moment.

Trying to think herself into Maggie Yates's head, Marie went through to the kitchen and filled the kettle to make coffee. Okay, she was a divorcee. A strong woman, an intelligent woman. A woman brought up to live on the edge of the law, surrounded by wide-boys who made a living wherever and however they could. Treated badly by a husband who'd depended on her more than he'd been able to admit. She'd taken her revenge and made her escape. Mid-thirties. Ready to start anew. To do things on her own terms, not taking any crap.

How did that sound? Well, like a start, she supposed. It meant that she could begin to get inside this person. But she needed more, the sort of detail that should have been supplied to her if Salter had prepared this properly. Like what sort of family Maggie Yates might have. She could imagine a father, maybe brothers, operating in the same semi-legitimate territory as her ex-husband. Maybe that was why she'd been allowed to get away with taking the cash out of the business and heading north. Perhaps her ex knew what would happen if he tried taking on the Yates family.

She poured the coffee, laughing at the way her imagination was starting to run with the half ideas she'd been playing with. But it didn't pay to be too clever. The hard part, as they'd repeatedly reminded her during training, was remembering which lies you'd told. The best strategy was to keep close to the truth, to reduce the risks of a slip-up. A nice theory, but not so easy when you were stuck in the world of Maggie Yates.

It was nearly four in the afternoon. Friday. In any normal life, she'd be looking forward to the weekend, planning how to use the empty two days. She'd agreed with McGrath that she'd start work on the Monday, and she'd wondered whether to take the opportunity to go home. She'd been up here for a couple of weeks now and hadn't made a return trip to London. She knew from her previous experience how difficult it was to keep stepping in and out of character, and her grip on the mysterious Maggie Yates felt too tenuous to risk further loosening.

But she knew that Liam needed her. She couldn't fool herself that his condition hadn't deteriorated. The physical decline was unavoidable. He was largely confined to the wheelchair, the adjustable armchair she'd bought for him, and his bed. When they'd last spoken over the phone, he'd seemed vague and had complained repeatedly about feeling exhausted. She knew that the carers came and got him up, prepared him some breakfast and lunch, and came round in the evening to help him get to bed.

Marie worried about the practicalities of Liam's existence. She worried about the risks that he might have a fall from his chair between the carers' visits. They'd organised for him to have a portable alarm, so that he could be in contact with social services if anything did happen. But what if he fell and hit his head? Or, the way he was now, if he simply forgot about the alarm.

But her greatest worries were not solely practical. She worried about his mental state, about how he must be feeling, stuck on his own all day, struggling to paint or, worse still, recognising that painting was beyond him. As far as she knew, he hadn't made a serious attempt to work again since she'd left, and she didn't know whether or not she should encourage him to try. During their phone calls, she was detecting more of the passivity, the unreal calm, that she'd noted in their last face-to-face conversations. His condition seemed to come and go, and some days were better than others. But the bad days were increasingly frequent.

She pulled out her personal mobile and thumbed the home number again. She'd grown accustomed to the under-cover protocols around mobile phone usage, ensuring no potentially compromising linkage between her two lives. In the past it had been frustrating for Liam that she wasn't easily available at the end of a phone line. Now, each time she switched on her personal phone, she was afraid that there might be a message bringing bad news – an accident or a worsening of his condition.

She listened to the ringtone, expecting no answer. Then, as she was about to end the call, the phone was picked up. 'Yes?'

It took her a second to recognise the female voice. Sue, the lead carer. 'It's Marie, Sue. Just calling to check on Liam.'

There was a pause at the other end of the line, as if Sue had forgotten who Marie was or, more likely, was silently registering her disapproval at Marie's absence. 'Not so good today,' Sue said at last.

'Oh. I'm sorry,' Marie said, unsure whether she was expressing regret or offering an apology. 'What is it?'

'Probably just a cold. Has a bit of a temperature. But it's really knocked him back.'

'It always does, anything like that. Can I have a word?'

Another pause. 'He's asleep at the moment. Seemed completely whacked.'

'Right. Well, okay. If you're still there when he wakes, tell him I called. I'll try again later.'

'I will.'

Marie ended the call, feeling oddly wrong-footed. She could sense Sue's disapproval down the phone. That was no surprise. But Marie was also left with an unreasonable sense that she'd been usurped, that Sue had taken on a role that was rightfully hers. Well, in a sense, that *was* exactly what she'd done. Taken on the role that a more traditional wife might have occupied. Marie couldn't have it both ways. If she wanted the freedom to pursue her career, she had to accept that others would need to step into the role she'd vacated.

The real issue was Liam. She'd seen how a normally trivial illness – a cold or a fever – could knock him sideways. And even though his state of health usually improved once the illness had passed, each incident brought him a little lower, caused a further deterioration. She wondered again whether she ought to return home this weekend. She'd see how Liam was when she called later, and head back in the morning if he seemed no better.

She was slipping the phone back in her handbag when it buzzed in her hand. She glanced at the screen. It was the code, designed to look like a junk text advertisement, that indicated she should call Salter on the secure line. The arrangement was that an undercover officer should have a single designated point of contact, who would both act as a conduit for information and provide a 'buddying' role, keeping an eye on the physical and psychological health of the officer in the field. Normally, the contact was another officer of equivalent grade so the relationship was free of hierarchical pressures. Salter had been her previous contact, but she'd assumed that, following his promotion, he'd allocate the role to another officer. Instead, he'd decided to continue. She didn't much care – after all, she'd never been unduly intimidated by Salter's supposed seniority. But it was another factor which fed her suspicions.

She dialled the number and went through the usual ritual of exchanged codes. 'You wanted me, Hugh?' Strictly speaking, she wasn't supposed to use his name, but given that he'd flouted most of the relevant protocols in setting up the assignment, she couldn't see that one more trans-gression would hurt.

'How's it going, sis? You making progress?'

'Well, I've got the job with McGrath if that's what you mean.'

'That's good. We'd have been well and truly scuppered if he'd turned you down. Mind you, you came highly recommended.'

'I don't think it was my references that he was interested in, to be honest, Hugh.'

'No, well. I'd heard that about him. One reason I was keen for you to flash a bit of cleavage.'

'Ever the professional, Hugh. I start Monday. And I can't wait.' She paused, thinking that she might as well push Salter a bit harder. 'You're sure he's worth it, Hugh? He strikes me as pretty small-time.'

'That's not what the intel says. He's not a massive player, but he's growing. Building up market share, as they say. And he's got some interesting contacts. Now's the time for us to get in there, before he gets too big and powerful.'

'If you say so. So was that why you called? Just to enquire about my well being?'

'You know how much it matters to me, sis. But, no, actu-ally. I've got someone who'd like a chat with you.'

'How lovely. I assume it's something important, given that I'm undercover and everything?' She was growing increasingly concerned about Hugh's apparently casual approach to her role. This wasn't how it was supposed to be.

'Could be,' Salter said. 'Might be relevant to McGrath, as well.'

'Go on.'

'Got a guy here on secondment. DI from Greater Manchester Police. Working as evidence officer on the Pete Boyle case.'

This was interesting, she thought. If Salter really was in Boyle's pocket, why would he bring in an outsider to support the investigation?

'Don't know how useful it'll be. If we hadn't got this extra resource foisted on us, I'd struggle to justify it.'

'Foisted on us?'

'Long story. But, yeah, it means we can pay Boyle a bit of extra attention. There've been a spate of killings across the north west. All apparently gang-related, but not obviously linked to each other. Could be Boyle marking his territory. Telling the competition to get the fuck out of there.'

'Better than saying it with flowers.'

'They all look like pro jobs. It's another possible route into Boyle. Thought it might be a good time to up the ante a bit'

'And where do I come in? Why'd you want me to see this guy?'

'Background, really. You got closer to Boyle than most of us.'

'Not much. You sure it's worth the risk? If he's a DI with the GMP he's likely to be recognisable.'

'He's recognisable, all right. But if he meets you outside Manchester, the risks are pretty limited.'

'Don't you think we should set the threshold a bit higher than 'pretty limited', Hugh? We can't afford to compromise the operation. Or me.'

'There's no risk. Anything that gives us any more chance of nailing Boyle has to be worth it.'

'Okay, Hugh. Against my better judgement and all that. When did you have in mind?'

'How about tomorrow?'

'Tomorrow? Christ, Hugh, you really do push things to the limits, don't you?'

'Well, if you don't like working weekends—'

'For God's sake, Hugh, it's not that. I just think we ought to set up a meeting properly.'

'It's not an international summit. Just meet him for a coffee. Give him your thoughts on Boyle.'

'But what's the rush?'

'We've only got this guy for a month or two, I imagine. Want to make the best use of his time. Once you get started with McGrath, it'll get harder to pull you out for things like this.' Salter paused in a manner that she recognised. He'd saved up some last little titbit for last. 'Anyway, you should be flattered. It was his request to speak to you.'

'Piss off, Hugh. He can't even know I exist.'

'Well, he wouldn't, except that young Hodder's helping him out. I imagine he mentioned your involvement in our little escapade last year.' Little escapade, she thought. One dead villain, one corrupt cop, and the two of them escaping by the skin of their teeth. She wondered what Hodder had said. Wet behind the ears he might be, but he was no fool.

'And he asked to see me, this DI of yours?'

'Very keen. He's just trying to pull together whatever background we've got. He's been through all the files, but he thinks you might be able to give him some more personal stuff.'

'I can't see I can give him much, Hugh. Most of what I know will be in the files anyway.'

'He's a smart cookie, this guy. You know what it's like. Half the time in this job you don't know what you're looking for. If you just take him through your impressions, he might come up with something.' Another pause, this time indicating that Salter was building up to one of his attempts at humour. 'Anyway, you don't want to pass up the opportunity. He's not my type, but the girls in the office think he's a bit of a looker.'

Girls in the office, she thought. Salter used that kind of phrase with a supposed edge of irony, but it reflected his view of the gender divide. Present company perhaps just about excepted. 'Well, we've few enough of those,' she said. 'What's his name, this guy?'

'Brennan. Jack Brennan.'

She was silent for a moment, holding her breath, but couldn't prevent herself from laughing. 'Jack Brennan, Hugh? That would be *the* Jack Brennan?'

'I imagine we've the same one in mind, yes.'

'No wonder they've foisted him on you. I bet they won't be in much of a rush to take him back.'

She thought she'd pushed him too far. Salter was rhino-skinned in most respects, but he never responded well to being laughed at. But finally he gave a forced laugh to match hers. 'Well, maybe. But he's a good cop. A good *detective*.'

'I know that, Hugh. A bit too good, some might say. But he's not made many friends.' She succeeded in restraining another laugh. 'That why you've taken him on, Hugh? There but for the grace of God and all that?'

'I didn't have much choice about taking him on. They

were keen to get him out of the heat. And you're know what we're like for manpower. Thinner than a supermodel on hunger strike. We'll take anything we can get. But you're right – he's not that different from me.'

'I'll judge that when I meet him, Hugh. Difference was you risked your life to expose a corrupt bastard who'd put all our lives at risk. Everybody says Brennan grassed up a popular cop to save his own skin.'

'Not how he tells it. He'll probably bend your ear on the subject. Seems to do that with most people he meets. By the way, speaking of the devil, I hear Welsby's making progress. Not enough for them to take the bugger out of hospital and stick him back in Belmarsh where he belongs, but enough that's he's likely to stand trial after all. Maybe there is a God.'

'I thought it was God who'd left him in limbo,' she said. She didn't want to think about Keith Welsby, not just now. She didn't want to think about what might happen if he stood trial. She and Salter would be key witnesses, even if she were allowed to retain her under-cover anonymity. She'd have to relive everything. She'd have to give answers under oath. Most of what she'd said in her witness statements at the time had been accurate. But Salter had inveigled her into bending the truth about one or two aspects of his own role. Salter wouldn't have too many scruples about perjuring himself on issues that weren't, in the end, even particularly germane to the case against Welsby. But she might have more difficulty. 'So what's the news?'

'Apparently he's getting more responsive. Be a while before he's fit to stand up in court, though, I'd guess.'

'Justice for all,' she said, sardonically. 'Okay, so when do you want me to meet Brennan?'

They spent a few more minutes sorting out the details. Saturday lunch, she suggested, in a cafe-bar just outside the city walls in Chester. A bit off the main drag, less risk of them being spotted together. She was even more concerned now she'd discovered Brennan's identity. His picture had been in the newspapers once or twice when the story first broke. Not exactly a celebrity, but someone whose features might be familiar to those who, for whatever reason, were interested in such things.

She switched off the phone. It was still early, not yet five. She sat silently in the anonymous room, conscious of the silence of the deserted estate outside. Earlier, there'd been the odd car passing, mums bringing their children back from school. Soon, working husbands and wives would start arriving back, settling in for the weekend with a take-away and a bottle of wine. But for the moment there was peace.

For Marie, it felt less like a moment of rest than the calm before the storm. She walked over to the front window, gazing out at the monotonous view, house after house bathed in the late afternoon sunshine. Nothing to see, no sign of human life. Further along the road, she could make out the rear of a dark saloon and, for a second, felt a frisson of anxiety. She moved to get a better view. Not a Mondeo. Empty. Nothing to worry about.

Her head was filled with too many things. Salter. Brennan. Welsby. McGrath. Peter Boyle. And, of course, Liam. There was no chance now of returning home this weekend. She told herself that she'd had no choice. But she knew that she'd offered only token resistance to Salter's request. And what did that tell her? That she was afraid to go home?

Well, maybe. But she had a job to do. A serious job that she couldn't just step away from because things weren't going well in her personal life. A job that might literally be a matter of life and death. A job that needed her full concentration.

Yet at the moment she felt she was giving it anything but.

8

When he woke, it was already dark. There'd been nothing else he could do in the meantime. Better to get some rest. Stay sharp for what was to come.

He fumbled in his rucksack for the things he needed. A bottle of water, a couple of cereal bars. Keep his energy levels up. He climbed out of the sleeping bag, carefully rolled up the bag and the thin foam mattress and stuffed them into the rucksack. He'd leave a few traces, but there was no reason they'd even think to look in here. And he was confident that nothing, not even his DNA, could be linked to the person he now was.

He glanced at the luminous dial of his watch. Nearly eleven. Time to prepare himself, then he could watch and wait until the lights went out. Allow time for her to get to sleep. Not crucial, but it would make everything easier. There was no power in here, so he'd have to wait in darkness. He could see but not be seen. He was used to darkness.

He stood in the middle of the room, stretched his arms above his head, and began his usual exercise routine. It was partly just another superstition by now, like holding the photograph to his forehead. If he kept everything the same, it would all work out. But it was good sense, too. He kept himself fit, but this was about priming himself for the moment. Making sure he was alert for anything that might get thrown at him.

He spent ten minutes with the stretches and bends. Then, slightly out of breath, he picked up the water bottle and made his way to the window. There were lights in most of the houses, but otherwise no sign of life across the estate. Cars were parked up for the night. Soon, there would be a few people returning from evenings out. He wouldn't make a move until after midnight.

He could see the house clearly from here, its outline visible through the sparse leaves of one of the trees that lined the road. An attempt to make the estate seem more like somewhere you might actually want to live.

There were still lights on in the house. He was fairly sure she was alone. He'd been watching for several days now, and had seen no sign of visitors. She'd come and gone as he expected. Sometimes he'd followed her. Most times, after a while, he hadn't bothered. He knew where she was likely to go, and she'd sprung no surprises.

Even if there was another person there, it would be an added complication, but nothing he couldn't handle. He had everything planned out. He didn't know the exact floor plan of the house – he hadn't dared to make himself too visible to any watchful neighbours – but it would be similar to this one, with the layout inverted.

When he'd first arrived here, days earlier, he'd been unsure how to manage the surveillance. The estate was too exposed, too uninhabited, too fucking middle class. He couldn't afford even to be seen driving up and down too much. Some bastard from the neighbourhood watch was bound to report him as a potential house-breaker.

The first couple of times he'd left his car in the unobtrusive spot he'd identified, hidden among a cluster of cars overspilling from the neighbouring houses. But he knew that someone would eventually spot his unfamiliar car and start wondering who owned it. Then, after a day or two, he'd found a better solution. A few doors down from his target, on the opposite side of the road, there was an empty house, with a 'For Sale or Let' sign outside. The owners had presumably relocated for some reason and had not yet been able to sell their current property. He'd returned, late one night, having left his car tucked away in a backstreet half a mile away, feeling his way across the meadow that backed on to the back garden of the uninhabited house. He'd climbed the rear gate and let himself in. Neither the locks nor the alarm system had delayed him very long.

The place was ideal. It had clearly been unoccupied for a few weeks, and most of the furniture had been removed. He travelled light when on an assignment, his rucksack containing only the essentials for sleeping, eating and hygiene. The place still had running water, so he had everything he needed.

He'd been there for a couple of days, keeping out of sight during the day. It gave him the ideal vantage point to watch her comings and goings, with little chance of his being spotted. The only risk was that someone – the estate agent, the owners – might turn up unexpectedly. But even if someone came, he could hide himself from any superficial search of the place, and he'd left no obvious sign of his presence.

He'd been able to keep a good eye on her, waiting for the word to come down. And now it had. He'd received the signal that afternoon – the usual untraceable text sent to a mobile he'd discard once the assignment was complete.

Tonight. Time to complete the job. It was a relief. He prided himself on his patience, taking time to ensure that everything was in place. But now he'd done all that. It wasn't a difficult assignment logistically. She lived and spent most of her time alone. Her movements were relatively predictable. She was living in an ordinary house which would provide no access problems. All he needed was the signal to proceed.

Even so, he didn't rush. He waited till after midnight. The lights had been extinguished in most houses. Wageslaves who needed their sleep. A solitary car had passed by just before twelve, but now everywhere was silent. The lights in her house had been turned off forty or so minutes before.

He methodically finished packing up his rucksack, had a final check around the house to make sure that he'd left nothing behind, and pulled on his short black jacket. Everything was black – jeans, T-shirt, jacket. He wore a black baseball cap with the peak pulled down over his face, just to render identification more difficult if he should be inadvertently caught by CCTV. But his garb was ordinary; if you passed him in the street, you wouldn't register him.

He let himself out of the rear door, securing it behind him. He'd reset the alarm before exiting, so there was no obvious trace that anyone had been there. He took a deep breath of the chilly night air, and made his way down the side of the house, out into the street and across to his target.

The roads were deserted, but it was important not to

become careless. All it needed was for some late night busybody to spot him acting suspiciously and the police could be on their way before he knew it. But once he was out in the street, he walked confidently down the centre of the pavement rather than skulking in the shadows. If anyone caught sight of him from one of the overlooking windows, they'd assume he was making his way home from a night out. Even here, there must be a few residents – teenage children, for example – who didn't assume that every journey had to be made by car or taxi.

As he reached the house, he paused, as if to adjust the rucksack on his shoulder, taking the opportunity to glance quickly around and make sure he wasn't being observed. Then he moved quickly up the driveway and made his way to the rear of the house.

He peered in through the kitchen window, making out the small glows of red and green indicators on various kitchen appliances. As he'd expected, the layout of the house was an inverted equivalent of the house he'd just left. He spent a few minutes examining the locks on the rear doors and patio windows, working out what sort of alarm system would be in place. He'd already registered that there was a security spotlight activated by a movement sensor. He stuck close to the wall, outside its range.

He reached into the rucksack and brought out his small, neatly arranged box of tools. It took him only a few silent minutes to unlock the rear door, and little longer to ensure the alarm was disabled. The alarm was, as he'd expected, a relatively sophisticated model, but well within his capability. Once inside, he propped the rear door slightly ajar to provide a rapid exit route.

He stepped through the kitchen into the hallway, pausing to reconnoitre the interior of the house by the dimmed beam of his small flashlight. There was nothing unexpected. The main living room off to the right. A slightly smaller living-cum-dining room to the left. A small downstairs lavatory and washroom. All very bland, impersonal. The house of someone who had been here for only a short time, and was not expecting to stay much longer.

He made his way slowly up the stairs, keeping his feet close to the wall to minimise any risk of creaking wood. The main bedroom was directly ahead at the top of the stairs, and he assumed that this was where she would be sleeping. The door was slightly open and, moving silently, he eased it wider and peered inside.

He was momentarily disconcerted to see that the large double bed was unoccupied and apparently undisturbed. There was an en suite bathroom at the far end, and he carefully flashed his torch towards it, wondering if he'd timed his arrival to coincide with her getting up.

He held his breath and heard the rhythmic breathing from behind him. He stepped back out on to the landing. There were two more bedrooms, with a bathroom between them. He moved forward a step or two, listening hard. The breathing was coming from the further room, which overlooked the road. He wondered whether she'd picked the room because it made her feel more secure; with the vain hope that she might hear someone approaching. Like that grassing bastard up in Yorkshire – he'd picked the perfect spot, upper windows looking down on any intruder approaching up the only footpath. He'd kept a shotgun primed and ready, like a medieval king protecting his fucking castle. Fat lot of good it had done him.

He gently pushed open the door. She was lying asleep, half covered by a flower-patterned duvet. Her head was to one side, facing towards him. She was wearing some kind of nightdress, her shoulders bare, and she looked, he thought, quite striking. If you liked that kind of thing.

He always thought, at this moment, that it was best simply to trust your instincts. He'd had his approach ready, but he liked to respond to circumstances, use what the scene presented to him. Another superstition, perhaps, but it meant that he was less predictable. There was no recurring pattern for some smartarse profiler to spot.

It was a double bed, slightly smaller than the one in the main bedroom. There was a spare pillow lying on the empty half of the bed, inches from her head. As if fate had placed it there.

He stepped forward and carefully picked up the pillow.

He carefully moved her head until it was facing up towards him. Then he took the pillow between his hands and lowered it on towards her face.

At the last moment, she opened her eyes. She stared at him for a moment. There was no sign of recognition in her gaze and, as far as he could judge, no sign of fear or even surprise. Perhaps it was simply that she was not yet fully awake. But it felt almost as if she had been expecting him, or someone like him. As if she had been waiting for this.

Their eyes locked for a long moment. And then he pressed the pillow against her face. Pressed and held it hard.

She struggled then, finally, as if she had suddenly recognised the need to resist. Her body jerked violently as she tried to drag herself from under the weight of his unyielding arms, and one of her flailing hands caught him glancingly across the side of his face.

But he was too strong for her. He moved his head back out of her reach, but held the pillow firmly, still pressing down on her face. He remained in that position, crouched awkwardly across her body, forcing all his weight on to the pillow until at last, all her movement ceased.

PART TWO

9

'Sorry, mate. Not allowed in here without permission, whoever you are.' The taller of the two looked appropriately threatening in his uniform and starched white shirt. His younger colleague, still sitting with a copy of *The Sun* across his lap, looked as if he would do whatever it took to avoid any trouble.

Salter stepped forward and held out his Agency ID, complete with the warrant card in the adjoining pocket. 'I've got permission, *mate*. Just a quick visit.'

The officer leaned forward and peered at the ID. His expression suggested that he didn't understand its significance, but recognised its authority. 'Police?' he offered, finally.

Salter nodded, even though it wasn't strictly true. Close enough for a prison officer. For this prison officer, at least.

'You won't get much out of him, anyway,' the officer said. 'He's sparked out. Sedated. Not that he's exactly a barrel of laughs at other times.'

'No,' Salter said. 'Not much to laugh about.' He peered at Welsby's supine body. 'Just come to see how he is, really.'

The officer glanced at his colleague. 'You know him?'

'Only to work with,' Salter said. 'I helped put him in here. Well, not in *here*. But in Her Majesty's safe custody.'

'Right.' The officer took a moment or two to work this out. 'Bent,' he said. 'That's what we heard. Corrupt bastard.'

Salter moved past him and took one of the plastic seats next to the other officer. He looked closely at Welsby's face, as if expecting the older man to react in some way. Welsby was breathing steadily, an oxygen mask clamped across his mouth and nose. Drips and wires protruded from beneath the bedclothes. 'We mustn't prejudge the due process of law,' Salter said. 'But, yes, I'd have said that "corrupt bastard" sums it up.' He looked across at the seated officer. 'How's he doing?'

The officer held out his hand for shaking. 'Eddie Brady,' he said.

Salter ignored both the hand and the name. 'He looks like shit,' he observed, gesturing towards Welsby.

Brady looked up at his colleague, who shrugged and moved to stand by the door, staring out into the corridor as if hoping that the cavalry might turn up from that direction. All yours, son, seemed to be the implicit message.

'I think "shit" pretty much sums it up,' Brady said. 'They reckon he's improving,' Brady went on, 'but I suppose that depends where you're starting from.'

'He say much?'

'Bugger all that I've heard.' Brady gestured towards the oxygen mask. 'Though it's not easy to tell. Grunts the occasional yes and no if you ask him a direct question.'

'Understands what you say, then?'

'Seems to. Basic questions, anyway. Can't say I've tried to engage him in conversation.'

'You reckon he's the full shilling, then, mentally?' Salter was leaning over and peering at Welsby's bulky body, as if he might glean some clues to his condition.

'I've no idea, mate. I'm just a screw. You'd be better asking the doctors, I'd have thought.'

'If I can find one,' Salter said. 'Could only see one bloody nurse out there. Health Service, eh? You two here permanently?'

Brady shook his head. 'My first time on this detail. Greg over there's been over here a few times before, though. We rotate. Governors don't let us out of their sight for too long.'

'Must be costing the Prison Service a bloody fortune, having you two stationed out here all the time. It's not like he's about to do a runner.'

Brady shrugged. 'Regulations, isn't it? They haven't got the facilities to treat him inside, so they've had to bring him out here. But he's still a prisoner, so he needs a bed watch. Pain in the arse, but there you go.'

'Bugger's only on remand, anyway,' Salter mused. 'He was refused bail because they thought he might bugger off. You'd have thought he might be granted it now, but he's not reapplied. Heard his lawyer was trying to get the case struck out because he was unfit to stand trial, but he scuppered that by starting to recover. Can't do anything right, poor bastard.'

'Stroke, was it?' Brady said.

'That was what did for him in the end. Tried to top himself first. He messed that up as well, but when they were cutting him free he collapsed anyway. Not a surprise. He was always an aneurism waiting to happen.'

He pushed himself slowly to his feet. 'Anyway, just here to pay my respects.'

'Don't they have to be dead before you do that?' Brady said.

'Wishful thinking, son. Right, I'll go and see if there's any trained medical staff around to shed some light on his condition. Won't hold my breath, though.' Salter made his way toward the door. As he exited, he turned back to the two officers. 'Take care of him, won't you, lads? Don't go disconnecting any tubes or anything.'

'Jack Brennan?'

He looked up from his newspaper and squinted at the light from the entrance. 'That's me,' he said. 'All too recognisable. You must be Maggie Yates. Hugh Salter gave me a description.'

'Of course he did,' she said.

He smiled. 'Probably didn't do you justice, though.'

She ignored the compliment and looked around the cafe, which was surprisingly busy given its location. 'Fancy going somewhere where we can talk more easily.'

'Fine by me,' he said. He had half a cup of coffee left, which he finished in a mouthful. 'Where'd you have in mind?'

'How about a walk in the park?' she said. 'Given the sun's shining for once.' They were only a short distance from Grosvenor Park, which ran along by the river. Out there, there was less chance of being overheard, even if it marginally increased the risk of her being spotted with Brennan.

'Why not?' Brennan folded up his newspaper and rose

from the table. 'Can't think of a better way to spend a summer's afternoon.'

She was half-expecting him to add some flirtatious follow-up and found herself almost disappointed when nothing materialised.

Salter had been right about Brennan's looks, though. He was even better in the flesh, and she suspected he knew it. There was more than a touch of vanity about his appearance. He was dressed casually, but the clothes were expensive. If she'd been more knowledgeable she'd no doubt have recognised the discreet logos on his polo shirt and jacket. His hair was styled in a manner than looked casual, but had taken a while to achieve.

It was the kind of look she normally found unattractive – she preferred men who were more interested in her appearance than their own. But there was something about Brennan that suggested he might be more fun than he initially appeared. Something in his eyes. A sense of humour, or even a sense of mischief. Someone who was bright enough to be aware of his own weaknesses and who wouldn't be afraid to laugh at them. Or perhaps she was already being half-seduced by those ruggedly handsome good looks.

They walked back into the sunshine and made their way into Grosvenor Park. It was an attractive spot – a Victorian park, lined with trees and dotted with intriguing features, the River Dee lying just beyond. There were a few people about – parents with small children heading for the miniature railway, young couples, dog walkers – but the place was hardly crowded. They found a bench in the sunshine and sat watching the passers-by.

'Hugh said you asked to see me,' Marie said.

'I hope it's not inconvenient,' Brennan said. 'I didn't realise you'd just started a new assignment.'

'Only just kicked off,' she said. 'No, it's okay. I'm not sure I can really help you, though. I don't know that I can tell you anything that's not in the files.'

'My experience is that there's only so much you can get from the files. They give you the facts. But they don't give you – I don't know – the colour, I suppose. They don't tell you the things that are really important.'

'What is it you want to know?'

He paused, as if trying to think how best to phrase the questions. Then, to her surprise, he said, 'What do you think of Salter?'

She twisted on the bench and looked at him. 'I thought we were here to talk about Pete Boyle.'

'I'm just looking for a bit of context. You know what it's like in a new job. You don't know anybody. You don't know the dynamics. Who hates who. Who are best pals. Which couples are shagging in the stationery cupboard.'

'I'm not aware Hugh's shagging anyone in the stationery cupboard,' she said. 'Except possibly himself. Though, with respect—'

He gazed back at her, and suddenly laughed. 'Okay, I'm the last one to be raising that particular topic. Though you shouldn't believe everything you hear. I'm just trying to get a sense of how things work around here.'

'And why do you think I'm the one to give you a view on that?'

'I've been talking to Andy Hodder. You know him?'

'Andy? He's good. You're lucky to have him working with you.'

'Yeah, that's my impression. Enthusiastic, and no fool. He said you were worth talking to. Not just about Boyle, but generally. Said you'd give me a straight view.'

That didn't surprise her. She'd chatted to Hodder a few times over the past months. She liked him. He was smart, keen and, as far as she could tell, honest. She knew that Salter had co-opted Hodder into helping with his freelance move against Jeff Kerridge. Salter had used Hodder's unauthorised involvement to persuade her not to tell the whole truth about how Salter had carried out the operation. *Don't want to land young Hodder in any hot water, sis.* Marie had the impression that Hodder's views of Salter were similar to her own.

'I hope he's right,' she said. 'Question is, Mr Brennan, if I give a straight view, how do I know what you'll do with it? I've no particular reason to trust your discretion.' She paused. 'Or your integrity, if what I hear is true.'

His face was expressionless. 'Like I say, don't believe everything you hear. Though I can see why you might.'

'What I heard,' she said, 'was that you were shagging the Chief Super's wife. And when he found out, you shafted him – just as you'd been shafting her, I suppose.'

Finally, his expression softened and he laughed. 'Yeah, that's the story. Have they told you how I shafted him?'

'Exposed him for taking backhanders is what I heard. Ended his career.'

'Interesting, that, isn't it? Not something I could have invented, really. Him taking backhanders. He either was or he wasn't. And if he was, don't you think it was right to expose it?'

'I suppose. Doesn't make your motives any more honourable, though.'

'Not if the story was true. But it's not quite the way it happened.'

'Go on.'

'Chief Superintendent Craddock's a popular guy. One of the lads. Also, bent as the proverbial and a total bastard. Not at work – well, only when it suited him. But at home, to his wife and kids. Beat the crap out of her, and probably them as well. Yeah, I did have a brief thing with the wife. It was stupid – after some office do. She'd been abandoned there by her dear hubby who'd buggered off to screw a young WPC. She'd had too much to drink – we both had – and I didn't think she was safe to get home by herself. So I organised a taxi, went with her to make sure she was okay, and – well, you know. She poured her heart out about what a bastard her hubby was, and I ended up staying a bit longer than I'd intended. We met a couple more times. She was a nice woman and I felt sorry for her. But we both realised it was bloody stupid and ended it. Over a year ago.'

'So where does the corruption allegation come in?'

'A few months back, a grass let me in on a little secret. He'd been fucked over by someone and was looking to get his own back. So he told me a bunch of stuff about the someone in question, most of it bollocks. But part of it was that 'the someone' was paying a nice little retainer to our friend Craddock. And that he wasn't the only one. That bit of the story rang true because it tied in with rumours I'd picked up from other sources. I wasn't the only one who suspected, but most didn't want to rock

124

the boat, given what a popular guy we were dealing with. Being the bone-headed pillock that I am, I did a bit more digging, found more evidence, and in the end felt I had no option but to turn the whole thing over to Professional Standards.'

'And all this was after you'd finished with his wife?'

'Insofar as I ever started, yes. Months after. I thought Standards would kick it into the long grass in any case. But there was too much evidence for them to ignore. They brought disciplinary action against the Chief. And he started muddying the waters. His wife had obviously let something slip – probably one of those nights when she was accidentally banging her head on the kitchen door. He claimed I'd been having an affair with his wife. Said that when he'd found out and tried to stop it, I'd threatened to expose his dodgy dealings. It was all bollocks, but it cast doubt on my motives, especially as he scared his wife into backing up his story. He couldn't avoid the central allegations, of course, but a lot of the evidence was circumstantial and he managed to play it down quite successfully. Yes, he'd made some serious errors of judgement and allowed himself to become too close to the wrong people. But he didn't accept that he'd behaved corruptly and – blah, blah, blah. Standards didn't believe a word of it, but didn't want to crap on their own doorstep. In the end he was allowed to retire quietly on a full pension. Poor bugger. And then he did everything he could to shift the blame on to me – the bastard who'd fucked his wife and his career.'

'Right,' she said, not knowing quite how to respond. 'And as punishment they've sent you to work with us? Jesus, they're ruthless.'

He laughed, this time with genuine humour. 'Just wanted me out of their hair. They can't sack me. I'm too far off retirement. So all they could do was move me sideways to somewhere where I can't do too much damage.'

It could all be a pack of lies, she thought. The grapevine could be right, and this might just be Brennan's way of ingratiating himself. But she was inclined to believe him. His story matched her own experience of police politics.

'Okay, you've persuaded me,' she said. 'So what can I tell you? You were asking about Hugh.'

'Yeah. I don't know what to make of him. I don't know whether he's stuck me on some half-arsed wild goose chase or whether this Pete Boyle stuff really matters.'

'Hard to say. It generally is where Hugh's concerned. He's a smart guy but he looks out for number one.' She was conscious of trotting out platitudes, skating round her real thoughts about Hugh Salter. 'Boyle's a big deal, though. You've heard the background to all that?'

'I heard something. But tell me your version.'

'I was working undercover in Manchester, trying to get some grift on Jeff Kerridge. We'd already arrested Boyle, on what seemed like good evidence from a grass—' She paused for a moment, as her mind drifted back to the grass in question. Jake Morton, her former lover. Killed by Boyle. And the biggest skeleton in her own particular closet. 'The plan was to use Boyle to build a case against his boss, Kerridge. But we knew that intelligence was leaking somewhere. Turned out that Keith Welsby, who was the senior running mine and Hugh's team, was in Kerridge's pocket. Salter took it on himself to expose Welsby. Nearly got both of us killed in the process. But in the end it worked. We got Welsby bang to rights. And Kerridge was killed. By Hugh. In self-defence. Supposedly.'

Brennan looked at her with interest. 'Supposedly?'

'Let's go and look at the river.' She rose and they began to walk across to the corner of the park that overlooked the Dee. 'It's not my place to start spreading rumours about Hugh Salter,' she said. 'I've no evidence.'

'But?'

'I don't trust him. Like I say, he'll always look out for number one and will screw you over if it's in his interests. But it's not just that. I don't trust his integrity.'

Brennan nodded. 'Hodder implied the same thing.'

'I shouldn't be saying this to you. But ever since what happened last year, I've suspected that Hugh is on Boyle's payroll. I think – no, that's too strong – I've *wondered* if that's why he shafted Jeff Kerridge and Keith Welsby. Not for honourable motives. But to advance the cause of Peter Boyle.'

Brennan gave a low whistle. 'But you've no proof?'

She glanced across at Brennan, wondering if she'd said too much. Christ, she didn't know that Salter hadn't sent Brennan here precisely to winkle this out of her. How had she allowed herself to be so indiscreet? Those baby blue eyes again?

'Of course not,' she said. 'And half the time I think I'm wrong. I've been watching Hugh like a hawk for the last six months and I've seen no evidence of anything untoward.'

They had reached the edge of the park. They crossed over the road and stood together looking at the water sparkling in the afternoon sun. 'Begs another question,'

Brennan said. 'If he is on Boyle's payroll, why's he employed me to help on the case?'

'Good point. When the powers-that-be dropped the prosecution last year, Hugh made out he was furious. Said we shouldn't let the bastard off the hook. Result was that he was given the Boyle file. I wondered whether he'd engineered that to keep control of it. Could still be true. He's made some progress in building a case against Boyle, but we're still a long way from anything that would stand up in court.'

'But the fact that he's brought me into it suggests he might be serious after all?'

'Maybe. A more cynical view would be that, well, you're damaged goods. He's given you a role that involves you trying to coordinate with the very people who've offloaded you, possibly chasing up links that don't exist. Trying to build a case that might be tainted just by your involvement.'

'You really know how to build someone's self-esteem, don't you?'

'You wanted me to be straight,' Marie pointed out. 'I'm just saying that Hugh's smart enough to play that game.' She paused, staring out across the water. 'Might even be that he's using you to spread the word about Boyle. Boyle doesn't even need to do much, if he's got the police linking every gangland killing back to him. Good way to put the wind up the competition.'

'That really is a cynical view. Ever thought of a career in politics?'

'However cynical I am, you can bet that Hugh Salter's more so. That's the trouble with this business. You end up not knowing what to think or who to trust.' She decided to chance her arm. 'You, for example. I've opened up here, told you precisely what I think of Hugh. Probably a really stupid thing to do. Maybe he's sent you here just to find out what I'm thinking.'

Brennan turned back from the river and took a step or two away from her. 'If you think that, there's no way I can persuade you otherwise, I suppose. But it's not true. I wanted to speak to you – well, partly to get some context and background, like I said. But mainly because I don't trust Salter either. I've no real grounds for it. Just something about the whole thing that doesn't feel right to me. I feel I'm being used. Even if I don't know quite how.' He paused and glanced at his watch. 'We haven't even talked about Boyle, yet. Fancy getting that coffee now? Lunchtime rush should have died down.'

'Why not?' she said. 'Live dangerously.' She began to follow him back across the park. 'Look, all that stuff about not trusting you. It's just that – well, in my life of work you can't afford to be too trusting of anyone. I've just taken a big risk. I hope my instincts are right.'

He smiled. 'They are, even if I can't prove it. Look, we should—'

She never discovered what he was about to say, because there was a sudden burst of music from his jacket. His mobile ringtone. The Clash, she noted, with slight amusement. 'Police and Thieves'.

Brennan pulled out the phone and glanced at the screen. Then he frowned, gave her look that she couldn't immediately read, and took the call. 'Brennan.'

He listened without responding for a minute or two.

'Jesus,' he said. 'Yeah, I'll give it a go, though I don't expect they'll slaughter the fatted calf or anything when I turn up. But if you've cleared it, they might at least let me in. Okay. Cheers.'

He thumbed off the call. 'Talk of the devil,' he said. 'That was our friend and colleague, Hugh Salter. Apparently he's just had a call from on high bearing news from Manchester. Jeff Kerridge's widow. She's been murdered.'

10

'Well, well, well. Look what the cat's thrown up. Didn't think you'd have the nerve to show your face around here for a while.'

Brennan gazed at DCI Renshaw impassively. 'Fuck off, Rob,' he said amiably.

Renshaw laughed. 'Well, those are some of the more polite comments you'll hear, I imagine.' They were standing by Renshaw's car outside the crime scene. Inside, the SOCOs were finishing their work. 'Giving you a friendly warning, that's all.' He gestured over to where a small cluster of DCs were gathered round the rear doors of the police van. 'Giving you the evil eye, already.'

'I can live with it.'

'You'll have to, old son, if you're still hanging round like a bad smell. Thought we'd seen the last of you.'

'Can't tear myself away, Rob. Must be love.'

'Sod's law, isn't it? I can see why the Agency are interested in this one. And I can see why they might want to use you to liaise with us. Even if you are the worst fucking choice in the world, in the circumstances.'

'I don't think they see it as their role in life to make

131

me feel comfortable.' Brennan smiled. 'I've got a thick skin, Rob.'

'I'm sure you have, old son. I'm sure you have.'

Brennan had been slightly relieved to discover that Renshaw was the Senior Investigating Officer on the case. He got on pretty with Renshaw. The DCI was a few years older and several lifetimes wiser than Brennan himself. He'd seen through all the bollocks with Chief Superintendent Craddock from day one. 'You have to accept it, Jack,' he'd said. 'You get the buggers cornered, they start throwing the shit around. And most of the numbskulls round here are too dim to recognise a total bastard when they see one.'

Renshaw had done the best he could to shield Brennan when the waste-products had hit the air-conditioning. There hadn't been much he could do, except counter some of the more slanderous accusations flying around. Brennan suspected that Renshaw might have had a hand in fixing up his secondment but the matter had never been discussed between them.

But if Brennan had to start sticking his nose in a Greater Manchester Police murder case, it helped that Renshaw was the man in charge.

'So what's the story?' Brennan said. 'I only got the bare bones over the phone.'

'Helen Kerridge,' Renshaw said. 'Widow of the late unlamented Jeff Kerridge of this parish. Supposed to meet her sister for coffee this morning. Didn't turn up, which is apparently unprecedented. Didn't answer her mobile or home phone. Sister gets worried. Comes round here. Can't get an answer. Checks round the back and finds the door open. Goes inside and finds Mrs Kerridge dead in her bed.

Panics and calls an ambulance. Who call us. Asphyxiation, apparently, though the quacks are still checking on that.'

Brennan looked at the estate around them. Moderately upmarket, he supposed, but still a row of identical boxes. 'This where she lived? Wouldn't have thought this was Jeff Kerridge's style, from everything I've heard.'

'Christ, no. Kerridge wouldn't have been seen dead in a place like this.' Renshaw paused. 'If you'll pardon the expression. No, this wasn't his scene at all. He was a man for the overpriced exclusive gated community. Keep the likes of us out.'

'So how come his widow ended up here?'

'Not because she was short of a bob or two. Kerridge did well enough for himself, and Mrs K's kept the old business ticking along very nicely since Kerridge went.' He shrugged. 'She sold up the old mansion a couple of months back and bought this place instead. Probably looking for a bit of anonymity. Get her head back below the battlements. Kerridge was all swagger and image. He loved all that pillar of the community crap. She wasn't into all that. Just wanted to get on with the job.'

'That why she'd been topped, you think? Because was getting on with the job?'

'Seems likely, doesn't it? There was a struggle to hold the old empire together once Kerridge was off the scene. Lots of people jockeying for position. But Mrs K seems to have managed it. She's taken a few hits, but word is that she's hung on to most of what Kerridge had in place. Probably surprised a few people.'

'Hence the topping.' Brennan said.

'Looks like a pro job. It was an expert break-in. She had

pretty decent security as you'd imagine, but it doesn't seem to have delayed our chap for long. It's still early days, but we haven't found a significant trace of evidence so far. There'll no doubt be some DNA in there other than hers, but I'm willing to bet now it won't show up on the database.'

'Any sign that she was being threatened? Someone trying to warn her off?'

'Not that we know of. Most of her associates have gone to ground, as you might expect. Sister reckoned Mrs K was her usual self when they'd met last week. Not unduly worried or out of sorts. But she wouldn't necessarily share any worries of that kind with her sister. Sister's straight, as far as we know. Doesn't even seem to know quite what the Kerridges got up to.'

'Any leads?'

'Scores of associates and competitors we'll need to follow up. But it could be any one of those, or someone else entirely. We don't know of any specific deal or activity that might have prompted this. Not yet, anyway.'

'What about Pete Boyle?'

Renshaw regarded Brennan for a moment. 'Well, they *have* brought you up to speed quickly, haven't they? Yeah, Boyle's got to be in the frame. It's always sad when true love dies, but Boyle and Kerridge were at each other's throats at the end. Boyle had gone from trusted protégé to thoroughly untrusted competitor. If Kerridge had lived, one of them would have shafted the other before too long. Though I'm not sure which way I'd have bet. Boyle's gradually been building his empire, so he wouldn't have been happy with Mrs K's persistence in keeping Kerridge's business going.'

'Not exactly a motive for murder, though, is it?'

'Not in your book or mine. But these people don't necessarily think like ordinary sane human beings.'

'So you'll be going after Boyle for this, then?' Brennan
looked across to where the DCs and a couple of uniforms
were standing. Waiting for the SOCOs to finish so they
could carry out a full search of the house. Most were looking
in his direction, though he couldn't read their expressions
from here.

'Unless you lot are telling me we shouldn't,' Renshaw
said. His tone suggested that he was only half-joking. They
both knew that there'd been occasions when overzealous
police work had messed up some covert operation by the
Agency.

'Not as far as I'm aware,' Brennan said. 'Though you
shouldn't assume the powers-that-be share all their secrets
with me. As far as they're concerned, I'm still one of you
lot.'

'Betwixt and between, eh?' Renshaw nodded sympathetically.
'Must be hell. But, yeah, we'll be interviewing Mr Boyle. Can't
imagine that we're going to find much of a link between him
and this, though. Even if he was behind it, he'll have covered
his tracks.'

'Another of the long list of unsolved gangland killings,'
Brennan intoned. 'Been a few recently, from what I hear?'

Renshaw looked at Brennan with more interest. 'That
what you hear, is it? Can't say I've noticed.'

'I'm just fishing, Rob. I've heard rumours that Boyle's
been flexing his muscles.'

'Maybe. There's no doubt that he's ambitious. And in his
business that's bound to mean rubbing up a few people the
wrong way. But I can't say I've noticed much more than

135

normal. Though that's plenty, of course.' He smiled. 'That what they've got you chasing up, is it? Pete Boyle's empire building?'

'Among other things,' Brennan said, vaguely. 'They're just trying to build a sustainable case against Boyle.'

'I heard they fucked it up first time round. Hope they manage to do better with you on board. Can't help thinking they'd do even better if they were prepared to share information from time to time.'

'Good point, well made.' Brennan smiled. 'I'm not holding anything back, Rob. You remember Hugh Salter, the guy that was involved in the business with Jeff Kerridge last year? He's got some theory that Boyle's behind a number of killings across the north west.' He briefly recounted the cases that Salter had described to him. 'Reckons that Boyle's got a personal grudge against each one of these, so he's been settling a few personal scores as well as sending out a message about his business ambitions.'

'And Helen Kerridge would make four? You think there's anything in this?'

'No idea. Salter's seen as a high flyer, but there's something about him. There are one or two reckon he's on the take.'

Renshaw laughed. 'Jesus, Jack. You've only been there five minutes and you're starting again? Don't you know when to leave well alone?'

Brennan shook his head. 'I'm doing nothing. Keeping my nose squeaky clean. I'm just trying to work out where I stand. If Salter is dodgy, I don't want to find that I'm being used as the dummy.'

'That's the problem when you've screwed up as royally as you have, Jack. You become fair game for every shyster.'

'Thanks a bunch for that.' Brennan was watching the house, where the SOCO team seemed finally to have finished. A couple of them in their white suits were standing on the doorstep chatting to the DCs waiting to go in. He could see one of them gesture in his own direction, clearly offering some observation about Brennan's presence. 'You were right about communication, though. All I want is to be kept informed. I'll do the same with you. I'll let you know anything that emerges on Boyle. I'm not sure I'm even supposed to do that. Salter didn't exactly swear me to secrecy, but he won't be overjoyed that I'm sharing everything with you. But in return I'd like you to keep me up to speed with this. Anything that comes up from your interviews.'

Renshaw gazed at him for a moment. 'You know, for a smart guy, you can be very naïve, Jack. Our lot and their lot are both chasing the same prize. If we start sharing information, there's a danger they might get there first. And, judging from past experience, they're not too keen to share the glory.'

Brennan had noted that he hadn't been categorised as one of 'their lot'. 'I'm on your side, Rob. I'm not going to shaft you.'

'Too right you're not, Jack. Not if you don't want to find your softer parts spread on toast. Okay, I'll keep you in the picture. But don't feed back any of it to Hugh fucking Salter without my say-so. I'm running this investigation, and I intend that it'll stay that way. That clear?'

'Pellucid,' Brennan said.

Renshaw was gazing over Brennan's shoulder. A police car was turning into the far end of the estate, blue lights flashing but without sirens. 'Looks like the top brass are here to make a token appearance for the media. Make yourself scarce, Jack. Before your fan club arrives.'

When she finally turned on her personal mobile, there were three messages waiting. She listened to the most recent first. Sue, Liam's carer, her voice dripping acid. 'Just having another go at getting hold of you, Marie. Liam's stable, but they want to keep him in overnight for observation. I'll keep you posted.'

Shit. The previous two messages told the full story. Liam's condition had worsened that morning and, by the time the carers arrived, he seemed to be having some difficulty breathing. Sue had left a first message seeking Marie's agreement to call Liam's GP. Receiving no response, she'd called the GP anyway, and the GP – almost inevitably, in Marie's experience – had decided to get Liam checked out in hospital.

She dialled Sue's number but the phone was busy or turned off. Maybe she was at the hospital with Liam. Double shit. She left a short apologetic message and ended the call.

Marie paced up and down the tiny living room of her new house, wondering what to do. It was four o'clock, Saturday. There was time for her to drive back down to London, check how Liam was, and – assuming he was okay – head back up here sometime on Sunday, ready for McGrath and the start of the working week.

It wasn't what she wanted to do, though, unless it was really necessary. As it was, she felt grossly under-prepared for kicking things off with McGrath. She'd been hoping for another day of thinking herself into the mind and body of Maggie Yates. The last thing she needed was a day of being

Marie Donovan under pressure, worrying about Liam, making sure he was being properly looked after. And what would happen if she got down there and discovered that he really wasn't well enough to be left? Could she face telling Salter that she was abandoning her assignment? What would be the implications of that?

Part of her mind was still distracted by her earlier meeting with Jack Brennan. He'd rushed off after taking the call about Helen Kerridge's murder, and she'd been left with a frustrating sense of unfinished business. They hadn't begun to talk about Pete Boyle, Brennan's purported reason for wanting to meet her. But she'd felt an empathy with Brennan. Maybe it was just that he'd echoed her concerns about Salter. Or maybe it was that, like her, he seemed out on a limb, feeling his way in unfamiliar territory, unsure who to trust.

Or maybe it was just that he was the best-looking policeman she'd come across in a while. She'd never claimed to be deep.

Whichever it was, she'd instinctively liked him more than she expected. She could see that there was some vanity there, and some ego, but it was offset by a self-deprecating good humour. She also sensed a warmth and generosity of spirit that had been missing from her life since – well, since Liam had fallen ill. It was only now, as she saw the contrast with Brennan, that she realised how much the illness had affected Liam. She didn't know who he was anymore, but she was increasingly sure that he wasn't the man she'd once loved.

She also knew how dangerous these thoughts could be. She'd recognised in her previous assignment that one of the real problems with this job was the loneliness. There was no space for real friendships. You couldn't afford to get too close to people. Couldn't allow them to spot the chinks in your fictional armour. Even going for a casual drink or a meal was fraught with risk.

But the loneliness could cloud your judgement. She knew that all too well. She knew how serious the consequences could be. That was how she'd ended up in bed with Jake Morton.

She was distracted from these thoughts by the buzz of her mobile on the table. She'd left it turned on after trying to call Sue, hoping that the carer might respond to the message she'd left. But the number on the screen was unfamiliar.

'Yes?' Never give your name, that was one of the rules. Never give too much away until you're sure who you're talking to. She'd given very few people this number – Liam, her parents, now Sue – and most of them had strict instructions. Don't mention Marie's name in any messages, don't leave your own name or return number. Think about the consequences of the phone being lost or stolen. Only Sue, who knew nothing significant about Marie's work, had not been given this guidance, and Marie had winced when she'd heard her name being spoken in the messages earlier. The risk was minimal, but it was still a risk that Marie normally avoided.

'Sorry to call you on this line. Thought the secure one was a little too close to home.' She recognised the voice now. Brennan.

'How'd you get this number?' she said, conscious that she sounded more accusatory than she'd intended. On the other hand, how *had* he got this number?

There was a pause, which she interpreted as signifying embarrassment. 'From your personnel file, actually. I went into the system and dug it out.'

It was her turn to pause as she thought through the implications of this. 'What did you mean about the secure line being too close to home?' she asked, finally.

'Just felt that if I wanted a private chat with you, this one might be a bit more discreet. I thought that Salter might have access to the records and wonder why I'd called.'

'Good question. Why are you calling me?'

'Felt we hadn't finished today. Wondered whether we might continue another time.'

'Look, Jack. I was uneasy about agreeing to the meeting in the first place. I don't know if I can justify meeting you twice.' Even though, she thought, it's exactly what I'd like to do. 'Especially if you're looking to do it behind Salter's back.'

'It's Salter I want to talk about. Among other things. We seem to have some common views about him.'

'Neither of us trusts him,' she said. 'Let me break this to you gently: that doesn't make us members of any exclusive club.'

'I'm guessing that the Society of Hugh Salter Shaftees is probably a pretty broad church. But I'd rather not be one of them. And at the moment I have the sense that I'm being set up.'

'And where do I come in?'

'Maybe I'm just looking for a receptive ear. Someone who knows Salter better than I do, and who can tell me if I'm talking bollocks.' He paused. 'Someone to give the new kid a bit of support. I've screwed up royally once. I can't afford to do it again.'

It was tempting. She wanted to nail Pete Boyle. And she wanted to know what Salter's game was. Brennan might help her achieve both objectives. He was certainly in a better position to do anything than she would be once she'd got her feet under McGrath's desk. She'd at least have an ally.

Assuming she could trust Jack Brennan.

'Let me think about it. I've got to be careful. I'm starting the new job tomorrow and I've got to keep my head clear. Give me a week or so till I'm settled in. Then – well, maybe we could meet up again. I'll call you.'

She ended the call and stood for a moment, staring at the screen. She had the sense that she'd just committed to something more serious than her words had implied. The story of her life. Leaping before she looked.

She was startled by the sudden buzzing of the phone in her hand. Sue the carer this time. 'Hi. Marie.'

'I've been trying to call,' Sue said, accusingly, 'but it just went to voicemail again.'

'Sorry. Somebody called me. I've just got off the line. How is he?'

There was a pause, in which Marie imagined Sue mouthing the words 'As if you care.' Sue said, 'Like I say, stable. They want to keep him in for observation, though. He's still not well. Seems very unresponsive. We were struggling to get any fluids down him, so he got a bit dehydrated as well. They've got him on a drip now.'

'What do they think the trouble is?'

'Something and nothing, they say. Probably just a cold. But you know the way that knocks him back.'

Of course I do, Marie wanted to say. I live with him, for Christ's sake. Except that, just at the moment, that wasn't

142

quite true. She wasn't living with him. 'Any little thing seems to, these days,' she said. 'Okay, I'd better head back down. I'm due to start the new job up here on Monday, but I can at least come back for tomorrow. How long do they reckon he'll be in for?'

'They're not sure. If he improves overnight, he could be out tomorrow. But they might keep him in longer if he's showing no signs of improvement.' There was another hesitation which again seemed to convey a wealth of meaning. 'Look, it's up to you, obviously. But I don't know there's that much point in you rushing back tonight. By the time you get down visiting time will be finished, so you won't be able to come in here anyway. Why don't you wait until the morning? If he's okay by then, maybe they'll discharge him anyway.'

'He'll still need someone to look after him. Get him home.'

'Well, I was going to say that, if it's needed, I could do that.'

'That's very kind of you, Sue. But the care arrangements won't cover that, will they?' The core support from Sue and the other carers was largely funded through the local authority, although Marie and Liam paid for some additional hours out of their own pockets.

'Don't worry about that,' Sue said. 'It's not covered my time today, either, but when these things happen you just have to deal with them.' The tone, to Marie's ears, managed to be both martyred and accusatory.

'Yes, but we can't expect you to—'

'It's what I do, Marie. I do it to make a living. But I also do it because I want to. I won't let Liam down.'

The subtext there was unmistakable. Marie was on the point of saying: 'No, sod you, I'm coming, whether you like it or not.' But she bit back the words, recognising that, whatever her own feelings might be, Sue was indispensable to Liam. Even if Marie could help Liam tomorrow, she was still going to have to return up here on Monday. 'Well, if you're sure you can manage, Sue.' she said, finally.

'I'll be fine,' Sue said. 'I'll give you the number of the ward, so you can phone directly and check how he is in the morning. Then you can decide whether it's worth coming down.'

There was a finality in Sue's words that allowed no space to disagree. Marie muttered more thanks and ended the call. Christ, she thought, it's getting worse. We're playing tug of war over poor Liam's struggling body, trying to show which of us cares more.

And the worst thing was that it felt as if she'd already lost. As if Sue was already dragging Liam away, pulling him unresisting into the warmth and security of her caring heart.

11

Another one down. Another job completed.

It had turned out pretty easy in the end, for all his initial forebodings. Apart from that small jitter at the start, he'd handled it perfectly. He sat back, thinking through the detail of the night before. Checking that he'd got it right, and had left no evidence that might come back to bite him. He felt confident enough. He'd left barely a trace of himself in the house. Apart from the dead body and the unlocked rear door, there was no obvious sign that he'd been there. And there was nothing – fingerprints, DNA – that could be traced back to the person he now was. There would be more in the house he'd used for reconnaissance, but no one would have a reason to look in there.

And the killing had been remarkably simple. He'd somehow expected that she would give him more trouble. But she'd hardly woken. Just that moment when her eyes had opened and she'd looked directly at him. He wondered whether she'd recognised him in that split second. Probably not. Their paths had crossed only infrequently in the days when he worked for her husband.

But she knew what was about to happen to her. Even

though she'd struggled, fought back against his weight pressing down on her, that had seemed almost an after-thought. In her eyes, she'd seemed almost resigned to it. Something she had been expecting for a long time. Perhaps something she wanted.

They were often like that. That one up on the moors. He knew what was going to happen, and he seemed simply to accept it. Perhaps it had been a relief. He'd been running for a long time, and now he was able to stop.

So now everything was done. He'd texted the code to the anonymous number to confirm it was finished. No need for more contact than that. After a short time, the remainder of the money would arrive. Clean cash sent to a designated PO Box, that he'd pay in instalments into a range of bank accounts. No sums large enough to excite any suspicion.

For once, he already had another job in place. Usually he had to wait. He was good at the job and had a reputa-tion in the right places, so the commissions came in often enough. But it was a niche service. And there were risks in being too busy. He might get careless, cut corners. Usually, he was happy to get a job done, and then slip off the radar for a month or two.

But this had been a golden period. One commission after another, but with freedom to work at his own pace. He knew, or at least he thought he knew, who and what was behind it. But it wasn't his business to care about that. The requests came through the usual channels, and the required upfront retainer was paid. That was all he was bothered about. After that, it was just a job.

Even this one.

He admitted to himself, though, that this one was

different. It would be foolish to pretend otherwise. There was nothing wrong with feeling some emotion. But you had to recognise the fact. You had to make sure it didn't cloud your judgement.

So there would be a personal dimension to this one. He would feel something, for sure. The question was what.

That was his real worry. That he couldn't be sure of his own feelings. He felt anger, resentment. A sense of humiliation. But also something more positive. A lingering affection. Love even. He didn't know what love felt like, but there had been times when he had thought, just maybe, it might feel like this.

'It's a mess, I'm afraid,' McGrath acknowledged ruefully.

He could say that again, Marie thought. Not just a mess. A towering heap of crap that had clearly just been allowed to grow for years. If nothing else, it ought to mean that she had a job here for as long as she wanted it. 'It would benefit from a little organisation,' she offered, tentatively.

They were standing in the room that McGrath had designated as her office. It was approximately a quarter of the size of McGrath's own, and largely filled with piles of unsorted documents. Invoices, bills, letters, company brochures. And almost anything else you cared to name. There were two battered filing cabinets, both empty. Beside those, squashed into the corner of the room, there was an equally decrepit desk, with an ancient-looking computer perched on top. Without moving some of the papers, it would be impossible for her even to sit at the desk.

'Well,' McGrath said, 'that's why we need you. This isn't really Lizzie's strong point.'

'We all have different talents.' Marie preferred not to think about where Lizzie's might lie. She picked up a handful of papers from the nearest file, examining them as if they might offer a solution to McGrath's administrative problems. 'You'd like me to sort these?'

'As best you can, anyway.' McGrath was already backing towards the door. 'I imagine a lot of it can be thrown.' He leaned over, apparently to peer at the documents she was holding, although also securing a lengthy look at her cleavage in the process.

'I imagine so.' The papers were clearly in no kind of order, chronological or otherwise. Some dated back several years, others were relatively new. She wondered whether the bills had actually been paid. 'Should keep me out of mischief, eh?' She raised her gaze back up to McGrath, who hurriedly averted his own from the upper half of her body. 'Is there anything else I need to know?'

McGrath had said that there was a lot to hand over to her. She suspected she was probably looking at most of it. She wondered whether the material related solely to the legitimate side of McGrath's business, or whether it might contain evidence relating to his shadier affairs. Given McGrath's disorganisation, anything might be possible.

'Don't think so. Lizzie can show you all the domestics. Tea and toilets and all that. I've got a few bits of business to attend to. See you later.'

He'd left the room before she could make any response. That was a relief in one respect, at least. She'd had a fear that McGrath might spend the day breathing down her neck – or some other parts of her body – as she tried to get on with things.

She stood back and regarded the pile of papers. Several weeks' work there, without question. It might be an evidential treasure trove, or it could be the pile of rubbish it appeared. There was only one way to find out.

She decided to postpone the evil moment a little longer and wandered back to the office where Lizzie was sitting at her computer, perusing the online gossip pages of some tabloid.

'Andy said you could show me where to make myself a coffee,' Marie said.

Lizzie looked up, her expression suggesting that Marie had raised some issue relating to quantum mechanics. 'Coffee? Um, yeah, there's a kitchen at the end of the corridor. Water heater thingie. Coffee and mugs in the cupboard over the sink. Milk's in the fridge. I've got ours labelled. If I don't, the techies upstairs nick it.' An IT company occupied the floor above them, with various other small companies scattered through the rest of the building.

'Thanks. Want one?'

Lizzie looked genuinely surprised. 'Yeah, thanks. Look, I'll come through and show you.'

Marie followed the young woman into the small kitchen at the end of the corridor. There was a sink, fridge, row of cupboards, a cheap-looking dishwasher. Marie busied herself preparing the coffee. 'Been here long?' she asked, idly.

'Nearly two years.'

'Straight from school?'

'Worked in a shop for a bit. Chemist's. But this is a lot easier.'

I bet, Marie thought. 'How are you finding it?'

'All right. Left to myself a lot of the time, when Andy's out and about. So I just get on with things.'

'Andy okay to work for?'

Lizzie nodded. 'Yeah, really good, actually. Easygoing, generally.' She filled the cups from the water heater. 'Don't know how he makes any money, though.'

Marie looked at Lizzie with interest. Maybe not quite as dizzy as she appeared. 'Doesn't seem busy?'

'Dunno really. I mean, I'm no expert. He gets some business through. But it doesn't seem like much.' She paused to hand one of the mugs to Marie. 'Maybe there's stuff I don't see.'

Marie nodded, her face expressionless. 'Probably handles a lot of it himself. Anyway, let's hope he manages to keep us in work, eh?'

Back in the office, she sat on the floor, the coffee beside her, and began to look through the piles of paperwork. Sitting with the mass of documents at eye-level, it seemed like a Herculean task.

It was too much. Not just this – filtering through the world's biggest haystack in search of a needle that might not even be there. But everything.

Especially Liam.

That was the real issue. That was why she was feeling bad. She hadn't driven down to the hospital on Sunday. She'd phoned in the morning and been told that Liam's condition had improved significantly. They were keeping him in for another night but, assuming there was no further relapse, expected to release him on Monday. Ten minutes later, Sue had called and reassured her that everything was in hand. 'He's been asleep most of the time. I'll pop in again at visiting time.'

'I think I should come down—' Marie had begun.

'Well, that's your decision,' Sue responded. 'But you really don't need to. I know how busy you are.'

'I can get down for the day.'

'They won't allow anyone in except during the designated hours. And he's most likely to be asleep. It's a long way for you.'

'What about tomorrow?' Marie said, wanting to move the conversation on. 'If he's released. Is everything okay for him at home?'

'I can be there when he gets home tomorrow. I've spoken to the social worker. She's going to come tomorrow afternoon and do an assessment. See if we need to increase the care package. But it's all under control.'

Marie had noted the 'we', but wasn't sure who Sue was including in that first-person plural. She was feeling increasingly excluded, even though she knew that she'd chosen to exclude herself. 'I still think I should come back,' she said, though the offer sounded insincere even to her own ears.

'There's nothing you could do. Liam probably wouldn't even be aware you'd been.'

'Well, if you're sure . . .'

'Absolutely certain. If anything changes, I'll contact you straight away. But there really is nothing for you to worry about.'

'You'll let me know if there's any change for the worse?'

'I've just said I will. I'll call you tomorrow morning to update you anyway. If you can't answer, I'll leave a message.'

'Thanks. That's great. I'll be back next weekend, then.'

'Whatever you think best.'

Marie had ended the call and stood, in that poky little living room, staring at the phone in her hand. She was tempted to call back, say she'd changed her mind. Head off down the M6 and back home.

But she'd known that she wouldn't. She couldn't cope. She couldn't face the thought of dealing with someone who was growing more and more disabled, more and more dependent. By contrast, Sue seemed unfazed by whatever Liam's condition might throw at her. She'd dealt with clients whose condition was far worse, she said. You just had to get on with it.

Marie told herself that it was easy to be blasé when you could walk away. For Sue, Liam was a professional challenge, not a dependent. But Marie thought she saw signs that Sue's relationship with Liam was changing. That, for good or ill, Sue was beginning to get personally involved. That Liam was something more than just another client.

That was the trouble with this job, Marie thought. Externally, she had to present herself as Maggie Yates. Marie Donovan was locked in her own head, stuck with her own thoughts and imaginings. She sat here, on the dusty floor of this crappy office, concocting fantasies about what might or might not be happening two hundred miles away. She'd no reason to suspect Sue's good intentions. For Christ's sake, the woman had made it possible for her to continue to work and live as she wanted. She could hardly resent her for that.

She wished there was someone she could talk to about all this. Once, Liam would have been there to offer support and reassurance. Now it was Liam she wanted to talk about, and there was no one to listen.

Her thoughts went back to Jack Brennan. Maybe she should meet up with him after all. Salter could hardly complain, given he'd set the whole thing up in the first place. She couldn't talk to Brennan about anything personal – Christ, no – but she could allow herself to be Marie Donovan for a short while. Get outside her own head.

'How's it going?' Lizzie was peering round the door, staring at Marie and the piles of paper in something approaching awe. 'Wondered if you wanted another coffee?'

Marie looked at the papers in her hand, and realised that, although she'd worked systematically through more than half of the first pile, she'd taken in almost nothing of what she'd been reading.

'Not so good, really. Only just scratched the surface.' She sat back on the hard floor and looked at the stacks of paperwork. 'Coffee would be good. A really, really strong one.'

12

'Hello?'

'Jack Brennan?'

Brennan took the phone from his ear and glanced at the screen. Number withheld. 'Who's asking?'

'Colin Barker. DS in Renshaw's team. Rob tells me you're all right.'

'I think so. Not everyone would agree.'

Barker laughed. 'You the guy who shafted Craddock?'

'So they say.'

'Makes you all right in my book. Not everyone loved that bastard.'

'Plenty of people seemed quite fond of him at the time.'

'Protecting their own, weren't they? Worried what else might come to light once you'd turned over the stone.'

'I dare say. How can I help you, Colin?'

'More a question of how I can help you. Rob tells me you're interested in Pete Boyle?'

'More than a bit. You've got something?'

'I've got a grass who's close to Boyle's team.'

'Sounds ideal. Any info gratefully received.'

'You reckon Boyle's flexing his muscles?'

'That's the theory on this side of the house. One person's theory, anyway. I'm keeping an open mind.'

'Could be right. Been a bit of tension on the streets. Not exactly open warfare. But things a bit more heated than usual. Couple of assaults on known dealers. Places burnt out. Sporadic, so far, and no obvious pattern. But enough to suggest that something's going on.' Barker paused. 'And then there's Kerridge's missus.'

'What impact has that had?'

'Too early to tell. It's left a definite vacuum, though. Doing bloody well, was Ma Kerridge. Taken over Jeff's reins very nicely. Lots of people reckon she was the brains behind Jeff Kerridge anyway.'

'Who'll succeed her?'

'Far as we know, there's no obvious number two. Ma Kerridge learned from what happened with Pete Boyle. If you groom a successor, they end up trying to usurp the bloody throne.'

'But not having a successor brings other problems,' Brennan pointed out.

'Too right. But you probably don't care too much once you've gone. We'll get some serious jockeying for position now. All the big players will want in.'

'Including Pete Boyle.'

'He'll have been camping out all night, waiting for the sale to start,' Barker said.

'You reckon he was behind it?'

'High on the list. But not the only possibility. Mrs K

didn't go out of her way to make friends. May never find out for sure. Looks like a pro job. Not left much for us to go on.'

'Don't suppose it matters much. Real question is what happens next.'

'Why we're keeping our ears close to the ground.'

'This grass. He told you much about Boyle's plans?'

'Not recently. But we've not been asking much. Boyle's not really been on the radar since he got out. Kept a low profile. Might have just been building up his reserves. But the topping of Helen Kerridge is a game-changer, whoever was behind it.'

'So what are you suggesting?'

'Thought it was time for a more in-depth chat with our informant. Renshaw thought you might like to tag along.'

'Will he talk with me there?'

'Christ knows. He's a big-mouth. Tries to impress. Acts tough and makes out he knows more than he does. If there's two of us, he'll probably play up to that. It'll make him feel important. He talks some crap, but if you filter that out, most of what he comes up with is pretty kosher.'

'Worth a shot, anyway. Where and when?'

'I'll try and get him tonight. Let's go for the Wetherspoon's place by the Town Hall. Somewhere big and anonymous, and away from his stamping ground. He'll feel more comfortable. About six, so the office crowds are still in there. Give me a call when you get there and I'll tell you where we're hiding.' He gave Brennan a mobile number, then added: 'Mind you, you'll probably spot us, anyway.'

'Why's that?'

'Because we'll be the ones who look like a copper and a grass. Why else?'

'Bloody hell,' McGrath said. 'You've made progress.'

She sat back on the floor and looked around her. It didn't feel as if she had, given how much work she'd put in, but she supposed he was right. She'd ploughed through perhaps a quarter of the accumulated junk, working as systematically as she could manage. Much of the paperwork had been little more than rubbish – age-old copies of invoices and receipts, old brochures, unenlightening correspondence. Some of this material might be of interest to the Revenue, but it was small-scale stuff. She'd found a few documents that could relate to McGrath's more clandestine activities. Nothing that would constitute evidence, but the names mentioned might open up a few leads for the intelligence people. She'd secreted the relevant documents into the side of her briefcase, trying to persuade herself that she wasn't wasting her time.

The rest she'd sorted as well as she could. On the shelves in Lizzie's office, she'd found a stack of predictably unused box files, and she'd sorted the paperwork into various categories, filing it away chronologically. She couldn't imagine that her day's activities had served any real purpose, other than helping to clear the floor and beginning to build some credibility with McGrath. He'd been absent for most of the day, out on some unspecified 'business'.

'Well, I've made a start,' she said, pulling herself slowly to her feet. Her smart business suit was dusty and her limbs felt as if they'd lost contact with her brain. McGrath shrugged. 'Didn't expect you to get quite so far, to be honest.'

'I've been quite ruthless,' she said, gesturing towards an already overfull bin bag. 'Thrown away anything that didn't look as if it was likely to be useful. Hope you don't find you're missing anything important.'

'If it was in this pile, I've managed without it long enough.' He took a few steps forward and gazed around the room, with the air of a monarch surveying his kingdom. 'Yeah, you've done a bloody good job.' He looked back at her, smiling. 'Enough for today, though, Maggie. You must be knackered. How about a drink?'

Inwardly, she groaned. It had been inevitable that McGrath would renew his efforts to ask her out, and she'd known it would be impossible to reject him entirely. The trick would be to get close enough to secure McGrath's confidence, without getting so close that she gave him any wrong ideas. Not an easy trick, given the appraising glances that McGrath was already throwing in her direction.

She glanced at her watch. 'Bit early, isn't it?'

'You've been working hard. You deserve the break,' he said.

Might as well get it over with, she thought. 'Just a quick one, though. I'm still trying to sort the new house.'

They left Lizzie to close up the office, and Marie walked with McGrath out to a pub on the main road, near the entrance to the business park. Lizzie had watched them with an expression that, as far as Marie could tell, mixed amusement with relief.

The pub was the usual plastic hostelry found on the edges of business parks, selling microwaved fake gourmet meals to besuited men in the nearby offices or the adjoining budget hotel. At five o'clock it was still relatively quiet, though beginning to fill up with workers grabbing a quick pint before heading home.

McGrath bought her a red wine and himself a pint of lager, and led her to a table in a quiet corner. 'Nice place,' he said, gesturing around them. 'Decent food, too. We'll have to do lunch sometime.'

She nodded noncommittally and took a sip of her wine. 'Do you come here a lot?'

'Well, you know, business lunches. That kind of thing. Useful place to have on the doorstep.'

'You must have to do a lot of entertaining. With clients, I mean.' She was trying to find a line of conversation that would allow her to probe a little, without putting him on his guard.

'What it's all about,' McGrath said, taking a deep swallow of his lager. 'Build up the networks. Get to know people.'

'Is that where you were today?' she asked. 'With clients?'

He glanced at her with what might have been suspicion. She distracted him by stretching out her stockinged legs. Sure enough, his gaze drifted uncontrollably to where her skirt was beginning to ride up her thighs. She moved to adjust it, and his eyes flicked back to her smiling face. Not subtle, but it achieved the intended effect.

'Yeah,' he said, finally. 'Clients. Bit of this, bit of that, you know. Bit of schmoozing.'

'Successful?'

'Hard to tell.' She could sense that he was warming to the subject, his desire to impress her outweighing his instinct for caution. 'But, yeah, I think so. There'll be one or two bits of business coming out of today. Nothing major, but a couple of little deals.'

'Importing?'

His eyes met hers again, but any suspicion seemed to have vanished. 'You know how it is. Got fingers in all kinds of pies. Can't afford to limit yourself in the current climate.'

'Must be tricky times,' she said, sympathetically. 'With the economy the way it is.'

'Bloody tough. Last couple of years have been a nightmare. Banks won't give you an overdraft. One or two customers went to the wall so we lost orders. Others are cutting back. Bloody nightmare. Can't afford to have all your eggs in one basket.'

'No, I can see that.' She eased out her legs again, feeling like a conjuror engaged in a particularly clumsy piece of misdirection. 'What sort of things do you get involved in, then?'

His eyes were fixed on her legs. 'Well, like I said, anything where I can turn a profit. You can't be too choosy. If you have too many scruples, you might as well kiss the business goodbye.'

'I imagine you have to be quite ruthless,' she said, in what sounded to her own ears appallingly close to a simper. 'To survive, I mean.' She picked up her glass, ensuring that McGrath received a good eyeful of cleavage in the process. Talk about not having too many scruples, she thought.

'Ruthless,' he agreed. 'And not too worried about the letter of the law.' He leaned back in his chair and smiled at her smugly. 'You wouldn't believe some of the stuff I get involved in.'

Jesus, she thought, he really is an idiot. First flash of leg, and he's shooting his mouth off to some woman he barely knows. 'Really?'

'Christ, yes. I mean, a lot of it's above board. But I take a few risks when I need to. Sail a bit close to the wind.'

'Sounds very – exciting,' she offered.

'Can be. I mean, a lot of it's just transactions. But if the goods are – well, not strictly legit, then it does add a bit of a thrill.' He leaned over and smiled at her conspiratorially. 'I heard your ex was in a similar line of work?'

'Not quite my ex yet,' she said. 'I'm still working on that.' No harm in reminding McGrath that she was supposedly still married to the fictional philandering husband. 'Not sure he's fully accepted that I've walked out yet. Keep expecting him to turn up on the doorstep. He could be a jealous so-and-so. Violent, too,' she added, mischievously.

McGrath involuntarily leant away from her, glancing towards the pub doorway as if he expected the non-existent husband to appear at any moment. 'He doesn't know where you are, though?'

'Hope not,' she said. 'Sounds like he was in a similar line of business. I used to do all his admin. Legit and non-legit. Part of the trick was to launder some of the non-legit money through the other side of the business so it came out clean.'

McGrath regarded her with an expression that, compared to his previous lecherous glances, seemed almost respectful. 'Didn't know you were that involved,' he said. 'Though you came highly recommended. Capable and discreet.' He intoned the last three words as though reading a reference. 'That's what I was told.'

'Sounds about right,' she said. 'You learned the fine art of discretion, working for my husband.'

'I can see you're likely to be an asset to the business.'

McGrath paused to take another peer at her legs. 'In more ways than one.'

'I'll do my best.'

He took another deep swallow of his pint. 'Need all the help I can get, just at the moment, I can tell you. Things are moving. Lots of opportunities. But lots of threats, as well.' He spoke with the air of a management consultant reviewing a business plan. 'Tricky times.'

'How do you mean?'

He hesitated, glancing around the bar as if afraid of being overheard. There was no one sitting near them and the hubbub in the room was loud enough to ensure that his words wouldn't carry. 'I reckon there's a chance to expand. Build market share. Some of the competition's – well, run into difficulties. Chance to steal some business before they regroup. Trouble is, there are plenty of others out there with the same idea.'

'I'm not sure I follow.'

He paused again and took another look around. 'You heard of a bloke called Jeff Kerridge?'

It took an effort of will to keep her face expressionless. She shook her head. 'Means nothing.'

'You're from down south,' he said. 'He was a big deal up here. Lord of the manor, you might say.'

'Was?'

'Yeah. Don't know the whole story, but he was shot by some copper. Was all hushed up, but they reckon Kerridge had been paying off the filth. Maybe someone wanted him silenced.'

'So what's this about?' she asked. 'Carving up Kerridge's empire?'

'Sort of. But it's a bit more complicated. Kerridge was killed last year. Everyone thought his business would fall apart, but it didn't. His wife took over and made a bloody good job of it, by all accounts.' McGrath's tone suggested that he couldn't quite bring himself to believe it. 'Held everything together. Even carried on growing the business.'

'So what's changed now?'

'What's happened now is that the old lady's also kicked the bucket. Police are keeping a lid on it at the moment, but the word is that she was topped. Professional job.' McGrath looked up and caught her eye, as if he'd just realised that he might be talking too freely. 'If you know what I mean.'

'I know what you mean,' she said. 'So you think someone's looking to take her place?'

'Looks that way. Means that there might be opportunities to pick up some crumbs from the table.'

'Suppose it depends who's dishing up,' she said. 'If they're prepared to have Kerridge's wife killed, they sound pretty ruthless. Would you want to risk crossing them?'

McGrath looked uncomfortable. 'Christ, no. That's not in my league. At the end of the day, I'm just a businessman. Got to be careful. I'm happy to sweep up anything I can, but I don't want to put anyone's nose out of joint. Like I say, there are opportunities and threats. There's some bad stuff going down out there.'

'Like what?'

'Nasty stuff. Killings. Beatings. Arson. People throwing their weight about.'

'The same people who killed Kerridge's wife?'

McGrath shrugged. 'Seems likely. But it's not just Kerridge.

I've heard of a few small players – people like me – who've had problems. I just want to keep my head down and mop up any bits of business I can. I like a quiet life.'

'Maybe you're in the wrong business, then,' she smiled.

'Yeah, maybe,' he said, looking gloomily into his nearly empty glass. Then he looked up at her and laughed. 'Couldn't do anything else, though. I like the ducking and diving. Keeps me young. Another?' He waved his glass in her direction.

'Better not,' she said. 'Not if I'm driving.' She realised, too late, that this sounded dangerously close to an invitation for McGrath to give her a lift. 'And I've still got a stack of stuff to sort out at home.'

She was beginning to warm slightly to McGrath. He was a small-time grifter, but at least he knew it. He remained relentlessly buoyant in the face of whatever the world might throw at him, even if he was only just keeping his head above water. Even his lechery was straightforward. He'd chance his arm once or twice, she thought, and when she knocked him back he'd shrug and move on to another quarry.

He peered regretfully into the empty glass. 'You know what, Maggie? You're too sensible to be working for me. Mind you, a dose of good sense is exactly what I need. There are some nasty people out there.'

'Tell me about it,' she said. 'I married one of them. And there's plenty more where he came from.'

'Too right. Don't suppose you've come across Pete Boyle?' He asked the question as if it were just a casual follow-up, but he glanced nervously towards the pub entrance as he asked it.

She shook her head, adopting the poker-face again. 'Another local big shot?'

'Used to be Kerridge's dep. They had some falling out. Word is that Boyle got shafted and ended up inside, but they couldn't make the case stick. Now he's out, and they reckon he's one of those throwing his weight about.'

'Would make sense,' she agreed. 'If he thought he'd been shafted by Kerridge. Would give him a motive for taking out a contract on Kerridge's widow, I suppose.'

McGrath gave another glance towards the door. 'He's a nasty bit of work, anyhow.'

'Is there a problem, Andy?' She realised that she'd used his name for the first time. She couldn't help herself. One whiff of a lead and she found herself deploying all the tricks and techniques she used with informants. Gain their confidence. Lure them in. Get them relaxed. It was made her good at her job, but there were times when she hated herself for it.

'Might be. I've had a few deals go tits up recently. People crying off at the last minute. Contacts who've dropped off the radar, you know? Today. I heard one got his stock destroyed in a fire at some storage place in Liverpool. Then someone tells me that Boyle and his associates have been clocked around these parts over the last week or so. This isn't his territory. Wasn't, anyway. But they reckon he sees everywhere as fair game these days.' McGrath had been looking for a way of offloading his anxieties, she thought. That was why he'd been talking so freely. Seeing her as someone to share the pain.

'The rumour mill might be wrong,' she said. 'It often is.'

'But it makes me nervous. Don't like to think Pete Boyle might have his beady eyes on me.'

'Have to keep your head down,' she said. 'Try not to draw attention to yourself.'

'Easier said than done.' McGrath gazed ruefully at his glass. 'I'm going to risk a second,' he said, finally. 'Sure you won't join me?'

'I need to get going, Andy. See you in the morning, okay?' She pushed herself up from the table. 'Stop at this one, though, eh? It wouldn't be smart to get done for drink-driving, on top of everything else.'

'Yeah. I usually manage to avoid being a total dickhead, with a bit of encouragement.' He laughed. 'Sorry. Not like me. One of nature's optimists, usually. Just got me a bit rattled, that's all.'

'You'll be okay?'

'Yeah, of course. You get off. Plenty more chances for me to buy you dinner, eh?' He laughed, with a glint of the familiar mischievous lechery back in his eyes.

She smiled back. 'You know what, Andy? You carry on asking and there's half a chance I might say yes. See you in the morning, eh?'

She made her way to the exit. At the door she paused and glanced back towards McGrath. He was still sitting there, empty glass in front of him, as if waiting for someone to arrive.

13

He watched as she left the pub, noting her confident stride across the car park. It's the wrong sort of car for her, he thought. She was built for a flash little sporty number, something with a roof you could lower when the sun came out. He'd imagined her blonde hair caught by the wind as she sped down an empty country road, like a model in a car advertisement. Not stuck in some prosaic black Japanese saloon.

She looked different, though. Not so different that he hadn't recognised her. He would have known her anywhere, however different she might appear. In any case, the changes were superficial. She'd dyed her hair a lighter shade of blonde. She was wearing a different style of clothes. More make-up. Tarty, he thought. That was the word.

But, underneath, she was the same person. Pretty, neat, smart in every sense. The same person. She was just doing a job.

And she was good at it, too. This would be a challenge. She was clever and streetwise. She was used to keeping her eyes open. More than that, she was *trained*. She'd be expecting – well, not him. Certainly not him. But someone. She'd be expecting that someone might be behind her.

But he liked the idea of having some competition, a real test of his ability. Something to keep him on his toes, help him hone his skills.

He'd parked his car three rows back in the busy car park, where there was no danger that he'd be seen, even if she stopped to look around. Even if she suspected that someone might be here.

He'd seen no sign of that, though. She'd seemed relaxed enough. She'd glanced round before getting into her car, but that was just force of habit.

He had it all under control. A couple of days earlier, in the small hours of the morning, he'd visited her house. He'd parked half a mile away, off the estate, and made his way silently through the surrounding fields. When he'd reached her house, he'd fixed a magnetic electronic tracking device under one of the wings of her car.

He hadn't really needed to go to those lengths. He could have managed to slip the device unobtrusively under the car even in broad daylight, even if the car was parked in a busy shopping street. That stuff wasn't difficult. If you looked confident enough, people just ignored you. They assumed you were going about some legitimate business, and they didn't trouble themselves too much about what it might be.

It was harder in the dead of night. If anyone caught you, they would know you were up to no good. But he'd done it to test himself. It was just a game. Setting yourself a personal challenge, make the work more interesting.

He'd thought about not using the tracker for the same reasons. But the risks were too great. Keeping a tail on a vehicle was never easy, even with less experienced targets.

You couldn't get too close. But if you kept too far back, particularly in a city, you risked losing the target. You found yourself doing stupid things. Jumping lights or overtaking on blind bends. Stuff that got you noticed. Stuff that might get you killed.

But he could follow the tracker through an app on his mobile phone without having to move a muscle. He could trace the little green blob on the electronic map, and know precisely where she was. He could let her go on ahead and follow at a discreet distance, waiting to catch her up. Easy.

He sat motionless in his car, watching as she pulled out of the pub car park into the main road. This time of the evening, she was probably just heading home. If so, he'd leave her be for tonight, unless she showed signs of going out again.

There was no hurry. He always made it clear to clients that, unless they had some urgent requirement – and he would charge extra if that was the case – he would work at his own pace. He had to observe, think, plan. For the moment, they just wanted him to watch. Report any movements that seemed unexpected or significant. Eventually, they'd want him to act. But not yet.

He reported any relevant information to an anonymous voicemail. He received no feedback as to whether his information was useful, and he didn't expect any. If it was valuable, they'd use it. If not, they'd ignore it.

He watched the trace of her movement on the screen of his mobile, checking that she was heading back towards her home. Just as he'd expected.

He smiled faintly, then dialled the number of the voice-mail. He left his message after the tone, as requested by the robotic voice. Just the basic details of what he'd observed. He ended the call, tossed the mobile on to the passenger seat, and started the engine.

'Where are you?'

'Back room. To the left as you face the bar. Table in the corner. I've a pint waiting for you.'

Brennan pushed his way through the bustling pub. Smart choice, he thought. A crowded Wetherspoon's joint, just off St Peter's Square, crammed full of office workers in the early evening. Not a place likely to attract any of Boyle's associates.

He found Barker and the grass easily enough. Their roles weren't quite as obvious as Barker had suggested, but Barker looked every inch a copper. He was tall, solidly built, obviously in decent shape. Probably late twenties, his hair trimmed short, his expression suggesting the right balance of enthusiasm and cynicism.

The grass was a different proposition. Short, overweight, with greasy greying hair flopping across his forehead. He had a couple of days' growth of beard and could have been anything from thirty to fifty. Nearer thirty, Brennan thought as he sat down, but thirty shitty years. He had the familiar look of the informant – shifty, nervous, ingratiating. He looked, as they always did, as if here was the very last place he wanted to be.

Brennan nodded to Barker then smiled at the grass. 'Brennan,' he said.

The grass nodded. 'I'm Kenny,' he said. 'Just Kenny.'

'Hello, just Kenny. Mr Barker here says you work with Pete Boyle.'

Kenny blinked, as if Brennan had taken a liberty in speaking the name out loud. 'Work for various people,' he says. 'Depends who's paying. I've worked with Boyle.'

'Working with him at the moment?'

'What do you want to know?'

'Off the scene for a bit, wasn't he?'

Kenny laughed. 'You lot fucked that up. Thought you had Boyle bang to rights. Ran rings round you.'

'He's a smart boy, Peter Boyle,' Brennan said. 'Must have caused a few problems, though. Being out of commission. Had to get back.'

'Can't say. But Jeff Kerridge's missus froze him out. Boyle thought that, with Kerridge out of the way, he could muscle his way to the top of Kerridge's empire. She had other ideas.'

'And now she's dead, too,' Brennan mused. 'Boyle behind that?'

'Christ knows. He's not telling the likes of me.' Kenny looked apologetically across at Barker. 'I could make out I knew. But Mr Barker here knows I tell the truth.'

'Course, Kenny. More or less. No mileage in bullshitting Mr Brennan here. He's too smart.'

'But, yeah, most people seem to think Boyle was behind it. He'd plenty of reasons to want her off the scene. Not the only one, though.'

'Boyle's looking to take over, is he? That what people are saying?'

'Seen it myself. Started throwing his weight around over the last couple of months. Show people he's back.'

'What people?'

'Anyone who's likely to get in his way. He's in a hurry. Won't care who he crosses.'

'So what's he doing?'

Kenny looked up, as if suddenly conscious he was in a public place. 'What I've *seen*,' Kenny said, finally, 'is stuff designed to scare people off. Some low rent dealer picked off the street and given a beating. Not because he gives a bugger about the dealer, but because he's telling whoever's supplying that this is Pete Boyle's territory. Shops burnt out, places trashed. That kind of stuff.'

'Making some big enemies, then. Not everyone's easily frightened.'

'Working so far. Expanding his territory nicely as far as I can see.'

'You got any evidence? Anything we could use in court?'

Kenny looked at Barker with a smile. 'You said he was smart, Mr Barker. I'm a grass, Mr Brennan, not a fucking idiot. I'll pass on titbits for a bit of cash in hand, but I'm not going to start collecting fucking *evidence*.'

'But you know that this is happening? Not just tittle-tattle.'

'I've seen it. Some of it. There's probably lots more stuff that I don't know about. I just do bits of business for Boyle when he asks me to.'

'Including beatings?'

'Jesus, man, look at me. Not my game at all. I'm a leg-man. Fetching and carrying. But I know some involved in the rough stuff. Names that Mr Barker would know.'

'I can guess,' Barker said. 'You reckon Boyle's taken anyone else out? Like Mrs K, if he was behind that.'

'That's what people are saying. Heard all kinds of stories, but I don't know how much is true. But Boyle's got people running scared. Even some of the big boys.'

'What about you, Kenny? You scared of Boyle?'

Kenny shifted uncomfortably on his chair. 'I don't scare easily, Mr Brennan. Wouldn't be here if I did. But, yeah, Pete Boyle makes me nervous. He's always been a fucking psychopath.' He paused. 'Smart bastard, though. One step ahead of you lot. Word is he's got some of you in his pocket.'

Brennan glanced at Barker. 'Any names, Kenny?'

'Well above my pay grade. But not small fry.' He shrugged. 'Could all be bollocks. Boyle likes people to think he's a big shot.'

'Anything else you can tell us, Kenny? Where's he had you fetching and carrying recently?'

'A few places,' Kenny said, vaguely. 'Told Mr Barker about a couple of deals I'm aware of. Small-time stuff. Boyle'll have bigger jobs in the pipeline, but I don't know any details yet. Can maybe get you some stuff.'

'That would be good, Kenny,' Barker said.

Kenny looked up and Brennan saw him give an almost imperceptible flinch. Something he'd seen. Brennan turned his head casually towards where Kenny had been looking. A knot of people at the far end of the bar. Men in suits, just out of the office. No one Brennan recognised. 'Something wrong, Kenny?'

Kenny's eyes had snapped back towards Brennan. 'Not with me,' he said. 'We done, then?' He was already making a move to stand up.

Brennan hesitated, wondering whether he would get any more out of Kenny. Kenny was looking even more uncomfortable than before. 'Suppose we are, Kenny. You hear anything else about Boyle, you'll keep Mr Barker informed, won't you?'

'Yeah. Course. I'll be in touch.'

Barker patted Kenny on the shoulder, slipping something into his hand in the same movement. 'For your trouble,' he said. 'Take care, eh, Kenny. Bad people out there.'

'Right enough.' Kenny had begun to push through the crowds of drinkers. He was looking back over his shoulder. Not at the two police officers. Beyond them, towards the far end of the bar.

'Got scared,' Brennan said. 'Saw someone.'

Barker was scanning the room. 'No one I know. But I thought the same.'

'How'd he strike you? Before that, I mean.'

'Not his usual cheery self, if that's what you mean. Usually pretty full of his own importance. Didn't see much of that tonight. Not particularly forthcoming about Boyle, either.'

'No. Well, didn't expect too much on that front. He confirmed what we'd been thinking, even if he wasn't brimming over with detail.'

'He was nervous from the start tonight. Twitchy in a way I've not seen before.'

'Maybe it was me,' Brennan suggested. 'Having a total stranger at the table isn't the best way to put a grass at ease.'

'That sort of thing doesn't usually faze Kenny too much. Looks to me like Boyle's got everyone nervous.' He paused, looking thoughtful. 'If he's right about Boyle having some senior coppers in his pocket, Kenny won't know who to trust.'

Brennan swallowed the last of his pint. 'In that respect,' he said, 'young Kenny can join the fucking club.'

14

'How's it going, sis? You fending off McGrath's advances all right?'

'I can handle you, Hugh, so I can handle Andy sodding McGrath. Well, I'm in. Feet under the table. Don't know how much we're going to find, though.' She was sitting in the poky little kitchen at the rear of the poky little house, a newly poured glass of some Australian Shiraz in front of her.

Bloody typical. She'd got in, kicked off her shoes, poured the wine and started to think about supper, when Hugh bloody Salter had texted her to call him. As she thumbed in the number – no significant numbers were kept in her contacts list – she realised how reluctant she was to make the call. Even the sound of Salter's voice made her uneasy.

'Know you won't let us down, sis.'

'Not planning to, Hugh. I just don't know how much we'll find there. He's small-time.'

'You never know. He's got connections. We'll get leads from him.'

'Maybe,' she said, doubtfully. 'You wanted something?'

'Just to check how you were.'

'Very thoughtful, Hugh. All heart.'

'All okay, though?'

'As well as can be expected. Don't worry, Hugh. I'm coping.'

'Well, if you need anything . . .'

Don't bother to ask, she thought. She supposed it was decent of Salter to enquire, but he was just going through the motions. He'd read somewhere that it was what bosses should do. 'Thanks, Hugh.'

'How'd you find Brennan?'

'All right. Smart, pleasant—'

'Good looking?'

'If you like that kind of thing,' she said.

'Able to help him?'

'Don't know. He was just trying to get some background.'

'Probably a wild goose chase, like you said. But he was keen to meet you. How did you leave it?'

She was tempted to let Salter know that Brennan wanted to see her again. But Brennan had clearly wanted to keep that to himself. 'Happy for him to get back in contact if he's any specific questions. But I don't know that he will.'

'You'll get another chance to gaze on those handsome features at some point, sis.'

'Bugger off, Hugh. Some of us are actually trying to do our job.'

'If you say so, sis. I'll be in touch in a week or so to touch base. Let me know if there's anything you need.'

'Don't worry, Hugh. You're always first on the list.'

She slipped the secure phone back in her pocket. Then she took out her domestic phone and dialled the home number. She was half expecting that it would ring out. But it was answered almost immediately. 'Hello?'

'Hi, Sue. It's Marie.' She glanced at her watch. Nearly eight. What was Sue still doing there? 'How are things?'

'He's back at home. That's the main thing. They discharged him this morning, once the consultant had seen him, so I drove him back.'

'That's very good of you, Sue. Thought you'd be working today.'

'I booked a day off. They could have brought him home in the ambulance, but I wanted to make sure things were properly ready.'

'I'm really grateful, Sue. But we can't expect you to keep—'

'I've told you, Marie. This is more than just a job for me. I do it to earn a living, but with the really needy cases like Liam – well, I don't mind going beyond the call of duty.'

Marie could feel herself bridling. 'Well, if you're sure it's not too much trouble.'

'No trouble at all. I enjoy looking after Liam. And he's very appreciative of everything that I do.'

'How is he?'

'Better than he was a few days ago. A bit more his old self. But it's really knocked it out of him.'

'Is he able to talk to me?'

There was the briefest of pauses, but enough to suggest that Sue had been considering her excuse. 'He's asleep at the moment. I gave him some food when he first got in, and then he dozed off. It's all been a bit of a strain. Even getting back today. You know how difficult it's getting to help him in and out of the car.'

'Well, maybe if he wakes up before you go, you could ask him to give me a call.'

'Of course. I can help him do it. Will your phone be switched on?'

Marie bit back a sharper response. 'I'll leave it on all evening. If you go before he wakes, could you leave him a note?'

Another pause. 'Yes, of course. Though I don't know whether he'll do it if I'm not here to prompt him.'

At first, Marie thought that this was another of Sue's coded attacks. Why would Liam want to call someone who wasn't even there when she was needed? But there was an awkwardness in Sue's voice.

'How do you mean?'

'It's just that, since we got back, he seems less responsive than before. As if he doesn't want to do anything. Even eating. I had to keep prompting him to take the next mouthful. He'd sit there, looking at the plate, as if he'd forgotten what he was supposed to be doing.'

Marie could think of no immediate response. This sounded worse, a lot worse, than when she'd last seen Liam. There'd been signs of the passivity that the neurologist had warned about. But only occasional and momentary. Small lapses where his attention would seem to wander, or when he'd fail to respond to something she'd said or done. Things you'd hardly notice if you weren't watching out for them. 'You think he seems different from before?'

'A bit, maybe. It's hard to tell. He's been very tired today. Maybe he'll be better tomorrow, when he's had some proper sleep. You know what it's like in hospital. You never get a decent rest.'

'Don't worry about him calling tonight, then,' Marie said. 'I'll call again tomorrow evening.'

'I'm back at work tomorrow,' Sue said, 'so I'll just be here for the three formal visits. Might be easiest if I call you when we get here for the evening visit. Then you won't disturb him if he's asleep.'

There was nothing Marie could say to this. She felt resentful, as if she were already being excluded from her own home. But Sue's suggestion was reasonable. 'Okay, Sue. I'll make sure the phone's on tomorrow evening as well. Hope he's a bit better tomorrow.'

She ended the call and took a large swallow from the wine glass. Christ, this couldn't go on. She was fooling herself, thinking she could continue in this role, trying to ignore what was happening with Liam. His condition was continuing to deteriorate, faster than she'd ever envisaged. He needed looking after, and she couldn't simply leave that to Sue, however well-intentioned she might be.

Without noticing it, she'd already finished the glass of wine. There was nothing she could do now. Not tonight. She could sit and think and brood, but that wouldn't help anyone. Better to put it off, drink some more wine, dig out a trashy DVD. Then think about it properly in the morning when her mind was less tired and fogged.

She poured herself a second glass of wine, raised the glass and stared at it for a moment. Then she downed it in one.

'What? Hang on.'

Marie rolled over in the bed, tangled in the duvet, trying to work out what time it was. She'd answered the phone before she'd woken properly, the shrill ringtone infiltrating her dream. She dragged herself to a sitting position. 'Sorry, who is this?'

'It's me. Lizzie.'

Lizzie? Who the hell was Lizzie? For a moment, the name rang nothing more than a vague bell.

'Lizzie from the office.'

Oh, that Lizzie. Lizzie who worked for McGrath. What the hell was that Lizzie doing calling her at – she squinted at the digital clock on the bedside table – 3.40 in the morning?

'Lizzie. Sorry. Still half-asleep. I didn't know you had my number.'

'Andy gave it to me when I was setting up the interview. I put in my phone so I wouldn't lose it.' It occurred to Marie, as her mind was gradually clearing, that Lizzie didn't sound fully in control. There was a shrill edge to her voice. A note of slight hysteria.

'Is everything okay?'

She could hear Lizzie gulping for air. 'Really, really sorry to disturb you, Maggie. I didn't know who else to call—'

'What's wrong?'

'It's the office. A fire. I've just had a call from the company who own the building.' Another gulp. 'Everything's gone, apparently. They're still fighting the blaze, but that part of the building's gutted.'

'Christ. Where's Andy?'

'That was why they called me. They've been trying to contact Andy for the last hour or so, but his phone's turned

180

off and there's no answer on his home line. They had my name and number as a backup, so they called me. Andy's still not answering.

'He's probably asleep,' Marie said. 'He'll have his phone charging or something. I'm sure there's no need to worry.'

'That's what I thought,' Lizzie said. 'So I came out to his house. He's not here. I've been ringing the bell. And there's no sign of his car. He usually leaves it parked outside. That's why I called you. I didn't know what else to do.'

'Maybe he's staying with friends or something. I'm sure there's nothing to worry about.' She spoke gently to calm the young girl's evident panic. But her own unease was growing. After her earlier conversation with McGrath, this felt like a hell of a coincidence. 'Why don't you get home, Lizzie? We'll know more in the morning. The police will have tracked Andy down by then.'

'I can't just do that. What if something's happened to him? I was going to head up to the office.'

'I don't know if that's a good idea. The fire service aren't going to want—'

'They called me, Maggie. The landlord wanted me to get Andy up there. If I can't find Andy, I should go myself.'

This was a different sounding Lizzie, Marie thought. Panic subsiding, beginning to rise to the occasion. Taking on responsibility in a way that wouldn't have seemed possible when Marie first met her. 'Okay, Lizzie. I'll come over too. At least we can give each other some moral support. Meet you up there.'

'Thanks, Maggie. I was really hoping you'd say that.'

'Don't worry. I'll see you in twenty minutes or so.'

Marie lay in the semi-darkness, watching the line of light

thrown through a gap in curtains from a street light outside. One *hell* of a coincidence, she thought.

It was unusual for him to be up late. But sometimes, like tonight, he would sit up into the small hours poring over the documents relating to his current assignment. He liked to work through it all systematically, make sure he'd covered every eventuality. He kept the documents no longer than he had to. He would spend the early days of a new assignment working through whatever material his clients had provided – background information, details of home address and place of work, photographs of the target and other relevant individuals. He committed those to memory. When he was confident he had memorised every line, every word in the files, he would painstakingly destroy them, shredding the papers and burning the remnants.

At the same time, he would be adding material of his own. He took endless photographs of the locations where he would be working – his target's home, workplace, the surrounding areas, places where he might choose to take action. He reviewed the countless images and created detailed, hand drawn plans of the key locations and buildings. He used online mapping tools and satellite images to explore the surrounding area, identifying suitable positions for his purposes. He made detailed notes of his surveillance, identifying patterns and routines of activity, preparing to choose the most appropriate plan of action.

That was what he was doing at four o'clock in the morning. Sitting at the rickety table in the shabby basement flat he was renting. He preferred a house or a flat on the lower floors so that he could come and go however he liked without arousing the interest of other residents. He had enough money to live wherever he wanted, but he had to select places where his temporary presence would not attract attention. These were usually downmarket, occupied by people whose lives were, for whatever reason, as transient as his own.

He didn't know what made him glance at his phone. It was late. He was finally growing tired. His head was beginning to feel fogged by the data that he'd systematically ingested. He walked through to the kitchen to get a glass of water, trying to decide whether to call it a night. As he stood running the tap, he looked idly at his smartphone. Something led him to open up the application linked to the tracking device on her car.

He'd checked it last around midnight. She'd been safely back at home. He was surprised now to see that the car was moving, the tiny blob making its way along the main road towards the centre of town.

He frowned. It looked as if the car had only recently left the house, probably just a few minutes before. What would have caused her to travel back into town at that time of the night?

For a moment, he was tempted to forget about it. But he couldn't, for the moment, think of any straightforward reason why she might be out and about at this time of the night. From what he'd seen and knew, she hadn't struck him as a night bird. She might have left something behind at the office, but he couldn't imagine what might be so important or essential that it would drag her out of the house in the smallest hours of the morning.

After a few seconds, he made up his mind. Yawning, he grabbed his coat from where he'd flung it on the sofa, pulled it round his shoulders and picked up his car keys from the table.

It might be well be nothing, this nocturnal trip. But it might be something. And if it was something, then he ought to know.

15

She could see a haze of blue lights and smoke between the buildings ahead. She turned off the main road into the business park. Further ahead, there was an array of fire engines and police cars, dark silhouettes standing or running between the vehicles, thick billows of noxious-looking fumes and, through the broken windows of the office building, a glare of flames. Jesus, it looked bad.

She slowed her car, knowing the police would prevent her drawing too close to the burning building. She saw Lizzie's aged Mini parked by the access road and parked behind it. Lizzie was standing a few yards ahead, outside the line of emergency vehicles, staring at the building. Marie left her car and approached the younger woman. 'Lizzie. You okay?'

Lizzie looked over her shoulder. Her face was drawn and exhausted, her eyes red. Her expression suggested that Marie was the person she'd most wanted to see in the world. After Andy McGrath anyway, Marie thought.

'Any word from Andy?' Marie knew there was no way of avoiding the question.

Lizzie shook her head. 'I keep trying his mobile, but it's

still off, and his home phone just keeps ringing out. I've called the owners – their guy's over there with the police – but they've heard nothing either.'

'They'll track him down, Lizzie. Don't worry,' Marie said, trying to convey more confidence than she felt.

'I keep telling myself that,' Lizzie said. 'It's not like he's Mr Domestic. He's always out on the tiles.' She looked a little calmer, as if Marie had provided the reassurance she'd been trying to conjure up for herself.

Marie laughed. 'Maybe he got lucky.'

'Yeah, maybe.' Lizzie smiled for the first time. 'Wouldn't be for lack of trying, anyway.'

Marie registered a figure looming out of the darkness towards them. One of the police officers.

'You two ladies okay?' he said, in a tone that clearly implied: 'And what the hell are you doing here?'

'A bit in shock, actually,' Marie said. 'We both work in the building. My colleague here was called out because the landlords weren't able to track down our boss.'

The policeman hesitated. 'Where do you work, exactly?'

Marie pointed towards the block still on fire. 'In that building. We've got the ground floor.'

The policeman glanced behind him. 'Bad news, then, I'm afraid. That area's pretty much gutted. They've got the fire under control now, but it's done a hell of a lot of damage.'

Marie thought about the paperwork she'd spent the day sorting. One way of dealing with McGrath's backlog, she thought. She was glad now that she'd removed the few documents that might have some evidential value.

'Can I take you two ladies' names and addresses?' the police-man added. 'We'll need to talk to you. And to your boss.'

'Why us?' she asked. The answer was obvious, but she was keen to find out how the police were viewing the fire.

'Just routine. Obviously, we need to investigate any incident of this kind.'

'You think it might not be an accident?'

'We can't rule anything out.'

'No, I suppose not.' It had already occurred to Marie that, unless she revealed her true role, her own presence was suspicious. First day in the new job, and the office gets burned to the ground. Any half-decent copper would at least want to investigate the coincidence. She'd leave that one to Salter. It wasn't her job to break cover.

The two women dutifully gave their names and addresses, and Lizzie added McGrath's details. 'You've no news of Mr McGrath?' the policeman asked, as he noted down the information.

'I've been trying to track him down ever since they called me,' Lizzie said.

'Lizzie knows him better than I do,' Marie said. 'But apparently it's not entirely unknown for him not to come home after a night out. If you know what I mean.'

The policeman glanced at the building. 'Hope he's had a good time. He'll need something to cheer himself up once he finds out about this lot.'

There was a shout from another police officer running towards them. He stopped short as he caught sight of the two women. 'Geoff,' he said, finally. 'You're wanted. Developments.'

The first policeman nodded to Marie and Lizzie. 'Okay, ladies. Can I suggest you get yourselves back home now?

There's nothing you can do here and, well, it's never helpful to have civilians cluttering up the scene.'

'No, of course not.' Marie was looking past him at the second policeman, trying to read his expression in the darkness. Developments. 'If we track down Andy – Mr McGrath – we'll get him to call the landlords, shall we?'

'Please.' The policeman was already turning away from them to join his colleague. 'Goodnight, now, ladies.'

Marie turned to Lizzie. 'I think we should try to get some sleep. There's nothing we can do here. Andy'll turn up in the morning.'

'Don't reckon I'll get much sleep.'

'There's a lot to think about. But no point in worrying until we know what the damage is. I presume Andy will have insurance?'

'You never know with Andy. He's not the most organised person.'

'I'll give you a call in the morning, see if there's any word from him. Then we can decide what to do next.' She gently led Lizzie back towards her car. 'You get off. I'll see if there's any chance of getting a word with the landlord's rep over there. See if he knows what the damage is likely to be.'

'Okay,' Lizzie said, doubtfully. She climbed into the car, started the engine and wound down the window. 'I'll keep trying Andy's number. In case he turns it on.'

'He'll be asleep, I should think. Wherever he is. But there's no harm in trying.'

She watched as Lizzie headed off towards the main road. Then she made her way towards the line of emergency vehicles, moving as silently and unobtrusively as she could.

There was a row of trees lining the car park. She moved

forward, keeping in the shadow of the trees, drawing as close as she could to the knot of figures clustered around the building. She strained her ears to try to catch something of the discussion taking place between the police and fire officers.

'. . . asphyxiation, as far as we can tell. The fire had scarcely touched that room apart from scorching round the door. My guess is he was in there, working or something, and then he heard the noise of the fire. Opened the office door and was met with a wall of flames.' The speaker, who seemed to be one of the fire officers, paused while someone said something Marie couldn't hear. 'Must have done the smart thing and shut the door again. Probably tried to get out through the window.'

'So why didn't he?' another voice asked. 'It's a ground floor room.'

'Christ knows. Maybe the smoke got to him quicker than he expected. Sometimes you don't notice it till it's too late. Maybe he thought he had more time than he did. Maybe couldn't get the window open. That's for you lot to try to sort out. All I know is we've got a body. Poor bugger.'

There was a jumble of other voices, then the fire officer spoke again. 'It's under control now. We'll have it out before long. But no one goes into the building until the structural engineer's had a look. Damage doesn't look too severe, but you never know.' There was another buzz of voices before the fire officer continued. 'Yeah, I understand all that. We'll get you in as quickly as we can. But I've got a duty to make sure nobody takes unnecessary risks. All I can tell you is that the body's male. Fortyish, probably. Dressed in a suit. I didn't stay long enough to see much more.'

Marie slipped away and managed to reach her car without anyone detecting her presence. Seated behind the wheel, she prepared to pull away from the swirl of blue lights and smoke.

A body. Fortyish. Dressed in a suit.

She had little doubt that it would be Andy McGrath.

One hell of a coincidence.

'Jesus, sis. What time do you call this?'

She glanced across at the alarm clock. 'Four thirty-seven,' she said. 'Thought you were an early riser, Hugh?'

'Not this bloody early,' he groaned. 'I hope this is important.'

'Might be,' she said. 'You tell me.'

'Hang on.' She heard a clatter as he put down the phone, then an indecipherable jumble of background noise. Christ knew what he was up to. 'Okay sis,' he said, finally. 'All ears.'

'There's been a fire tonight. At McGrath's place.'

There was a pause. She knew that Salter was already trying to work out the angles and decide how to play it. 'How serious?'

'I don't know exactly but pretty serious. And there's more.' She briefly recounted her suspicions about the body found in the office building.

'You don't know for sure it's McGrath?'

'I know what I'm telling you, Hugh. But who else is it likely to be?'

'Christ knows. I'll make a few discreet calls in the morning. See what I can find out.'

'Bloody big coincidence, don't you think? I start working

with McGrath, and immediately somebody comes along and tops him.'

Another pause, almost imperceptible this time. 'Even if you're right about it being McGrath, sis, we don't know that someone's topped him. Might have been an accident. Might have torched the place himself and ballsed up his own exit.'

'Still a bloody big coincidence.'

'Shit happens. Don't start jumping to conclusions until we know what's what.'

'So what about me, Hugh? You're going to let the local cops know who I am?'

'We don't need to make a decision on that yet. Don't want to break your cover unless we need to.'

'Why not? The job's finished anyway. If McGrath's dead, there's no reason for me to stay.'

'We don't even know that he is. I want to find out what's going on first. And even if McGrath's out of the picture, there may still be ways we can use you up there. Now we've got the legend established, I mean.'

'Christ, Hugh. With respect, that's ridiculous. I wasn't comfortable with how we rushed into the assignment in the first place. We can't just use me somewhere else to save a few pennies in your budget.'

'You don't have the full picture, sis. I need to think it through. Leave it with me.'

As if I've any fucking choice, she thought. 'And what if the police see me as a suspect? I work for McGrath for one day and his offices get torched. Aren't they going to think that's a bit of a coincidence as well?'

'There's nothing to link you to the fire. Even if they think it's dodgy, there's no case.'

'And if they start delving into the mysterious Maggie Yates? Surely the cover won't stand up to a proper investigation?'

'Local plods,' Salter said. 'Couldn't find a haystack in a pile of needles. Look, I know you think we rushed into this one, sis, but we did a kosher job. It'll hold together if we need it to.'

'But surely we should just tell them, Hugh. The cops won't be overjoyed when they find out we've been holding out on them.'

'*If* they find out. And if we do decide not to tell them. Look, sis, this isn't entirely my decision. I need to run it up the line and see what the bigwigs say.'

That made sense. For all his maverick inclinations, Salter was smart enough to make sure his backside was covered. 'So what do I do in the meantime?'

'Just carry on, sis.'

'Like any new starter would do if their office burnt to the ground with the boss inside? Start looking for another bloody job.'

'Just bear with me. I'll find out what the word is on McGrath. And then decide how to play things.'

'What if the police want to talk to me?'

'Just go with it. After all, there's not much you can tell them.'

It was Marie's turn to pause, allowing herself to take several deep breaths before responding. 'There's a hell of a lot I *could* tell them, Hugh. But I'll let it run, if that's the official line.'

'That's the line. But I'll sort it.'

'Just sort it quickly, okay?'

But Salter had already ended the call. Marie sat for a moment, reflecting on the conversation. There had been something in Salter's response that left her feeling uneasy. It was as if her news had genuinely taken him by surprise. As if it had somehow disrupted his plans.

All she could do was wait. Wait for the news on McGrath. Wait for whatever Salter's decision might turn out to be.

She lay back on the bed, still fully clothed, staring up at the ceiling. Waiting for daylight.

16

She'd expected to lie awake till morning, but at some point she drifted off to sleep. She woke to the sound of her mobile phone buzzing on the bedside table.

She fumbled for the phone, still half-asleep. 'Yes?'

She'd thought it would be Salter, but her fogged mind registered in time that it was the Maggie Yates phone ringing, rather than the secure line she'd used to call Salter.

There was a gulp and an intake of breath from the end of the line.

'Lizzie?'

'Maggie. I – I thought I should let you know,' Lizzie was crying, struggling to speak around her hiccupping breath. 'I just had a call.'

Marie desperately wanted to put Lizzie out of her misery. Instead, she had to keep silent, allow the girl to force out the words she was finding so difficult.

'One of the police officers who was there last night. They've found—' She stopped and Marie could hear her swallowing, fighting to keep control of her voice. 'They've found a body, Maggie. A man. They think it must be Andy.' She was sobbing properly now,

'Lizzie,' Marie said, as calmly as she could. 'I'll come over. Just wait there. I'll be as quick as I can.'

She succeeded in extracting Lizzie's address between sobs. She ended the call, and stumbled into the bathroom. Jesus, she felt awful. Her mouth was parched. Her head full of cotton wool. Her body had the clamminess that comes from sleeping in your clothes. She really wanted a good scalding shower, a cup of decent coffee.

Marie did the best patch-up job she could on her hair and face, conscious that she looked exactly like someone who'd been up most of the night. Outside, the sky was dark and heavy, threatening rain. It hadn't been a great summer, and as the season shifted slowly into autumn there was no sign of any improvement. The sooner she was back down south the better.

She found Lizzie's flat without difficulty. It was in a part of the city still not quite as salubrious as the property developers had hoped. The block had been built, maybe ten or so years before, with the expectation of attracting relatively upmarket residents. Now it looked rundown. When they'd been chatting over coffee the previous day – it seemed a lifetime away now – Lizzie had said that she shared the flat with an old school friend who worked in a customer service role in one of the local banks. They were struggling with the rent, but it was better than living with Lizzie's mother.

She found the bell and pressed. The door buzzed open and she made her way through the dimly lit lobby and up the stairs to the first floor. Lizzie was waiting for her at the top of the stairs, her eyes red and sore from crying. As she saw Marie, she burst into tears again, and Marie found herself cradling the younger woman in her arms as if comforting a small child.

She led Lizzie back into the flat and sat her down at the kitchen table. The flat was small, but looked homely. It was clear that the two flatmates had put some effort into making it a pleasant place to live.

Marie busied herself making a pot of tea for them both, hunting through the cupboards for teabags and mugs, while Lizzie sat silently at the table, staring down at nothing in particular. A gloriously English response to a crisis, Marie thought. A pot of bloody tea. But she wanted to give Lizzie time to recover herself, with no requirement to deal with Marie's presence.

Finally she sat down, pushing one of the mugs towards Lizzie. 'I've put sugar in it. Supposed to be good for shock.'

Lizzie looked up at her, her red-rimmed eyes blank.

'Tell me what happened,' Marie went on. 'You said the police called?'

'They were trying to find out if he had any relatives. Next of kin. Didn't even tell me what had happened at first. But I'm not stupid.'

'They found him in the office?'

'That's what they said. Must've been in his own office. He said it was the smoke.' She stumbled to a halt and for a moment looked as if she might burst into tears again.

'They didn't find him till they'd got the fire under control. After we left last night.'

'I'm so sorry,' Marie said. 'It's an awful thing.' As always in this kind of situation, there was really nothing to be said.

'Poor Andy,' Lizzie said, burying her face in her hands.

'He won't have suffered, anyway. If the smoke got him first, he wouldn't have known what was happening.'

Lizzie had begun to sob again, quietly into her hands. Marie put an arm around her shoulder. The best she could offer was a physical presence, reassurance that Lizzie was not on her own. She began to wonder about the mother Lizzie had mentioned and whether she should be contacted.

It was odd that Lizzie should be so affected by McGrath's death. Marie had warmed to McGrath during their conversation, but he'd still been little more than a small-time shyster. He'd simply been Lizzie's boss. A pleasant and easy-going boss, but still just a boss. Marie couldn't imagine becoming emotional about any of the bosses she'd worked for over the years.

Lizzie was just a teenager, though. At a similar age, or maybe a little younger, Marie could remember getting over-emotional about all kinds of things – supposed boyfriends, sentimental films, the end of school – in ways that were incomprehensible to her now.

'You were very fond of him?' she prompted, finally.

Lizzie lifted her head and stared at the older woman as if she didn't understand the question. 'You didn't know him, Maggie. He's kept me sane over the last couple of years. He was – well, not like a father, exactly.' She paused, as if considering the appropriateness of her last comment. 'Not like a father at all, actually. Not like my father, anyway. More like – I don't know – like a nice uncle. You know what I mean?'

Marie didn't really. Her own father, still living happily with her mother and quietly retired in suburban Surrey, was decent enough, if too reserved to show the love he no doubt felt towards his only daughter. Marie had a couple of uncles, but hadn't met them since childhood. But Lizzie clearly had some relationship with McGrath that went beyond that simply of boss and subordinate. 'He looked after you?'

Lizzie's eyes brimmed again with years. 'Had an awful time, couple of years ago.' She took a deep breath, calming her voice. 'Living with my mum. She's divorced. My dad left years ago.'

'That must be hard.'

Lizzie shrugged. 'I was just a kid when he went. What you've never had, you never miss, I suppose. Anyway, we were having a hard time. Mum had mental health problems. Depression. Spent half the day in bed, and the other half drinking too much. Not exactly violent, but she was a different person drunk. Insulting. Offensive. She'd say things – well, you know. She needed looking after, but the last place I wanted to be was home. I was working in a chemist's in town. Volunteered for any overtime going, just to spend more time out of the house. Then the shop went bust. The recession. There were rumours about some buyer. But it didn't happen. Closed us down almost overnight. Didn't even get my redundancy.'

'I'm sorry,' Marie said.

'It was a nightmare. There were no jobs going. I've got no real qualifications – they'd talked about me doing phar-macist exams, but it hadn't happened. No other shops were recruiting. Mum was on income support, so my wage had been keeping us going, really.' She paused, and Marie could sense that she was wondering how honest to be. 'Worst thing for me was that I couldn't get out of the house. I was stuck there all day with mum. I mean, love her to bits, but – well, she wasn't the best company just then.'

'Where did Andy come in?'

'He was some old friend or contact of my dad's. My mum had been talking to my dad about me losing my job and all that. She wasn't exactly proud of having to go looking for help from him. But Andy phoned and then came to see us. Said he could offer me a job if I wanted it.'

'That was nice of him,' Marie said, wondering what kinds of old acquaintances Andy McGrath might have had.

'I'd always thought Andy fancied my mum a bit. He was kind to her as well. Helped her get support with the depression, helped her off the drinking. He found her a job too, doing admin stuff for some mate of his. They got together for a bit, but that was never going to last. He took it in his stride when she met someone else. He was just a nice man—' She stared at Marie for a moment, and again her eyes dissolved into tears. 'It's not fair, Maggie. It's not bloody fair.'

'Life isn't, Lizzie. Too often it's the nice ones who go first.' Unbidden, an image of Liam flashed into her mind. Yeah, she thought. Not bloody fair. 'Sounds like he was a good man.'

'It wasn't just all that – the stuff I've just told you about. When I started working here, he was the same. He was patient. Helped me along. Even paid me a bit extra when we were having trouble at home.'

Marie felt a twinge of guilt. She'd assumed that McGrath could have only one motive in employing an attractive young woman like Lizzie. It sounded as if there'd been hidden depths to Andy McGrath. 'How'd he know your dad?'

Lizzie shook her head. 'I don't know. They went back a long way. Mum would never really talk about dad, except to tell me what a bastard he was. And how she was glad he'd got what was coming to him.'

'How do you mean?' None of her business, Marie told herself. Although she'd come here to comfort Lizzie, her professional instincts were kicking in. She could justify taking the opportunity to dig into McGrath's past; she couldn't justify any prurient interest in the rest of Lizzie's life and family. But she could see that the girl wanted to talk.

'Last year,' Lizzie said. She smiled faintly for the first time. 'Cheered mum up, really, though she felt bad about that. She wouldn't tell me any details. But dad had ended up in prison. And then he was ill. Very ill. A stroke, left him pretty much paralysed.' She shook her head.

Marie was staring at her, an absurd idea worming its way into her mind. Prison. A stroke. 'What did your dad do, Lizzie? His job, I mean.'

Lizzie looked up, puzzled, recognising a new tone in Marie's voice. 'That was the thing,' she said. 'That's why mum said he had it coming.' She hesitated. 'He was a policeman.'

Marie reached out and took Lizzie's hand. She gripped it as if to comfort the younger woman, but she knew she was simply steadying her own nerves. A policeman. Lizzie's surname was Carter. Presumably her mother's maiden name rather than her father's surname. But Marie suspected that she might know the father's surname only too well.

And if she was right, that was yet another coincidence. Another *hell* of a coincidence.

He stayed as long as he dared outside the line of emergency vehicles, watching the comings and goings, the clustered knots of figures, the movements growing less frantic as they gained control of events.

He hadn't known what to expect and had almost been caught by surprise as he turned the corner and saw the pulsing glow of blue lights. He pulled into one of the office units, tucking his car into an unobtrusive corner space, then continued on foot, his senses alert now for anything or anyone approaching.

Coming closer to the emergency vehicles, he'd recognised her parked car. There was a thick pall of smoke, and he could make out an occasional flicker of orange flame. He could almost feel the sense of organised urgency.

What was going on? Was this coincidence, or was some fucking freelancer trying to muscle in on his territory? Shit might happen, but there was usually a reason why it did. Maybe there were other interests at work here, people who were more impatient than his own employers. He didn't fully know or care what was motivating his employers. But he knew that they would be royally pissed off if someone had screwed up their plans.

He drifted silently round the edge of the site, until he was approaching the building from the opposite direction. He had little fear of being detected. He remained just outside the light, half-hidden among the trees, his dark clothing blending into the shadows. Even if someone should spot his movement, they would just assume that he was another emergency worker making his way across the site.

For the next hour, he simply watched. The fire teams had the blaze under control and were working towards extinguishing it completely. There was a sudden burst of movement among the fire and police officers that indicated some new development. He watched with interest as combinations of officers gathered, pointing towards the office building as they provided each other with information. At one point he glimpsed his target moving, almost as surreptitiously as he had done, to stand close to one of the clusters of police officers. She was listening, he thought, trying to find out what was happening. He watched as, apparently satisfied, she disappeared back into the night. He couldn't imagine that she would be going anywhere other than back home, but he would check in a while.

As the sky lightened in the east, he saw more police vehicles arrive, including a scene of crime van. There were long discussions between the police and fire officers as they waited for the building to be declared safe for entry.

He had seen as much as he needed to see. Once it was light, it would be much more difficult for him to remain undetected. A scene of crime van implied just that. A crime, or at least a potential crime. And, judging by its rapid arrival and the body language of the assembled police officers, a more significant crime than arson.

As the first crimson light of the sun began to show between the buildings, he slipped back between the trees and cautiously made his way around the site, back to his car.

17

'Hello?' A woman's voice, slightly cautious. With every reason to be cautious, Marie thought. What the hell was she doing there this early in the morning? She considered some acid response and then, just in time, bit it back. It wasn't early in the morning. It was nearly noon. Sue would be making her scheduled visit.

Marie had got back from Lizzie's a couple of hours before, stretched out on the sofa, and promptly fallen asleep. She'd woken feeling worse than she'd ever felt in her life, at least without the contribution of alcohol.

She was conscious that there were things she had to do. She should contact Salter, to see if there was news on McGrath and find out what the bloody hell she was supposed to do. She should try to discover the truth about Lizzie's father.

And she should check how Liam was. Through the events of the night, somewhere at the back of her head had been nagging anxiety about Liam.

She didn't know how much to trust Sue. Not her honesty or integrity, but simply her judgement. In Marie's experience, the carers tended to overstate Liam's illness. More than once, while she'd been working in London, she'd received frantic phone calls claiming that he'd had a severe relapse. She'd rushed back and generally found him only a little worse than usual. The carers had to protect their own positions. If he really was in a bad way and they ignored it, they'd be accused of negligence. If in doubt, they were right to call her. And she knew her own perspective tended to be over-optimistic. Part of her wanted all this to go away, for things to be like they'd been before. She didn't want to believe there was no future for them but this steady decline.

She knew that Sue had said she'd call her in the evening, rather than risk disturbing Liam. But Marie still resented this other woman interfering, however well-meaningly, in their relationship.

'It's Marie, Sue.' She immediately found herself apologising for phoning and hated herself for doing so. 'I was worried about him overnight. How is he now?'

'A bit better, I think. He managed to get down some breakfast. Bit more in control than last night. More his old self.'

As if you'd know, Marie found herself thinking. 'Is he still up?'

There was enough of a pause to suggest that Sue was weighing up Liam's best interests, rather than simply answering Marie's question. 'He's gone for a rest. He was asleep when I last looked in.'

There was no way that Marie could call Sue a liar. 'Thanks, Sue. I'll check back again.'

'I'll call you if there are any problems, obviously,' Sue responded in a tone which confirmed this was the preferable approach.

'Right. Goodbye, Sue.'

She wandered into the kitchen and prepared some toast and coffee while she thought about what to do next. She'd eventually calmed Lizzie down and persuaded her to get more sleep. The police would probably turn up to talk to Lizzie – and to Marie herself – before too long, but she hadn't bothered Lizzie with that. She tried to persuade Lizzie to go back home to her mother, but Lizzie had thought, maybe rightly, that the idea was anything other than calming. But she'd seemed all right by the time Marie left, contemplating the therapeutic benefits of a night on the town with her flatmate.

Which left the question of Lizzie's father. She'd considered raising the question with Salter. But that wasn't the way to go. Salter had assigned her up here. So if she was right, and it all wasn't just to be a *hell* of a coincidence, that meant he knew. And she couldn't begin to think what the significance of that might be.

She could try to find out from someone back at HQ or even at the local office up here. The answer would be in the files. But there was still the risk of alerting Salter if she started asking questions.

She hesitated and then reached into her handbag for her address book. She'd jotted down a number a few pages in, with no name attached. Now she keyed the number into her mobile. After a couple of rings, she heard a voice. 'Hello?'

'Hi, it's Marie Donovan.'

She found herself unaccountably disappointed by the second or two it took him to place the name. 'Marie. Wasn't expecting you to call this quickly. Or even at all, if I'm honest.'

'Shows you shouldn't underestimate people, Jack,' she said.

'Not usually one of my failings,' Brennan said. 'Though there are plenty more you could choose from. To what do I owe the honour?'

'Maybe I just fancied a chat,' she said, then regretted the mildly flirtatious tone that had crept into her voice. 'Actually, Jack, don't know if you've heard, but things have changed.'

'McGrath, you mean? Salter just called me. He sounded a bit – put out.'

'That's the impression I got. Mind you, Hugh never likes anyone screwing up his plans, even by dying.'

'Where does that leave you?'

'Christ knows. Hugh's ordered me not to break cover. Not yet, at any rate. Which I guess means that for the moment I might even be a suspect.'

'You reckon?'

'I start working there on the Monday. Monday night the office burns down and the boss is killed. You're the detective, Jack. Wouldn't you want to probe a little further?'

'If you were that unhappy in the job, you could have just resigned.'

'Very good. But it means I'm in the frame, at least for the moment.'

'It won't go anywhere.'

'Too bloody right it won't. I've been there before. Set up and left dangling in the wind. This time I'll make sure Salter pulls the plug.'

'That why you called? Want me to speak to Salter?'

'I'm looking for a bit of a favour, actually, Jack. Wondered if there was something you could check for me?'

'Go on.'

She briefly recounted to him her conversation with Lizzie.

'Bloody hell,' he said. 'You think her father is Keith bloody Welsby?'

'I don't know,' she said. 'But there can't be many incarcerated semi-vegetative coppers around.'

'I don't get it, though,' Brennan said. 'If you're right, where does Welsby fit in with McGrath?'

'God knows. Welsby was working with Jeff Kerridge. Maybe McGrath was one of Kerridge's associates. Would explain why he was so nervous about Pete Boyle.'

'But you've seen background intelligence on McGrath, presumably?'

'Some,' she said. 'No reference to Kerridge. As far as I was aware, McGrath was a small-time freelancer doing his own deals out of woolly-backed Chester. Doesn't mean that Kerridge wasn't there in the background.'

'For people like Kerridge, keeping your hands clean is part of the job description,' Brennan agreed. 'So you want me to check on this Lizzie?'

'It should be on Welsby's file. If I go in the office and start rooting about on the system, someone's bound to ask why I'm there. I don't want anything to get back to Hugh. At least not yet.'

'I should be able to do it without anybody getting interested. Even if you're right, though, what does it prove?'

'I don't know what it proves,' she said, 'but I think we should do a bit more digging on McGrath.'

'But you've been briefed on McGrath,' Brennan said. 'He was your target. What else could there be?'

'Everything I saw pointed to McGrath being small-time. A local freelancer who might just be a nuisance to the big boys. That's how McGrath presented himself to me, and I didn't see anything at his offices to contradict it . . .'

'But?'

'But why was Hugh so keen to assign me there? It never made much sense and it was all so rushed. Maybe there was more to McGrath than met the eye.'

'And maybe that's why he's dead? But, if you're right about Salter, why would he have assigned you up here if McGrath was going to be topped anyway?'

'Christ, I don't know, Jack. I still can't see Hugh as the type to be party to contract killings. If he is involved, maybe that stuff's out his hands.'

'That would be part of *his* job description as well, I suppose. Okay, I'll do some digging into Welsby and into McGrath as well. I go through the files this afternoon. How do I contact you? On this number?'

She'd called him on her personal mobile. Like Brennan, she'd felt uneasy about using the secure line in case Salter had it monitored, and she'd thought it too risky to call on the Maggie Yates phone. Now she could feel paranoia creeping up again. Any telephone contact felt too vulnerable to interception.

'Let's meet up tomorrow morning. Same place as before,' she said.

'A walk in the park,' Brennan said.

'If the weather's fine.' She paused. 'Thanks, Jack. See you tomorrow.'

She still didn't know if she was right to trust Brennan. She was a decent judge of character, but some characters were too good at manipulating your judgement. Brennan was working closely with Salter, maybe even owed Salter something. He'd made the running in calling her the other day. Maybe she'd been a fool to trust him.

It was too late now, and she had no other easy way of getting the information she needed. And there were other things she needed to worry about. Like the fact that the local police would soon be knocking at her door, wanting to interview her about the fire. She pulled the secure mobile out of her handbag and dialled Salter's number.

'Hi, sis. How's it going?'

I think that's the question I should be asking you, Hugh. You were going to sort things for me, remember? Since when there's been a deathly silence.'

'Jesus, sis. Give me a chance. I've hardly got into the office yet.'

'Some of us were up half the night, Hugh. And now I'm sitting here waiting for the police to call.'

'I've sorted that. At least for the moment. Got the higher-ups to pull a few strings. Told them McGrath was involved in one of our operations and we've got everything covered.'

'They can't hold off on a murder investigation.'

'Not even clear it is murder yet, sis. They've got the fire investigators looking at it, but it looks like there might have been a gas leak in the kitchen. Maybe poor old McGrath just lit up an illicit ciggy after hours.'

'Inside his office?'

'Maybe he ducked back in there when the whole thing went up. Anyway, that's what they're looking at.'

'And what was he doing in his office at that time of night, anyway?'

'You sound like you want to be investigated, sis. I can always put in a word for you. If we tell them to soft-pedal, they're not going to bust a gut investigating the death of someone like McGrath. They're only too happy to leave it in our capable hands.'

'If you say so, Hugh. So where does that leave me?'

'Where you are, for the moment. Best if you just stay put for a few days. The police might get a bit curious if you vanish off the radar suddenly.'

'But why not just tell the police who I am and let them get on with it?'

'Because we're telling them the truth, sis. McGrath was under surveillance. He was part of one of our operations. His death's a pain in the arse from that point of view, but it might shake something out of the woodwork. If he was topped, someone topped him. Might be interesting to find out what they plan to do next.'

'I can't see it, Hugh. He was small time. If someone topped him, it was just because he'd got up someone's nose.'

'We've nothing to lose by waiting a day or two to find out. If nothing happens, the plods can have their case back.'

'So what do I do in the meantime?'

'Enjoy the break. Enjoy the sunshine. Go for a walk in the park.'

She felt a chill down the back of her neck. Coincidence, or more Hugh Salter game playing? Letting her know that he knew? 'Don't drag this on too long, Hugh. I'll sit it out for a day or two. But then I'm heading back, and you can let the police know where I've gone.'

'Forty-eight hours,' Salter said. 'Or maybe seventy-two. No more.'

'Forty-eight.'

'Ciao, sis.'

She dropped the secure phone back into her handbag, her unease growing as she reflected on the conversation. She knew it was theoretically possible for him to intercept her mobile – after all, he had access to the technology – but she hadn't imagined that he'd have made the effort or taken the risk. On the other hand, it never paid to underestimate Hugh Salter.

At least the police were unlikely to come calling. The locals wouldn't take kindly to being told to back off, even if McGrath's death wasn't high on their priority list. It would have taken some high level arm-twisting. Salter must have a bloody good reason for wanting to stall the investigation. Something more substantial than the vague hope that something might come out of the woodwork.

It struck her that she'd eaten nothing since the previous night. She felt no real appetite, but she forced herself to make a sandwich with the last of the ham from the fridge. It was only when she took the first bite that she decided she couldn't face it. It was as if her brain had decided it had had enough and was preparing to shut itself down.

She made her way upstairs to the bedroom. The sensible part of her mind told her to get undressed, go to bed properly. But the exhausted part of her mind couldn't be bothered to do any more than push off her jeans and crawl into bed in the rest of her clothes. She lay back, still half-expecting that she'd lie restlessly awake for all her tiredness. But within seconds she was asleep.

She woke in semi-darkness. The bedroom window faced west, and bars of crimson from the setting sun stretched down the far wall. As she lay there, the reddened light inched towards the ceiling as the sun lowered behind the houses opposite.

She rolled over, fumbling for the clock. She'd been more tired than she realised. It was already mid-evening, the first street lights coming on in the road outside. She did at least feel rested, much better than after the morning's snatched sleep.

It took her a few moments, as her head cleared, to register her own unease. Something wasn't right. Something had disturbed her, maybe even woken her up.

She sat up, motionless, straining her ears for any sound. Trying to work out what felt out of place. She could hear only the occasional click from the radiators, the sound of the central heating coming on as the thermostat kicked in.

The central heating. Cold was the one thing this bloody house never was. It was a new build shrine to the virtues of double-glazing, cavity wall insulation and loft-lagging, with – according to the developers – a carbon footprint so small it could probably save the planet by itself. The heating thermostat was set to what she presumed was a comfortable level, but, even as summer drew to a close, the heating had stayed resolutely off since she'd been here.

And now it was on. Because there was a chill in the air. A recurrent breeze through the house that occasionally caused the bedroom door to bump gently against the frame. Something had allowed the cool evening air into the house.

Shit.

Moving silently, she pulled on the jeans and her flat-soled shoes. She picked up the handbag that she always left on her bedside table. It contained her mobiles and, in a concealed pocket, her warrant card and other key documents. She made her way to the door and peered out into the landing, her eyes adjusting to the dim light.

Nothing. No sound that she could make out. But definitely that chill that she'd detected, an unaccustomed movement of air through the house.

She moved across the landing, straining her ears. There was nothing more than the faint whisper of the breeze, the occasional soft thump of the bedroom door. The house was in near darkness, illuminated only by the last red rays of the sun and the first pale orange of the street lights.

She inched silently down the stairs and paused at the bottom, her back to the wall. If there was a door or window open, someone was inside. Had whoever killed McGrath come for her as well? If so, he wouldn't use the same method twice. If the police really did still harbour doubts about McGrath's death, a second fire at her place would quickly dispel them. More likely, she'd be killed somewhere away from here. Or they'd make her death look like suicide. Either way, the implication would be that the mysterious Maggie Yates was somehow involved in McGrath's death.

That wouldn't work, of course, once Salter revealed who Maggie Yates had really been. But the killer wouldn't know that. Unless the killer knew that only too well—

Christ.

She could still hear nothing. She looked around the dark hallway, considering her options. The kitchen first, she thought. She could find a weapon there. If some bastard had broken in with the intention of killing her, she wouldn't worry too much about the implications of defending herself.

She edged along the hall, keeping her back to the wall, eyes darting between the doors to the kitchen and the living room. The kitchen looked deserted. She eased back the door to ensure no one was hiding behind it, and then looked around. Now she saw the source of the cool breeze blowing through the house.

The rear door, which led out into the small back garden, was ajar. As far as she could see in the darkness, it appeared undamaged. So either she'd accidentally left it unlocked, and maybe even unfastened. Or someone had managed to get through it.

She'd spoken to Salter about wanting to get the security tightened on this place. It was standard domestic stuff, not even high quality. Nothing to keep out even a moderately skilled housebreaker, let alone a professional.

She stepped across the room and looked out into the garden. No sign of anyone, though the bottom end of the plot, backing on to the gardens of the next road, was lost in darkness. She turned back into the room and, still facing the centre, her eyes fixed on the door, she felt her way along to the drawer where she kept the kitchen knives.

Reaching behind her back, she began to fumble in the drawer, her fingers rummaging blindly among the contents. The drawer was filled with kitchen utensils – wooden spoons, ladles, a cheese grater. None of this stuff was Marie's own – it was an off-the-shelf job lot the landlord had supplied when the Agency had arranged the furnished let.

There had to be a knife in there. She was struggling to remember whether she'd used a knife earlier, whether it was sitting in the dishwasher waiting to be cleaned. With a wary glance towards the door, she decided to risk turning to look.

Her back was turned for no more than a few seconds, but she knew she'd made a mistake. She felt, rather than heard, the presence behind her.

When she turned, the man was standing in the doorway. In the dim light, she could make out nothing except that he was of average height, stockily built, running slightly to fat. He had a baseball cap pulled over his forehead and a black scarf wrapped round the lower half of his face.

Without speaking, he stretched out a gloved hand.

Balanced across the palm she could see two kitchen knives.

PART THREE

18

Marie took a deep breath and tried to suppress her rising sense of panic. Somewhere in her head, as if belonging to another person, her rational mind was continuing to work, assessing the options, trying to come up with any sort of game plan.

'Who are you?' she said, making an effort to keep her voice steady. 'What do you want?' She had no expectation of a response, but she knew the importance of trying to engage with a potential attacker. Of trying to turn a mechanistic process into a human encounter. If he was a pro, it would make no difference. If he wasn't, it might buy her a few minutes.

She was conscious of the external door, still ajar to her left. Could she reach it before he reached her? He was standing casually, the knives still balanced playfully on his palm, as if he felt fully in control.

'What the fuck are you doing in here?' she said.

There was no chance of provoking a reaction. The man watched her in silence, and she could sense that he was enjoying her discomfort, relishing her fear.

Not a pro, she thought suddenly. He wants to give that

impression, but he isn't. She couldn't immediately tell what made her so sure. Then she realised that the answer lay in what she'd just recognised. He was getting a kick out of scaring her. It was in his body language, the way he was standing, the way he was watching her. The way he was playing with the knives, trying to show how bloody clever he was.

She'd dealt with hit men in her career, interviewed one or two as part of investigations. For the real pros, it was just a job. Sure, most were psychopaths, lacking the basic empathy that oils normal human relationships. But they were in it for money, not for kicks. Get in, do the job, get out. Don't get caught. Leave no trace. Anything else was at best a waste of energy, at worst a dangerous distraction.

A real pro would have done the job by now.

If he wasn't the real thing, he might give her an opening. He'd already made his first error. He'd delayed, allowed her time to think, time to recognise his weakness.

If she made a break for the door, he'd get there first. The answer was to do the opposite.

'Not very talkative, are we?' she said. She took three deliberate steps towards him. 'Wonder who you are behind that cap and scarf? Someone I know, or a perfect stranger?' She took another step. She was only a few feet away from him. 'Shall I find out?'

It was a big risk. He might be an amateur, but that made him unpredictable. A pro would do nothing to compromise his anonymity. An amateur might do any damn fool thing. But she could sense her gamble was paying off. He looked wrong-footed, his posture suddenly less relaxed. He wanted to threaten her, regain control, but didn't want to speak.

'Let's have a look.' She took another carefully measured, step forward and, with brutal suddenness, kicked hard at the man's groin.

She'd trained in self-defence earlier in her career. She couldn't recall if this move had been on the curriculum, though the female instructor had been keen to emphasise the particular vulnerabilities of the male body.

It worked well enough. The intruder jerked back, then toppled forward like a suddenly deflating balloon, clutching his hands between his legs. As his head flew back, she caught a glimpse of his face between the scarf and the cap. No one she knew.

As he staggered forward, she launched another ferocious kick at his head. Her shoe caught him square in the face. He fell sideways, catching his head against one of the kitchen units.

She paused, weighing up the odds of finding some way to secure him. But she'd have to find some wire or tape and she didn't know how long it would take him to recover. And if she called the police, it would just open the whole can of worms around her and McGrath.

Clutching the handbag over her shoulder, she headed out of the open back door and made her way round the side of the house, fumbling for her car keys as she reached the front drive.

As she pressed the fob to unlock the doors, she could already hear footsteps behind her. She dragged open the car door and fell inside, slamming shut the central locking. To her left, she could see the man, still half-crouched in pain, moving towards her.

She jammed the keys clumsily into the ignition and

started the engine. Slamming the car into gear, she pushed the accelerator to the floor, the car screaming away from the curb just as the man reached the passenger door. Moments later, she reached the edge of the estate and turned on to the main road.

What to do now? She was tempted just to give it all up, tell Salter where to stick his bloody job, and head home. Back to Liam and away from all this crap.

But she didn't really want to do that. Not yet. Now, even more than before, she wanted to know what the hell was going on.

She headed towards the centre of town, her eyes flicking to the rear view mirror for any signs of pursuit. If she wasn't going to head home, where could she go?

She thought first of Lizzie. But the last thing Lizzie needed was more trauma and another reason to be afraid.

Which left only one other option. Jack Brennan. She knew nothing of Brennan's circumstances – whether he was married or single, where he lived. But she had no other bolt hole. He could only tell her to bugger off.

The other question was whether she could trust him. But then what had she to lose? For all her suspicions, she really knew nothing. Even if Brennan was trying to get her to spill the beans, she really had no beans to spill.

She pulled off the main road into a pub car park, found Brennan's number and dialled. The phone was answered almost immediately. 'Yes?'

'Jack. Marie Donovan.'

'Everything okay?' he said. 'I thought we were going to talk tomorrow.'

'There's been a development.'

'Not a good one, presumably.'

'You might say that. I think we need to talk.'

'Sure. You mean now?'

'Yes, and not over the phone. And Jack—'

'Yes?'

'There's one other thing. I need somewhere to stay.'

There was a pause, and Marie could sense him thinking through the implications of what she'd just said. 'Sounds like some development,' he said at last. 'You better come on over.'

19

She didn't know what to expect. In giving his address and directions, Brennan hadn't let slip any indication of his domestic circumstances. She didn't know whether she'd find some louche bachelor pad or a haven of familial domesticity. In the end, it was neither, but a neat backstreet semi in an unassuming corner of Cheadle Hulme. It had taken her longer than she'd expected to get here up the M56, but she'd at least put some distance between her and her intruder.

She rang the bell, still uneasy about the set-up she might be imposing herself upon. Coppers' wives aren't usually keen on their husbands bringing work home, especially in the form of a female colleague.

But she knew almost as soon as he opened the door that, whatever Brennan's circumstances might be, he lived alone. It was partly the ease with which he greeted her, but it was also that, even on first glance, the house somehow lacked a woman's touch. Neat enough, and well maintained, but with a functionality that struck her as quintessentially male. White painted walls. A few prints that looked as if they'd been bought from IKEA. An unsullied beige carpet.

'Have you eaten?'

It was only when he asked the question that she realised how hungry she was. Apart from the abandoned sandwich, she'd eaten nothing for the best part of twenty-four hours. 'Now you come to mention it,' she said, 'no.'

'I was just about to stick something on. Nothing fancy, but you're welcome to join me.'

'If you're sure?'

'I can spare a plate of pasta. Come through and we can talk while I get it going.'

She followed him into the kitchen. Again, it was neat and clean, with a surprisingly impressive cooker and range of kitchen equipment and utensils. The kitchen of a man who likes cooking, rather than the domain of a woman or even a couple.

Brennan busied himself chopping onions and garlic, and gestured towards an opened bottle of red wine on the table. 'Help yourself. In fact, help both of us. I'd just opened it when you called. Glasses in that cupboard.'

She filled two glasses and handed one to him, watching his hands as he prepared the food. A touch of vanity permeated everything he did. She could see he was conscious of working in front of an audience and there was some showmanship in his movements – the rapid chopping of a practised chef, the demonstrative way he tossed the ingredients into the pan. But he might have behaved the same way even on his own. As with the way he dressed, it was the style of a man conscious of his impact on the world. It was even mildly endearing.

Most importantly, he made her feel at ease. For the first time since she'd encountered the intruder – for that matter, for the first time since McGrath's death – she began to relax. She felt safe here. She trusted Brennan, even knowing that there were risks in doing so.

Brennan glanced up at her, as if he'd been reading her thoughts. 'You okay?'

'I am now.'

'So what's happened? You were pretty cryptic on the phone.'

'Someone broke into my house. I think they were trying to kill me.'

He stared at her for a moment. 'Christ. Tonight?'

'Just before I called you.' She described how she'd discovered the intruder and managed to make her escape.

'You left him there?'

'I don't think he wanted to steal the DVD player. He might have taken my laptop, but I keep that clean. I imagine he'd have made himself scarce pretty quickly.'

'You reckon this was the same person who killed McGrath?'

'Well, I don't *know*. But like everything else in this, it's a hell of a coincidence otherwise.'

'But why would he come after you?'

'Because he knows who I really am? But that takes us back to Salter's involvement. Why would he send me up here to have me bumped off?'

'He might,' Brennan said, thoughtfully. 'If you're right about him, I mean. If he – or Boyle – wanted McGrath out of the way for whatever reason, maybe you were set up to be the scapegoat. If you'd gone missing, or killed in a way that looked like suicide, the police might have decided to look no further.'

'I'd thought of that. But I can't see it. It's too risky for Hugh. Too many loose ends. He couldn't have concealed who I was, not for long. Too many people knew. Including you.'

Brennan frowned and resumed shredding a bunch of basil leaves. 'I suppose,' he said. 'But if not that, then what?'

'I don't know. Maybe someone else saw me as a scapegoat.'

'But it only works if McGrath's killer knew something about you. He wouldn't just pick a random new employee. So either he knows who you really are, or he knows about the legend for the mysterious – what was your name?'

'Maggie Yates.' She stared gloomily at her half-empty glass. 'Yes, I can see that. You might make Maggie Yates fit the profile of a contract killer. You might even be able to pin it on the semi-real Marie Donovan. But it wouldn't work if I was just a local housewife doing a week's temping.' She swallowed the rest of the glass in one mouthful.

Brennan pushed the bottle towards her. 'You were right, though,' he said.

'Was I? There's always a first time.'

'About your Lizzie and Keith Welsby.'

She looked up. 'Really? I'd begun to think that was just another case of me putting two and two together and making seventeen.'

'Not absolutely certain,' he said. 'But it fits. I had a delve through the personal files this afternoon. Welsby's been married twice. Divorced both times. He's got one child by the first marriage. A girl. Would be in her early twenties. Elizabeth Rose.'

'Sweet,' she commented. 'Don't imagine that was Welsby's choice. Fits though, doesn't it?'

'Question is, what does it tell us?'

'Did you find out anything about McGrath?'

'Something. Certainly not as small-time as you were led to believe. Or if he was, there's been a lot of interest in him over the years.'

'Go on.' She took the liberty of pouring herself another glass of the wine, then dutifully topped up Brennan's glass.

'I found the files on McGrath. He's been under surveillance for some time. Five or six years at least.'

'And?'

Brennan paused to take a swallow of wine and give the sauce a stir. 'That's the thing. I can't tell you much more. There was a lot a data in the files. But it was all restricted. Authorisation required. Guess who?'

'Salter,' she said. 'Doesn't prove much. I was undercover with McGrath. Salter had every right to keep that confidential, even within the Agency. Chinese walls.'

'I can see he's got to protect the operation,' Brennan said. 'Not to mention you. But would that involve restricting everything in there?'

'I don't know. Probably not the earlier stuff. But he might err on the side of caution.'

'There was loads of stuff on McGrath. You could see the file sizes in the directory. It must have included PDF files. Scans of documents. But I couldn't get access.'

'It doesn't square with what Salter told me,' she agreed. 'But then what Salter told me didn't square with making McGrath the target of a full-scale undercover operation. There wasn't much background material in the briefings I was given.' She paused. 'It's not exactly a smoking gun, but it does suggest that Salter's not on the level.'

'Doesn't get us very far, though,' Brennan said, spooning pasta and sauce on to two plates. It looked pretty good, she thought. Several notches up from student spag bol. A male copper who could cook. Whatever next?

They ate at the kitchen table. The food was simple but tasted as good as it looked. Brennan even produced fresh Parmesan with an elegant-looking grater. 'Like I say, nothing fancy. Just what I was throwing together for myself.'

She was feeling more at ease than she'd felt for days. The earlier terrors had already begun to fade in her memory. She felt she deserved a brief respite.

Brennan topped up both their glasses. 'Then there's Jeff Kerridge,' he said.

The words instantly dispelled the peace she'd momentarily enjoyed. Jesus, she thought. Jeff Kerridge. The last man she wanted to think about. The man who, along with Keith Welsby, had been nearly responsible for her death a year before. 'In connection with McGrath?'

'Maybe.'

'You found a link between McGrath and Kerridge?'

'Nothing definitive. Like I say, I couldn't even get into McGrath's files. But Kerridge's were mostly accessible. I'd be interested to see the paper files. There's a hell of a lot of stuff there.'

Marie knew only too well how much evidence they'd gathered on Kerridge. Much of it provided by her former lover, Jake Morton. It had cost him his life.

'We'd have put Kerridge away, if Salter hadn't killed him first,' she said. 'No question. And Boyle too, probably.'

'Makes you think, doesn't it?'

'It certainly made me think. Though I still don't know quite what.'

'I couldn't spend all day on the files,' Brennan said. 'I was already attracting attention. But I skimmed through as much as I could. And I found something.' He leaned over and reached into the pocket of a smart-looking sports jacket slung over the back of one of the kitchen chairs. He unfolded a sheet of A4 paper and handed it to her.

She looked up quizzically. 'A copy of a passport.'

'Recognise him?'

She squinted at the passport photograph. It was a black and white print of a scanned document. The image was blurred, but she had no doubt. 'McGrath.'

'Passport in the name of one Paul Kavanagh.'

'You found this in Kerridge's files?'

'There was a whole stack of fake documentation. Passports, driving licences, you name it. Stuff pulled together for various members of Kerridge's team.'

She had seen the material on the data stick Morton had sent her just before his killing. 'I remember.' She held her voice steady. She'd put Jake Morton behind her now. She recalled his face, his warmth, the feel of his body in bed. But she no longer knew how it had happened, why she'd allowed herself to have a relationship with him. Loneliness and insecurity. Nothing stronger than that. A stupid mistake made by a different person. But, just occasionally, something unexpected brought him back to her mind, and for a moment her feelings for him felt stronger than she allowed herself to believe.

'This was just one document among all that,' Brennan

went on. 'I was lucky to spot it, but that handsome face caught my eye. Far as I could see, there was nothing else relating to McGrath.'

'Suggests he was on Kerridge's team at least, doesn't it?'

'Doesn't tell us how big a player he was, though. Or how close to Kerridge.'

'I can't see Kerridge getting a fake passport made for just anyone. He must have had some significant dealings with Kerridge. You find anything else?'

'No. Took me a while to plough through the documents. I was getting a bit paranoid. Thought people might be wondering what I was up to.'

'It's a start, though,' she said. 'Means that Salter could have had some ulterior motive for planting me with McGrath.'

'Keeping an eye on one of Kerridge's former associates? Makes more sense if McGrath was a bigger fish.'

'Didn't see much sign of that in his business. But maybe he was smarter than he seemed.'

'It's a hall of mirrors, this, isn't it? Is this what life's like for you lot all the time? Thought standard policing was tricky enough.' He emptied the last of the wine into their two glasses.

'It's undercover work,' she said. 'Out in the field, you can't afford to trust anyone. You need a safe anchor back at base. Someone to rely on when everything starts shifting around you.' She paused, realising that she had almost begun to see Brennan himself as that anchor. Stupid, she thought. She still couldn't be sure whether to trust him. 'That's why it's such a nightmare with Salter. It's not just that he might be bent. It leaves me out here twisting in the wind.'

'But this one's done now, presumably? Now McGrath's no longer in the picture?'

She couldn't tell whether there was a note of regret in his voice. 'Salter's playing silly buggers with that as well, though. Stringing me along.'

Brennan gestured towards the wine bottle. 'You want any more? I can open another bottle.'

'Tempting, but I'd better not. My head's not very straight as it is. I'm feeling all in.' She felt as if she'd been sleeping all day but was still unrefreshed. 'You sure it's okay for me to stay over?'

'Fine by me. Happy to offer you a bed for the night.' If there was any double-meaning in his words, he gave no sign. 'Nice to have female company, to be honest. Civilises the place.'

She was tempted to ask about his domestic circumstances, but couldn't think of any question that wouldn't seem intrusive. Or that wouldn't give the impression that she cared. 'You haven't seen my place. Do you mind if I turn in? I'm feeling pretty knackered. Not the best company, female or not.'

'I'll show you where things are. Can't offer you a change of clothes, I'm afraid, unless you fancy cross-dressing. But I can lend you a dressing gown.'

'Thanks, Jack. I'm really grateful for this, you know.'

'What else would you expect me to do? I hope you'll do the same for me next time some bastard breaks in here with a knife.' He laughed. 'Seriously, it's nothing at all. Just get a decent night's sleep.'

He led her upstairs and showed her round the small upper floor. The second bedroom was, endearingly, set up as a guest room, with a small selection of toiletries and even a tray with tea and coffee. She could see Brennan as the kind of punctilious soul who would keep a guest room prepared for unexpected visitors.

'All yours,' he said. 'Do you want waking? I usually head off around eight.'

'Whenever suits you,' she said. 'Once it's daylight, I'll be happy to get back home and find out if my visitor left any signs.'

'Sure that's wise?'

'He didn't strike me as a pro. My guess is that he made himself scarce as soon as I legged it. Can't see him coming back straight away.'

Brennan gazed at her face for a moment, as if he were trying to think what to say. 'Just be careful, for Christ's sake, Marie. We don't know who we're dealing with.'

She looked back at him, a little surprised by his concern. 'I'll be careful, Jack. This time I'm going to be bloody careful.'

He had watched from the shadows, wondering what to do. His instructions were clear. Observe, monitor, report back. Take no action until told to.

It was only luck that he was out here this evening. He had intended to leave her once she was safely home. However careful he was, if he spent too much time in the proximity of her house it inevitably increased his risk of being detected.

But as the evening came, although he knew that her car had never left the drive, he began to feel uneasy. Maybe it was the arson attack. He'd reported that back. The text he'd received in reply had instructed him to carry on as before. But he'd detected something, even in the terse syllables of the text message, that suggested the news had been unexpected.

That wasn't a surprise. If they'd wanted McGrath killed, he'd have been given the job. So McGrath's killer was some third-party. Which raised some interesting questions. He sensed that the job had just become more complicated.

So he'd come out here again tonight, impelled by some sixth sense. Feeling that something would happen. Something that might complicate things still further.

He was checking over the front of the house when he registered the car arriving further down the street. It had parked some distance away, near the main road. Moments later, he'd seen the driver walking down the street towards him.

This wasn't how people behaved in an estate like this. You didn't park your car at one end of the road and walk to your destination. This place was built for cars. You parked outside your own house or the house you were visiting.

He moved a step or two further back into the darkness, watching the figure approach. The body language wasn't right either. There was an air of wariness about the move-ment. The gait of someone who wanted to be unobtrusive.

He waited silently as the figure drew level with the house, stopped, looked cautiously around, and made its way down the side of the building to the rear garden.

He watched, wondering what to do. The house was in darkness. She'd probably been exhausted after her disturbed night. Maybe gone back to bed, or fallen asleep in a chair. Either way, she wouldn't be prepared for an intruder.

He stood and watched in the chill night air, as patient as ever in his reconnaissance, listening for any disturbance within the house. Long minutes went by, but he saw nothing. The house remained unilluminated, and it was too dark to discern any movements inside.

When the movement finally came, it almost took him by surprise. He heard a clatter of footsteps up the side of the house, heading towards the street. It was her, running breathlessly towards her car. He watched as she thumbed open the locks, clambered inside and, after an agonised second or two, started the engine. The car sped off, initially unsteadily, towards the main road.

The intruder had reached the car just too late. But she was already gone and the silhouetted figure – his own car parked too far away for any chance of pursuit – was left staring morosely after her.

Amateur. Caught up in the moment, the intruder had made no effort to conceal his presence or even appear inconspicuous. He clearly had no intention of returning to the house. Instead, he shuffled his way back down the street to where his car was parked.

It was disturbing. Not just that this had happened but that they – whoever they might be – had entrusted the job to such a buffoon. They'd underestimated her, though he knew how easy it was to do that.

In the distance, he heard the sound of the intruder's car starting, and wondered whether to follow it. But he had his instructions. He would report back on what had happened and allow them to make the decision.

For long minutes he remained motionless, his eyes fixed on the empty house, until he felt safe to move.

Finally, he concluded that any residents drawn to their windows by the two cars pulling away would have returned, unenlightened, to their televisions or evening meals.

Then, hidden in the shadows but moving with an unhurried nonchalance, he made his way out of the estate towards the nearby pub where his own car was unobtrusively parked.

20

She was woken at seven by two competing sounds – a gentle knocking at the bedroom door and the furious buzzing of her mobile on the bedside table. Half-awake – these days, it felt as if she spent most of her life half-awake – she rolled over and grabbed the phone, simultaneously calling towards the door; 'Yes?'

'You ready to wake up?' Brennan asked from outside.

'Yes. Thanks.' She peered at the screen. A missed call. Lizzie. Why the hell was Lizzie calling her at seven in the morning?

'Shower's free if you want it,' Brennan called. 'Cooking bacon butties, so don't be long.'

Jesus, she thought. A domestic god. Or maybe trying a bit too hard to impress. If only he knew how easy she was to impress these days. Or how few people were trying.

She dragged herself from the bed and threw on the dressing gown. A woman's dressing gown, too small for Brennan. None of her business. Definitely none of her business.

She soaked herself for a few minutes under a scalding shower, as hot as she could bear it. She felt as if the previous evening's events had left her with a need to cleanse herself, literally to wash the scent of fear and anger off her body.

She'd slept better than she'd expected, too. Now she felt – well, some fear, certainly. Some bastard had tried to kill her and might have succeeded. But mostly she felt anger. A cold fucking fury at the man who had broken into her house and come so close to taking her life. And at those who had paid him to do it.

Brennan was in the kitchen, already dressed in a slightly-too-smart pastel shirt and expensive-looking trousers. Marie knew and cared little about clothes, at least by comparison with most other women that she knew, but she could recognise quality when she saw it.

He was arranging rashers of freshly grilled bacon on neatly sliced bread. 'Thought you might feel like something solid after last night,' he said.

'You mean the wine or the attempted killing?'

He pushed one of the laden plates towards her. 'I was thinking mainly of the killing thing,' he said. 'But you might want to soak up the wine, too. Coffee?'

'Please. I think I'm okay. As well as can be expected, anyway.' She took a grateful bite of the sandwich. It was exactly what she needed. Something simple, salty, filling. Something *ordinary*.

He poured coffee from a filter machine into two mugs, then sat down opposite her and began to chew on his own sandwich. 'You sure you're ready to go back there? It wasn't just the wine talking?'

'No, I'm fine. Really. He won't come back. Not today, anyway.'

'You can come back here tonight if you like. Hope that doesn't need saying.'

She smiled. 'That's kind of you, Jack. I'm very grateful. I don't know. I need to find out what Salter's got in mind for me.'

'You think he'll try to keep you up here?'

'Depends what his game is, doesn't it? I was very conveniently positioned last night for someone to have a go at me.'

'Even if that's true, he can't try it twice,' Brennan pointed out. 'Once you tell him what happened – put it on the record, I mean – he's got to take you out of the field.' He paused. 'You are *going* to put it on the record?'

Until he'd asked the question, she hadn't even thought about it. 'Yes, of course. I've got to. I couldn't call the police last night because that would have set too many hares running. But I've got to tell Salter. Make sure it's made formal. And you're right. Salter will have to take me out of the field. Whoever's behind this – whatever's behind it – I've been compromised somehow.' She paused. 'I'm going to tell him I'm heading back home whether he likes it or not.'

'That's good. And make it official. Quickly. If Salter is involved in all this, you want to make sure it can't happen again.'

'I can get into the secure network on my laptop. File a report online. I'll do it before I speak to Salter.'

Brennan glanced at his watch. 'I need to go in a minute. Stay as long as you like. You can let yourself out. And if you decide you want to come back here tonight, that's fine.'

'Thanks, Jack. Once I've spoken to Hugh, I think I'll just pack up and head back south. Whatever he says. He can sort out the police up here.'

Brennan looked at her for a moment, and she thought that there might have been a trace of regret mixed in with his obvious relief. Maybe his offer of shelter hadn't been entirely altruistic. And maybe, sitting here in yesterday's grubby clothes with her wet hair unbrushed, she was indulging in some mild wishful thinking.

'Anyway,' Brennan said, 'keep me posted. About everything. I'll do the same. Whatever Salter's up to, I still feel my chain's being jerked. It's not a feeling I like.'

'I'll keep you posted,' she promised. 'And thanks again, Jack. Really. You kept me sane last night. I was more shaken than I realised.'

'Didn't do much except pour you a glass of wine. But you're welcome. Anytime.'

After he'd gone, she sat in the silent kitchen, chewing the remains of her bacon sandwich, helping herself to a second coffee. She had to decide what to do next. It felt strange. She'd hardly got herself into this job, hadn't even properly thought herself into the character of Maggie Yates. And yet now she felt as if a rug had been pulled from under her. She'd been geared up for months of life undercover, creating a new personality, a new life. The slow painstaking work needed to make a covert operation work. Without realising she was doing it, she'd already begun to adjust her thinking, get herself ready for immersion into a new world.

And now she was being dragged back into real life and everything that went with it. Especially Liam. And everything that went with Liam.

Okay, she had to get back to her house. Get on to the secure network – assuming that last night's murderous bastard hadn't waltzed off with her laptop – and submit

240

her report before Salter could do anything to prevent it. Then speak to Salter. Then call home and see how things were with Liam.

And Lizzie.

Shit, she'd forgotten Lizzie's call. She couldn't begin to think, even now she was wide awake, why Lizzie should have called her. She'd left no message. It wasn't a good sign if the only person she could think to call was someone she'd only known for a couple of days.

She pulled out her mobile and found Lizzie's number. The phone rang a couple of times and then a voice said: 'Yes?' She sounded tense, suspicious. The voice of someone expecting an abusive phone call.

'Lizzie?' Just in time, Marie remembered to revert to her undercover identity. 'It's Maggie. Are you okay? Did you try to call me?'

There was a pause, and then an indrawn breath. 'Maggie. Oh, thanks for phoning back.'

'What is it? Is something wrong?'

"I'm probably just being stupid. It's just – well, you know, everything that's happened. I'm not thinking straight.'

'Where are you? Are you still at the flat?'

'Yes. That's just it. I was here alone last night. Katy decided to stay over at her boyfriend's.'

It felt as if someone had run a cold finger slowly down Marie's spine. 'What is it, Lizzie? Did something happen?'

'I'm probably just imagining it—'

'What, Lizzie? What happened?'

'I woke in the night. Don't know why – I'm not usually a light sleeper. But I got up to get some water. As I was going through the hall, I heard a noise at the front door.

241

A scraping.' She paused, gathering her breath. 'I thought it was someone trying to break into the flat.'

'What happened?'

'It went on for a bit, and I was wondering what to do. Whether to call the police. Then it suddenly stopped. The people in the next door flat have a dog, and I could hear it barking. Whoever it was probably got scared off.'

Marie took a deep breath. 'Did you call the police?'

'No, I just waited. I listened hard but there was nothing else. I thought the police would think I was making a fuss about nothing. That I was under stress.' She gave a not-particularly-convincing impression of a laugh. 'I probably am. I'm not sure I wasn't just half-asleep and just imagined the whole thing. I'm just feeling a bit messed up, Maggie.'

'You've been through a hell of a lot in the last few days. What time did all this happen?'

'Threeish, maybe. In the end, I went back to bed and hid under the bedclothes. I don't think anyone could get in through that door anyway. It's pretty solid and we had some strong locks put in because Katy's dad was worried about us living here on our own. I kept telling myself that.'

'You should have called me straight away,' Marie said.

'I thought you'd just think I was being hysterical as well,' Lizzie said. 'I didn't want to disturb you at that time of night. Not two nights in a row.' Her laugh this time was slightly more genuine, even if tinged with bitterness.

'I'll come round,' Marie said. 'Make sure everything's all right.'

'You don't need to, really—' Lizzie stopped. 'But I'd like it if you did.'

'I'll be there as quickly as I can,' she said. 'I'll be a little while because I'm up in Manchester. Long story,' she added, conscious that it wasn't a story she could share with Lizzie.

It took her the best part of forty minutes to reach Lizzie's flat. On Marie's previous visit, Lizzie had buzzed her in immediately. Now, in response to the doorbell, Lizzie's voice emerged cracklingly from the speaker by the door. 'Who is it?'

'It's me. Maggie.'

Marie made her way slowly up the stairs. By the time she reached the first floor, Lizzie was standing at the door of the flat, scrutinising the face of the wood and the edges of the doorframe. 'I've not dared come out till now,' she said.

Marie peered past her at the door. There were minor scratches in the door and frame next to the lock. If someone had tried to break in, it looked as if they hadn't got very far. 'Are those new?' Marie asked.

'I think so.' The door was in need of a new coat of paint, so the damage round the lock wasn't initially obvious. The lock itself was new and looked solid. 'I'm pretty sure that wasn't there last night.'

'Looks like you were right, then,' Marie said. She straightened up and looked around her. 'How would they have got into the lobby?'

'It's not all that secure. If you buzz a few bells, someone will open the door without checking. Or you hang around outside until someone else comes in and you give the impression you're visiting someone or you've left your downstairs key behind. I've done it once or twice when I've forgotten my key. Most of the flats are rented so people come and go all the time. Nobody knows who else lives here.'

'But it was the middle of the night,' Marie pointed out. 'Who'd let someone in then?'

'You'd be surprised,' Lizzie said, leading them inside the flat. 'We've got some students. A few unemployed. You see lights on all times of the night.'

'What do you think, then?' Marie asked. 'Attempted burglary?'

Lizzie continued through to the kitchen, while Marie closed the front door behind them. Lizzie seemed a different person from the distraught young woman she'd sat with the previous day. Not as if she'd overcome the shock of McGrath's death – let alone the additional terrors of the previous night – but still much more in control. Older, almost. It was an odd transition, especially since the events of the night could hardly have helped her feel more comfortable.

Lizzie was already at the sink filling the kettle. 'Tea or coffee?' she asked, without looking back.

'Tea, please.' Marie lowered herself on to one of the kitchen chairs. She watched Lizzie carefully, trying to read her body language. Even that seemed different. The previous day she'd been hunched, fearful, her thin arms wrapped around her chest as if to protect herself from harm. Now, Lizzie was standing upright, as if she were ready to take whatever the world might throw at her.

She brought the two mugs of tea to the table and sat down opposite Marie.

'You sure you're okay?' Marie asked.

Lizzie nodded, eyes fixed on Marie's face. 'Thanks for

244

coming round. It means a lot. More than you know, maybe.'
She paused. 'I've not been entirely straight with you.'

'How do you mean?'

'I told you about Andy. About what he did for me. And
for my mum. All of that was true. He was a decent man,
underneath it all. Decent to me, anyway.' She paused, and
a regretful smile played across her face. 'But I didn't tell
you the whole truth. I said Andy had been a contact of my
dad's. He was more than that. They were business partners,
except that my dad was – what do you call it? – a sleeping
partner. Because of what he did.'

'I don't understand,' Marie said.

Marie thought she could detect a note of amusement in
the younger woman's eyes. 'Because he was a copper,' Lizzie
said. 'You must have worked out that Andy's business wasn't
all legit.'

'I'd assumed that. It was why he took me on. Because I
had a bit of experience in that direction.'

There was an expression in Lizzie's eyes that Marie
couldn't read. 'Thing was, Andy was a crap businessman.
He had the contacts, and he had the blarney. He knew
how to pick up good deals and some of the time he
knew how to sell them on. He just didn't know how to
make money in the process. Or how to hold on to any
money he did make.'

'Can't say that entirely surprises me, either,' Marie said.
'I wondered how well the business was doing.'

'Better than you might think,' Lizzie said. 'That was my
job, you see. Keeping tab on the finances.'

Marie was already feeling disconcerted. This was a
different Lizzie, not just from the distraught young woman

245

she'd comforted the day before, but also from the confused and self-effacing person she'd first met in McGrath's offices. 'Your job?'

'Yeah. Don't get me wrong. I was grateful for the admin help you were going to give us. But most of that side of things was already under control.' Lizzie allowed herself a full smile. 'I didn't entirely tell you the truth about my work experience either. I did a business studies degree and qualified as an accountant. I don't claim to be Bill Gates, but I can read a balance sheet.'

Marie shook her head, trying to reconcile this information with the impression she'd had of Lizzie until this morning. Maybe Marie had been guilty of sexist and ageist stereotyping herself, assuming that an attractive young secretary's most important physical asset wouldn't be her brain. But it was more than that. Lizzie had gone out of her way, even when they'd been talking the previous day, to give the impression that she hadn't contributed anything to the business beyond making McGrath his morning coffee.

'I didn't get the impression that McGrath had his filing under control,' Marie commented.

Lizzie laughed. 'Andy didn't know how to file his nails. Didn't worry me too much. I removed anything that was important and made sure it was stored safely. The stuff you were going through needed sorting, but most of it was – well, just rubbish really. We liked to give the impression that everything was a bit of a shambles. Helpful in all kinds of ways. Revenue didn't suspect that Andy was living above his means. Competition tended to underestimate his operation. And it was useful for me to play the dim little secretary. Used to find out stuff without anyone even noticing I was there half the time. Amazing how gullible people are – well, men are – when they see a short skirt. They assume you haven't a clue what they're talking about.' She smiled again, this time with a discernible touch of fondness. 'And Andy never wanted to believe that it was me keeping the business afloat. He liked to play the big businessman, and I was happy to let him.'

'What about your dad?' Marie asked. 'Where does he fit into all this?'

Lizzie hesitated for a moment. 'What I told you was more or less true. He and mum were at loggerheads. She didn't want him anywhere near her or me. But he wasn't that bad. At least not to me. He helped fund my degree course and gave me money from time to time when I needed it. Not that I told mum that. He knew that Andy was struggling so, when I needed a job, he suggested to Andy that I might be able to help out. So I came and – well, it worked out.' Her smile changed in tone. 'And it's not dead yet, you know. The business is still there. I've got a shareholding – it was something my dad fixed up – and, as far as I know, Andy's left the rest to me. He had no one else.'

As Lizzie spoke, Marie wondered again about the burning of McGrath's office. The police might have a different view once they'd discovered the ownership structure of the business. She wondered whether Keith Welsby had had any shareholding, but she thought it unlikely. Welsby wouldn't leave those kinds of ends dangling. She couldn't envisage Lizzie as a killer, or even as an arsonist. But until the last few minutes she hadn't envisaged her as an accountant either. 'You think you can keep the business going?'

'I don't have Andy's sales skills or network. I'd be more interested in building up the legit side of the business.'

Marie decided to chance her arm. 'And what about Jeff Kerridge? Where did he fit into all this?'

Lizzie stared at her for a moment, and then laughed again. 'Interesting question. What makes you ask that?'

'I keep my ear to the ground. I heard Andy had some dealings with Kerridge.'

There was an expression of amusement on Lizzie's face. 'Yeah. Andy had dealings with Kerridge. You might say he was part of Kerridge's team. Not an intimate member, exactly. But close enough. Kerridge put a lot of business Andy's way.'

'And was your dad a member of Kerridge's team, too?' Marie asked, and immediately knew she'd opened her mouth once too often.

The amusement on Lizzie's face was unconcealed by now. 'Another interesting question. Why are you so interested in my dad, Maggie Yates?'

Suddenly, it was crystal clear to Marie. Lizzie knew. She knew who Marie was. She knew why Marie had been sent to work with McGrath. She'd known all along. Christ knew how she'd found out. But she'd known. Marie had no doubt of it.

'I'm listening to your story,' Marie said. 'And wondering why you're telling me it. Why now?'

'Because we live in interesting times, Maggie Yates. Andy McGrath was killed when someone torched his offices. I have an intruder trying to break into my flat. Have you been disturbed at all?'

Marie thought she'd kept her face expressionless. But she

could see immediately that Lizzie had read her thoughts. 'Well, that's interesting again. If all these incidents are connected, why would they be interested in you? You'd only just joined the company.'

'You've lost me, Lizzie,' Marie said, aware of the coldness in her voice. 'Doesn't sound as if you're in great need for my support. Maybe I'd better be going.' She made a move to leave the table.

Lizzie remained motionless. 'I can see how you might feel you've been misled. But my lying's quite small beer compared with yours. Isn't it, Marie?'

Marie had already decided that Lizzie must know her real identity, so the use of her real name shouldn't have come as a shock. But it did, as if a mask had just been physically torn from Marie's face.

She lowered herself back on to the chair. 'Okay, Elizabeth Rose. You tell me what this is all about.'

Lizzie nodded. 'I assumed you'd be thorough. You know who I am. Who my father is.'

'And you've known who I am. All the time?'

'No. Andy was a bit suspicious at first. You'd been recommended as someone who might be right to help out in the business. Your lot had put the word about in the right places, so that by the time it reached Andy, it sounded legit enough. Almost sounded too good to be true, so we did a bit of digging. But everything checked out. It was only with the fire that I began to get really suspicious. It all seemed too much of a coincidence. You turn up, and everything goes to hell in a handcart. Yesterday, when you were here, I managed to get a photo of you on my phone without you noticing. Sent it off to a few people to see if your face rang any bells. And it rang one.'

Marie could think of only one explanation, improbable as it seemed. 'Your father? They wouldn't let him anywhere near a mobile. And I thought he was in no state to recognise anybody?'

'He's making something of a recovery. Has been for a while. Better than he's letting on, but not over keen to stand trial any time soon. They've got him on bed watch in hospital with a couple of prison officers. But you must know how my dad can twist people round his little finger. They're pretty lax with him because they think he's incapable anyway, the state he's in. I've got a number to contact him so I texted over your picture and he knew you straight away. I was gobsmacked. I thought there was something dodgy about you, but I never had you down as a cop.' She paused. 'Though why the hell you were wasting your time on a two-bit operation like ours is beyond me. Who did you think we were? The bloody Kray Twins?'

'Good question,' Marie agreed. 'Short answer is I haven't a clue. Made no sense to me from the start. I thought there must be more to the business than met the eye.'

'There is,' Lizzie said. 'Or was. But not that much more. Nothing that merits the attentions of a full-time undercover cop, I'd have thought.'

'Except that Andy McGrath had links with Jeff Kerridge. Like your dad.'

'That's history. Kerridge is dead. Even his wife's dead.'

'She is now. There's another coincidence. We keep stumbling across them. Just how close was Andy McGrath to Jeff Kerridge?'

She felt rather than heard the movement behind her. 'Close enough,' the voice said.

She turned slowly, her throat dry. He was standing in the kitchen doorway, with at least the decency to look mildly embarrassed. 'Sorry,' he shrugged. 'Must be a bit of a surprise.'

'Just a bit,' she said. 'You're looking remarkably well. For a dead man.'

Andy McGrath made his way slowly into the kitchen and lowered himself on to the chair next to Marie. He was limping and there were bruises on the side of his face. Not in the best of nick, you might say. But not bad for someone who'd supposedly been burned to death a day or so earlier. 'A bit of a misunderstanding.' He began to cough suddenly, retching violently. Lizzie quickly filled a glass with water from the sink. McGrath swallowed most of it in one gulp, but it was a few more minutes before he was able to speak.

'Smoke,' he croaked. 'Got into my throat. Getting better but still left me hoarse.'

'I don't know what game you're both playing. But you've lost me.' Marie fixed her gaze on McGrath. 'Is this some sort of scam?'

McGrath shook his head. 'It wasn't me in the office. The police assumed it probably was, because no one could track me down. They'll have worked out by now that it isn't.' He took another sip of the water. 'But it was meant to be me in there. I'd had a text, earlier in the evening, supposedly from one of our customers. Said he'd got a bit of a crisis on. Could I meet him at the office, help sort things out.'

'You're accustomed to late night business meetings?'

'Depends on the business. This was the kind of customer who prefers to work outside office hours, if you get my drift. My guess was he'd screwed up some deal – not delivered what he'd promised – and was looking for me to come up with the goods. It happens. Sometimes I'm on the other side of the counter. Never does any harm to do the odd favour.'

'So you went back to the office?'

'Sat around for half an hour, twiddling my proverbials. No bugger turned up. Got fed up waiting, decided I was being messed about, so called it a night. I was heading out when somebody jumped me. Hit me over the head with something big and heavy. Probably blacked out for a few minutes. Next thing I know I'm being dragged back into the office, and I can smell gas. Lots of fucking gas. We got a couple of heaters in there. Whoever it was had turned on the gas and was waiting for it to fill the room.' He suddenly stopped, as if he'd only just registered the significance of what he was describing. 'Jesus. I was on the floor, half conscious, trying to work out what the fuck was happening. Took me a few minutes, but then I looked up and saw this bastard standing near the door, waiting there with a box of fucking matches.'

It was clear that Lizzie had already heard McGrath's account, but the equanimity she'd displayed minutes earlier seemed to have deserted her. She was looking much more like the anguished Lizzie of the previous day.

'You don't knock me down easily,' McGrath went on. 'I thought, fuck this, and launched myself at him. Took him by surprise, but I was a bit too slow. Heard this *whoomph* behind me as he threw a lit match into the room, and then

I was on him. I could hear the papers on the desk catching fire. There was another Calor gas cylinder in there that would go up if the fire took hold. I wasn't thinking straight, and this bastard was fighting back as hard as I was. He caught me on the side of the face with something – not sure what – but then I was back on to him. I was battering him with my fists, trying to force him back into the room. Then he slipped and caught his head on the corner of the desk. Really nasty blow. There was another almighty bang – maybe the cylinder going up. I didn't stay to find out. Just legged it out, jumped in my car and got away as fast as I bloody could. I thought the whole place was going up.'

'So who was the body? The guy who jumped you?'

'I'm assuming so. If he was out cold, he wouldn't have had any chance. There was already enough smoke in there to catch my throat. Chances are he wouldn't have come round.'

'So who was he?'

'Christ knows. I didn't get to see his face. He jumped me from behind, and everything's a blur after that. But there was nothing that rang any bells.'

Marie made her way over to the window. Outside, she could see the mundane backstreet on which the apartment block was situated. Just a row of dull Edwardian terraces. Workman's cottages, they'd have been originally. Probably they'd been the same on this side of the road until someone had demolished them to build this modern edifice. The housing you'd find in any semi-industrial town or city across England. A mundane world, which she was sharing with someone who'd returned from the dead, armed with some half-arsed story that just might be true. She turned back into the room. 'So why didn't you go to the police, Andy? Let them know you'd not been fried to a crisp.'

'Not my favourite people,' he said. 'Present company maybe not even excepted.

I didn't know what the hell was going on. All kinds of thoughts were going through my head. Not least the coincidence that you'd started working for us the very fucking day this happens. I didn't go home. I went off to a – well, a girlfriend, let's say. Someone who'd give me an alibi for the night if needed it.'

'In case someone didn't believe your story about being jumped from behind. In case someone thought maybe you'd been the one doing the jumping. That you might have a reason for torching your own office.' She was conscious of the anger in her voice. She was getting tired of being jerked around.

'You know the way police minds work,' McGrath said. He paused and smiled. 'Yeah, you know exactly how their minds work. Just wanted to make sure I'd got the bases covered, in case it was needed.'

'And what about Lizzie? You didn't bother to let her know you hadn't been incinerated?' She remembered how distraught Lizzie had been after the fire. Surely that hadn't been just an act?

'Yeah, you're right. It was shitty of me. I wasn't thinking. Or maybe I was.' He glanced across at the younger woman. 'Poor Lizzie left me message after message trying to track me down. She said she was with you at the office. And – well, like I say, I didn't know who the fuck you were or what you were up to. I knew Lizzie was straight, but I thought maybe you were stringing her along somehow. So

I decided to lie low for a bit. Work out what was going on. Not that I got very far. In the end, I called Lizzie yesterday and asked about you.'

'Scared the bloody life out of me,' Lizzie said. 'Thought it was some sick bastard playing games.'

'Thing was,' McGrath said, 'once Lizzie calmed down, it was clear we'd both come to the same conclusion about you. That it was all a bit of a bloody coincidence that you'd turned up just when all this happened.

'Life and soul of the party, that's me,' Marie said. 'So you decided to find out who I was?'

'Yeah, exactly.' McGrath glanced across at Lizzie. 'Think you took us both my surprise, though. Undercover cop. Infiltrating my business. I almost feel honoured.'

'Just doing my job,' Marie said, unsmiling. 'Whatever you might think of it.'

McGrath shrugged. 'It's all a fucking game, isn't it? You lot have it harder than we do. You play by the rules, mostly. Real question is why you were bothered with a tinpot operation like mine. Must be bigger fish out there.'

'But maybe not bigger fish with links to Jeff Kerridge? Maybe you're selling yourself a bit short. I don't think you're as small-time as you'd like people to believe.'

McGrath laughed. 'I like people to underestimate me. I'm not the best money-man in the world – I leave all that to Lizzie these days – but I've done all right. It's like any other business. It's who you know. And I know the right people. Me and Jeff went way back. I was never one of his real inner circle – not like Pete Boyle, which is a laugh, seeing how that turned out. But I was close enough. He

255

put business my way, and I put a few opportunities in his direction.'

'What about his widow?' Marie asked. 'You close to her?'

McGrath gave another laugh. 'Not the way that sounds. Don't think anyone got close to Helen Kerridge in that way, other than Jeff. Not even sure that Jeff did, come to think of it. Not that often, anyway. But, yeah, after Jeff went, I kept up contact with Helen. Got a few opportunities out of it. She was even more ambitious than Jeff, but she was less paranoid. She was happy to work with me to build up business in this neck of the woods, without worrying that I was stealing it from under her nose. Jeff was a control freak. Always assumed the worst of everyone. Rightly, in Pete Boyle's case, but there you go.' For a moment, he looked almost wistful. 'Could have been good with Helen. She knew what she was doing, and with me and a few others she was starting to build an operation. Could have been running the whole fucking north west, given a year or two.'

'But she wasn't given a year or two,' Marie said. 'Someone took her out.'

'Not someone,' McGrath said. 'Pete fucking Boyle took her out. No fucking question.'

'And what about your office? Was that Boyle as well?'

McGrath frowned. 'Well, that's it, isn't it? I mean, it must be fucking Boyle. But it doesn't feel right. Boyle's been throwing his weight about for months. But it's been professional. Real pro hit jobs. Enough carnage to make his point, without getting to the point where the police felt obliged to do much about it. All targeted to scare the shit out of the likes of me. Working a treat, I should think. Even killing Helen Kerridge – well, it was tastefully done, if you get my

256

drift, and I don't think the police were going to lose much sleep over the Kerridge family.'

'But torching your office was different?'

'There've been one or two other arson attacks, but handled with more finesse. The guy who jumped me was a fucking clown. The whole thing was fucking amateurish. What sort of pillock ends up incinerated in his own fire? And the whole thing was over the top. Everyone knows I'm not the bravest fucking soldier. If someone warns me off, I stay warned off. Helen's death was enough for me. I was treading fucking warily. I didn't need anyone to come and set fire to me.'

'What about last night?' Marie asked. 'Was there really an intruder, or was that just a story to get me over here?'

'There was an intruder.' This time it was Lizzie who answered. She'd been sitting in silence, listening to Marie and McGrath, her face suggesting she had plenty of thoughts of her own. 'Andy stayed the night here, in the spare room. I wasn't sure that was wise, in case the police came looking, but, well,' she glanced across at McGrath and smiled, this time with genuine warmth, 'the old bugger was genuinely worried about me. And just as well he was, as it turns out. The story was a bit different from what I told you. I was woken by someone trying to get in the front door. Again, not exactly subtle. Someone with a bloody great crowbar. I woke Andy. He went into the hallway and banged like hell on the inside of the front door. Must have frightened the shit out of whoever was out there.'

McGrath shrugged apologetically. 'Didn't know what else to do, to be honest,' he said. 'I mean I couldn't exactly call the police, could I? And I wasn't going to open the door.

'Like I say, courage isn't my strongest point. But I was banking on it being another fuckwit. By the time I opened the door, he'd buggered off down the stairs. I went after him, but he'd legged it to a car waiting outside. I was happy to let it go at that.'

'And you were attacked as well?' Lizzie asked.

Marie nodded. 'Yesterday evening.' She briefly described what had happened. 'Jesus,' McGrath said. 'You're a tough one, aren't you?'

'You don't know what you're capable of till the adrenaline kicks in.'

'I know what I'd have done,' McGrath said. 'And it wouldn't have been that.'

Lizzie was watching them both, her expression increasingly impatient. 'Yeah. well. So you're fucking brave. But in the space of twenty-four hours, someone's had a go at each of us. Maybe Pete Boyle. Maybe someone else. Maybe half-arsed, but that doesn't mean they won't have another go and get luckier next time. And Andy's in the shit, anyway, because there was a cremated fucking body in his burnt out office and he's done a runner—'

'I've got an alibi,' McGrath said. 'I got all that sorted.'

Lizzie turned to McGrath, her face that of a despairing teacher faced with another feeble excuse for missing homework. 'Andy, you got an alibi from a girlfriend who's got convictions for shoplifting and benefit fraud. How long do you think it's going to take the police to pull that one apart?'

McGrath opened his mouth as if to speak. But he could clearly think of nothing worthwhile to say and, after a moment, he closed it again and shook his head.

Lizzie turned to Marie. 'What are your plans now? I

presume this means the end of your assignment.' She placed the lightest ironic emphasis on the final word.

'I'd say so, wouldn't you?' Marie agreed. 'My orders were to stay put for a day or two. My bosses were going to square things with the local police, but they didn't want me to disappear before that was sorted.' It was a précis of the truth, she thought, but close enough for the moment. 'But last night put an end to that as well, as far as I'm concerned. I don't want to stay up here and let someone have another shot at me.'

'So you're heading back to London?' Lizzie was looking thoughtful.

'As soon as I can bloody well manage it.'

Lizzie nodded, as if Marie had just confirmed some idea that had been gestating in her own mind. 'That's great,' she said. 'That's perfect. Because my dad says you're just the person he wants to talk to.'

21

'Inappropriate?' she said, finally. 'What was inappropriate, exactly?' She felt, for a moment, as if all the breath had been knocked from her. As if someone had physically kicked her in the stomach. She wasn't sure what she'd been expecting exactly, but it wasn't this.

Salter leaned back in his chair, his face giving nothing away. He's been reading one of those crap management books, she thought. Leadership secrets of Adolf Hitler. He allowed the silence to build for a few moments, the way he might have done when conducting an interrogation. That was what it felt like. As if he were trying to worm the guilt out of her.

At last, he sat forward, his face assuming an expression she presumed was supposed to look businesslike. 'Well,' he said, 'since you take the trouble to ask, pretty much every-thing.' The expression looked more smug than anything else, though she suspected that wasn't the look he was aiming for. But maybe she'd done him more of a favour than she knew.

There was no point in arguing with him just yet. He was going to have his say and she might as well let him have it. 'Everything,' she repeated, trying to inject some scepticism into the word.

'Let's start at the beginning, shall we? Disobeying a direct order to stay put. How's that for inappropriate?'

'Oh, for Christ's sake, Hugh. Someone broke into my house and tried to kill me. What was I supposed to do?'

'You were supposed to obey instructions. Or at least let me know what you were doing. Rather than just buggering off.'

That at least was a fair point, she conceded. She couldn't see what else she could have done, but she hadn't handled it well. She'd been pissed off with Salter for landing her in this mess, and she hadn't felt inclined to go chasing him up. 'I didn't just bugger off,' she pointed out. 'I tried to get hold of you. I left you a message telling you what I was going to do.'

'Which I received when it was too late for me to do anything about it.'

As if it was my fault you were avoiding my calls, she thought. Out loud, she said: 'Aren't you listening, Hugh? Someone broke into my house and tried to kill me. I was bloody lucky to get out alive. Should I have just sat there and waited for it to happen again?'

'You should have got in touch and asked for support,' Salter said. 'We'd have made sure you were safe. We should have followed up the attack. We might have found out something useful.'

'Like who tried to kill me?'

'Or why. Christ, it's all fucked up now. I had to come clean with the local cops about what you were doing up there. That created the mother of all shit-storms.'

'You'd have had to tell them anyway,' she said. 'It's a murder investigation now. They'd have wanted to know who the hell Maggie Yates was.'

'Maybe,' Salter conceded. 'Though they're much more interested in tracking down Andy McGrath. The guy in the office was some small-time punk who did bits of dirty business for all and sundry. Not the brightest bulb on the chandelier, apparently, and quite capable of setting himself on fire. But McGrath's gone to ground, so they want to talk to him.'

She could feel him watching her intently as he spoke. Not for the first time, she had the uneasy sense that Salter knew what she was thinking. She'd last seen McGrath the previous morning in Lizzie's kitchen. She'd tried to persuade him to go to the police himself. McGrath had pointed out that the police were never going to cut any slack for the likes of him. 'Even if they can't pin the arson or the killing on me, they'll find some reason to bang me up. My inclination's to make myself scarce, maybe start over somewhere else. If I don't make it too easy for them, they won't worry themselves too much over me or the bastard who tried to kill me.' She'd said nothing, though he might well be right. Small war between two lowlifes. One dead. Who was going to care?

'Not sure I see McGrath as a killer,' she said. 'But then I can hardly claim to have got to know him.'

'One of our shorter undercover assignments,' he said, in a tone that implied the fault was hers. 'Still, the way things were going, it's probably as well you got out before you did any more damage.'

'What's this about, Hugh? I was expecting sympathy and support, not a bloody dressing down.'

'That right?' Salter was flicking through a sheaf of papers in front of him. From her side of the desk, she couldn't make out any of the content. 'We've already talked about disobeying a direct instruction. Coming out of the field without permission. Do you know how serious it is to disregard procedure like that?'

'For God's sake, Hugh, it didn't make any difference. You'd have had to recall me anyway.'

'Then there's Jack Brennan,' Salter went on, as if he hadn't heard her.

'Jack Brennan? What's he got to do with anything?'

'That's what I was going to ask you. You seem to have spent a fair bit of time in his company.'

She opened her mouth to respond, but then stopped. As always with Salter, the question was how much he knew. 'You put Brennan in contact with me,' she said. 'If you remember, I wasn't all that keen to meet him.'

'You were keen enough to meet him again.'

So that answered that question, she thought. Partly, at least. Salter knew she'd been in contact with Brennan after that first, officially sanctioned meeting. 'He wanted my input,' she said, conscious how feeble her explanation sounded.

'You said it yourself, Marie.' The use of her name was always a bad sign. 'If you're undercover, you can't come in and out of role when you feel like it. It's not just that you risk compromising yourself. You put the whole bloody assignment at risk.'

She could feel her anger stirring. 'What bloody assignment, Hugh? I still don't even know what I was doing working in that cowboy outfit. What was McGrath involved in that's of interest to us?' Even as she spoke, she felt she was saying too much. The only way to play Salter was to let him make all the running. Say nothing that will give him more ammunition.

'It was your job to find that out, Marie, wasn't it? Now maybe we'll never know.' He spoke as if it had been her fault that McGrath's office had been torched, as if she'd somehow been responsible for terminating the assignment. Which, of course, technically she had, since she'd aborted the mission before Salter had formally issued the order. She could see the way his mind was working.

She took a deep breath and made the effort to contain her annoyance. There was no point in expecting Salter to be reasonable. Salter's way was to twist and turn everything till it shone the best light on Hugh Salter. 'We're going round in circles. Okay, so maybe I should have made more of an effort to get hold of you before I came back. I'm sorry. But it's changed nothing—'

'Jack Brennan,' Salter said. 'Your relationship with Jack Brennan.'

She opened her mouth but, for a moment, nothing came out. Relationship? What the hell was this all about? 'What are you talking about, Hugh? I barely know Jack Brennan.'

Salter was flicking slowly through the papers on the desk as if he'd forgotten he was in the middle of a conversation. After a few seconds he stopped and stared at one of the sheets. 'And yet,' he said, without looking up, 'you spent the night at his flat.' He looked up and met her eyes. 'Do you often do that with men you barely know?'

She stared back at him, her mind taking too long to come to grips with what he'd said. 'What the fuck is this,

Hugh? Am I under surveillance? Can't be the best use of your resources.'

The faint, almost imperceptible smile was back. Like catching an occasional glimpse of a basking shark beneath still waters. 'Not you under surveillance, sis. Jack Brennan.'

'Brennan? I thought he was one of yours.'

The smile became more definite. She could almost see the shark's teeth. 'Not one of mine, sis,' he said, as if with regret. 'Never one of mine. Tell you the truth, I'm not sure what to make of Mr Jack Brennan. I was hoping you might be able to enlighten me.'

She hesitated for a second, trying to work out where Salter was taking this. 'Let's get this straight. Like I say, I barely know Jack Brennan. In any sense. I went to his flat because, as I keep reminding you, someone broke into my house and tried to kill me. It was late at night. I was probably in a state of shock. I didn't know what to do or where to go. So I went to Brennan's. And maybe that wasn't the smartest thing to do, but I'm not quite sure what the alternatives were. I was in no state to drive back down here.' She paused, conscious again that she was saying too much. She could feel Salter's blank eyes staring at her from behind his steel-rimmed spectacles and, as so often with him, she felt he was peering into her head. 'Anyway, that's what I did. And Brennan was very helpful. He calmed me down and gave me somewhere to stay. And, not that it's any of your business, that somewhere was his spare room. Okay?'

The smile was still there, unconnected to any warmth of feeling. 'If you say so, sis. Like you say, none of my business.'

His tone implied that it was she who'd dragged the conversation into over-intimate territory. 'I'm just interested in Jack Brennan and what he's up to.'

'And what do you think he's up to, Hugh?'

'You know he joined us with something of a tarnished reputation?'

'I think everyone's aware of that. More sinned against than sinning was my impression.'

Salter shrugged. 'Depends who you talk to. That's the way that Brennan tells it. Just doing his honest job. No choice but to blow the whistle. All that crap. Not, of course, the way that former Chief Superintendent Craddock tells the tale. You pays your money and you takes your choice.'

'But Craddock was bent.'

'Not as clean as the proverbial whistle,' Salter agreed. 'But you could say that of a lot of people.' Salter paused, as if mentally compiling a list of individuals who might fall into this category. 'Maybe even Brennan himself.'

'A bent whistleblower?'

'People do things for all kinds of reasons, sis. You must have realised that by now.' His tone had changed. He was coaxing, gently inveigling her into some kind of complicity with him. 'There's more to Brennan than meets the eye. I brought him over in good faith. Always happy to give someone a second chance. Brennan had a good reputation as a detective. He knows the lay of the land up in that neck of the woods.' Salter spoke as though the north west were some kind of uncharted territory. 'I thought he might be just what we needed to pin down Pete Boyle and his cronies.'

Like hell you did, she thought. You thought that a copper

with Brennan's reputation would be just what was needed to destroy any lingering credibility the case retained in the eyes of the CPS. 'And you're saying that he wasn't?'

'I made him Evidence Officer for the case,' Salter went on. 'I wanted someone who would properly coordinate all the material we had. Assess its strengths and weaknesses. Work out where the gaps were, and advise on what was needed to fill the gaps.'

'And he's not done that?'

'Up to a point. He's spent a lot of time researching the background.' Salter gave the last word a heavy overtone of irony, as if the notion of background research was absurd in the context of detective work. 'One reason why he was so keen to meet you. But not much seems to have emerged from all this. In fact, quite the opposite.' He stopped and again flicked slowly through the pile of papers. She couldn't work out whether the papers were genuinely pertinent to their discussion, or whether this was simply another of Salter's theatrics. 'He seems to have rejected most of the evidence as irrelevant or unhelpful, leaving us with more gaps than substance.' He pulled two sheets of paper out from the larger pile and spent a few seconds carefully arranging them side by side on the desk in front of him. 'More worryingly, there seem to be signs that evidence has actually been destroyed or amended. And that the records have been changed in an attempt to conceal the fact.' He best forward to study the two sheets for a moment, and then picked them up and slid them back into the remaining papers. Theatrics, she decided. Nothing but bloody theatrics.

'You're saying that Brennan has destroyed evidence?'

'That's what we want to know, sis. You know how these things are. It's so easy for things to be misunderstood or misinterpreted. Maybe Brennan's been trying to do an honest job to the best of his abilities. Maybe he wasn't up to it. I think we sometimes underestimate how difficult our job can be compared with traditional policing.'

She could feel her rage bubbling up again. It was easy to imagine Salter deploying this 'more in sorrow than in anger' voice at some future disciplinary hearing while he gently skewered Brennan's career. It was clear now where this was heading. And it was equally clear how Salter had typically muddied the waters.

She could believe that Brennan had been assiduous at rejecting any supposed evidence against Boyle that he'd felt to be unconvincing or unhelpful. He thought that Salter was setting him up to fail, and he wouldn't have wanted to present anything to the CPS that was less than watertight. She could imagine that Salter himself would have been happy to include material that would fall at the first hurdle.

The second part of the accusation was much more serious. If Brennan had been destroying or amending evidence, that would imply he was corrupt. That would imply that he was on Boyle's payroll. She didn't believe it for a moment. But others might be only too pleased to do so. Brennan had made enough enemies who'd use any weapon against him. This would play right into their hands.

'You can't believe that, Hugh,' she said. 'You can't seriously think that Brennan's been destroying evidence.'

Salter leaned back in his chair and looked at her appraisingly. 'Look. sis, I know we don't always see eye-to-eye. I know you don't think much of me. Which is a pity, as it happens, because I've rather a high regard for you. And you don't trust me all that much. Which is fair enough, I guess. I've never denied being ambitious. And I've never hidden the fact that I prefer to look out for number one—'

'Is this going somewhere, Hugh?' This was Salter shifting gear yet again, into the 'cards on the table' mode he used mostly when just about to pull the wool over your eyes. He was bloody good at it, she knew. What better way to get someone to trust you than by acknowledging that they didn't?

He sighed. 'All I'm trying to say, sis, is that, though you probably don't think so, I've got your best interests at heart. I don't know or care what kind of relationship you might have had with Brennan—'

'I've told you, Hugh—'

He held up his hand. 'None of my business, sis. But you need to know that Jack Brennan's bad news. I can understand why you feel a need to protect him, but I'm telling you it's not a good idea. Not for you. Not for me. The powers-that-be are taking a long hard look at him. He's already been suspended, and the expectation is that he'll be disciplined. Or worse.'

It took a moment for this to sink in. 'Suspended? When?'

'Yesterday. Not so long after he said his fond farewells to you, I should imagine. When he got into the office, he was called in by the Chief up there and given the news. Sent home on full pay while the investigation's carried out.'

She sat for a moment in silence, trying to come to grips with this news. She felt, unreasonably, that someone should have told her before now. But why would they? Brennan was nothing to her, other than the focus of whatever salacious rumours their surveillance efforts had prompted. Perhaps she was disappointed that Brennan himself hadn't called her. But he wouldn't have wanted to risk implicating her in whatever he was being accused of.

'The long and short of it, sis, is that you'd do well to steer clear of him. The investigation will take a few weeks, I imagine. Professional Standards are starting to look at the material.' He shrugged. 'A lot of it may be circumstantial. He can probably come up with a good story as to why he disregarded evidence, but the tampering will be harder to explain. My bet is that, at the very least, Brennan's on his way out. But of course, if he was destroying evidence, the real question is why.'

She felt treacherous for not protesting Brennan's innocence. But there was no point. She wasn't going to persuade Salter, for Christ's sake, and all she'd do was reinforce the impression that she was close to Brennan. 'So what's this got to do with me, Hugh?' she asked, determined that he should spell it out.

'You're on thin ice, sis. Like I say, you've disobeyed orders. You've broken cover without authorisation. You got rather closer than was wise to Brennan. However innocently. The people upstairs have their eyes on you.'

That was one of the many things she despised about Salter. The way he always shifted responsibility onto some unnamed authority. If senior management really did have their eyes on her, it would be because he'd made damn sure she was in their sights. 'I've done nothing, Hugh. You know that.'

'And for the moment,' he said, his voice oozing

magnanimity, 'I'm accepting that and taking no action. I'm just warning you that Professional Standards are watching. They know you were in contact with Brennan. They know you spent the night at his flat. They probably know every step you've taken since then.' He sat back, the cold smile once again spread across his face. An insincere TV quiz host who'd just given away the star prize.

She felt the cold finger on her spine again. Every step she'd taken since then. Which would include her meeting with Lizzie and McGrath. If they'd had Brennan's flat under surveillance, it was possible they'd followed her when she left. But if that were the case, why was no one asking her about her movements? She supposed that there was nothing intrinsically suspicious about her visiting Lizzie – the two women had been through a traumatic night together, after all. There was no reason for anyone to know that McGrath was there. Unless they'd subsequently seen him leave . . .

Stop it, she thought. This is exactly what Salter wants. He's a master at putting you on the back foot. Saying enough to sow a seed of doubt and then letting you squirm until you inadvertently tell him what he wants to know.

'I've got nothing to hide,' she said, as calmly as she could manage.

'Never thought for a minute you had, sis. But you know those bastards in Professional Standards. If they decide you're worth looking at, they'll trawl through every last detail of your private life. Anything that's going on at home. Anyone you might once have had a relationship with . . .' Again, he stopped and left the words hanging in the air.

She felt another momentary chill, but knew he was just throwing out bait in the hope of getting her to bite. He might have suspicions about her past relationship with the informant, Jake Morton. But there was no way that he could know for sure that she'd allowed herself to be compromised. That bit of dirty linen had been safely packed away with Morton's murder. All Salter was doing was stirring the shit, and hoping that something juicy would float to the surface.

'Are we done, Hugh?' she said. 'Like I say, I've nothing to hide. If Standards want to talk to me, officially or otherwise, that's fine by me.' She made a move to rise from her chair, conscious now that she was keen to escape Salter's presence.

'Okay, sis,' he said. 'Look, I'm not a monster. I'm taking a hard line on this for your own good. There are people upstairs who wanted me to do more than rap your knuckles, and I can't promise they won't still want to pursue this. At the very least, you can expect that Professional Standards will want to interview you about Brennan. I'm sure you've got nothing to hide, but you'd do us both a favour if you kept a low profile. I'll make sure Standards don't do anything stupid.'

You're all heart, Hugh, she thought to herself. 'Thanks, Hugh. I know you're just doing your job.' Jesus, no wonder she was good at this work, if she could lie through her teeth like that.

'Good girl. Look, you've had a tough time over the last few days. And I know things are tough at home, too. Why not take the rest of the day off? Tomorrow we can get out heads together and decide what we do with you next. I'm afraid it'll be more backroom stuff for a while, but we can sort something out.'

In other circumstances, the 'good girl' might have been

the last straw. Today, she knew it was wiser to cut her losses. 'That's kind of you, Hugh. I'll be in bright and early tomorrow,' she said. 'Can't wait to get back to those old files.'

'That's my girl,' Salter said, beaming across the desk.

She took a deep breath and swallowed any response she might have been tempted to offer. She turned to leave the room, being careful not to look back.

Not in a million years, Hugh Salter, she thought. Not your girl in a million fucking years.

22

'Christ. How long's he been like this?'

'It's been up and down. Some days better than others. But he's not been the same since he came out of hospital.'

Marie realised she'd been staring at Liam. He didn't seem to mind. He didn't even seem to notice, just at the moment. But that just made it worse. She tore her gaze away and looked over at Sue. 'He seems a hell of a lot worse even than when I left.'

She was half-expecting Sue to respond with some acid jibe, but the carer seemed to have moved beyond that. Beneath her professional exterior, she seemed as distressed as Marie herself. 'It's hard to tell,' Sue said. 'Like I say, there've been good days and bad days. Today's probably the worst he's been.'

She's fooling herself, Marie thought. Or maybe it's because when the decline happens in front of you, even in a matter of days, it's less obvious than if you haven't witnessed the progression. 'He wasn't like this when I left. Not as bad as this.'

Sue said nothing. Marie looked back to where Liam was sitting, slumped awkwardly in one of the armchairs. He'd looked up once when she'd first entered the room, and she'd been buoyed by the warmth of his smile. He'd looked as if he was genuinely pleased – relieved, even – to see her. He'd croaked out her name; 'Marie. Hi, love.'

But almost immediately she knew that something was wrong. More wrong than when she'd left. He'd stared at her for a long moment, the broad smile fixed on his face. But the light had faded from his eyes. He'd been staring blankly at her, almost through her, as if he'd already forgotten she was there.

'How are you feeling, Liam?' She'd lowered herself on to the chair next to him, taking his hand gently in hers. His posture seemed worse than before, too. Previously he'd sat upright in the chair, whereas now he was leaning to one side. He didn't look as if he'd be capable of dragging himself upright as he had before.

He looked across at her, and she detected a faint note of surprise in his eyes. It took him a second to focus. 'I'm— you know, not too bad. Mustn't grumble.' For a second, there were traces of the old humour in his voice. But it felt like someone responding by rote. Saying the things you were supposed to say in a conversation. Not Liam at all.

'I'm back now, Liam,' she said. 'I won't be going away again for a while.' She could feel Sue watching them from across the room.

Liam was looking ahead again now, his gaze unfocused. 'That's good,' he said. 'That's very good.'

The conversation had continued on the same lines. Marie offering breezy platitudes, Liam giving little, if any, response. Finally, she rose and stepped across the room to where Sue was standing.

'What did the doctor say?'

'What do they ever say? Not much. Seemed to think it was what we should expect.'

'But this isn't Liam. Maybe it's a psychological thing. It's as if he's retreated into himself. Switched off from the world. I mean, it would be understandable enough –'

Sue was shaking her head. 'They did tests while he was in hospital. Had one of the clinical psychologists visit him. They seemed pretty sure that this is – well, just the result of the illness. Just the next step.'

Marie opened her mouth to protest, but she knew she was clutching at straws. She couldn't deny what Sue was saying. Whatever was wrong with Liam, it wasn't simply a psychological problem. She'd been warned that this was the direction in which he was heading. She just hadn't expected to be heading there so quickly.

'But everything I've read about MS,' she continued, knowing that now she was really speaking only to help order her own thoughts. 'It never mentions this kind of development. They talk about minor mental impairment – forgetting words, that sort of stuff – but they don't talk about this.' She knew she was merely rehearsing the same discussion she'd had with Liam himself, weeks before. He must have known then that something was wrong. Seriously wrong. He must have realised that his mental capacities were slipping away, already begun to feel the fog closing in. Shit. What must it have been like for him?

And he'd not told her. He'd dropped hints but she'd been too slow or stupid to pick them up. But he hadn't come out and told her exactly what he feared, what he thought was happening. She'd left him here to face it on his own.

The only consolation was that at least now he seemed calm enough. There was no sense of distress or fear.

'They reckon it's the short-term memory that's affected most,' Sue said. 'You can ask him something and he'll respond. But five minutes later he's forgotten about it. You don't realise at first. He's become quite skilled at covering it up. Always gives you the right kind of polite response.'

Marie wondered how long that had been going on, too. With hindsight, she could recall incidents where he seemed to have forgotten something obvious. But he'd made light of it. Said he'd always been scatterbrained. It was strange how she'd failed to spot what was happening. Perhaps she hadn't wanted to see it.

'Christ,' Marie said, finally. 'This is really it, isn't it? This is where it gets serious.'

She realised now that Sue had known all along how much Liam's condition had deteriorated. Perhaps she hadn't wanted Marie to come rushing back. Or, more charitably, perhaps Sue had been shielding her from the real gravity of the developments.

'I've spoken to the social worker,' Sue said. 'She's going to do an assessment. See whether she can get some more support. It won't be easy. They're cutting back everywhere. But Liam must be a deserving case.' She paused, as if unsure how to articulate her next thought. 'I shouldn't say this, but in a way he's getting easier to care for. I worried that he was pushing himself too hard, trying to prove he could still do the things he used to. I used to get worried that if I left him by himself, he'd have an accident . . .' She stopped again, shaking her head. 'I'm sorry. You know all this. It must be awful. I mean, I've grown fond of Liam. He's a lovely man. But for me it's just a job. At the end of the day, I can walk away, pour myself a glass of wine, forget about it till morning. You can't do that. He's your partner. You have to watch this happening. Shit—'

Sue had turned away, and Marie realised that the other woman was crying. It occurred to Marie for the first time that she'd misjudged Sue. She was only doing her job – rather more than her job, in fact. Marie had been projecting on to her all her own guilt and self-criticism. 'I've been hiding from it,' Marie said, articulating her thoughts out loud. 'I wanted to pretend it wasn't happening. That I could just continue like before. That everything would still be all right. But it's not going to be, is it?'

Sue was wiping her eyes, looking awkward, as if she'd allowed her guard to slip more than she'd intended. 'Is that why you've come home?'

For a moment, Marie was tempted to lie. Instead, she shook her head. 'No, not really. Just a work thing. But I'd have been back, anyway. Now that I've seen how he is.'

Sue nodded, her face expressionless. She was a good looking woman, Marie thought, but even in other circumstances she wouldn't have ever been Liam's type. Liam would never have fallen for the kind of woman who would want to take care of him. Instead, he'd fallen for a woman like Marie.

'I don't know what to say to you,' Sue said, finally. 'I mean, there's nothing you can say, is there? Not when things are like this.' She walked over to where Liam was sitting. His upper body had gradually been slipping sideways and he was twisted awkwardly in the chair. She took his hand and eased him back upright. For a moment, his eyes remained unfocused, then he blinked and glanced up at her. 'Thanks,' he whispered, frowning. 'Thanks. Sue.'

His mind wasn't entirely gone, then, Marie thought, and then felt guilty that she was already thinking that way. But that was how it was. It was happening. It was real. The Liam she loved was already slipping away from her.

'I was going to get Liam some soup,' Sue said. 'He seems to find that easier to eat. Shall I get some for you?'

'No, I'm fine. It's not your job to look after me. Just do the best you can for Liam.'

As Sue disappeared into the kitchen, Marie took Liam's hand. He looked up at her and smiled. Just in that moment – in the shape of his lips, the expression in his eyes – she caught a glimpse of how he once had been. 'Marie,' he said. 'You're back.'

She smiled, struggling hard to keep her eyes from watering. 'Yes, Liam,' she said. 'I'm back.'

It was only later, after she and Sue had helped Liam into bed, that she noticed the text message.

While Marie had been away, Sue had made some changes in Liam's living arrangements. When he'd returned from hospital, it had become obvious that he would be unable to climb the stairs even with the carers' help. Fortunately, one of the two sofas in their living room was convertible into a sofa bed – they'd used it to accommodate occasional visitors before Liam had moved his studio downstairs. Sue had dragged that into the dining room and moved Liam's painting gear into a corner. It was hardly an elegant solution, but it at least meant the carers been able to help Liam into bed each night.

'He needs a proper bed,' Sue said. 'One of those electric gizmos that go up and down, so we can get him in and out easily and make sure he's comfortable. I've asked social services to look into it, though God knows how long it'll take.'

Liam had looked comfortable enough, though, and he was asleep almost immediately. He'd been getting increasingly tired, Sue told her, frequently nodding off as he sat in the chair during the day. She'd rearranged the visit times slightly so that the carers could get him to bed as soon as he'd eaten in the evening.

Jesus, Marie thought, after they'd finished and Sue had departed for her next call, was this what it was going to be like? She still felt slightly in shock. It was difficult to come to grips with the speed with which all this had happened. When Liam had first been diagnosed, she hadn't known what to expect and the supposed experts had hardly been able to enlighten her. It was the great unknown, the neurologist had told her. Things might remain unchanged for years, or there might be sudden declines. The general direction was downwards, but the speed was unknown.

Even so, she'd been assuming it would take years. But this was – what? Hardly two. And suddenly she was having to deal with something beyond her imaginings.

She made her way into the kitchen, deciding that this was probably an appropriate time to crack open a bottle of wine. As pulled out a bottle and fumbled in the drawer for a corkscrew, she pulled out her phone to check messages.

There were no messages, but there was a text. It was short and cryptic. An unfamiliar mobile number and the brief message: 'Call. Use another phone.' She stared at the message for a minute, as if she somehow expected it to yield some more detail. Then she finished opening the bottle and picked up Liam's phone from where it had been left charging – for who knew how long – on the kitchen work-surface.

Would Liam's phone be safe? Probably. It was just a pay-as-you-go device he'd picked up after he'd mislaid a more expensive model – the loss probably another example, she realised now, of the way his memory had been declining.

The call was answered almost immediately, but there was silence at the end of the line.

'Hello,' she said. 'Who is this?'

'Marie? Jesus, thanks for calling. I need a friendly voice.' Jack Brennan. 'I'm in the shit, Marie. Deep, deep in the shit. Not sure how I'm going to extricate myself.'

'Salter told me you'd been suspended. I should have called,' she said. 'But I thought it might make things worse.' That was at least half true. She'd contemplated calling Brennan on leaving Salter's office, but had concluded it wouldn't help either of them if she appeared to be confirming Salter's suspicions about their relationship. Or had it just been cowardice? Either way, the idea had melted from her mind as soon as she'd been faced with the reality of Liam's condition.

'You were better not to,' Brennan said. 'Turns out they've had me under surveillance for a while. I've not managed to spot anyone yet, but I suspect I still am. And I think there's an intercept device on my landline and mobile. I'm using a pay-and-go thing I borrowed off a mate. Hope you're not using your own.'

'No, I'm using – someone else's. Should be safe enough.' She couldn't bring herself to mention Liam's name to

Brennan. Not because she wanted to conceal anything, but because she couldn't face whatever questions might follow. 'Look, Jack, it can't be all that bad. Okay, there'll be an enquiry. But you've done nothing wrong.'

'Not sure it's that simple. I've got history. There are plenty of people out there gunning for me. All they need is ammunition. And Salter will make sure they get it.'

'But he's got nothing,' Marie said. 'And he's taking a big risk if he makes all this too public. He's not going to want to put himself in the spotlight.'

'He's smart, Marie. And I've not been as smart as I thought I was. Shit . . .'

'What's the story, Jack?' She was beginning to realise that there was more to this than Brennan had been letting on.

'I've underestimated Salter,' Brennan said. 'I can't believe I've been so dumb. I mean, when he took me on, I was suspicious. Salter's got himself a reputation out there.'

'As bent, you mean?' It was a long while since she'd had contact with the wider policing world. Once or twice, her old friends in the Force had told her obliquely to watch herself in dealing with Salter. But she'd never needed reminding of that.

'Not exactly,' Brennan said. 'Or not necessarily, anyway. People have mixed feelings about him. Some people think he's a hero for exposing Keith Welsby. Some people think he's a bastard for the same reason.'

'People have mixed feelings about you, too, Jack,' she reminded him.

'Yeah, but with me people think it was personal,' Brennan said. 'Nobody thinks that about Salter. Whatever they think about the Welsby case, they're all in agreement that Salter's a ruthless, cold-hearted shit.'

'Not bad judges of character, then.'

'Well, you should know. Everyone thinks that Salter has one priority in life and that's Hugh fucking Salter. He'll do whatever it takes to protect his own backside and screw everyone else over.'

'Sounds right. So what made you agree to work for him?' It was the same question that might be asked of her, she thought.

'I didn't have many options,' Brennan said. 'They couldn't pension me off, and no one knew what else to do with me. I'd probably have ended up being shunted into some admin role or even back into uniform. When Salter's offer turned up, it was a lifeline – not just for me but for everyone trying to decide what to do with me.'

That was interesting, Marie thought. Salter had told her that he'd been asked to take Brennan. Brennan was saying that Salter had come actively looking for him. 'But?' She could sense a qualification in Salter's tone.

'So I didn't have a lot of choice. And I was suspicious of what Salter was up to. Why come looking for me, for Christ's sake?' He paused. 'But I wasn't entirely sorry the offer had been made. I'd been following the Welsby case quite closely.'

'Because it paralleled your own?'

'I suppose. Like I said to you, the ironies weren't lost on me. Salter had blown the whistle on a corrupt cop, just like I'd done. Salter was a hero. I was a pariah. So, yes, I followed the story in the newspapers. Did a bit of asking around. Mostly just idle curiosity.'

'"Mostly"?'

'Well, I was intrigued. Don't get me wrong. I wasn't exactly burning with indignation at Salter's treatment. I could see there were differences. I knew he'd risked his life in dealing with Welsby and Kerridge—'

'He risked *my* life, more to the point,' Marie interjected. 'Though, in fairness, he probably saved it as well. So why the interest in Salter?'

'At first, as I say, just curiosity. Fellow feeling, maybe. Someone who'd been through what I'd been through but come out in a better place. But the more I asked, the more interesting the story became.'

'Go on.'

'Salter polarises opinion. Everyone agrees he's a total bastard. Some people think he's an honest total bastard, and others think he's a corrupt one. But the more I talked to people, the more the name of Pete Boyle cropped up. It surprised me at first. It didn't fit with the way we saw things in Manchester. Even after he got out of prison, we thought Boyle was a lame duck. He was shooting his mouth off about getting back in control, taking over Kerridge's territory, but we couldn't see it happening.'

'Why not? Boyle had been Kerridge's number two. Till they fell out, anyway.'

'And they fell out because Kerridge was looking for a scapegoat to take the heat off him. He shafted Boyle because he and Welsby knew that if the authorities got the scalp of one local bigwig, they'd probably lose interest in chasing up any more. For a while, anyway.'

'That wasn't how we saw it,' Marie protested. 'Everyone was talking about Boyle as the first step to prising open Kerridge's organisation.'

'I'm sure they were. I'm sure that's how Welsby positioned it. But you know how these things are. What the Chief Constable's looking for is a good news story he can sell to the local media, *How we snared local crime lord*. The thing about Boyle was that, in truth, he wasn't much more than Kerridge's muscle. A tough guy, but not much up top. Kerridge kept him as part of his inner circle, even designated him as his deputy, because he knew that Boyle wasn't much of a threat. I suspect that Kerridge kept him well away from the serious stuff, and Boyle hadn't the brains to realise it. If Boyle had gone down, he'd have shot his mouth off all over the place, but he probably wouldn't have taken anyone down with him, except a few other small-fry. Kerridge would've made sure of that.'

Marie took a few moments to digest this. She'd assumed that Boyle had a higher status than Brennan was suggesting, but then they'd all been indoctrinated in Keith Welsby's skewed view of the world. 'So why would Salter have thrown his lot in with Boyle – if that's what he's done. Salter's a lot of things, but he's not dumb.'

'They don't come much smarter. That's what intrigued me. I thought it might be interesting to find out more about Salter and Boyle.'

'So this is a great personal crusade, is it?' she asked. 'What were you hoping? That you could expose Salter and resurrect your own reputation?'

'Hardly. I may not have Salter's intellect, but I'm not stupid enough to think that I'd be thanked for exposing yet another popular hero. No, like I say, mainly curiosity.' He allowed himself a small laugh. 'When I was a kid, I was the one who went poking about under stones, just to see what might crawl out.'

'And what crawls out has a tendency to bite you. So that was why you were pumping me about Boyle when we first met?'

'I suppose,' he said. 'I'd got the impression from everyone I'd spoken to that you were seen as pretty straight—'

'Well, gee, thanks,' she said. 'I should treat that as a compliment.'

'It's intended to be one,' he said. 'You've a good reputation out there. And you were much more straight with me than I expected.'

'That just shows how dumb I am,' she said. 'Pity you weren't as straight with me.'

'I haven't kept any great secrets back from you. And – to be honest – I wasn't sure how far I could trust even you. You were very open with me when we met. But that might have been another of Salter's games. You acting indiscreet to get me to shoot my mouth off.'

Marie recalled that she'd had similar fears about Brennan. Jesus, this was how it was dealing with Salter. He generated an air of mistrust wherever he went. Everyone was so busy suspecting everyone else that Salter could sail serenely through the middle of it. 'So what have you been holding back?'

'I started snooping around right from the start. That was why I wanted to meet you, to see if I could identify some leads, some way of digging whatever dirt there was on Salter.'

'I wasn't much help in that regard.'

'Salter covers his tracks very well. Part of this was about covering my own backside. I didn't know why Salter had invited me on to his team. He gave me a lot of guff about being a good detective, putting the past behind me, all that crap. But I never really bought it. I thought he was setting me up to fail. There I was, reputation already half in tatters, trying to build an evidential case against Boyle. Half the evidence in the files was as thin as cheap bog paper. Much of the other half looked dodgy. Some of it potentially concocted stuff that would dissolve under the scrutiny of a half-decent defence council. I thought the idea was that I'd do my best to pull this stuff together, submit it to the CPS, and they'd laugh in my face. Salter would shift the blame on to me, and the case against Boyle would be quietly dropped. If that's what he wanted, I was the perfect fall guy.'

'Salter told me you'd been sifting through the evidence. Discarding stuff.'

'That was just me trying to do my job properly. Weed out the crap and see what we had left. Which wasn't much. But while I was doing that, I was trying to find out whatever I could about Salter. Trying to get some purchase on him. I was digging into the Agency's computer files, pulling up anything there was.' There was a pause. 'That's where it gets tricky. I went further than I should have. Persuaded someone in HQ to help me, and I got hold of a couple of passwords. Got access to some more confidential files—'

'Jesus, Jack. Not a smart thing to do, no matter how good your intentions. Apart from anything else, the way I understand, you leave your fingerprints all over the system whenever you look at anything.'

'I was hoping to leave someone else's fingerprints,' Brennan said. 'But I'm no expert. Anyway, Salter sussed that I was dabbling in areas I shouldn't have been.'

'Have you been told that? I mean, is it part of the case against you?'

'It's worse than that,' he said. 'After a while, Salter must have worked out what I was doing and when. From what's been said to me, it looks as if he must have entered the system shortly after I did each time, used the same access route and made changes to the files I'd looked at. Deleting and amending stuff. Important stuff about Boyle.'

'But that's crazy. The systems are designed to be secure. And our forensic IT people must be able to tell what was changed and when. They can probably show that the changes were made from a different workstation from the one you used. It wouldn't achieve anything.'

'It's about throwing suspicion in my direction. Salter would know there was no point in making those sorts of changes, but I wouldn't necessarily. I'm new to the Agency. I've not worked with the IT experts. That's obvious from the fact that I was stupid enough to access the material in the first place. I didn't use my own workstation, but I had to use one in the Manchester office. It doesn't take Sherlock Holmes to make the link. And I don't know how or where Salter made whatever changes he made. Maybe he did it while he was up here. In any case, they think they've got enough of a case to bring a misconduct hearing. And they've said it might go further than that.'

'Shit. But, even so, most of that's circumstantial. They can't prove it was you that made the changes.'

'They don't need to. Not for the misconduct hearing, anyway. They just need to satisfy themselves that I'm guilty on the balance of probabilities. This would be construed as gross misconduct. Which means that dismissal's the most likely outcome, even if they decide not to take it further.'

'But, Jesus, why would he go this far?'

'Because he's a ruthless bastard, Marie. He can feel me sniffing too closely to whatever relationship he's got with Boyle. So he ratchets his plan up a notch. Not just position me as the scapegoat who carries the can when the case fails, but actually paint me as a bent cop out to screw the case against Boyle. The case against Boyle won't just be dropped, it'll be buried so deep that it'll take another decade to uncover it. And any suspicion that might have fallen on to Salter's nearly deflected on to me. Like I say, deep, deep in the shit.'

'I don't know what to say, Jack. If there's anything I can do . . .'

'I think you're better off keeping your distance. I bet Salter's already warned you off, hasn't he?'

Her silence answered his question. She knew that it was sensible advice – maybe the only possible advice – but it still made her feel disloyal.

'It's better for both of us just now,' he said, as if trying to persuade himself as well as her. 'There's no point in tarnishing your career by association with mine. Apart from anything else, you're more likely to be able to do something about Salter if your reputation's not sullied.'

It was a fair point, but she could feel despair beginning to overwhelm her. 'Christ, I don't know what I can do, Jack. I've had this half-baked idea of trying to expose Salter since all the stuff with Kerridge and Welsby, but I've got nowhere. I don't even know where to start. I keep hoping that some opportunity's going to pop up, but Salter's too smart for that. And when I do find someone who seems like he might be an ally – I mean, Christ, see what he's done to you –' She could feel the emotion rising in her voice. She stopped and took a breath, trying to calm herself.

'He's a smart bugger,' Brennan said, calmly. 'Maybe smarter than me. But maybe not smart enough.'

'What are you saying, Jack?'

'I'm saying I've got some stuff. On Salter. Not enough. Not yet. But maybe enough to put the wind up him.'

The full wine glass had been sitting untouched on the kitchen surface in front of her. She picked it up and took a large swallow. 'What kind of stuff, Jack?'

'If you go through the files over the years, it's interesting how often evidence just seems to fall into Salter's lap. As long as it's a case involving one of Boyle's rivals. And it's interesting how little substance there is in any of the evidence against Boyle.'

'With respect, Jack, that's not going to get you very far. It might confirm your suspicions and mine, but it's not going to cut much ice with a misconduct panel.'

'But that was just the start. I went out and called in some favours from mates in the Force up here – I've still got a few. Got them to put out feelers with their inform-ants. Wasn't easy because a lot of people clammed up when they knew what I was after. Boyle's got people pretty nervous up here.'

She had a sense that this might be going nowhere, that Brennan was clutching at straws. 'So did you get anything?'

'Yeah, I did, in the end. I got a couple of grasses who were prepared to talk. On the record. I've got taped testimony, and I've got their commitment that, if we promise them protection, they'll say it again in a formal statement.'

'Are you sure about this, Jack?' She knew from experience how often such promises melted away once informants realised what they'd agreed to. 'What's in it for them?'

'Boyle's made plenty of enemies over the years. There are enough people around who want to get back at him. And nobody likes a bent cop.' The last sentence was expressed with some feeling. 'I know it's a long shot. But I think I could land them, with a bit of internal help. But that's not the best of it.'

'Go on,' she said, cautiously.

'After I'd got people to put feelers out, I received a package in the post. Sent anonymously. A CD-R. Just a few files on it. But all of them interesting. A handful of photographs of Salter meeting people whose faces I recognised. Not the kind of people you'd expect Salter to be meeting.'

She found herself holding her breath. 'Including Boyle?'

'Sadly not. Smaller fry. But awkward enough for Salter.'

'It's good,' she agreed. 'But probably not good enough. You know Salter. He'll talk his way out of it. They'll suddenly become his informants. He'll come up with perfectly legitimate reasons why he had to be talking to them.'

'There's still more. A couple of audio files. Tapes of conversations. One of the voices unmistakeably Salter. The file names suggest that the other parties were among those in the photos, though I don't know the voices myself. But the subject matter isn't the kind of thing that someone in Salter's position should be discussing. Accepting payments for favours rendered. Or blind eyes turned.'

She realised that, without noticing, she'd finished the

glass of wine. Phone in one hand, she poured herself another. 'That's better,' she said. 'But still not great. We'd have to prove for certain that it really is Salter. We'd have to be certain who he's talking to. And we'd have to ensure there was no context that might provide a legitimate explanation for what he appears to be saying.' She was familiar enough with the lengths that defence councils went to in casting doubt on the quality of prosecution evidence. She had no doubt that Salter would know all the same tricks.

'It's not perfect,' Brennan acknowledged. 'But it never will be. Not with someone like Salter. It's going to be a question of scraping together whatever we can find and hoping we get enough to make it stick.'

'Okay,' she said. 'So what are you going to do with this?' She could suddenly envisage some great tit-for-tat corruption battle between Brennan and Salter. Or, worse still, Brennan attempting to blackmail Salter into dropping the misconduct charges. Salter would make mincemeat of Brennan, she suspected. It wasn't just that he was smarter, or at least more cunning. It was that he had the whole of the Agency's resources behind him.

It was clear that Brennan thought the same. 'I don't think I can do much,' he said. 'I'm too compromised. It'll look as if I'm just throwing mud to see if I can get any to stick. It'll be too easy for Salter to pull it apart.'

It was all too clear where this was heading, she thought. She took another large mouthful of wine. 'You want me to do something with it?'

'I don't know. But it seems to me that you've got more chance of being listened to than I have. You're still trailing clouds of glory from dealing with Kerridge and Welsby.'

From where Marie was sitting, none of it felt glorious. Brennan was right, up to a point. The problem was that she didn't know what dirt Salter might have on her. How much did he really know about her relationship with Jake Morton? Did he or didn't know that she'd met with Andy McGrath after his disappearance? What kind of innuendo would he spread about her night at Brennan's flat? If she tried to confront Salter, she could imagine he'd have an armoury of ammunition to use against her.

On this other hand, this was what she'd been wanting for the past year. Surely she could do something with it. She had a duty to help Brennan. The misconduct hearing would be weeks or more away. There had to be an opportunity to use the material Brennan had to build a real case against Salter.

'Look, Jack,' she said, 'I'm making no promises. Like I say, it's good stuff but it's maybe not good enough. If we're going to make anything stick against Salter, we need to have something substantial. Not necessarily something that would stand up in court. But enough to make the powers-that-be take a really serious look at him. Do we have that?'

There was a silence. 'I don't know,' Brennan finally acknowledged. 'I mean, you're right. It's not definitive. I don't see how Salter could talk himself out of all of this, but I can see he'd have a damn good try. Look, Marie, I'm too close to all this. It's been a shock, the last day or so. Just when I thought I was getting somewhere, the whole fucking rug gets pulled from under me. I'm not sure I'm thinking straight –'

'Make a copy of the disc. Stick it in the post to me, special delivery. I'll look at it and tell you what I think. See if it's got legs.'

'That would be good,' Brennan said. 'You know Salter much better than I do. You know how he'd react to this stuff.'

'I don't think anyone knows Hugh Salter,' she said. 'Not even Hugh Salter. Okay, Jack, I'll do my best. If I can nail Salter and help you out of the shit, I will. But no guarantees.'

'No, of course not. But I need all the help I can get at the moment.'

'I'll do what I can. Should I call you on this number when I've had chance to look at the disc?'

'Yes, use this one. Don't want any risk of Salter keeping tabs on me.'

'Okay, Jack. Trust me, I'll do my best with this.'

She picked up the bottle of wine. It was half-empty already. She stared at it for a moment and then refilled her glass. She wasn't sure how she felt. For the first time since the Welsby affair, there was at least the possibility of building a case against Salter. But she felt a growing unease. Maybe it was the fear that, once again, Salter would be one step ahead. Maybe it was anxiety that Brennan was pinning his hopes on not very much. Whatever it was, she thought, it just didn't feel quite right.

23

Things had changed, that was obvious.

No one had briefed him, but that wasn't a surprise. Nor was he much bothered. He didn't like to receive too much information from the client. In principle, it was good if the client kept him in the picture. In practice, even in the early days of a job, he soon knew more than the client did. So he made a point of finding out for himself.

And, as this case showed, clients weren't brilliant at keeping you up to speed. When things went pear-shaped, or just took a turn they hadn't been expecting, they tended to have problems of their own to deal with. They forgot that you were out there, working on their behalf, representing their interests. By the time they remembered, it might be too late.

He took all that in his stride. He kept watch, made his own judgements, and decided what to do next.

A day or two before, he'd watched her return to the house. He'd kept watch on her movements the previous night, guessed from the tracker location where she'd spent it and wondered about the significance or otherwise of that. He wondered whether she knew that the policeman was under surveillance and had been for some days. That was interesting too. The surveillance looked official – if less expert than his own efforts – and he could guess who had ordered it. Something was brewing here. It was like the first moments of subsidence or decay in an apparently sound building, the point where the first cracks appear. There might be nothing obvious to the naked eye, but the slow destruction has already begun.

He was becoming philosophical in his middle age, he thought. A dangerous tendency in this job. Better to stick with simple pragmatism. His instincts told him he needed to take care. Get this job done, whatever it now turned out to be, and then get away for a while.

He noticed that, on the way back from the policeman's, she'd made another stop. He'd done his research and knew whose flat she'd stopped off at. He knew who lived there and, more than that, who was staying there at the moment. Another interesting development. He wondered whether that flat was also under official surveillance. He thought that it was quite possible. If so, he was not the only one joining these various dots. In the circumstances, he wondered whether his own presence here was strictly necessary. But that wasn't his call. And, after all, his role was different.

He'd been back waiting outside her house when she'd returned. He could see she was nervous from the way she parked, a few hundred yards down the road, and from the cautious way she approached the house. He could have told her there was no need to worry. Last night's intruder had not returned.

Half an hour or so later she'd re-emerged, this time lugging two large suitcases. She left them by the front door for a moment while she moved the car next to the house, then slung both the cases into the boot. This looked pretty permanent, he thought. He wasn't surprised she wanted to vacate the house after the previous night's events. And there was no reason for her to continue the assignment up here. Presumably, she was returning to base.

He watched as she locked up the house, returned to the car and set off down the road. Well, that was it, he thought. From this point, his instructions were unclear. He'd been told to keep watch on her up here, that was all. He hadn't even known whether his other services would be required. In a way, he was sorry that they hadn't been. It would have been interesting to test whether he could maintain detachment. He would have done the job successfully, but it would have required a little more effort than usual.

He assumed there would be no requirement for him to follow her back south. Not for the moment, at least. He would send in his anonymous report as usual – the intruder, where she had spent the night, her visit this morning, her apparent departure. He would keep an eye on the tracker, just in case her leaving was only temporary. He would wait patiently for his next instructions, whatever they might be.

If this really was the end of this case, he probably would act upon his thought, which had come to him only that morning, to take a break. Not for long. Just a month or two. Somewhere warm, where he could just relax, lose himself. Just long enough for this, whatever it might be, to come to a head.

'Yes?' It was the Maggie Yates mobile. That was interesting. Even though the mission had been effectively aborted, the

297

line hadn't yet been cancelled and no one had asked for the phone to be returned. Perhaps Salter had wanted to discover what calls she might receive on it. She picked the phone up from the table and carried it out of the back door into the cold night.

The caller's number was withheld, but from the first spoken syllable Marie recognised the voice. Lizzie. She interrupted hurriedly. 'Sorry,' she said. 'The battery on this is nearly dead. Can you call me back on another line?' Not giving Lizzie the chance to speak, she gave Liam's number and then repeated it more slowly, hoping that the Lizzie would have the nous and the means to take it down. She cut the line.

That probably meant that she couldn't continue to use Liam's line as an alternative. If Salter was having the Maggie Yates line intercepted, he'd very soon be trying to do the same for the number she'd just given. If she was right about Salter, she wondered if he was doing it all by the book. Whether he was getting warrants to justify the interceptions. Probably, at least as far as Brennan was concerned. And maybe she was just being paranoid about her own position. Salter wouldn't go any further out on a limb than he had to. On the other hand, the Brennan case probably provided him with the justification he needed to spread the net more widely. There was no point in taking chances.

She began to worry that Lizzie had failed to take down the number. Then Liam's phone buzzed on the desk and she picked it up.

'Are you okay to talk?' Lizzie said.

'Yes, I'm fine. Just being cautious.'

'You think the other line's bugged?'

'It's possible. It's an Agency phone.' After her conversation with Brennan the previous evening, it had occurred to her that they might also have planted some surveillance devices in her home. The very thought made her angry, though she recognised that, in her line of work, it would be hypocritical to complain about invasion of privacy. It was this that had made her take the phone out into the small back garden.

'I'll keep it brief,' Lizzie said. 'I told you that Dad wanted to see you.'

Marie was silent for a moment. She had no desire to meet Keith Welsby again. The last time she'd encountered him, he'd been threatening her life. Part of her still hoped that, in the end, he wouldn't have gone through with it. That he'd have found some other way of extricating himself from the mess he'd created with Jeff Kerridge. She'd respected Welsby once. For a time, she'd almost thought of him as a model of what a policeman should be – iconoclastic, challenging, difficult but still fundamentally honest. As it had turned out, while he might have had the first three of those qualities, he'd certainly lacked the last. 'I don't see how it's going to be possible, Lizzie. He's still technically on remand.'

'I've checked. Because he's on remand and hasn't had a chance to plead, they're more lenient than they might be otherwise. And they know that, the condition he's in, there's no real risk. They've let me see him as family. Surely you won't have any difficulty, given your position.'

'I'm not so sure about that, Lizzie. In the circumstances, the authorities might have reasonable suspicions about why I'd want to see your father.' In her mind's eye, Marie was contemplating the prospect of seeking permission from Salter to see Welsby. It would be too risky to see Welsby without letting Salter know first. But, actually, the more she thought about that, the more interesting the idea seemed. 'We've got to make it formal,' she said. 'Your dad's got to put in an explicit request for me to visit him. Tell them he's got something to say, but he's only prepared to speak to me. That way, they won't say no.'

'Okay. He wants to talk to you.'

I'll bet he does, Marie thought. She said polite goodbyes and ended the call. Welsby's condition was obviously improving. On the grapevine, she'd heard that he was likely to stand trial after all, although his lawyer was still trying to play the sickness card. Welsby was no fool. He'd have dirt on Kerridge's empire, and that meant that he'd have dirt on Boyle. And that, as surely as the hungover morning follows the drunken night before, meant that he'd have whatever dirt there might be on Hugh Salter.

If Welsby was going to go down – and there was little doubt that he would, unless his health decided otherwise – he'd make damn sure he took as many as possible down with him. That wouldn't even be about trying to mitigate his own sentence. It would be revenge, pure and simple. It was questionable whether his evidence against Boyle would cut much ice, given Welsby's history with the Boyle case. But any accusations against Salter might be more damaging. Even if he had nothing definitive, he could probably dish enough dirt to do serious harm to Salter's career. If Welsby made credible accusations, Professional Standards would be duty bound to investigate. And that, combined with whatever evidence Brennan had been able to muster, might start to put the skids under Salter's progress.

Marie stood silently in the garden, feeling the increasing chill of the autumn evening. She could hear the sounds of cars on the main road, the shouts of teenagers knocking back cider or worse in the park behind the terraced houses. In the back of the house opposite, she could see a woman standing washing up at her kitchen sink.

There were people out there who had lives. Maybe not happy lives. Maybe tough lives. But normal lives. Not the kind of life where you have to take calls in your back fucking garden because someone might be listening in. Not the kind of life where someone breaks into your house and tries to kill you. Not, she thought, the kind of life where your partner, the love of your life, is slowly slipping away from you, but still has to take second place to your work.

Not her kind of life.

So she had to change it. And change it now. And Keith Welsby seemed the best place to start.

24

'I can't allow it. It's too risky.'

She watched him coolly across the table, enjoying the discomfort he was trying hard to conceal. 'What's the risk, Hugh? He's a sick old man.'

'A sick old man who tried to kill us both.'

'Seriously, Hugh, we can't just let this go.'

'He's playing with us, sis. You know what he's like. The devious old bugger. I thought we'd got rid of him, but he even comes back from the dead to bloody haunt us.'

'It might be serious, Hugh. He's not well. Maybe he wants to clear the decks before it's too late. If we can get him to cough up what he knows, it won't just make his trial easier. It might open doors for us.'

'And what's Welsby's testimony worth? He's a bent cop, sis. Whatever he comes up with won't be worth the time you spend listening to it.'

He looked rattled, she thought. Salter was a good actor – he'd worked undercover himself – and he was putting on a good show of being his usual urbane, cynical self. But he wasn't quite pulling it off. He was saying a little too much, and saying it a little too quickly.

'You know that's not true, Hugh. Okay, it might not be useful, or even admissible, as evidence, but it'll be critical intelligence. You're not telling me that Welsby couldn't provide us with more leads than we'd know what to do with if he wanted.'

'If he wanted. That's the point. And – if he wanted – he could bugger us around till three weeks after doomsday. You know Keith Welsby.'

'Jesus, Hugh. What have we got to lose? If I see him, the worse that happens is I spend an hour listening to fluent bollocks.'

'The worse that happens is that he tries to save his own arse by sending us off on a wild goose chase.'

'He's not going to pull the wool over our eyes for long, is he? If we follow up what he gives us and it turns out to be nonsense, we just abandon it.'

'We don't even know he's going to give us anything,' Salter pointed out. 'He might just want to beg your forgiveness in his last days on earth. Or, alternatively, tell you he's sorry he didn't finish the job properly. Knowing that bastard, it could be either.'

'But Welsby's not going down without a fight, is he? He's going to muddy the waters with as much dirt as he can dish.' She paused, looking to play her advantage. 'If it comes out at the trial that he wanted to squeal and we said no, what kind of ammunition would that give to a defence council?'

Salter stared back at her as if he were construing her words as a threat. For a moment, she thought that he might lose his temper, something she'd never witnessed in her years of working with him. Then he shook his head. 'It's your funeral. Go and have a chat with him. See if he drops any pearls of wisdom in your ear. You're much more likely to get an earful of abuse.'

'Wouldn't be the first time, Hugh. I'm a big girl. And I think this is worth a shot.'

'If you say so, sis.' He looked down at the papers on the desk in front of him, in what was clearly intended as a gesture of dismissal.

'Thanks, Hugh. You won't regret it.'

He looked sharply up at her. 'I bloody well hope not. Just get it over with. And Marie?'

He still looked tense, but she couldn't read his expression. 'Yes, Hugh?'

'Give the bastard my regards, won't you? Tell him he's always in my thoughts.'

She returned from Salter's office thinking that she ought to feel pleased with herself. She'd secured Salter's permission for her visit to Welsby, and had dislodged his usual equanimity in the process. Things were moving.

But she felt uneasy at meeting Keith Welsby again. In her head, Welsby had transformed from a near father figure into a man who had intended to kill her. Almost fairytale territory. Maybe the meeting would bring what Winsor, their in-house shrink, would no doubt describe as closure.

Even so, it wouldn't be a comfortable meeting. It was a fashionable idea. Restorative justice. Putting the perpetrators of a crime in communication with its victims. It was supposed to be helpful to both parties. But Marie suspected that, when she met Welsby, her overwhelming desire would be simply for retribution.

The rest of the day passed uneventfully. Salter had

allocated her to back room tasks, working through yet more intelligence records. He'd told her to take a few days off, and she knew she should take up the offer. As it was, she spent the day staring into a computer screen, correlating numbers, trying to spot patterns of calls that might be worth investigating further, reviewing the trends that the computer analyses had identified. Getting nowhere slowly. She exchanged a few words with colleagues she barely knew, got up now and again to fetch water from the cooler, stretch her legs, grab a sandwich from the restaurant. Part of her wanted to spend the rest of her working life like this. Another part of was screaming inwardly at the very thought.

On the dot of five, she called it a day and took the Northern Line home. Autumn was well set in now, and it was growing dark as she walked back along the High Street from South Wimbledon station. Only a few weeks until the clocks went back. She was feeling a growing sense of anxiety. More than once she glanced over her shoulder, almost convinced that she was being followed. More likely, her paranoia was simply growing.

Sue and a fellow carer were still in the house, preparing an evening meal for Liam. They were running late because of some minor crisis with another client, and Marie found that she was grateful for the other women's presence. Their domestic bustling in the kitchen gave the house a more comfortable, homely feel, reassuring after the nagging concerns of Marie's day.

Even Liam seemed a little better. He was still sitting in the armchair, his posture slightly twisted and awkward. But he looked up and acknowledged her presence with a smile. 'Hi,' he said. 'Good day?'

'Not bad,' she said. 'Just in the office. You know.'

He nodded. 'That's good,' he said. 'Wanted to paint today.' He shrugged. 'But – well. Watched TV.'

For a moment, she could feel tears welling in her eyes. It wasn't just the sense of loss. It was that, for the first time, Liam didn't even care about what had gone. His mind is likely to slow down, the doctor had said. He'll become more passive, more apathetic. Now she could see it in front of her.

Marie left Sue to deal with helping Liam eat the soup and bread that she'd prepared, and made her way out into the hallway. She hadn't noticed on entering, but there was a small package on the floor by the front door. It had been sent special delivery, so must have been signed for by Sue on one of her earlier visits. Marie tore open the Jiffy bag and tipped the contents into her hand. A CD in a slim plastic wallet. Brennan's evidence.

She took it upstairs to the spare bedroom at the back of the house. Liam's old MacBook was sitting on a table in the corner, unused now for months. It would be wiser not to look at this on her Agency-supplied laptop, in case its presence could be traced later. She booted up Liam's machine and inserted the disc.

If anything, she thought, Brennan had undersold this. There were the photographs he'd described, and more of them than she'd expected. Blurred and distant for the most part, but unmistakably Salter and, in one or two cases, other figures that she recognised. One photograph, clearly a few years old, showed Salter enjoying a drink with Jeff Kerridge.

She played some snippets of the audio files. Unmistakably Salter's voice. She had no idea who the other speakers were, but the content was potentially incriminating.

There was probably nothing here that would stand up as evidence, and certainly not unless the identity of the various speakers could be confirmed. Most of the conversations sounded as if they'd been gathered from surveillance devices. But at least one was clearly a telephone conversation which would be inadmissible as evidence in any case. And a smart defence lawyer would challenge the rest unless their provenance could be proved.

But the material was better than she'd feared. It might not be enough to support a criminal trial, but it might be the foundation of something that could be presented to Professional Standards.

'Marie?' Sue's voice from downstairs. 'We're going to help Liam get to bed, then we'll be off. Is there anything else you need?'

She ejected the disc and stepped over to the door. 'I'm fine, thanks, Sue. How is he?'

'Seems more responsive today.'

We're already talking about him as if he were a child, Marie thought. She stood for a moment with the disc clutched in her hand, unsure what to do with it. She felt almost as if Salter were watching her, as if, whatever she did with the disc, he'd know.

She felt reluctant to leave the disc in any of the obvious places – in her handbag or a pocket. She contemplated hiding it in plain sight among the rows of discs – largely copies of his own work – that Liam had left piled on the bedroom table. As she considered the matter, another thought struck her. She sat down at Liam's laptop and picked up an unused CD-R from the half-empty box beside the computer. She burnt a new copy of the original disc, double-checked its contents, and ejected it. After a moment's thought, she knelt by the table and found a join in the carpet. She reached up to the desk where she'd noticed one of Liam's pallet knives. She slid the knife blade into the join, and, lifting up one side of the carpet, gently slid the disc, inside its wallet, underneath. She patted down the carpet and leaned back to inspect her work. There was no sign that the carpet had been disturbed.

'I'm off now.'

Marie jumped to her feet just as Sue pushed open the door. 'You okay, Marie?'

'Yes. Thanks. Just sorting out some of Liam's bits and pieces.'

Sue looked past her to where a couple of Liam's paintings were propped against the wall. 'He was good, wasn't he?' Then she caught herself and added: 'Is good, I mean.'

'You were right the first time,' Marie said. She gestured towards the pictures. 'He's not going to get back to this, is he?'

Sue shrugged. 'Who knows? All we can do is hope.'

'You're right, though,' Marie said. 'He was bloody good. Let's hope that others recognise it too, eventually.' She shook her head, staring at the canvases. 'Poor bugger.'

'Both of you,' Sue said. 'You need support too.'

Marie glanced at the dark space under the table where the duplicate CD-R was concealed. 'More than you know,' she said. 'More than you bloody know.'

25

The first sight was a shock. He was lying on the bed, apparently asleep. There was a thin blanket over him, and he was dressed in an old pair of pyjamas. Even watching from the doorway, she could see he'd lost weight since she'd last seen him. His thinning hair was bone-white. It occurred to her that he must have dyed it in the old days. She'd never associated Keith Welsby with vanity.

But then she'd never associated him with corruption either.

She paused in the doorway and looked at the two prison officers sitting by the wall. Both of them looked bored out of their heads. What a farce, she thought. Two officers deployed full-time to keep watch on a man scarcely capable of dragging himself out of bed. But that was the system. Prisoners are most at risk of escaping when they're outside the prison environment – being escorted to court, being moved between prisons, in hospital. So these two were stuck on bed-watch to make sure that Welsby didn't abseil down from the second floor window.

'Hi,' she said. 'Marie Donovan. You should be expecting me.' She held out her ID card and warrant.

One of the officers – even prison officers are getting younger, she thought – peered at the card. His colleague continued to flick through the *Daily Express*, apparently uninterested by her presence. 'Thanks, Ms Donovan.' He held out his hand; 'Eddie Brady.'

She smiled and shook his hand, wondering how long it would take for the enthusiasm to be knocked out of him. His colleague had clearly already suffered that fate. 'Hi, Eddie. Okay if I talk to Mr Welsby?'

'Yes, of course. We'll have to stay in the room, of course.'

As he spoke there was a rustling from the bed. Welsby had turned on his side and was glaring at them. For all his white hair and emaciated frame, he looked at least a shadow of his old self. 'Just fuck off for a few minutes, you two, and let me talk to the lass. I'm not going to vanish. Apart from the fact that I can barely walk three steps, you've got me chained to the fucking bed.' He shook his arm, confirming that his wrist was manacled to the bed frame. 'Last time that happened, I had to pay for the fucking privilege.'

Brady turned to his colleague, who shrugged and folded up his newspaper. 'This is strictly against regulations,' Brady said. 'If you tell anybody—'

'If I tell anybody,' Marie said, 'I'll get busted too. So why would I?'

Brady nodded, apparently satisfied by this logic. 'We had one of your colleagues in here a week or two back.'

'Oh, yes?' Marie responded casually. She could feel Welsby listening intently behind her.

'Hugh something. Slater?' Brady grinned, awkwardly. 'Bit of a smart-arse, if you'll pardon the expression.'

Marie shook her head. 'Know the name,' she said. 'But it's a big place. Wonder what he was doing here. Did he say anything?'

'Not much. Not much polite anyway. Seemed to be checking up on Mr Welsby here.'

'Probably just concerned for my health,' Welsby growled from the bed.

The young man nodded, his gaze flicking between Marie and Welsby. 'Well,' he said, finally, 'if you need us, we'll be just outside.'

'Thanks,' Marie said. 'And thanks for being so helpful.'

As the door closed behind her, she turned towards Welsby, who was lying on his back once more, his eyes half-closed. 'Hi Keith,' she said. 'I'd like to say it's good to see you, but I'm not sure it is.'

He nodded, as if she'd just offered a pleasant greeting. 'And you were such a polite, well-brought-up little thing, as well.'

'And you used to be someone I respected, Keith. What went wrong with us, eh?' She sat down on the plastic chair by his bedside.

'You've every right to be angry with me, Marie,' he said.

'Well, thanks for that, Keith. Funnily enough, your opinion on the matter isn't of much interest to me.'

He nodded, wearily, his eyes closed. 'Not going very far, this conversation, is it?'

'Maybe not,' she said. 'But we have to have it. You were going to kill me, for Christ's sake, Keith.'

He shook his head. 'It wouldn't have gone that far, Marie. I wouldn't have let it. I had stuff on Kerridge. I'd have sorted things out.'

'Like fuck, Keith,' she said. 'It had already gone too far.

That's only part of it. I trusted you. I looked up to you, for Christ's sake. And all the time you were fucking bent.'

'Nothing I can say to that, Marie. Except sorry. And I don't expect you to accept that. It's the way it is.'

'Why?' she said. 'For the money?'

'Partly. But this goes way back. There was a lot of it about. That's not an excuse. But it's an explanation. It was part of the culture. There were a lot worse than me.'

'Spare me this crap, Keith.'

'I'm just saying that once you're in, you're in. Once you've done enough to let them blackmail you, it's all or nothing. There were plenty of others. Most have buggered off by now.'

'Whereas you hung about long enough to become Jeff Kerridge's bagman.'

'I always thought of myself as his fucking conscience,' Welsby laughed, bitterly. 'But, yes, something like that.'

'Until Salter exposed you?'

'That little gobshite. Yeah, he exposed me because it took the spotlight off him.'

'You're saying Salter's bent, too?' She sat back in the chair, watching Welsby's expression.

'Oh, for fuck's sake, girl. Don't treat me like an idiot. You know exactly what Salter is. You know he shot Kerridge in cold fucking blood.'

'So why'd he shoot Kerridge?'

'Because he's on Pete fucking Boyle's team. What is this, girl? Fucking Mastermind?'

'No. Keith,' she said, slowly. 'It's just that I want you to spell it out for me. Word by fucking word. I'm sick of guesswork. I'm sick of innuendo. Tell me the fucking story.'

He stared at her for a moment, as if he were seeing her in a new light. 'Okay. Let me tell you how it is. You might despise me, girl. That's fair enough. I probably deserve it. But Hugh Salter's a whole different animal. People like me – well, we got into this to make a few bob on the side. I never did a lot of harm. A few tip-offs to Kerridge. The odd blind eye turned—'

'I get it, Keith. You were on the side of the angels.'

'Salter's not like that. You know Salter. He's ambitious. He's driven. Whatever he's doing he wants to be top dog. So he threw his lot in with Pete Boyle. Not because he thought Boyle was destined for great things. But because he knew that Boyle wasn't the brightest bulb in the Christmas tree.'

'You've lost me,' she said. 'Why would he do that?'

Welsby closed his eyes for a moment, as if the effort of narration was proving too much for him. 'Because Boyle's his puppet. It's not Pete Boyle who runs that operation. It's Hughie fucking Salter.'

'You're saying that Salter's running a criminal operation?'

'That's exactly what I'm saying. That was what was getting Kerridge so rattled. He knew that Boyle was angling to take over the business, but he hadn't seen Boyle as a threat. But then Boyle's moves starting getting cleverer and Kerridge guessed that someone else was involved, though he didn't know who. He leaked the evidence that we tried to use to put Boyle away, hoping that it might smoke out the other party.'

'Which, in a way, it did. Jesus.' She remembered how Salter had shot Kerridge, supposedly in self-defence.

'Yeah. Salter was too smart for all of us. Killed Kerridge. Got me banged up. Then tried to have me murdered.'

'I never saw you as the suicidal type,' she said, for the first time recalling the affection she'd once felt for the old bugger. 'You reckon that was Salter, too?'

'No way to prove it,' Welsby said. 'But who else? After Kerridge died, Salter thought the business would fall into his and Boyle's laps. But Mrs K was more resilient than they'd expected.'

'Until she was taken out, too. Christ.'

'Salter's been putting the frighteners on everyone up there. Gradually expanding the business. Helen Kerridge was the biggest and most important competitor. Boyle's taking over the whole territory.' Welsby coughed suddenly, and gestured for her to pass him a glass of water from the bedside cabinet. 'God, I'm not well. They reckon I'm going to stand trial now my condition's improved, but I don't know if I'll make it that far. I'd planned to do my damnedest to take Salter down with me.' He shook his head. 'My guess is that he's starting to get jittery.'

'Why?' she said. 'Sounds like it's all falling into place for him.'

'And that's when it gets dangerous. Pete Boyle's no Einstein but he's not completely dumb, either. He won't be happy playing second fiddle forever. He'll take on Salter.'

'I wouldn't give a lot for his odds, would you?'

'Maybe not. But Salter's vulnerable. He's the bent cop. Spends his life walking on thin ice.'

'It's all just guesswork,' she said. 'We don't know what Boyle's up to.'

'Lizzie told me about your intruder. Didn't sound like a pro.'

She frowned. 'Wouldn't have said so. All a bit half-cocked.'

'And why do it at all? Who was behind it?'

'I've been trying to work that out.'

'And who torched Andy McGrath's office? Another half-arsed job. None of this sounds like Hughie Salter. Doesn't sound like the carefully planned campaign of intimidation that's been going on up there till now.'

'You're saying Boyle was behind the recent stuff?'

'Like you say, it's guesswork. But my hunch is that things are not hunky-dory between Messrs Salter and Boyle. I think Boyle's throwing his weight about, looking for a bigger slice of the pie. Probably wasn't an accident that those incidents both involved you. Sounds like a message to Salter. Which will make Salter twitchy. He knows that Boyle could shaft him if he chose to.' He stopped, and then said, 'I heard on the grapevine that Jack Brennan's been set up.'

In the old days, she had always been astonished by Welsby's ability to absorb information as if from the ether. If there was something worth knowing, Welsby managed to know it before anyone else. Whatever his medical condition, he clearly hadn't lost that gift. 'Apparently,' she said.

'Just like he did with me,' Welsby said, ruefully. 'Makes sure the spotlight is firmly fixed on someone else.'

'So why did you want to see me?' she asked. 'Old times' sake?'

'I want to fuck over Hugh Salter,' Welsby said. 'That's the long and short of it. Like I say, you can think what you like about me. But Salter's a ruthless, dangerous bastard. He's not just taking the odd back-hander. He's in the thick of it. And he'll do – he has done – whatever it takes to further his ambitions. I want to stop him.'

'Is this just revenge, Keith?'

'Not just. But, yeah, in part. Why not? Bastard wrecked my life, and then tried to kill me. One reason I've not reapplied for bail and played up my illness is that I'm safer in here with those two screws sitting outside than I am out on the streets, or mixing with Christ knows who in prison. If I get to stand trial, I'll do everything I can to expose Salter. But I'm a tainted witness, so my credibility's shot. And I don't know if I'll even get that far. I'm not a well man, anyway, and I suspect that, one way or another, being sent back to prison won't be good for my health.'

'So you want me to do something?'

'You're the only person I'd trust, Marie. You're not just straight. You're also bloody good. I need someone on my side.'

He looked like an old man on the way out, she thought. He was a pale, thin shadow of the ebullient Keith Welsby she'd once known. Now he was gaunt, dark-eyed, scarcely able to sit up in bed without assistance. Hugh Salter had done that. She'd never forgive Welsby for what he'd done and been, but she could pity what he'd become.

'I've got some stuff on Salter,' she said, finally. 'Not enough. Certainly not enough for a court. Maybe not even enough for Standards, though it might force them to have a hard look at him. But something.'

For a moment, Welsby's expression again reminded her of the man he'd once been. She'd seen that look once or twice when they'd made a breakthrough on a case. It struck her that, for all Welsby's failings, at heart he'd always been a real copper. 'How come you've got this stuff?'

'Just a source,' she said. 'Salter has plenty of enemies.'

'Too right. But you reckon what you've got isn't enough on its own?'

'I doubt it. If only because Salter's such a slippery customer. Some of it's decent stuff, but there's nothing there he couldn't talk his way out of.'

'Even so, it means the net's starting to close. If enough mud gets thrown at him, some of it's going to start to stick. There are only so many times he can talk his way out of a corner.'

'I'm guessing he's got a few more lives left yet.'

Welsby gazed back at her, and she could feel that he was thinking through what she'd been saying. 'Well, then,' he said, finally, 'seems to me that we ought to be encouraging him to use up one or two of them.'

26

There'd been silence for a day or two, which had surprised him. He'd reported back what he'd seen and deduced – the intruder, the night she'd spent at the policeman's flat, the visit she'd made on the way back. The way she'd packed her cases and left the house.

He'd expected a quick response, either new instructions or confirmation that the mission was finished. He was feeling increasingly uncomfortable with this assignment. Something had gone wrong somewhere, and he still didn't quite know what or how. He could feel his careful planning, his professionalism counting for nothing as events slowly drifted out of his control.

The prospect of slipping away, taking a break for a while, was becoming ever more attractive. Grab himself a little sun and warmth before the winter came.

For the first day or so, though, there was no response. That worried him even more. Silence suggested delay, hesitation. Another sign that things weren't right.

Twenty-four hours later, he finally received new instructions. Head south, back to London, and maintain observation. More to follow.

The mission was moving into unplanned territory. There was no time for him even to carry out his usual research. He would have to wing it. He was good enough to do that, but it was far from ideal. And 'more to follow' worried him. This felt like operating on the hoof.

But the instruction was there so, for the moment, he felt obliged to follow it. It would be a big step to abort his involvement so late in the day. He'd been paid for his earlier work, but he'd get the full payoff on completion. Whatever that meant. The goalposts were shifting all the time now. But it would be expensive to pull out. And not his style. He was a pro. He'd carry on unless he felt that the risks were too great.

So he'd head south. Find a bed and breakfast somewhere in South London. Gather as much intelligence as he could, and try to be prepared for whatever was coming.

More to follow, he thought. But how much more?

Walking up Merton High Street, Marie felt the same gnawing paranoia as she had on the previous evening. It was beginning to rain slightly, and there were few pedestrians out in the early evening. At one point, she stopped and peered into the window of the Cypriot greengrocer, as if contemplating buying one of the more exotic vegetables displayed inside. She looked back along the street. There were a couple of figures, hidden under umbrellas, who might conceivably be suspicious, but no one had paused with her. One of the figures disappeared into an off-licence, shaking his umbrella out into the street. The other continued walking, maintaining a brisk pace.

When she reached the house, she found it silent,

empty-feeling. Liam was already in bed in the former dining room, sleeping soundly. There was a note from Sue on the kitchen table saying that he'd seemed very tired so they'd helped him to bed early.

Was this her life from here on? Dull days at work followed by solitary evenings, Liam sleeping in the next room?

She'd stopped on the way back from the hospital to buy another pay-as-you-go mobile. The brief optimism she'd felt on leaving Welsby had melted away during the journey back. Whatever she thought of Welsby, even in his current state he somehow still displayed an enthusiastic pragmatism that remained infectious. There'd been a moment, as she said goodbye to him, when she'd really felt they had a chance of bringing Salter down. Now, the whole idea seemed faintly absurd.

She texted the new number to Brennan and Lizzie and then, wrestling with her willpower for no more than a few seconds, she dug out another bottle of wine from the diminishing store in the kitchen cupboard. She was aware that she was beginning to drink more than was good for her. Just tonight, she thought. Christ knows I've deserved it. I'll pour a glass, run a bath, wash out all the crap of the day.

She'd completed the first part of this task when the new mobile rang. Number withheld. But it had to be one of two people.

'Hello?'

'Marie. It's me, Jack. See you got a new phone.'

'Hang on a sec,' she said. As on the previous night, she opened the back door and stepped out into the garden. The rain was still coming down, though little more than a thin mist blurring the street lights beyond the small back yard. She stood in the shelter of the porch. 'Sorry. Just wanted to get out of the house. I'm paranoid that Salter might have planted some intercept devices in the house.'

There was a moment's silence. 'I'd put nothing past that bastard,' Brennan said. 'I'm sure my phone's been bugged. Don't know about the house. But it's possible. Jesus.' She could hear him take a breath, as if he were finding the stress of the situation almost too much. 'Just wanted to check you'd got the parcel.'

'Safely received,' she said. 'Copied and hidden.'

'What did you think?'

'It's good, Jack. Better than I expected, to be honest. I still don't think it's cut and dried by any means, but it's good start. Where the hell did you get it?'

Another brief silence. 'You're not seriously asking me to tell you that? Let's just say that Salter probably has more enemies than friends.'

'I don't doubt that,' she said. 'And, no, I'm not asking you to reveal your sources. But if we're going to make this stick, we have to be confident of its provenance.'

'I'm confident,' he said. 'And there may be more where that came from.'

'That would be good.'

'Do you think you can do something with it?'

'I don't know, Jack. Like I say, it's good stuff. But I'm not convinced that Salter wouldn't still be able to wriggle out of it. Even the taped conversations aren't definitive. He's still pretty circumspect on those tapes.'

'Because he's a man who's constantly watching his own back.'

'I don't doubt it. But that doesn't help us. I think our

biggest hope with the material as it stands is that it might force Standards into conducting a proper investigation.'

'But?' Brennan said.

'But I don't even know if that will work. Salter might be getting twitchy but as far as the Agency's concerned he's still a rising star. Welsby was a big embarrassment for them. My guess is that they'll be reluctant to lift up any more stones unless they're forced into it.'

'You mean they'd rather turn a blind eye than risk another public humiliation?'

'Jesus, Jack, I don't know. But it's all political, isn't it? Some politicians have already got the Agency on their hit list because we're supposedly not cost effective or we're not delivering the goods or whatever the hell other stick they decide to beat us with. The other Forces don't like us because we challenge their authority. The powers-that-be won't be rushing to provide any of those parties with more ammunition.'

'It'll be far more embarrassing if Salter gets exposed and they've done nothing.'

'That's a big if at the moment.'

'So what do you suggest?'

She was silent for a moment, wondering how much more to say. 'I went to visit Keith Welsby today,' she said, finally.

'Welsby?' Brennan said. 'That must have been interesting.'

'You might say that. Not as painful as I'd feared in the end.'

'How is he?'

'Improving, but not great. He's expecting to stand trial, but he reckons he won't last that long. One way or another.'

'Jesus.'

'Whatever happens, he wants to make sure Salter goes down with him.'

'Everybody's gunning for Salter, then.'

'So it seems. And according to Welsby there might be one more.'

'Oh yes?'

'He reckons Pete Boyle might be after him, too.'

'I thought Salter was on Boyle's team.'

'More like the other way round, according to Welsby. But he thinks that all might not be well between them. Salter's getting rattled, doesn't trust Boyle entirely. And Boyle's tired of playing second fiddle.'

'Well, it's a theory,' Brennan said. 'Does Welsby have anything to back this up?'

'Not much, as far as I can tell. Just the old Welsby intuition. Mind you, the old Welsby intuition was a powerful beast in its day.'

'Probably was, when he was being tipped off by Jeff Kerridge. But presumably that's not the case now, unless Welsby's already secured his hotline to heaven.'

'More likely the other place, I'd have thought. But, yes, fair point.'

'So what do we do then? Are you going to take the disc to Standards?'

'I think we need leverage on this. With the best will in the world, I'm not convinced that evidence will cut much ice on its own. Just like I'm not convinced that it'll do much good if Welsby stands up in court and denounces Salter. Salter's as slippery as they come and Welsby's hardly a credible witness.'

'So what then?' She could sense the disappointment in

Brennan's voice. It was familiar to her – the sense that you'd almost pinned Salter down, and then he was off and running again.

'Look, Jack,' she said, 'I'm not letting go of this. This is the closest we've come to nailing Salter. We can't afford for it to go off half-cocked. If we don't get him this time, we'll never get another chance.'

'So what then?' Brennan repeated, his voice more insistent.

'I think we need Welsby,' she said. 'He's got nothing to lose. He's got a grudge against Salter the size of Manchester. And, from what I saw today, he's just about desperate and determined enough to make sure we get a result.'

27

She ended the call to Brennan and stood for a moment in the steady drizzle. It was only now she realised quite how cold she was. Even in the shelter of the porch, she'd been dampened by the drifting misty rain, her hair clinging to her face. And, for the first time since she'd returned home, she was beginning to feel scared.

Up there, out in the field, she'd expected to feel threatened, anxious. It wasn't just because you might have to face something like her mysterious intruder. It was because, day in, day out, you were operating on alien territory, working out the rules, pretending to be something you weren't.

Coming back here, even with all the problems she was having to face, she'd initially felt comforted. Whatever she might have to deal with, she was at least home. She'd felt safe.

But that sense of security had melted away. She was afraid the house had already been invaded, infiltrated. She had no idea whether Salter really had placed surveillance equipment here. Maybe it was a far-fetched idea. Liam had been in the house since his return from hospital, and Sue and the other carers had been coming and going. But maybe

Salter had taken advantage of Liam's absence, or maybe, even after his return, Liam hadn't been in a state to recognise that someone was in the house. She knew full well how skilled the technical support team could be. They could be in and out in the blink of an eye and, short of tearing the place apart to find whatever they might have concealed, there was no sure way to confirm whether they'd ever been.

More than that, though, she was afraid of Salter. She'd seen how ruthlessly he'd treated Brennan. And, if Welsby was even half right, that was only a fraction of what he was capable of. She hadn't believed it before, not entirely. Even when he'd killed Jeff Kerridge, she'd half-accepted his claim of self-defence. For all her suspicions, she still hadn't fully believed he'd gunned down Kerridge in cold blood, just to further his own ambitions. At worst, she'd thought, it must have just been Salter's usual mixture of opportunism and blind luck.

Now she had begun to believe that Salter was capable of anything. If he really was the driving force, the brains, behind Boyle's operations, that implied that he was behind all the killings that had taken place in recent weeks. That he'd been systematically, callously picking off the competition. That he'd actively commissioned one murder after another.

She drew the curtains in the small living room and poured the glass of wine she'd been promising herself. She ought to be hungry. She'd eaten nothing since a sandwich she'd grabbed at the office before leaving for the hospital.

But somehow the prospect of food seemed less attractive than the prospect of wine. Not a good sign. Apart from anything else, she needed to keep her wits about her if she was going to have any chance of dealing with Salter. She paused for a moment, considering what dealing with Salter might entail, then swallowed half of the glass in a mouthful.

She re-entered the kitchen and forced herself to make and eat a sandwich, her head already dizzy from the effects of the wine on her previously empty stomach. She felt restless, caught in limbo. She wanted this to end, but knew that any way out was bound to be painful. Pouring more wine, she prowled the house with the air of a caged animal. Twice, she stopped in the living room, tempted to start scouring the walls, the skirting board, the carpets, for any sign that surveillance equipment had been placed in the room. But that would be a sure route to madness. If it had been done by tech support, she'd never find any definitive evidence and would be reduced to examining every last scratch or mark as evidence of infiltration.

Finally, she opened the door to the dining room where Liam lay sleeping. The electric bed had already turned up, less than twenty-four hours after the social worker had ordered it. Marie didn't know whether this was evidence of local authority efficiency, or a sign that they recognised how quickly Liam's condition was deteriorating.

His former mobility, the ability at least to do what the social worker called 'furniture walking' – progressing around the house finding support as he went – already seemed like a distant memory. On a good day, he could just about stand for a minute or two unaided. On a worse day, like today, he'd almost had to be carried between bed and chair by the carers. The last couple of days he'd spent slumped in the armchair, eyes fixed on the flickering glare of the television screen, with no sign that he was taking anything much in. He woke in the morning, ate breakfast with help from the carers, dozed off mid-morning, had lunch, watched more television in the afternoon, and was helped to bed in the early evening. Already, it was no kind of life.

Now, in the late evening, he was sleeping soundly. She pulled up a chair and sat by the bedside, watching the rise and fall of his chest under the single duvet. Even the sight of the duvet brought a catch to her throat. When she'd first set up the sofa bed down here, she'd dug out some old bedding he'd had when they'd first met, while he was still at art college and she was at university. Those days seemed like little more than a dream now, a set of vibrant images fading against the relentless glare of real life.

His breathing sounded slightly rough. Sue had thought he had a cold and had suggested calling out the GP. But they'd agreed that, in the circumstances, a cold was the last of Liam's problems, and they couldn't face the thought that he might get taken into hospital yet again.

He was already beginning to have some difficulty in swallowing and even the ward consultant had agreed that, from here on, Liam would be better off at home unless his condition became very serious. Marie had had a lengthy telephone conversation with the neurologist the previous day. Even now, there seemed to be no definitive prognosis. But it was clear that the rate of progression was accelerating, perhaps even more rapidly than the specialists had expected – though, looking back now, she suspected that their non-committal judgements had always concealed an underlying pessimism about the likely outcome.

In the short time he'd been in hospital, Liam had

noticeably lost weight. Even though Sue had visited him there twice a day – significantly exceeding her official remit – to try to help feed him, the ward staff had been unable to offer the level of care he'd experienced at home. And since he'd returned home, it had been increasingly difficult to get him to eat or drink. He'd take a mouthful, then lose interest in the meal. When the carers tried to feed him, often he'd just sit with the food in his mouth for minutes at a time before finally swallowing. She could see him shrinking and weakening almost before her eyes.

She'd asked the consultant whether it was feasible for Liam to be fed automatically. There had been an almost embarrassed pause. 'It's not the policy now,' the doctor had said at last. 'We call it the PEG system. Percutaneous endoscopic gastrostomy. But it's a relatively intrusive process. The view is that it's appropriate in cases where there's a decent chance of recovery or significant improvement. A stroke, for example. But in cases like this . . .' As so often in these discussions, the prognosis had been left hanging in the air.

'You'll let him starve to death?' she'd said bluntly.

'That's not quite how it is. PEG feeding can cause its own problems. Infection. Vomiting.'

They'd talked further, but her impression had been that the outcome was already determined. Automatic feeding wasn't recommended, and – short of a pitched battle with the authorities – it wasn't likely to be provided. For Marie, the implications of that decision were clear, even if in theory they told her nothing that she didn't already know. Liam's condition was terminal. It was likely to be terminal relatively soon. Whether that meant weeks or months or years, she had no idea. But that was the way it was. The way it would be.

She felt numb, and it struck her that there was something wrong with her emotional state. Her partner, the man she'd thought of as the love of her life, was lying dying in front of her. And yet for days her mind had been fixed on bloody Salter. She felt nothing but numb about Liam, and yet she could feel a growing anger burning in her about what Salter had done. Winsor, the Agency psych, would no doubt witter on about transference, and he'd probably be right. There was nothing she could do about Liam's condition, except look after him as best she could. However much she might rage against the dying of the fucking light, it would change nothing. So maybe it was reasonable to concentrate her energies where she might just conceivably make a difference.

Or perhaps she was just trying to avoid dealing with what was stretched out here in front of her.

Liam gave a small cough and, for a heart-stopping moment, he seemed to cease breathing. Then he coughed again, and the rhythmic motion of his breath continued as before, perhaps slightly wheezier.

She leaned forward and kissed him gently on the lips. To her slight surprise, he stirred in his sleep and his lips unmistakably kissed her back. His eyes flickered and she heard him murmur, 'Marie—?'

'I'm here, love,' she said. 'Taking care of you.' She kissed him again. This time his eyes were closed and there was no response.

She waited, gazing at him. He seemed so calm, she thought. Looking at him like this, you'd never know there was anything wrong.

She sat for a few moments longer, listening to the slight rasp of his breathing. Then she rose, turned off the light in the dining room, and made her own way upstairs to bed.

The second message had come earlier that evening. Unusually, it had been a voicemail, the number withheld, the voice electronically distorted. The instructions, as always, crystal clear. He was a little reassured by that. It suggested that his client was back in control. Perhaps it had been a mistake to read the silence as implying hesitation or uncertainty. He, of all people, knew the benefits of thorough planning.

Nevertheless, he'd been taken aback by the instruction at first. It was a step or two beyond anything done previously. Understandable, no doubt, if he were aware of the full circumstances. But still slipping into territory that seemed riskier, more uncertain, perhaps more questionable.

He was surprised, in fact, to find that a part of him had recoiled at the instruction. An instinctive reaction. The kind of emotion he thought he had cauterised in his drive towards professionalism. Sentimentality. But he supposed that, ultimately, he was only human. However, much he might discipline himself, he still had to overcome the same weaknesses as others. That was part of the challenge.

It was important for him to see this task in the same light. As a challenge. A challenge in more than one way, given the target. He knew he had already come to grips with one part of that challenge. The rest would not be problematic. When the moment came, he would be in control.

He had kept her under surveillance all day. It hadn't been difficult. She was good, but he was better. He'd trailed her to that hospital, speculating about what might have been discussed there. He'd trailed her back on the tube, keeping in the darkness as she'd walked up the main street back to her house. She'd stopped at one point, looking back, clearly suspecting that someone might be following her. He'd wondered momentarily whether he'd failed, whether he'd allowed himself to be seen. But she was bound to be anxious about the possibility of surveillance. A minute or two later, she continued on his way, and he was confident that he hadn't been spotted.

He'd left his own car parked in the next street from her house. This was an area where, once the local residents had departed for work, other commuters from further afield parked to use the local tube station. He watched her go into the house, and then returned to his car. No one registered his presence as he started the ignition and pulled away.

The previous day he'd cased the house itself. He'd been armed with a clipboard, some official-looking papers, and a story about the local authority planning department if anyone had thought to question his presence in the alley behind the rear garden. But of course no one had. This was commuter land. Most of the locals would be out at work at this time, other than the odd young mother or retired elderly man. Her house was one of the few occupied. He'd parked his car further along the same street on that occasion, and had watched the comings and goings of the uniformed carers. In mid-morning, he'd watched them bring the young man out briefly in his wheelchair – apparently just a turn around the block to give him a breath of air.

These houses were little more than slightly extended two-up, two-downs, built around the turn of the last century to house the workers in the Abbey Mills over the river. The mill complex was a craft and heritage centre now, cluttered with bijou restaurants and bars, and the area was supposedly 'up and coming', though he doubted it would ever really get there. For his purposes, the size and design of the houses made it relatively easy to work out their interior layout. As always, he could plan his movements in advance.

But he continued to feel a degree of unease. It was the same feeling he'd had for days. He had no evidence to support it. His own role was, by definition, one of detachment and deniability. He'd didn't know what was going on and he didn't want to. But something felt wrong. He still had the sense that something was slipping out of control, and he didn't want to be around when that happened.

Just this one, then. Just the one, and then a long break.

28

At first, it felt like déjà vu. It was as if she was back in the north, in that bland estate house, reliving the night when she'd faced the intruder.

She had woken, suddenly, deep into the night, unsure what had disturbed her. Her mouth was dry from the after-effects of the unfinished bottle of wine. Her brain was struggling to disentangle the dissolving remnants of some dream from the reality of the darkness into which she'd awakened.

She sat up, fumbling on the bedside table for the glass of water she'd left there. She took a mouthful, then lay back, turning over in the double bed, preparing to go back to sleep.

The same as the previous time, she thought, her mind suddenly alert.

The chill in the air. The sense that the house was colder than it should rightly have been.

She was losing her marbles. This house wasn't the same as the place in Chester. That was a newly built eco-friendly box, every part of it sealed to help save the planet, or at least to minimise the heating bills. She'd noticed the cold that night because it was so unusual. In that house, even in the small hours with the heating off, the house had still retained its residual warmth.

This place was different. It was a jerry-built nineteenth century worker's cottage, draughts coming in from all directions. She knew full well that in the middle of a late autumn night the place could easily turn into an ice box. There was no reason to think that anything was wrong.

Even so, her mind was fully alert by now, and she knew she'd struggle to get back to sleep. Better to get up, make herself some hot milk, settle down to watch some late-night TV or read a book. Relax herself again, if relaxation were even possible. With everything that was happening, it probably wasn't surprising that her sleep was disrupted. She remembered that other time she'd woken in the night, in Jake Morton's quayside flat. The night he had been murdered. The night that all this had started.

She climbed out of bed, turned on the bedside lamp, and pulled on her dressing gown. It was cold, certainly, but no colder than she'd expect at this time of the year. She made her way slowly downstairs and into the kitchen. She realised that, just for a moment as she turned on the kitchen light, she'd held her breath, half-expecting to see the kitchen door standing open. But it was closed, of course. Still closed and locked. Irritated at her own foolishness, she tried the handle but the door didn't give.

She took some milk from the fridge and poured it into a saucepan, standing by the cooker as the milk heated. From this room, she couldn't even hear the rumble of the passing cars on the High Street.

She tipped the warm milk into a mug, and began to

make her way through into the sitting room, contemplating whether it was worth turning on the heating. She hadn't switched on the light in the hallway, and, as she flicked off the kitchen light, the house was momentarily plunged back into darkness.

She froze.

As she stood in the kitchen doorway, she was looking directly towards the front door. The bottom half of the door was plain wood, but the upper half comprised two parallel stained-glass panels.

Framed in the panels, silhouetted against the orange of the street light opposite, there was a figure. A figure standing motionless, apparently facing the door, like a caller who had just rung the doorbell.

She held her breath and glanced down at her watch. Two thirty-five. Not the time for casual callers. Not the time for Jehovah's Witnesses or unemployed young men flogging sub-standard dishcloths.

She would almost certainly be invisible to whoever was out there. Nevertheless, he – and she somehow had no doubt that it was he – would have seen the kitchen light extinguished and would know that someone was here.

Her mobile phone was in her handbag upstairs. The landline phone was in the living room. She could probably make it safely through into there, but there was no way of knowing whether the line had been disconnected.

She was weighing up her options, knowing that she had to make a move, when, to her surprise, the figure turned and moved back away from the door, apparently heading back down the short path to the street.

She released her breath. Just a coincidence? Some

small-hours drunk who had made his way to the wrong house? Not so far-fetched among these rows of identical terraces.

Or someone who was considering trying to enter the house from another direction?

Now that the figure had moved away from the door, she decided that her best option was to head upstairs. She could find her phone, keep watch on the street from the upstairs window, call the police if there was any sign of anything wrong.

Moving as silently as she could, her eyes still fixed on the glass panels in the door, she reached the stairs and dashed up two at a time. In the bedroom, she left the lights off and fumbled in her handbag for the phone. Clutching it tightly in her hand, she made her way across the darkened room to the window. Carefully, she eased back the curtain.

At first, she thought the street was deserted. The road was lined with parked cars, and the rows of houses cast deep shadows, broken only by the evenly spaced orange glare of the street lights.

The man was standing just beyond the glare of one of the lights, perhaps only fifteen or twenty yards down the road. He was dressed in a dark coat, a baseball-cap pulled low over his face, but he seemed to be staring back towards her.

Even at that distance, there was something familiar about the figure. Something that sent a chill finger down her spine.

As she watched, the figure stepped slowly forward, moving into the glowing circle, with the air of an actor entering the spotlight. As he did so, he removed his cap and raised his face to look in her direction. In that instant, she became certain.

Joe Morrissey.

Joe Morrissey. The man who had worked for weeks by her side in her first undercover role. The man she had chattered amiably to over pints in the pub. The man who, at first, had been her only companion when she'd first gone out into the field.

The man who, months before, had lured her out to a deserted beach and tried to kill her.

Salter had intervened and apparently saved her life. She had discovered, then, that Morrissey was a psychopath and a hired killer. A pro and a good one. She'd assumed that he'd been hired by Kerridge. But, in retrospect, murder – at least, that kind of cold-blooded, businesslike murder – obviously wasn't Kerridge's style. It was Boyle, and presumably Salter, who'd been polishing off potential witnesses.

So maybe Morrissey had been Salter's man all the time. Salter had claimed he'd turned up in the nick of time because he'd been on her tail all day. But maybe it was simpler than that. Maybe he'd been able to arrive just in time because he'd already known exactly where Morrissey was going to take her. Maybe that was why he'd waited so long before calling out the authorities to pick up Morrissey.

Maybe that was why, despite all their supposed efforts, Morrissey had succeeded in going to ground between then and his appearance before her just now.

She took a breath, her mind racing through the implications of all this. The spate of professional executions across the north west. Welby's supposed attempt at suicide. Further back, the question of who had carried out the skilfully executed torture and killing of her former lover, the informant Jake Morton.

And the question, above all, of what Morrissey was doing, here and now.

For a long moment, ringed in the street light's halo, Morrissey continued to stare back at her, his face clearly visible now in the pale orange glare. She could sense, somehow, that he knew she was watching.

She continued to stare back at him until, to her surprise, he suddenly turned on his heel and, with what appeared to be a valedictory wave of his cap, began to stride off down the street, heading back towards the High Street.

She watched, baffled by what she was seeing, until he reached the corner and vanished from sight.

There was no question, she thought. It was Joe Morrissey. And he had wanted her to see him, wanted her to recognise him. He had waited by the door until he knew he'd been spotted. And then he'd stood with his face in the light until he was certain that she had identified him. And then he had simply left.

Why? Just to scare the shit out of her?

Well, possibly. Maybe it was a warning. Lay off Salter and I won't come back.

But she couldn't believe that. It was too low-key, too unreliable. Morrissey might be good, but even he couldn't have been absolutely confident that she'd recognised him. His final gesture felt more like the departing flourish of a great performer who can't resist one last moment on the stage. It was an embellishment to the act, not the act itself.

She was holding her breath again, she realised, her chest suddenly tight with fear. As she'd grabbed the phone from her handbag, she had seen something, though she hadn't consciously registered it at the time. She hurried across the room and picked up the bag, rooting frantically around inside.

Brennan's disc was gone.

The chill had reached her heart now.

If the disc was gone, Morrissey had been in the house. Had been in her bedroom. Had been in there, standing over her, and then had left, without her even being aware of his presence.

She rushed through into the spare bedroom and fell on her knees in front of the table fumbling around in the darkness. She could still feel the shape of the disc concealed under the carpet. Morrissey hadn't found that. She had to keep reminding herself that, however skilled he might be, he was only human. There was no way he could have discovered the concealed copy.

But it didn't matter. If Salter knew that she'd received this evidence from Brennan, he would also know that Brennan had the original. And Brennan would no doubt have made his own copies, probably located more securely than this one. Salter's aim wouldn't have been to destroy the evidence. He would simply have wanted to get his hands on it, find out what was on there. Prepare his own defence and alibis before she or Brennan had a chance to do anything with it.

She stumbled to her feet, still shaken by the realisation that Morrissey had been so close to her. That, if he'd wanted, he could have shut off her life just like that . . .

Afterwards, she didn't know where the thought had come from. But, as soon as it entered her mind, she had known instantly that it was true.

It felt now as if Morrissey had somehow managed to reach into her body, grasp her heart in his cold fingers, and squeeze it until she could no longer breathe. She raced down the stairs, stumbling as she neared the bottom, catching herself against the front door. She turned and slammed open the door of the dining room, fumbling for the light switch as she did so.

At first, she thought there was nothing wrong. Liam was lying as peacefully as ever, his eyes closed, one hand tucked under his cheek.

But the room was silent. Utterly silent.

As silent as the grave.

29

The DI was holding her hand between both of his, in a gesture which, in other circumstances, might have seemed unduly intimate. 'We've done everything we can, Marie. Believe me.'

She did believe him, though she knew that he hadn't believed her. She knew him a little, DI Warrington. They'd done basic training together, a long while ago. He was obviously making decent progress. A bright career ahead of him.

She knew they'd made a concession in even sending a DI out, let alone all the other stuff they'd done that morning. The SOCO had crawled all over the dining room, painstakingly gathering any shred of evidence that might be there. The only difficulty was that he, like Warrington, clearly didn't believe there was any evidence to be found.

'There'll be a post-mortem,' Warrington said. 'Then we'll know for sure.'

'But you don't believe me.'

He stared at her for a moment as if unsure how to respond. 'Jesus, Marie. I know you. You're a copper. A good one. If you say something, we're going to move heaven and earth to check it out.'

'And I'm very grateful. But you still don't believe me.' She was aware that she was beginning to sound, in the circumstances, inappropriately petulant. Shit, Marie, she thought, get a grip on yourself.

Warrington looked around him, perhaps hoping that one of his colleagues might come to his aid. 'It's an emotional time for you, Marie. Of course it is. I mean, Christ knows how you've coped with all this—'

'If you tell me it's a fucking blessing, I might be forced to punch you in the teeth,' she said.

'No, of course not. It's awful. But that's the point. You're not in a position to think about it rationally yet . . .' He caught the look on her face and trailed off. 'I'm not handling this very well, am I?'

She shook her head. 'No, you're doing fine, Rob. You've done it all by the book and more. The doctor's been and concluded that it was most likely natural causes. Asphyxiation caused by fluid on the lung. Not that unusual in MS cases that have progressed as far as Liam's. And, yes, he did have a chest infection, though we didn't think it was serious. And, no, there was no obvious sign of a break-in. And, yes, all I did was catch a glimpse of a figure standing on the far side of the road in the middle of the night.' Almost without realising it, she discovered that she was crying. She buried her face in her hands, embarrassed at losing control among people she thought of as her colleagues.

Warrington awkwardly passed her a box of tissues from the coffee table in front of them, waiting while she regained control. 'Look, I'm not writing it off, Marie. I know what you do – well, something about what you do – and I know it must put you at risk. We're taking this seriously. If there's any evidence in that room, the SOCO will have picked it up. We're following up Joe Morrissey, though there's not much on the record about him.'

'There wouldn't be,' she said. 'He's a pro.' It was good of them to go through the motions, she thought, but she knew they'd find no evidence in the dining room and Morrissey would have long made himself scarce. Probably with a pay-off and the prospect of a nice long break in the sun. Somewhere where the talents and resources of the Met were unlikely to track him down.

She couldn't even be certain herself that Liam had been murdered. Sitting here, with the bleak autumn sunshine streaming through the grubby sitting room window, it all seemed unreal. All just a horrible coincidence. Maybe she hadn't seen Morrissey last night. Maybe she'd just let her imagination get the better of her.

She wiped her eyes with the tissue and looked back up at Warrington. 'I know you'll do your best, Rob. I'm probably just overwrought. Like you say, it's been a strain. And now he's gone – I don't know what to think.'

'You need a break,' Warrington said. 'They'll give you compassionate leave. You should get away somewhere.'

That was it, she thought. Salter's grand plan. He'd insist on her taking compassionate leave, show what a fucking caring boss he was. Get her well off the scene before any of the stuff with Brennan came into view. And if she started challenging Salter with Brennan's evidence, he'd let everyone know that, well, she was under enormous stress, wasn't she? Not surprising, after everything she'd been through. He'd probably get Winsor to conclude that she was perhaps a little unbalanced at the moment. Not quite getting everything in proportion. She'd even suggested that her partner, Liam, had been murdered, even though there was absolutely no evidence and he'd clearly been in the terminal stage of multiple sclerosis. It was terribly sad, but there you were. You had to ask whether she'd ever really be capable of resuming an operational career.

She nodded to Warrington. 'Maybe you're right,' she said. 'It's been a tough time. Not just this. Lots of stuff. Work as well. Maybe a break would do me good.'

Warrington nodded, with the relieved air of a man who had just managed to extricate himself from unfamiliar and uncomfortable emotional territory. 'Think about it, anyway. I'm sure it would help to get away.'

'I'm sure it would,' she said. She looked around the room, and it struck her that she was already beginning to forget that this was her home. With Liam gone, that sense of domesticity seemed to have melted away. She almost wondered why this furniture, these ornaments, the picture on the wall, had ever meant anything to her. Now, suddenly, this house seemed as bland and anonymous as the places they'd allocated to her in the field. 'Think you're right, Rob,' she went on. 'I think I'll get away. As soon as I can. Once I've tied up a few loose ends.'

It was another half hour or so before Warrington and the others left, though they were all clearly itching to get away. There'd been a stream of calls across the morning – her parents, Liam's parents, friends who knew them well, friends she hadn't seen for years but who somehow had picked up the news on the grapevine. She knew there was a hell of a lot to think about – organising the funeral, dealing with

345

the fact that Liam had left no will, sorting out the life insurance they'd had on the mortgage. She managed to phone the undertakers and put that side of things in train, but the rest she intended to defer to another day.

As the morning wore on, she'd increasingly ignored the phone and allowed the callers to leave messages, wearying of having to engage with the uncomfortable dialogue that followed the initial expression of sympathy. Somewhere in the middle, Salter had called. She'd let that one run to voicemail, and later listened, feeling nauseous at the sound of his voice. 'Very sorry to hear the awful news. Give us a call when you're able. Assume you'll be off for the next day or so anyway, but we should talk about giving you a longer break. We all know how much you've been through.' At least he'd refrained from calling her 'sis'.

After the police had gone, she fixed herself a coffee and stood staring into the empty dining room. Liam had been sleeping in that room for only a relatively short while, and he'd been increasingly uncommunicative, but the room's vacancy still felt strange and wrong. Social services would eventually be back to collect the bed and the room would, she supposed, return to its former use. Whether she'd be here to see that happen was another question.

As she returned to the sitting room, she heard one of her mobiles buzzing in her bag. She pulled out the pay-as-you-go phone she'd bought for calling Brennan and glanced at the screen. The number wasn't withheld but was unfamiliar. 'Hello?'

'Sorry to hear the news, girl. Bastard thing to happen.'

She managed to stop herself from answering immediately. Instead, she made her way quickly through the kitchen and opened the back door. 'Sorry, can you hang on a sec?' Once outside she said: 'Sorry, Keith. I don't know whether the house is bugged. I'm in the garden now.'

'Wouldn't put it past him to bug the bloody garden,' Welsby said. 'They've allowed me to use Lizzie's phone. Should be safe enough. How you doing?'

'Not great, Keith.' She'd phoned Lizzie earlier to break the news to her, but had given no real details. 'I don't think it was natural. I think Joe Morrissey was involved.'

There was a long pause. 'Jesus. That psycho for hire. He's certainly had links with our friends over the years.'

'He tried to kill me before,' Marie said. 'I thought he'd been hired by you and Kerridge.'

'Christ, girl, you really do have a low opinion of me, don't you?' He paused. 'Not Jeff's style, either. Might be prepared to turn a blind eye to it. But wouldn't commission it. That was what Boyle was for. You got evidence he was involved?'

'No, of course not. Nobody believes me. But Morrissey wanted me to know.' She described what she'd seen during the night.

She could almost hear Welsby's mind working and reaching similar conclusions to her own. 'Jesus, he's a ruthless bastard, isn't he? Our friend, I mean. I never thought he'd go that far.'

'He'll go anywhere he needs to. I realise that now. Should have realised it before.' She could feel the emotion building again. 'Christ, Keith, how do we stop him?'

'We need to do it by the book, I reckon, girl. You need to take that stuff you've got to Standards.'

'They won't take it seriously. Salter will have come up

with smart answers to all of it by now. I'll just make an idiot of myself.'

'No, you won't. You just got to take care how you do it. You raise it as something that's come into your hands. Something you've got concerns about. That's just you doing your job. It's up to them to look into it. But if you do that, it puts him on their radar. It obliges them to do something about it. Even if it goes nowhere in the short term, it'll start to put some pressure on him.'

'And is that the best we can do? Put some fucking pressure on him? Jesus, Keith—'

'Just trust me, girl. We'll get the bastard. One way or another.' He paused, and she could hear his rough breathing down the line. 'I'll get that bastard, girl, if it's the last fucking thing I do.'

30

'Ms Donovan? Come in. Take a seat. First of all, let me offer my sincere commiserations.'

He didn't sound particularly sincere, she thought, but he'd clearly done his homework. That was impressive, but slightly worrying. Did that mean he'd spoken to Salter? She decided there was no merit in being tentative. 'I'm impressed,' she said. 'Who told you?'

He frowned and looked momentarily puzzled. 'It's the talk of the building, I'm afraid, Ms Donovan. I'm sorry these things get spread as tittle-tattle, but I'm sure people's intentions are good.'

So that was it, then? Not good research. Just the usual grapevine. She wondered whether everyone also knew she'd asked them to treat Liam's death as murder. Quite probably. Shit. 'I'm sorry,' she said. 'It wasn't entirely a surprise, given his condition, but it was still a shock. I think I'm a little over-sensitive.'

'We can never entirely prepare ourselves for these things, can we?' He had the air of an Anglican vicar, she thought. Never more than a sentence away from a comforting platitude. 'Jonathan, by the way,' he added, holding out his hand, 'Jonathan Caulfield. I'm in charge here. Jon.'

'Please,' she said, 'call me Marie.' She could feel herself wanting to scream at the suffocating politeness of it. No doubt Caulfield was the one they wheeled out to the press when they wanted to demonstrate that one bad apple hadn't caused the whole barrel to decay.

'I must confess, Marie,' Caulfield went on, treating her name with the nervous care of a scientist handling a radioactive specimen, 'I was a little surprised that you asked to see us today. I'd rather assumed you'd be taking a few days off.'

'I was offered the opportunity,' she said, conscious that she was coming close to mimicking his circumlocutory style. 'And I'll probably take it. That was really why I wanted to deal with this now. So that I could take some leave with a clear conscience.'

'I see. And would this be concerned in some way with the sad death of your, um, partner?' The ecclesiastical air was again evident in the awkward emphasis he gave to the final word. But his question suggested that he was aware of the questions she'd raised about the nature of Liam's death.

She shook her head. 'No. This is something different.' She felt almost treacherous in denying the link to Liam, but she knew that it was better to present this as objectively as possible. She didn't want to give Caulfield any excuse to dismiss her as hysterical or unbalanced.

'I understand that there are some potentially serious allegations against a senior officer?'

She shook her head. 'I'm making no allegations.'

He blinked. 'But I'd understood from your phone message—'

'Mr Caulfield – Jon – I've worked regularly as an investigating officer and as an evidence officer. I understand the standards of evidence required to sustain a criminal conviction or even to bring a misconduct case. I don't think that anything I can give you will meet those standards at present.' She'd prepared this speech in her head while waiting outside for Caulfield to see her. She hoped that she was striking the right note. 'But I also know what kinds of issues would prompt us to begin an investigation. And I think what I've got to say at least merits your attention.'

Caulfield nodded slowly. 'But your – comments do involve a senior officer?'

She nodded. 'Yes. Relatively senior.'

'Have you read our policy on whistleblowers, Marie?' His tone implied that their policy might involve throwing them into a prison cell and tossing away the key.

'Yes, I have.' She'd skimmed it quickly on the intranet when she'd arrived at the office at the start of the afternoon. She'd attracted a few odd looks from her co-workers for appearing at the office on the day of Liam's death. 'I needed to get away from the house,' she'd said, wondering quite why she felt the need to make excuses. 'Just for an hour or two. Thought I'd come in and tie up a few loose ends. Then I can take some time off properly.' They'd all nodded sympathetically, clearly thinking that grief affected people in strange ways.

'We take whistleblowing very seriously,' Caulfield went on. 'First, if there's any potential substance in what you're telling us, I can promise you it will be investigated thoroughly.'

'There's substance,' she said. 'Enough to merit an investigation.'

'I don't doubt it,' he said. 'You've a good reputation, Marie. I took the liberty of looking at your file when you called. So I'm sure you're not wasting our time. You'll appreciate that, once in a while, we do get what appears to be a malicious accusation so we have to take care. But I'm sure this won't fall into that category.'

At another time, she might have felt offended at Caulfield's innuendo. Now she was thinking; you wouldn't begin to believe quite how much malice there is in my accusation, Mr Caulfield. Doesn't make it any less true, though. 'As I say, Jon, I'm not making any allegations. I don't think it's my position to do that. All I'm doing is bringing some intelligence to your attention. I'll leave it to you to decide how significant or otherwise it is.' Christ, she thought, can we stop dancing around this? She was beginning to understand why there were so few misconduct cases.

'I should just spell out a few ground rules,' Caulfield said. 'We'll deal with anonymous allegations, but we much prefer it if people come forward openly as you have. But equally, from our side, we'll guarantee your confidentiality, if that's what you prefer.'

'For the moment,' she said. 'At least until you've decided whether there's anything worth pursuing further. If you think not, that's fair enough. If you think there is, then I'm happy to discuss what you need from me.'

'So what's this about? I have to confess I'm intrigued.'

She reached into her handbag and, between her forefinger

and thumb, she brought out Brennan's disc. She'd made another copy before coming out. 'It's about this,' she said, placing the disc carefully before Caulfield.

He looked back at her and raised his eyebrows. 'And this is what?'

'It's a disc that – well, let's just say that it came into my possession. It contains various files which I think raise questions about the behaviour of a certain senior officer.'

'And can I ask who the officer is?'

'Hugh Salter.'

The eyebrows remained elevated. 'Your manager, if I'm not mistaken.'

'You're not mistaken. I'm assuming that's why the material was sent to me.'

'And may I enquire about the provenance of this – material?'

'You'll appreciate I have to protect my sources,' she said. 'Again, at least for the moment. If you decide to take the investigation further, I'll see what I can do.' She hoped that this would satisfy Caulfield for the present. She'd found that those who were away from the operational front line tended to have an excessive respect for the security of informants.

'Understood. So what's the nature of the material.'

'There are basically two types of files on the disc,' she said. 'First, there are photographs. Photographs which appear to show Hugh – Mr Salter – associating with – well, individuals on our target lists.'

'But there's no indication of the nature of this association?'

She shrugged. 'They're simply photographs. I

recognise Hugh, and I recognise some of the individuals he's talking to.'

'But there could be legitimate reasons for him to associate with those individuals?'

'Potentially,' she said, carefully. 'Although it would be odd for someone in Hugh's role to have extensive direct contact with those kinds of people.'

'Okay. And the second type of file?'

'Audio files,' she said. 'They appear to be surveillance tapes of Hugh in discussion with others. On the face of it, the content of the discussions appears to indicate that Hugh is involved in dealings which are inappropriate to his role or status.' Jesus, she thought, Caulfield's prolix style was catching.

'And you don't think the conversations might have an innocent explanation?'

'I don't know,' she said. 'I appreciate that it's all too easy to take snatches of conversation out of context. It's conceivable that there might be an explanation.'

'And who are the individuals involved? The other speakers, I mean.'

'There are names given in the file names. I recognise the names, again as individuals on our target list. I think I recognise one or two of the voices. But I can't say to you definitively that those are really the people on the tape. As far as I can judge, it does sound like Hugh speaking.'

Caulfield had been languidly making the occasional note as she spoke. Most of them seemed to be little more than one or two words, unreadable upside down. 'And do you believe the tape to be genuine? From what you know of its provenance.'

'I've no reason to doubt it,' she said, conscious that her reply fell short of an affirmative. 'In its own terms, I mean. I think it's unlikely that the photographs have been doctored or the tapes faked, if that's what you mean.' She hoped that he wouldn't ask her quite why she thought this. For all she knew, the files might be utterly phony. For her purposes, such as they were, that hardly mattered. 'But, as I say, that doesn't mean that there isn't a perfectly innocent explanation for them.'

'Quite,' he said. He picked up the disc and stared at it for a few moments, as if he might be able to read it without recourse to a computer. 'No, you were quite right to bring this to our attention. Corruption is always a concern.' He paused, and she could see that he was thinking. 'Salter was the chap who was involved in the Welsby case, wasn't he?'

She nodded. 'We both were. It was rather a bonding experience, as you can imagine. One reason why I'm finding this so difficult.'

He nodded sympathetically. 'Yes, of course. I suppose the Welsby connection could cut both ways. It's interesting that he worked closely with an officer who turned out to be corrupt. But equally it could be that there are people who're out to get him.' He gazed back at Marie, as if she might potentially fall into either category.

'That was very much my thinking,' she said. 'I'm struggling to see Hugh as corrupt. But then I'd never have guessed that Keith Welsby was bent. That's why I thought I ought to put it in your hands.'

'No. Quite right. You've done entirely the right thing. I'd rather think the best of our people, and it's quite possible there's an innocent explanation for all this.' He gestured vaguely towards the disc. 'But, as the Welsby case shows, we have to be vigilant.' He looked up at her. 'Rest assured that we'll take this seriously. If we decide to pursue it, you'll almost certainly hear from me again once we decide on next steps. If we don't, we won't risk compromising your confidentiality by coming back to you about it. So you can assume that silence means we've decided there's nothing to follow up.'

She nodded. That sounded to her rather as if he was intending to file the disc in the bin the moment she left the room. Disappointing, she thought, but not surprising. So much for doing it by the book. 'That's fine,' she said. 'I hope for Hugh's sake that it's the latter outcome, of course.' May God forgive me, she thought.

'But we won't let it lie until we've got a credible explanation for what's on the disc,' Caulfield concluded. 'Trust me on that, Marie.'

She returned to her desk, feeling even more deflated and miserable than before. Shit, she thought. That was all they had, and Caulfield was probably even now preparing to use the evidence as a drinks coaster. She was conscious that she'd been channelling all her grief at Liam's death into her quest to expose Salter. Now she was beginning to feel something close to real despair.

Worse still, Salter was back in his office, sitting gazing at something on his computer screen. As she walked back towards her desk, he caught sight of her and gestured for her to join him.

'Christ, Marie. What the hell are you doing here? I thought I told you to take some time off.'

She repeated the explanation she'd given earlier, aware that it sounded thin even to her own ears.

'What loose ends?' he said, and for a moment it felt almost as if he were accusing her. 'You need to look after yourself. You've been through a hell of a lot.'

She could almost bring herself to believe that he cared, she thought. 'I know, Hugh. It's just that things would have been hanging over me. I just wanted to make sure I'd cleared the decks before I went off.'

'Okay. But make sure you take some proper time off now. As long as it takes.' He paused, and she could sense that he was moving on to the issue that he'd really wanted to raise with her. 'By the way, Welsby's asked to see me now. He's obviously catching up on all his old acquaintances.'

'Are you going to go?'

'Why not? Maybe he really does have something to say. Have you done a report your meeting with him?'

'Not yet. That's another loose end.'

'Anything significant come out of it?'

'Hard to say. He's resigned to the fact that he's going to stand trial now, I think. But he clearly feels hard done by.'

'How does he reckon that? He was caught bang to rights.'

'You know how it is,' she said. 'People can bring themselves to believe anything if it puts them in the right. Or less in the wrong. Welsby accepts that he was bent, but claims he wasn't the only one and not the worst.'

'So who else did he have in the frame, then? Me? You?'

Salter's tone was dripping with irony, but she allowed the silence to extend for a moment before replying. 'He's not naming names. Not yet. But he reckons he'll denounce them all from the witness stand.'

'Terrific. That'll go down a storm with the judge, I imagine.'

'I don't suppose anybody can stop him though. Could be an uncomfortable process for anyone he does name.'

'Who's going to take that slimeball seriously?'

'But you're going to go and see him, anyway?'

'A fool to myself,' he said. 'But you never know. I'm going to head over this afternoon. You want to tag along?'

'Me?'

'It's on your way home. I want to make sure you really do leave the site. Besides, it might be useful to have a witness if Welsby starts throwing accusations around.'

She suddenly realised that he was scared. Scared of Welsby, of what he might do or say. He was concealing it well, but she could sense that his usual self-confidence was missing. It was as if he could feel that things were changing, that the ground was slipping from under his feet.

'Yeah,' she said. 'Why not? Like you say, it'll make sure I get out of here. Be interesting to see what Welsby's got to say.' Won't it just, she thought. 'What time are you going?'

He glanced at his watch. 'About an hour?' He was looking past her to where one of the team, standing outside the glass-walled office, was holding up a telephone receiver and gesturing to Salter. Salter nodded and waited while the call was transferred.

Salter mimed an apology to Marie and picked up the phone. 'Yes. Well, yes, of course. Does it have to be now? I've got one or two things I need to—Well, okay, but I need to be away by two.'

He put down the receiver and then looked back up Marie. His eyes were blank and expressionless, his gaze focused somewhere beyond her. He looked like someone in shock, she thought.

'Everything okay, Hugh?'

He blinked and looked at her. 'Yes. Yes, fine.' He looked back at his watch, as if hours might have passed since he'd last checked the time. 'Look, Marie. See you at the hospital around two fifteen, okay? Got a meeting first.' He paused and began gathering papers from his desk. 'Professional Standards,' he added. 'It's always bloody urgent with them, isn't it?'

'What are they after?' she asked, watching as he bustled at the desk, studiously avoiding her gaze.

Finally he looked up, blinking. 'Christ knows,' he said. 'Christ fucking knows.'

31

At the hospital Marie struggled to locate a parking space, finding herself repeatedly circling the perimeter road, waiting for someone to depart. Finally, she spotted a woman getting into a car in one of the most remote parking areas, and she drew in next to it, waiting for the woman to pull out. An elderly couple who had been similarly searching for a space had spotted the opportunity at more or less the same moment, and she could feel the old man silently cursing her as she pulled forward to assert her rights to the space.

She bought herself a ticket from the pay-and-display machine and looked at her watch. Two twenty-five already. She jogged into the hospital, heading along the corridors to the room where Welsby was located. She wanted to be present when Salter met with Welsby, though she had no idea what might happen.

But when she reached the room, Salter was still waiting outside, pacing along the corridor. The same two prison officers she'd met the previous day – Brady and his apathetic colleague – were sitting outside the door watching Salter stride anxiously up and down.

'What's up?' she said.

Salter looked at her as if he'd forgotten he'd invited her to join him. 'Welsby's daughter's in there,' he said. 'Seem to have having some kind of heart-to-heart.' He paused. 'Didn't even know Welsby had a heart.'

Marie peered in through the small window. Lizzie seemed to be concluding whatever she'd been discussing with Welsby. Seeing the two of them together, Marie could see a similarity in their appearance that she'd never have spotted unaided. She didn't know whether Salter had made any connection between Welsby's daughter and the woman who had worked for McGrath. If so, he gave no sign.

Lizzie gave Welsby a kiss on the forehead – an incongruous sight, Marie thought, to anyone who knew either party – and made her way to the door. She looked out at Salter. 'He's all yours,' she said. She glanced over at Marie, but her face gave no indication that the two women knew each other.

'Thanks,' Salter said. 'How is he?'

Lizzie shrugged. 'You know. Up and down.' She looked again at Marie, and this time the two women's eyes met. There was something in Lizzie's expression that Marie couldn't read.

Salter gestured to Marie. 'Come on, then. Let's see what he's got to say.'

Brady leapt to his feet. 'I'm sorry, sir. Only one visitor at a time.'

'Oh, for Christ's sake,' Salter said, 'you know who we are.'

'Even so, those are my orders. Strictly speaking we're not even supposed to leave the room. If I let two of you in, I won't have a job to go back to.'

Marie caught his eye for a moment, and detected a spark of amusement there. She had the sense that was extracting bureaucratic revenge for his previous encounter with Salter. 'I'll stay outside, Hugh. Don't want to get anyone into trouble.'

Salter glared at her for a moment. 'Okay. But I'll call you if I need you.'

'I'm sure you'll cope, Hugh.' She smiled winningly at Brady, who had signalled for his colleague to fetch her a chair from further down the corridor.

Salter said nothing but pushed his way into the room, letting the door slam behind him.

Brady arranged the seat carefully by the wall and gestured for Marie to sit down. 'I thought you might be more comfortable waiting out here,' he said.

'Too right.' Marie lowered herself on to the chair and stretched out her legs. 'Too bloody right.'

At first, Salter thought Welsby was asleep. But as Salter slowly lowered himself on to a chair by the bed, Welsby opened an eye. 'Afternoon, chum,' he said. 'Just like old times.'

'Not really.' Salter leaned forward to peer at the older man. 'I'd like you say you look well, but frankly you look like shit.' He glanced meaningfully at the saline drip attached to Welsby's arm, the bank of monitoring equipment behind the bed.

'You don't look so terrific yourself, truth be told, old son. At least I've got an excuse.'

'What's this all about, Welsby? Why'd you want to see me?'

Welsby was fumbling for a control device hanging down from the side of the bed. He eventually caught hold of it and pressed one of the buttons, raising the mattress beneath his head so that he was sitting partially upright. 'Thought it was time we had a chat, Hughie boy.' His gaze strayed past Salter to something on the floor by the bedside cabinet. 'God, this place is a shit heap. Can you pick that up, Hughie? Don't want anyone treading on it.' He gestured down to where an apparently used syringe was lying on the tiled floor.

Salter bent down impatiently, picked up the syringe and dropped it on top of the cabinet. 'Stop screwing me around, Welsby, and cut to the chase.'

'I thought we should have a chat about you, Hughie. You and your future.'

'What the fuck are you talking about? Have you brought me out here to waste my fucking time or is there some point to this?'

'Your future, Hughie. Or the absence of it. Because you don't have much of a future, do you?'

Salter started to rise. 'Just fuck off, Welsby. If you think I'm going to sit here—'

'You're in the shit, aren't you? Or at least that's how it seems to me. You've got Professional Standards sniffing round you . . .'

'What the fuck are you talking about?' Salter had involuntarily glanced towards the door when Welsby had mentioned Professional Standards. He was on his feet now, with the air of someone preparing to leave the room.

'You must be getting nervous,' Welsby went on. Standards wouldn't investigate without a reason. Wonder just what evidence they've got. And what other evidence might be waiting out there.'

'I don't know what game you're playing—'

'And Boyle's had enough of you, hasn't he? You used to be an asset, Hughie boy, but now you're just becoming a liability. Word is that Boyle's got someone else to do his thinking for him. You're yesterday's man, Hughie. Nobody can find a bargepole long enough.'

Salter glanced towards the door, clearly concerned that Marie or one of the prison officers might be watching. 'I know what this is, Welsby. You're just trying to wind me up. Get me to do or say something I'll regret.' He reached over and pulled the blanket from Welsby's chest. 'You got a wire in there?'

'Don't know how you could even think such a thing,' Welsby said. He pulled open his pyjama top to reveal his bare chest. 'Straight as a die, me, Hughie boy. Just got your best interests at heart.'

Salter stared back. 'So what the fuck is this all about? What are you playing at exactly?'

'Don't be too hard on me, Hughie. I'm a dying man.'

Salter gave a contemptuous grunt. 'You'll live long enough to stand trial. That's all that matters.'

'Now that's where you're wrong, Hughie, as it turns out. I'm a dying man, and you're the one who killed me.'

'What the fuck are you —?'

Welsby gestured behind him. 'This saline drip here. It's very unfortunate. But it seems that, just a little while ago, quite possibly just after you entered the room, it was injected with what I understand to be a lethal dose of morphine. The rate of flow was also turned up.

Difficult to imagine that anyone would do such a thing, isn't it?'

Salter remained motionless for a moment, clearly doubting Welsby's sanity. 'What are you saying?'

'I'm saying that someone's effectively injected me with a potentially lethal dose, old chum. Injected from that very syringe that's coincidentally has your finger prints all over it.' He paused, and for a moment it was as if he was struggling to continue talking. 'Of course, I've no idea how much has entered my bloodstream. Whether or not I'm beyond saving. Not that it matters much. If I survive, I'll have to testify that I saw you, while I was half-asleep, tampering with the drip. Too weak to call out for help. And if I don't survive, well, I imagine they'll work it out for themselves.'

'That's insane,' Salter said. 'Nobody's going to believe—'

'Don't you think so? With Standards snapping at your heels and me threatening to expose you on the witness stand. Wouldn't be surprising if you were feeling a little unbalanced, Hughie. Maybe not behaving entirely rationally. I mean, look at it this way. Who the fuck else is going to try to kill me? The doctors? My own fucking daughter?'

Salter continued to stare at Welsby for a moment longer, then unexpectedly launched himself across the bed, struggling to tear the drip feed away from the bottle. Welsby let out an almighty shout, the anguished cry of someone being physically assaulted.

The door slammed back and the two prison officers came storming in, dragging Salter off Welsby's body. Salter struggled with them for a moment. He had his hand around the tube of the drip, and he tore it away from the bag, leaving clear liquid dripping on to the floor. The two officers were pulling him back, struggling to keep a grasp on him. Under the weight of Salter's body, Welsby gave a sudden groan, his body jerking sideways on the bed. The lead officer, Brady, turned his attention to Welsby, and in that moment Salter broke free from their grip and sprinted towards the door.

In the corridor outside, Marie pacing up and down, waiting anxiously for Salter to emerge, wondering what was taking place between the two men. She'd been tempted to peer in through the door, and had taken herself off to the far end of the corridor, above the stairwell, in an effort to resist the impulse.

She'd turned as she heard Welsby's shouts and was in time to see the two prison officers storm into the room. Before she could make her way back down the corridor, the door burst open again and this time Salter came sprinting out, heading in her direction. Behind him, she could hear Brady shouting for him to stop.

'Hugh? What are you—?'

Salter cannoned into her, thrusting her off to one side. Driven more by instinct than rational thought, she clung on to his arm, trying to slow his pace. He reached back and tried to push her away, but she wrapped herself more tightly round him, burying her face against his back in case he tried to strike her. Salter slowed momentarily and looked back. Brady was emerging from the room.

Salter jabbed his arm fiercely at Marie's head, forcing her to loosen her grip, and then her was off again, heading for the stairs. She almost lost him, but she steadied her footing and launched herself at his legs, in an attempt at a rugby tackle. She caught his knees and hung on grimly as Salter tried to force his way forwards.

She never quite knew what happened in the final seconds of their struggle. Salter had almost reached the stairs and seemed to make one last effort to extricate himself from her grasp, throwing himself forward. She clutched tighter, and he toppled suddenly, losing his balance at the top of the stairway.

The weight of his falling body was too much for her and she lost her grip. She watched as he tumbled down, his shoulder crashing against the metal banister, his torso banging against the marble-tiled stairs. As he hit the first landing, his head struck the corner of the stairwell and his body twisted on to the hard floor. A pool of blood slowly spread across the pale polished surface.

'Jesus,' Brady said from behind her, peering down the staircase. 'He doesn't look so good.'

Marie lay on the floor, gasping for breath, staring down at the prone body below. 'You know what?' she managed to say at last. 'I'm really struggling to give a fuck.'

32

'How are things?'

'Sorry?' Brennan's voice echoed slightly, lost in a noisier space. 'I'm in the car. On the hands-free.'

'I said how are things?'

'Not so bad. They had to drop all the disciplinary stuff, obviously. Fully exonerated. No stain on my career. All that bollocks.'

'That's good,' Marie said. 'Are you back to work, then?'

'Will be soon,' he said. 'Need to talk to you about that. But they've let me take a couple of weeks off. Probably more to help them save a bit of face than anything else, but I'm not complaining.'

'Enjoy it,' she said. 'I'm off at the moment, too. Compassionate leave. Probably the best thing, but it's driving me mad. I'll be going back soon, I think. Not sure what to yet, though. They're still trying to work out what to do with me.'

'You and me both, then,' he laughed. 'Sometimes think they feel more comfortable with bent cops than straight ones. Speaking of which, what's happening with Salter?'

'He's on remand. Seems to have recovered okay.

Concussion, broken arm, several broken ribs. Some internal bleeding. But if you're going to throw yourself down a hard staircase, best do it in a hospital.'

'You reckon he threw himself?'

'Christ knows. The whole thing's bizarre. There was enough morphine injected in Welsby's drip to fell a horse, though only a limited amount had actually entered his bloodstream. Not much question that Salter put it there. His fingerprints are all over the syringe. Looks like he started to do it while Welsby was asleep and then Welsby woke up, saw what was happening and tried to stop it. And that was when we came in.'

'Salter couldn't have expected to get away with it, surely?'

'Don't see how. There are no other serious suspects. The only other possible culprits would have been Lizzie, the medical staff and the two prison officers. My guess is that it was just a last despairing gesture on Salter's part. He thought that Standards were on to him. He knew that Welsby was planning to denounce him at his trial. Things were closing in fast. I reckon his plan was to kill Welsby then top himself. That was why he threw himself down the stairs. Closest he could get in the circumstances.'

'Did it look like he threw himself?'

'Maybe. I don't know, in all honesty. I was trying to grab his feet. Maybe that made him trip. Or maybe he jumped. It's hard for me to care. All I care about is that he's going to stand trial. Probably for attempted murder or manslaughter. And certainly for corruption.'

'Standards have a decent case, then?'

'Cut and dried. They've dug up a whole network of bank accounts. He was getting payments all over the place. And he was smart. Never let it showed in his lifestyle. Mind you, from what they've found so far, it still doesn't entirely stack up with the idea that he was the real brains behind Boyle's operation. But maybe there's still more for them to find.'

'Or maybe Salter had covered his tracks too well.'

'Maybe. He's smart enough. Or was until the end.'

'Marie, just got to my destination. Got a meeting with someone. Maybe an hour or so. Can I call you back? Got a couple of things I want to talk to you about.'

'Yes, sure. I'm around all morning.'

Marie ended the call and sat back on the sofa. She looked around the small living room, mentally totting up the various items that would eventually need packing. It was a small house, but there still seemed to be an awful lot of them. Something to look forward to.

Was she doing the right thing?

Christ knows, she thought. She'd spoken to friends and family, and inevitably they'd given her contradictory advice. Some had said that it was too early for her to be making any decisions. You've got to allow yourself to grieve properly, some said. Whatever properly meant. It hasn't hit you yet. You're probably still in a state of shock. Take your time. There's no rush. Except that, if only in her own head, there was. It was only a week or so, but she felt already that she was in a state of suspended animation. A frozen body waiting to be reawakened

Some had said that moving was the last thing she should be doing. Too much change all at once, they said. You've lost Liam. You don't want to be casting away everything you associate with him. You don't want to be drawing a line under your whole life all at once. What about your friends?

Well, what about them? Few of them lived in this part of London, anyway. Some were north of the river. Others had moved away from London entirely. In any case she wasn't changing her whole life. She was going to continue with the same or at least similar work. She still had to have that conversation with the powers-that-be. They seemed keen for her to continue the undercover work. She had a natural aptitude for it. If they said so, she thought. It had never really felt that way to her. They'd also told her that, if she preferred, she could move back into standard investigations work. She was good at that, too.

Whatever the outcome, they'd left her in no doubt that she'd emerged unscathed, in career terms, from the debacle. She'd been unfortunate enough to find herself working with two officers who turned out to be corrupt, and she'd played a part in exposing both of them. She was exactly the kind of officer they wanted. When she returned, a promotion would be forthcoming in due course. Blah, blah, blah. She was happy to hear it said, but she treated the praise and promises with the scepticism they deserved. She just wanted to get back, do a decent job, keep her nose clean.

And she wanted to get away from here. Sell up this place and move – well, where? So far, she hadn't progressed much beyond 'somewhere else'. One or two friends agreed with her. They could understand why she didn't want to be rattling round this place, constantly reminded of Liam and what they'd had. What they'd expected always to have. She'd loved

Liam. She missed him. But she didn't want to be constantly haunted by his absence.

So she'd move. Soon. Somewhere. Maybe take the opportunity to transfer out of London. Maybe up north. Maybe Manchester, if the option was there. She'd have those discussions when she returned to work, and then make the final decision.

She rose and walked over to the sitting room window, looking out on the dull terraced street beyond. Beyond the lines of parked cars, she could see the streetlamp under which Morrissey had stood on the night of Liam's death. Morrissey was still out there somewhere. No longer working for Salter, but still killing for a living. She shivered slightly and turned away, resuming her restless pacing of the house. She was waiting for something to happen. Waiting for the phone to ring. Waiting for the future to get in touch. Waiting for life to restart.

'It's an e-ticket booking,' he said, brandishing the print-out of the confirmation.

The attendant behind the check-in desk scarcely glanced up. 'That's fine, sir. I just need your passport in that case.'

He nodded and slid the document across the desk towards her. Her head still lowered, she flicked briskly through the pages and then tapped on the keyboard in front of her. 'Mr Marshall. Travelling to Barcelona?'

'That's right.'

She looked up then, finally, and he smiled at her. After a moment, she smiled back. 'It's a good likeness,' she said, gesturing towards the open passport. 'The passport photo,

I mean. Usually, it looks nothing like the holder.' She laughed. 'It could be anyone standing in front of me.'

He nodded, still smiling. He'd decided to check in early and there was no queue behind him. The attendant obviously had time on her hands. It didn't worry him. There were times when he'd waited for a queue to build just to ensure that his presence wasn't registered. But today he felt relaxed, unworried. He'd done the job well and was confident that no one was on his tail. 'Got it done professionally,' he said. 'Hate those photo-booths. Make everyone look like a hired killer.'

He'd had the whole passport expertly prepared, in fact. Spent what was needed to get the best possible job. For the next two months at least, he was Geoff Marshall, a freelance engineering consultant.

'Or a terrorist,' she agreed, still laughing. 'Window or aisle?' She completed the check-in, tagging his luggage before it disappeared along the conveyor belt, waiting while the boarding cards printed. 'There we go. Should be boarding at three twenty. Security's slow today, so I'd recommend you make your way through as soon as you can.'

He wondered vaguely whether security was slow because they were still keeping an eye out for him. He thought it unlikely. He'd waited a month before arranging his departure. They'd have lost interest by now, if they'd ever had any. And even if they'd somehow acquired an old photograph of him, he'd never be recognised now. 'Thank you,' he said, pocketing the passport and boarding-card.

'Holiday?' she asked, clearly keen to string out the conversation.

'Bit of a break,' he said. He was dressed in a cream linen

jacket, a slightly over-garish shirt. 'Just finished a tough contract, so thought I'd get away for a few weeks. Enjoy the sunshine.'

'The way the weather's been here,' she said, 'you might be tempted not to come back.'

'I don't think so.' He paused, as if a new thought had just struck him. 'No, I'll definitely be back. I'm very lucky, you see. Because I really love my work. And I always like to finish the job.'

He nodded to her, still smiling, and then he turned and began to make his way unhurriedly towards Departures.

Brennan pulled into the entrance of the imposing new hotel. It was one of a rash of luxury hotels that were springing up on the edges of the city centre. He couldn't imagine how there was a market for them all, with the economy in its current state, but the developers seemed confident enough.

He pulled out of the wintry sunlight and followed the curving road down into the underground car park. It took him a few minutes to find a space and then cross to the lift that took him up to reception. He didn't have a room number, so he asked at the desk.

'Mr Douglas?' the efficient-looking receptionist said, tapping into her computer. 'Room 801. On the top floor. One of the suites. Would you like me to call up?'

He shook his head. 'He's expecting me. Don't worry.'

Brennan made his way to the lifts and ascended to the eighth floor, cocooned by plush padded walls and almost inaudible music. This place was a cut above even the most upmarket places available on a copper's expenses.

He tapped gently on the door of Room 801, and then a little harder as realised how the thickness of the wood swallowed the sound. A moment later, it was opened.

'Keep your hair on, Jack. Coming as fast as I can.'

'Wasn't sure you'd heard. Like knocking on the door of Fort Knox.'

Brennan followed Andy McGrath into the suite's living area. It was impressive enough, in a sterile kind of way, he thought. There was a wide picture window providing a panoramic view out over the city centre, from the CIS Tower to the Hilton spire, with countless more attractive buildings in between. Capacious well-stuffed sofas lined the walls. There was a large central table laden with a tray of coffee and tea.

A heavily built man was splayed across one of the sofas, dressed only in a disconcertingly gaping bathrobe. His head was shaven, his ears and one nostril studded with gold. He wore a Rolex which might or might not have been genuine. There was a glass of what looked like Scotch in his hand. He looked up as Brennan entered and gestured him to take a seat. 'Come in, Jack. Make yourself at home.'

Brennan nodded. 'Pete. How you doing?'

'Much better now, Jack, thanks for asking. Thought we'd all celebrate with a decent meal and a night in this place. Pity you weren't able to join us.'

Brennan shrugged. He wasn't aware he'd been invited.

Boyle waved the half-empty glass of Scotch towards Brennan. 'Drink?'

'Bit early for me. I'll stick with the coffee.'

'Help yourself. We're all in your debt, Jackie.'

Brennan shook his head. 'I didn't do much. She did the

hard stuff, in every sense. You okay, Lizzie?' Up to that moment, he hadn't registered her presence. She was sitting at a desk, tucked behind the door, tapping away at the keyboard of a laptop.

'Not so bad, considering,' she said, scarcely looking up.

'Sorry about your dad,' Brennan said, awkwardly. 'Not your fault.'

She shrugged, still gazing at the computer screen. 'No. And it was what he wanted, in the end. He didn't want to have to stand trial. Didn't want that kind of exposure.'

'They reckon it wasn't the morphine.' McGrath added. 'The coronary would have happened sooner or later. Probably sooner. And probably didn't help to have Salter leaping on top of him.'

'Still sad,' Brennan said. 'Decent guy.'

'Decent guy who got too near Jeff fucking Kerridge,' Boyle said. 'No offence, Lizzie.'

Lizzie seemed unconcerned. 'Just business, isn't it? You and Kerridge had a falling out. He had to choose. Maybe chose wrong. But you'd already got Salter under your wing. Which, looking back, maybe wasn't such a smart move in itself.'

Boyle laughed. 'All right, smart-arse. He got me a long way, Hugh Salter. Bright guy. Just that bit too ambitious in the end.'

'You reckon he'll try to stitch you up if it goes to trial.'

'Probably. Big if, though. Salter won't have many buddies in prison.'

'How much do you reckon Salter knew?' Brennan poured himself some coffee and lowered himself gently on to one of the sofas.

'About what was going on up here?' Lizzie asked. 'Not much. He knew there was something. That's why he sent that bitch Donovan up to keep an eye on Andy. But he didn't know about me. And he hadn't linked me to dad. Don't think he made the connection even when he saw me in the hospital. He'd never seen me face-to-face before.'

Boyle sipped on the Scotch and laughed. 'Getting some lowlife to torch Andy's place—'

'That lowlife was another one getting too big for his boots,' Lizzie said. 'Thought Andy was taking a risk sticking him back in his own fire, but it worked okay. Shifted the focus off Andy and me. Got a scapegoat to take the rap. Effectively kiboshed Donovan's assignment, especially when we got some other toe-rag to scare the shit out of her.' She laughed. 'Even claiming I'd had an intruder of my very own. Genius.'

'Pity about your dad, though,' Brennan said, again. There were times when Lizzie's hard-bitten callousness made him uncomfortable.

'Come on, Jack. He knew the risk. He wanted me to do it. He was looking for a way out, and he wanted to take Salter with him. If he'd survived that, I reckon he'd have topped himself some other way.'

Brennan couldn't argue with the logic, but he wanted to shout: 'He was your father, for Christ's sake. How can you talk like that?' He was locked into this now. He'd received too many favours. He was in too deep. 'Can't stay long, Pete. Was there something specific?'

'Just mainly wanted to say thanks, mate. For doing your bit. Getting that Donovan woman to pick up the dirt on Salter. That's what drove Salter over the edge.'

So you wanted to take the opportunity to remind me just how far I'm in the shit, Brennan thought. 'My bit was nothing,' he said. 'Not after all you've done for me, Pete. Giving me the dirt to shaft Craddock. Pity that backfired a bit. And pity Craddock's wife wasn't a bit more grateful, too. But there you go.' There you go, indeed, and there was never any going back.

'Yeah, well, we've got you nicely embedded in this new job now, Jack. Take it you're planning to stay there?'

'Don't see why not. You pulled strings to get me into the Agency.'

Boyle laughed again. 'Yeah, another example of Salter thinking he was using someone, while he was actually being used. Smart girl, our Lizzie.'

Brennan glanced across at the young woman sitting behind the laptop. No wonder Boyle had decided that Salter was dispensable. He'd found someone even smarter and more ruthless. He wondered how ambitious this one would turn out to be.

'Yeah, pretty damn smart,' he agreed. 'Yeah, well, I'd better be off.'

'Be good, Jack,' Boyle said. 'Or if you can't be good, remember who's paying you.'

'Don't worry, Pete. I won't forget.'

Back in the car park, Brennan started the engine and reversed carefully out of the space, then pulled back up the exit road out into the sunshine. Once he was back on the ring road, he flicked through the numbers on his mobile and picked the one he wanted.

'Marie? It's Jack again. Sorry I had to cut it short earlier.'

'No problem. You're obviously busier than I am at the moment.'

'Not much. Just a few domestics to sort out. Listen, I wanted to talk to you about work. Like I said, I'm going back in a few days. They've asked me to stay in the Agency,'

'So I'd heard,' she said. 'Not sure if congratulations are in order, though.'

'Suits everyone. The Force don't have to face the embarrassment of taking me back. The Agency want to do right by me for screwing things up. All fine by me. Thing is, they're asking me what sort of work I want to do. And whether I want to stay up north, or come and join you lot in the smoke. Tough choices.'

'Tell me about it,' she said. 'I'm wrestling with the same sorts of questions at the moment.'

'That right? Well, there you go. I'm just not sure I know enough about the place to make a sensible decision. So I was wondering . . .' He allowed his voice to trail off slightly, as if perhaps the signal had faded slightly.

'Jack?'

'Sorry, yes, still here. Anyway, thing is, I'm coming down to London for a few days next week to chat to various people about the options. Wondered if there was a chance of picking your brains while I'm about it?'

She laughed. 'If you think they're worth picking, yes, of course.'

'I thought maybe we could meet over dinner. Get to know each other a bit better. Future colleagues and all that.'

There was a long pause and for a moment he thought perhaps he'd lost the signal. Then she laughed again, this time with a note of genuine pleasure in her voice. 'Yes, okay, Jack. We can meet for dinner.'

'My treat,' he said. 'You just bring the brains.'

'Not a great bargain,' she said. 'And you'll find I'm not easily bought, Mr Brennan.' There was a mildly flirtatious edge to her tone now. 'But, yes. I'm all yours, then. Why not?'

Read on for case files
for our undercover agents

Case Files

Recruitment and Selection Report – Undercover Officer

Prepared by: Colin Mansfield, Head of Recruitment and Selection

Name of Candidate: Marie Catherine Donovan

Date of Birth: [redacted]

Place of Birth: Frimley, Surrey, UK

Summary Education History: Farnborough Sixth Form College, Hampshire, University of Hull (BA (Hons) in History, 2:1)

Summary Employment History: Metropolitan Police Force, Accelerated Promotion Scheme. Joined CID in [date redacted] as Detective Constable. Transferred to Agency as Investigating Officer in [date redacted]. Working in Intelligence since [date redacted]

Overview of Application (Interview and Assessment Centre)

Donovan's stated reason for applying to the Undercover Team is that she is seeking to move back into an operational role from her current role in the Intelligence Team. She joined the Intelligence Team as a career development move with the aim of broadening her skills. Her work there is well regarded and she clearly has an aptitude for the detail of intelligence gathering and analysis. However, she also had a strong reputation in her previous operational roles and it is recognised that her current position may not be using her talents to the full.

The Occupational Psychologist's report [see attached] confirms her general suitability for an undercover role, subject to the reservations described. She has been counselled about the potential challenges of undercover work, and appears to have a good understanding of its nature and demands. She has also made an effort to talk to current and past undercover officers about the realities of covert operations. In her panel interviews, she was able to talk cogently about her strengths and development needs in respect of undercover work, and she left the panel with no doubt of her overall capability.

Her performance on the practical assessment exercises was excellent. She handled the initial role-playing exercises without difficulty, and was able to sustain her 'legend', including some required improvisation, without difficulty. When she reached the final shortlist and had undertaken some preliminary training, she was subjected to the full 'role play' challenge. The exercise commenced immediately following an overseas trip on Agency business (during which she was not required to be 'in character') in order to maximise her potential disorientation. She was collected from the airport, without any prior warning, and subjected to intense questioning as if her role had been compromised. She handled the exercise admirably, with no exposure of her true identity.

On this basis, we have no hesitation in recommending the appointment of Donovan to an undercover role. She clearly has the ability and temperament to handle the work involved and we are confident that she will be very successful.

We would however highlight two potential concerns which should be kept under review as her assignment progresses. The first involves Ms Donovan's relationship with her partner, Liam Robinson. Robinson makes a limited living as an artist, but essentially is dependent on Ms Donovan's income. This might in principle create a vulnerability to bribery or similar approaches with security implications, but Robinson has been security vetted and there is no current cause for concern. However, Robinson has recently been diagnosed as suffering from multiple sclerosis. Our investigations into his diagnosis suggest that the severity and progression of his illness may be more serious than either he or Donovan appreciate. This may create additional pressures on Donovan which might affect her ability to perform effectively in her new role. We recommend that this is kept under review.

The second concern is Donovan's relationship with Hugh Salter, a former undercover officer who will act as her 'buddy' on this first assignment. Salter is highly regarded in terms both of his undercover work and his subsequent transition into a management role. However, as detailed in [report details redacted], he has been the subject of past investigation and scrutiny by the Professional Standards team as a result of concerns initially raised by his line-manager, Keith Welsby. Although the concern proved unfounded – and in turn raised questions about Welsby's own motivations – Salter remains under precautionary observation. It is clear that Salter's abrasive style causes tensions with his colleagues and that his relationship with Donovan is already under some strain. Our recommendation is that Welsby, Salter and Donovan are all kept under careful observation during the assignment to ensure that relationships remain constructive and mutually supportive.

Recruitment and Selection Event – Undercover Officer Psychological Assessment Report

Prepared by: Martin Winsor, CPsychol, Occupational Psychologist

This report summarises my findings in respect of the appointment of Ms Marie Donovan to the position of undercover officer. In my role as Occupational Psychologist, I was asked to conduct a battery of tests and exercises for potential candidates to help assess their suitability for the role. The exercises included, as well as standard numerical reasoning, verbal reasoning and critical thinking tests, a range of personality questionnaires intended to help evaluate the candidates' likely capability to handle the unique psychological and other pressures of the undercover role. A full list of the exercise and the detailed results are appended as Annex A [note: detail redacted].

Overall, my conclusion is that Donovan is likely to be well suited to the role. It should be stressed that no pre-assessment of this kind can be definitive. Although Donovan's responses to the questionnaires provide a valuable indication of her likely emotional and other responses, it is impossible to predict how an individual will respond in reality.

As a starting point, Donovan performed very well in the various reasoning tests. She has strong numerical and verbal reasoning skills and should have no difficulty in handling any relevant requirement in those areas (including any business management skills involved in her 'legend'). More importantly, her responses to the critical thinking test indicate that she has a highly developed capability to appreciate, analyse and deal with ambiguous language or material. This, combined with her ability to tolerate ambiguity and uncertainty, as indicated by her responses to the personality questionnaires, suggest that she is likely to be relatively comfortable in handling the unpredictability and lack of clarity often associated with an undercover role.

Overall, Donovan is a highly balanced individual who is likely to display the mix of personality traits most suited to undercover work. For example, she is capable of thinking independently when required, but is also comfortable working within the constraints of formal procedures. She is therefore unlikely to 'go native' while working in an undercover context, but should also be capable of displaying the required resourcefulness and ability to improvise. Similarly, she is comfortable in operating a team environment, but is also able to operate independently when required. She is not intrinsically suspicious of others or their motives, but tends to withhold trust until she is confident it has been earned. My only concern, looking as her overall profile, would be that. in the face of substantial operational pressures, her inclination might be to opt for an independent solution rather than having full confidence in the support of others. Clearly, the implications of this would depend on the circumstances involved!

In providing feedback on the results of the exercises, I took the opportunity to discuss informally her perceptions of the role. It is clear that she appreciates its challenges and risks, and she appears to have prepared herself as thoroughly as possible for these. I should add that she appears to be facing some pressures in her domestic life, particularly relating to her relationship with her partner. This may create some emotional vulnerabilities which will need to be kept under observation.

Undercover Team – Post Assignment Debrief

Prepared by: Simon Cottrill, Head of Operations

Name of Officer: Marie Catherine Donovan

Donovan has to date undertaken two undercover assignments. Both of these of these have proved highly problematic for reasons outside of Donovan's control, and it is likely that this will have a significant impact on her ability to undertake similar work in the immediate future. At this stage, I am drawing no firm conclusions about her capability and suitability to return to under-cover work. It is clear from her past performance that Donovan displays substantial resilience, as well as having an aptitude for this kind of assignment. At the same time, she has undergone some severe shocks and traumas in her initial exercises so care will be needed to ensure that she does not return to the field prematurely. Our decisions in this respect should take full account of Donovan's own feelings and preferences, as well as the professional opinions of the Agency Occupational Psychologist.

For the record, it is necessary to summarise some of the issues that Donovan has faced. These include:

- The recent unfortunate death of her partner. Mr Robinson suffered from secondary multiple sclerosis but the suddenness of his death was unexpected. Donovan's initial response suggests that her professional judgement was perhaps affected by the event. This is unsurprising and, in the view of the Occupational Psychologist, is likely to be a product of her grieving rather than a longer-term issue.
- The impending criminal proceedings against her former manager, Keith Welsby, prior to his recent death. We understand that Welsby served as an informal mentor to Donovan when she first joined the Agency, so she is likely to have been affected by the allegations of corruption

against him. It is not clear whether her reactions would have been alleviated or worsened by Welsby's subsequent illness and recent death.

- The impending criminal proceedings against her most recent boss, Hugh Salter. Although we understand that Donovan's relationship with Salter was very different from her dealings with Welsby – and, in fact, Donovan was the first to raise concerns about Salter's integrity – the accusations of corruption and his possible involvement in Welsby's death will undoubtedly have added to the stresses she is facing. It must be recognised therefore that her professional environment has become extremely destabilised over the past two years.

More significantly of all, however, Donovan has faced direct threats to her own life, apparently linked to the alleged corruption of both Welsby and Salter. She appears to have coped very resourcefully with these at the time, but there is no question that they will have left severe psychological scars. The view of the Occupational Psychologist is that these, combined with her recent bereavement and the disruption to her working life, may combine to create a significant emotional vulnerability. In the worst case, this might leave her open to emotional or psychological manipulation.

We understand that Donovan is planning to take some extended leave to resolve various domestic issues, but has expressed a wish to return to work in the near future. Our recommendation is that, for the present, Donovan is not returned to the field but is given an assignment in Intelligence or a similar field. This will provide us with an opportunity to assess her state of mind and suitability for a return to operational work in due course.

It's a race for the truth . . .

ALEX WALTERS
TRUST NO ONE

A terrifically fast-paced novel that has you hooked from the first chapter with a captivating central female lead who you can't help rooting for. Join Marie Donovan as she races for the truth . . .

As a covert officer specialising in 'deep cover' operations, Marie Donovan works amongst the most dangerous criminals in Manchester. It's a precarious life that puts Marie on the edge of the law.

When she begins an affair with Jake Morton, an informer due to give evidence against crime lord Jeff Kerridge, Marie knows she's breaking a cardinal rule.

Yet just as she comes to her senses and puts an end to their relationship, Morton is murdered. Suddenly Marie's undercover role is exposed and only one thing is certain – she can TRUST NO ONE.

An addictive read for fans of P.J.Tracey and Peter Robinson.

A V O N

£6.99
ISBN: 978-1-84756-285-2
ePub ISBN: 978-1-84756-292-2